VOLUME
14

Silver Spoon

HIROMU ARAKAWA

STORY & CHARACTERS

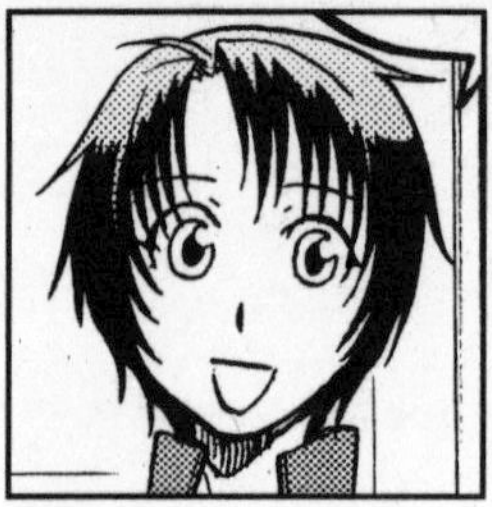

AKI MIKAGE

A third-year student at Ooezo Agricultural High School, enrolled in the Dairy Science Program. She's studying to get into Ooezo University of Animal Husbandry to get a job working with horses instead of carrying on the family farm.

YUUGO HACHIKEN

A third-year student at Ooezo Agricultural High School, enrolled in the Dairy Science Program. Former Equestrian Club member. Started a business with funds saved up from part-time jobs. His current project is raising and selling pasture pigs.

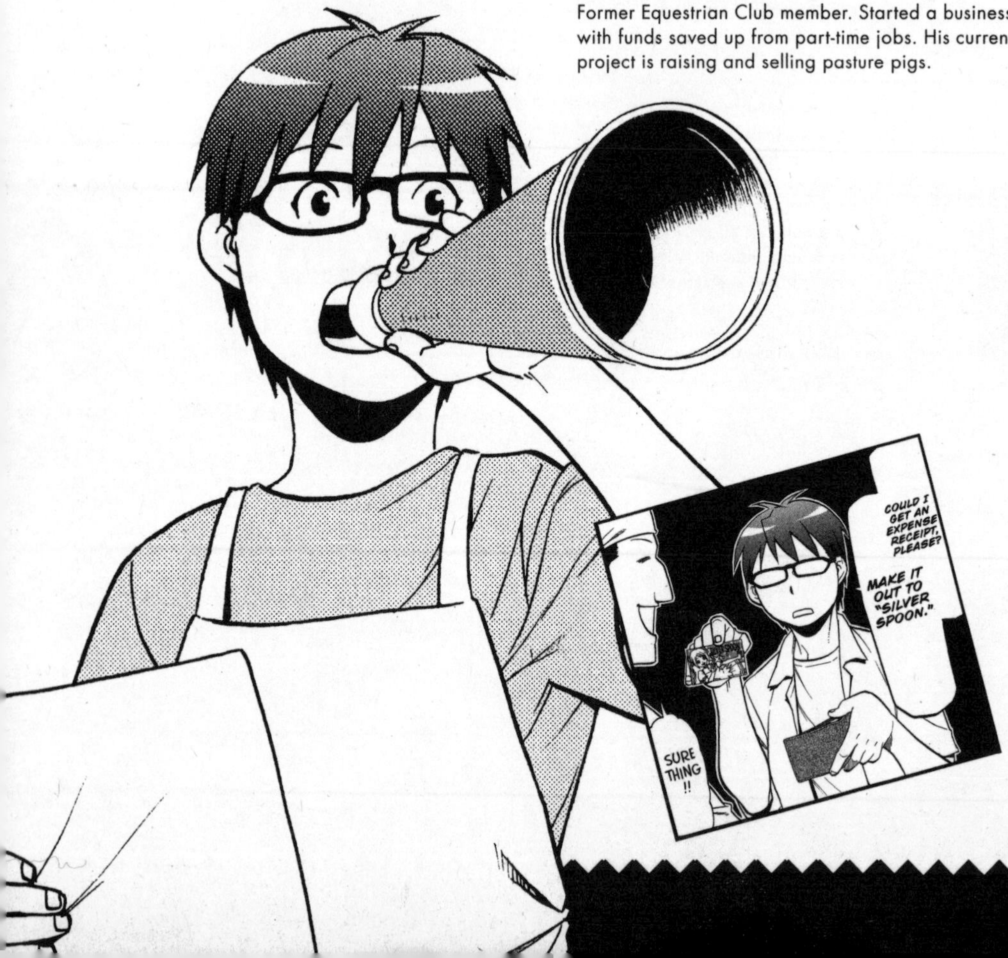
COULD I GET AN EXPENSE RECEIPT, PLEASE?
MAKE IT OUT TO "SILVER SPOON."
SURE THING !!

SHINNOSUKE AIKAWA

A third-year student at Ooezo Agricultural High School, enrolled in the Dairy Science Program. His dream is to become a veterinarian, and he aims to get into the same school as Mikage.

ICHIROU KOMABA

A former student at Ooezo Agricultural High School who dropped out when his family's dairy farm went out of business. Now he's working jobs far from home, saving toward a new goal.

The Story Thus Far:

Hachiken and his friends have reached their final year of high school. Impressively, the Ezo Ag Equestrian Club made it to the national championships in team competition, but when Hachiken goes brilliantly off-course at nationals, the team faces defeat all too soon... And so the season turns to fall. Mikage's crazy studying under Hachiken's guidance pays off, and she earns a recommendation for Ooezo University of Animal Husbandry! Meanwhile, Hachiken is busy preparing to sell pizzas at the Ban'ei stadium for his new business venture. Exam day and pizza sales day—both fall on November 30. As the pair's fateful day approaches, Komaba calls Hachiken for the first time with a surprising request...!

SHINEI OOKAWA

A graduate of Ooezo Agricultural High School. He is the president of the company he started with Hachiken. His personality has earned him the nickname "hardworking turd"...

CONTENTS

Silver Spoon

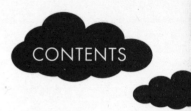

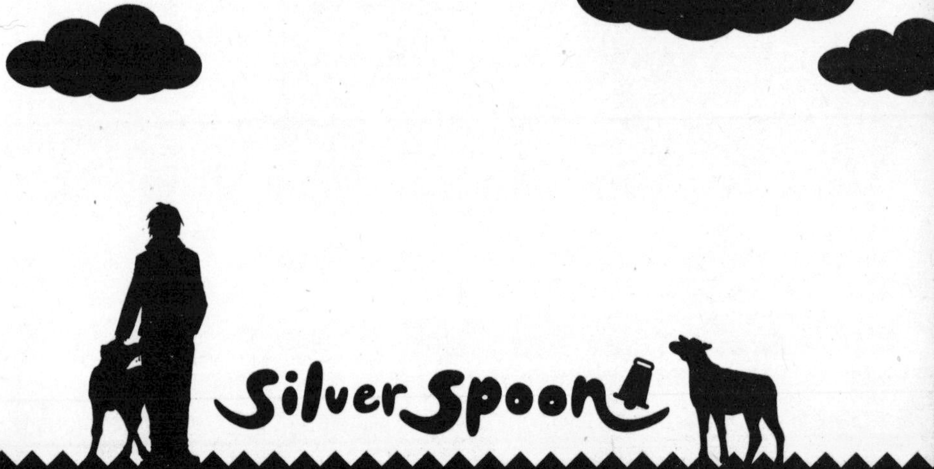

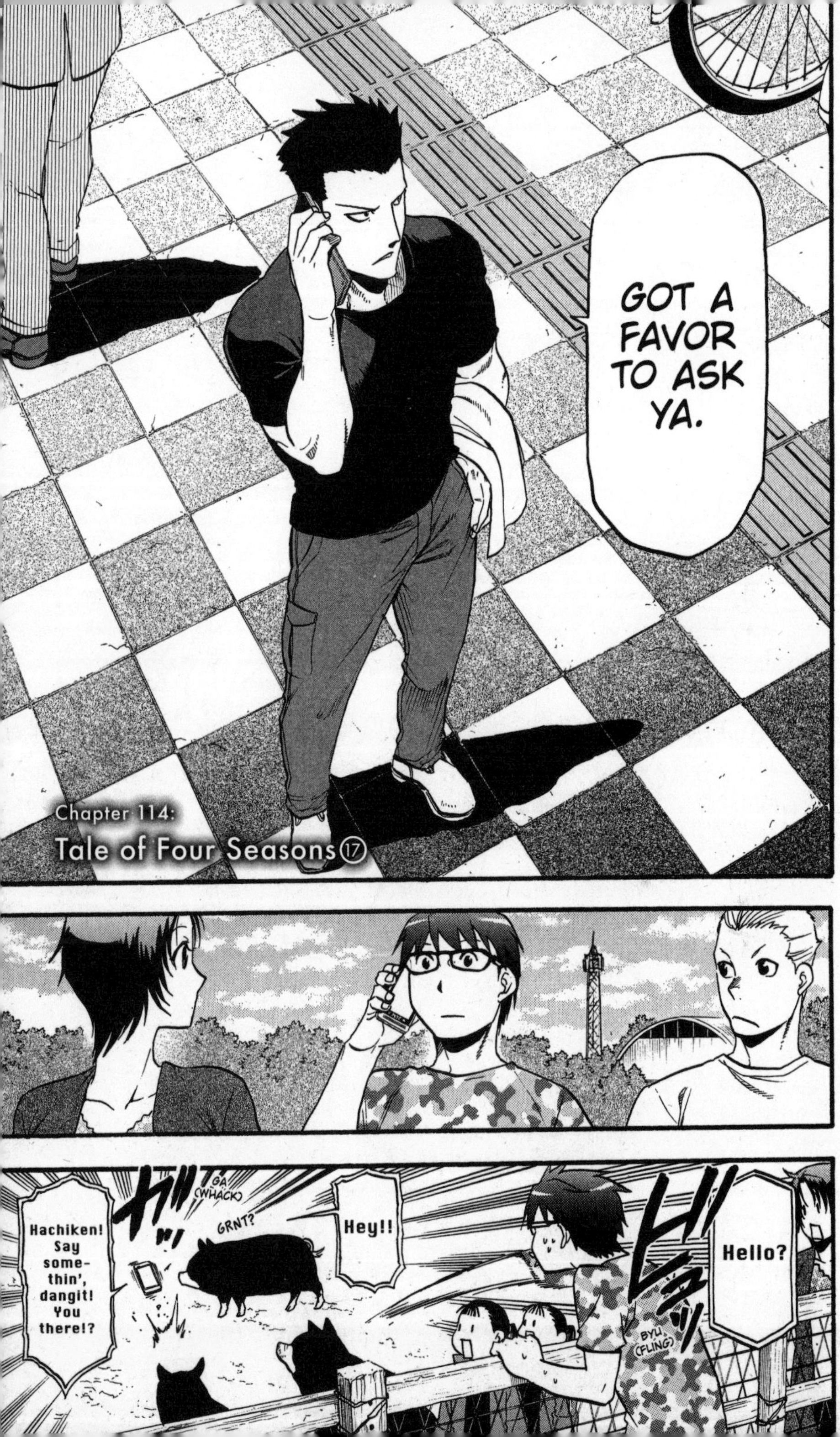
GOT A FAVOR TO ASK YA.
Chapter 114:
Tale of Four Seasons ⑰
Hello?
BYU (FLING)
Hey!!
GA (WHACK)
GRNT?
Hachiken! Say somethin', dangit! You there!?

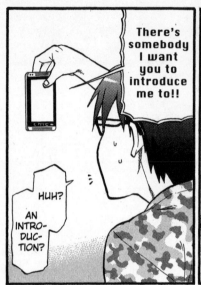

YOU HAVE A FAVOR TO ASK ME!?
DID YOU GET CAUGHT UP IN SOME TROUBLE IN THE BIG CITY!?
A PYRAMID SCHEME!? A SKETCHY CULT!?
What the heck do you think Tokyo is!? Sheesh!!
There's somebody I want you to introduce me to!!
HUH?
AN INTRODUCTION?
FROM ME?
Yeah.
From you.

Chapter 114:

Tale of Four Seasons ⑰

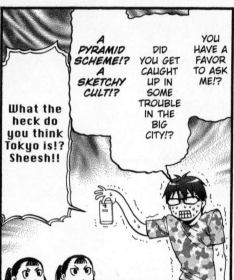

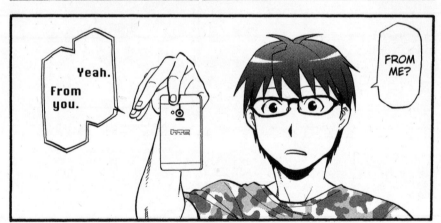

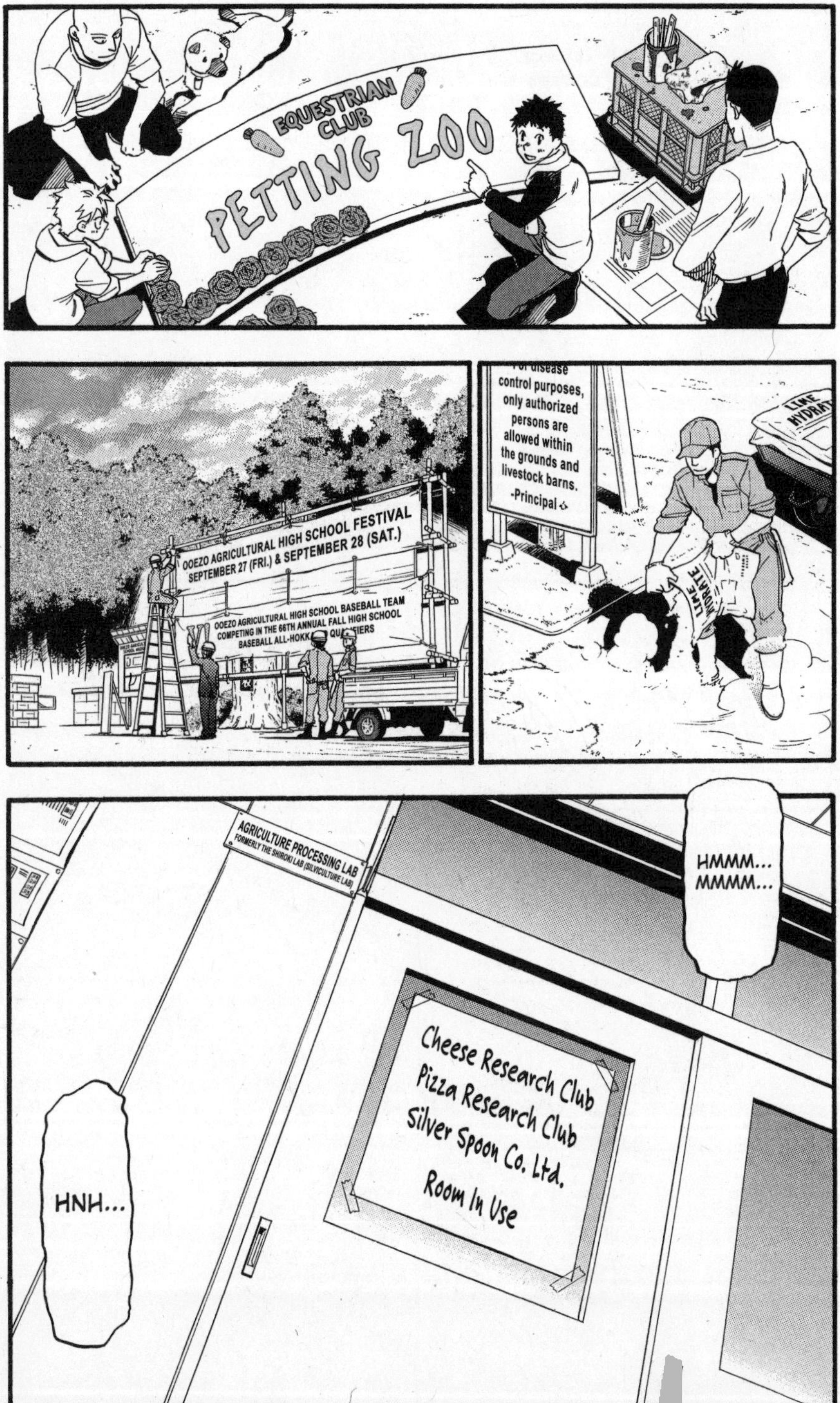
EQUESTRIAN CLUB
PETTING ZOO
control purposes,
only authorized
persons are
allowed within
the grounds and
livestock barns.
-Principal
LIME HYDRATE
OOEZO AGRICULTURAL HIGH SCHOOL FESTIVAL
SEPTEMBER 27 (FRI.) & SEPTEMBER 28 (SAT.)
OOEZO AGRICULTURAL HIGH SCHOOL BASEBALL TEAM
COMPETING IN THE 66TH ANNUAL FALL HIGH SCHOOL
HMMM... MMMM...
AGRICULTURE PROCESSING LAB
FORMERLY THE SHIROKI LAB (SILVICULTURE LAB)
Cheese Research Club
Pizza Research Club
Silver Spoon Co. Ltd.
Room In Use
HNH...

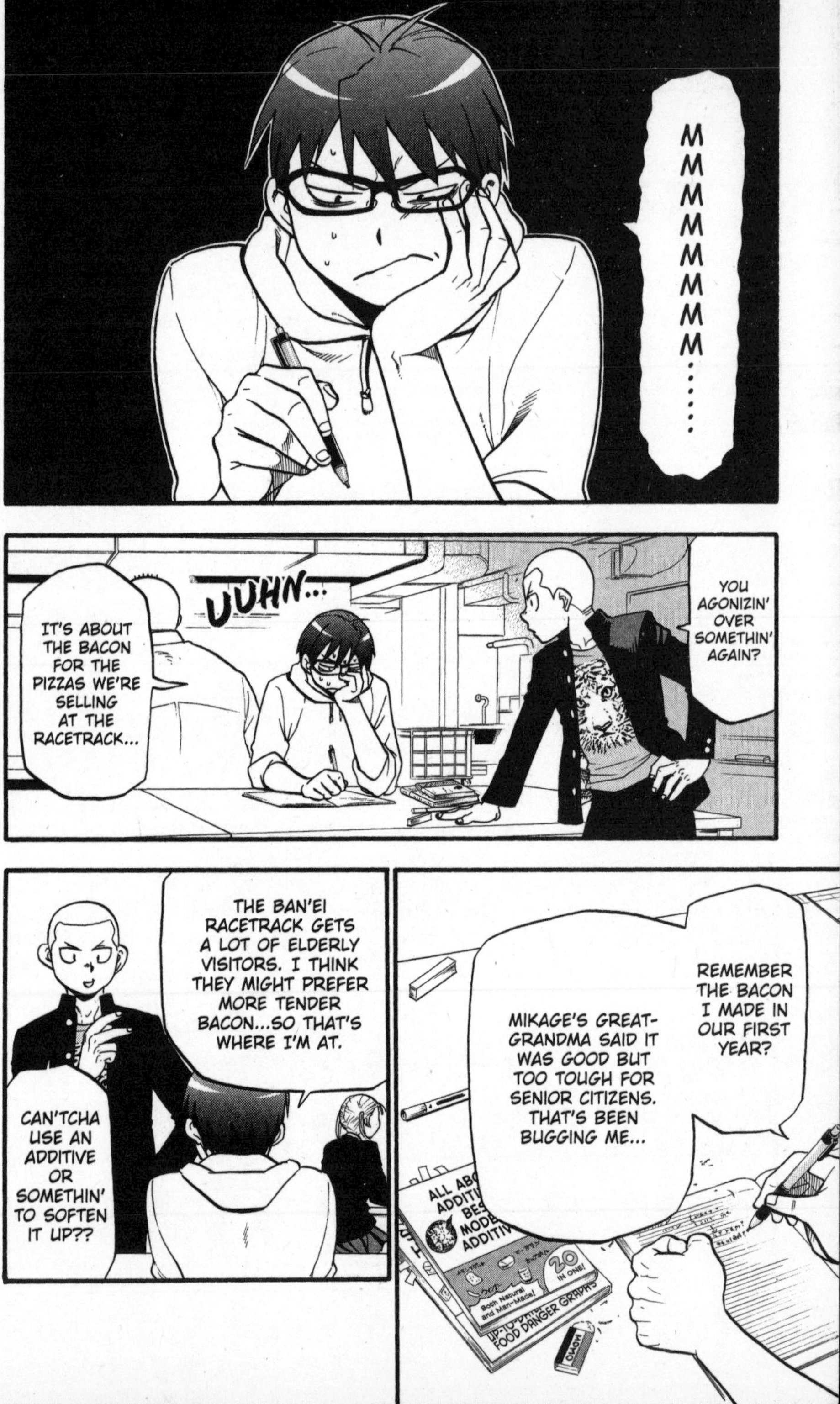
MMMMMMMM......
YOU AGONIZIN' OVER SOMETHIN' AGAIN?
UUHN...
IT'S ABOUT THE BACON FOR THE PIZZAS WE'RE SELLING AT THE RACETRACK...
REMEMBER THE BACON I MADE IN OUR FIRST YEAR?
MIKAGE'S GREAT-GRANDMA SAID IT WAS GOOD BUT TOO TOUGH FOR SENIOR CITIZENS. THAT'S BEEN BUGGING ME...
20 IN ONE!
Both Natural and Man-Made!
THE BAN'EI RACETRACK GETS A LOT OF ELDERLY VISITORS. I THINK THEY MIGHT PREFER MORE TENDER BACON...SO THAT'S WHERE I'M AT.
CAN'TCHA USE AN ADDITIVE OR SOMETHIN' TO SOFTEN IT UP??

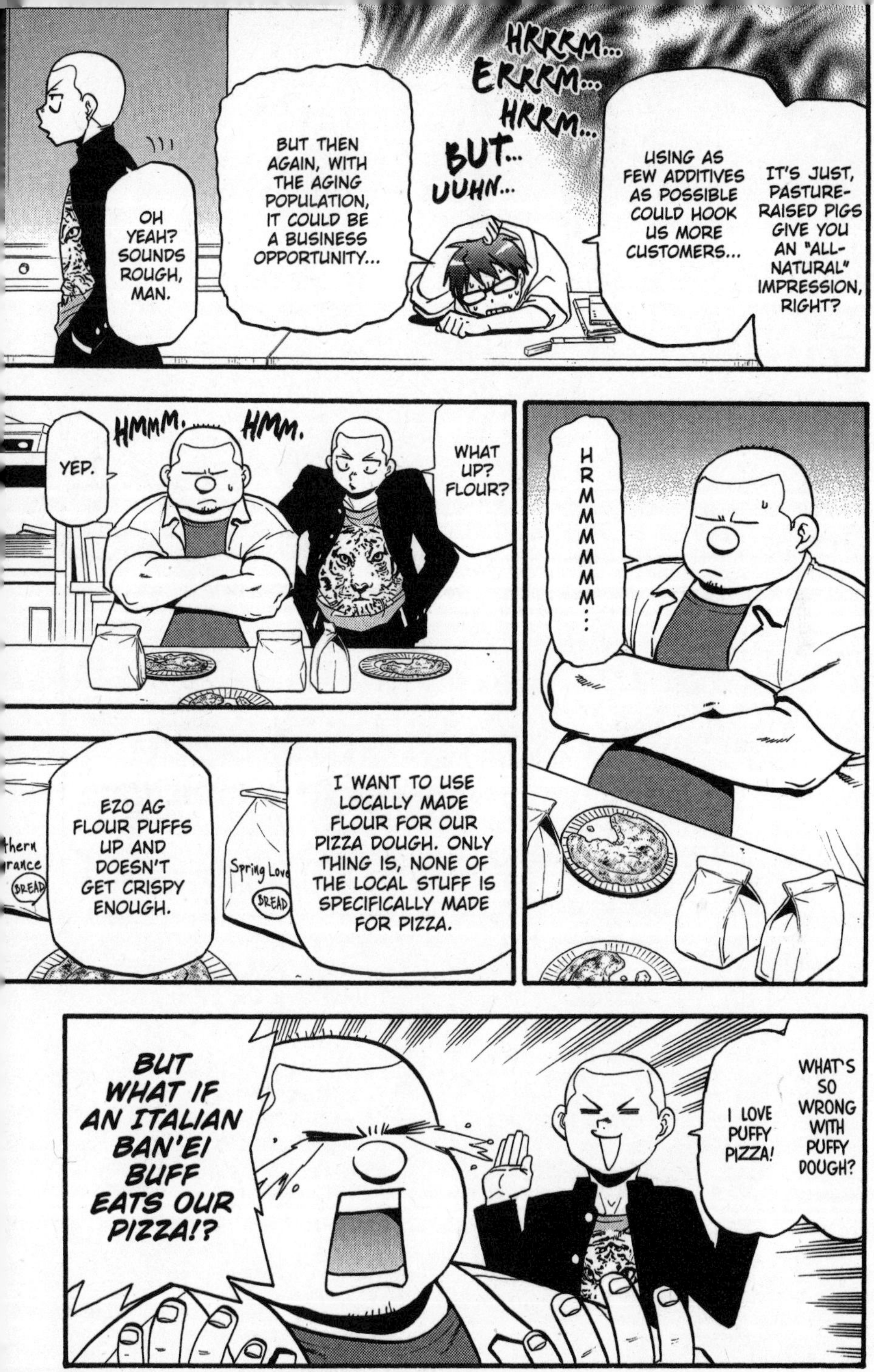

IT'S JUST, PASTURE-RAISED PIGS GIVE YOU AN "ALL-NATURAL" IMPRESSION, RIGHT?
USING AS FEW ADDITIVES AS POSSIBLE COULD HOOK US MORE CUSTOMERS...
HRRRM... ERRRM... HRRM...
BUT... UUHN...
BUT THEN AGAIN, WITH THE AGING POPULATION, IT COULD BE A BUSINESS OPPORTUNITY...
OH YEAH? SOUNDS ROUGH, MAN.
HRMMMMMMM...
WHAT UP? FLOUR?
HMM.
HMMM.
YEP.
I WANT TO USE LOCALLY MADE FLOUR FOR OUR PIZZA DOUGH. ONLY THING IS, NONE OF THE LOCAL STUFF IS SPECIFICALLY MADE FOR PIZZA.
Spring Love
BREAD
EZO AG FLOUR PUFFS UP AND DOESN'T GET CRISPY ENOUGH.
WHAT'S SO WRONG WITH PUFFY DOUGH?
I LOVE PUFFY PIZZA!
BUT WHAT IF AN ITALIAN BAN'EI BUFF EATS OUR PIZZA!?

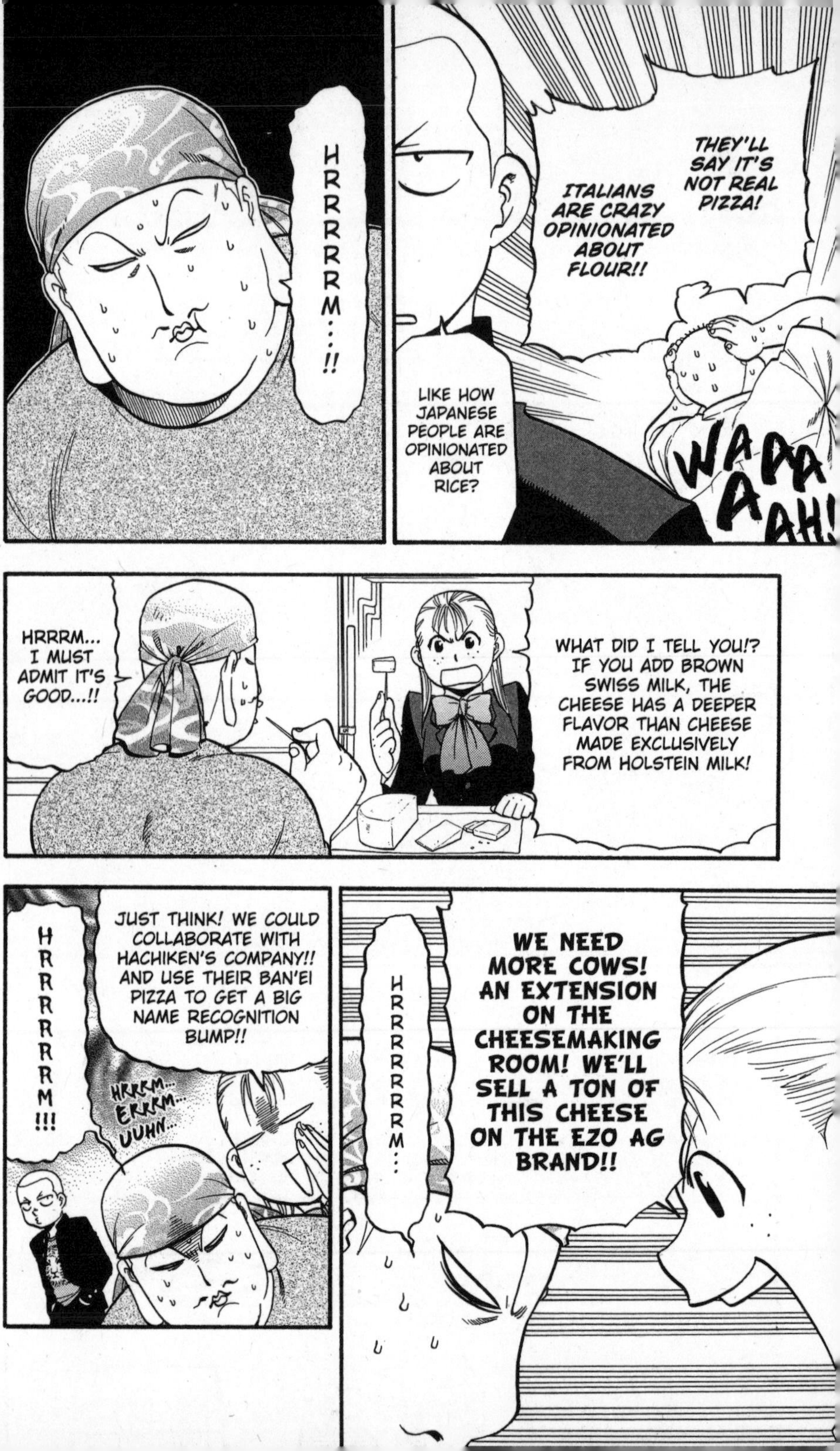
THEY'LL SAY IT'S NOT REAL PIZZA!
ITALIANS ARE CRAZY OPINIONATED ABOUT FLOUR!!
LIKE HOW JAPANESE PEOPLE ARE OPINIONATED ABOUT RICE?
WAPAAAAH!
HRRRRRM...!!
WHAT DID I TELL YOU!? IF YOU ADD BROWN SWISS MILK, THE CHEESE HAS A DEEPER FLAVOR THAN CHEESE MADE EXCLUSIVELY FROM HOLSTEIN MILK!
HRRRM... I MUST ADMIT IT'S GOOD...!!
WE NEED MORE COWS! AN EXTENSION ON THE CHEESEMAKING ROOM! WE'LL SELL A TON OF THIS CHEESE ON THE EZO AG BRAND!!
HRRRRRRRM...
JUST THINK! WE COULD COLLABORATE WITH HACHIKEN'S COMPANY!! AND USE THEIR BAN'EI PIZZA TO GET A BIG NAME RECOGNITION BUMP!!
HRRRRRRRM!!!
HRRRM... ERRRM... UUHN...

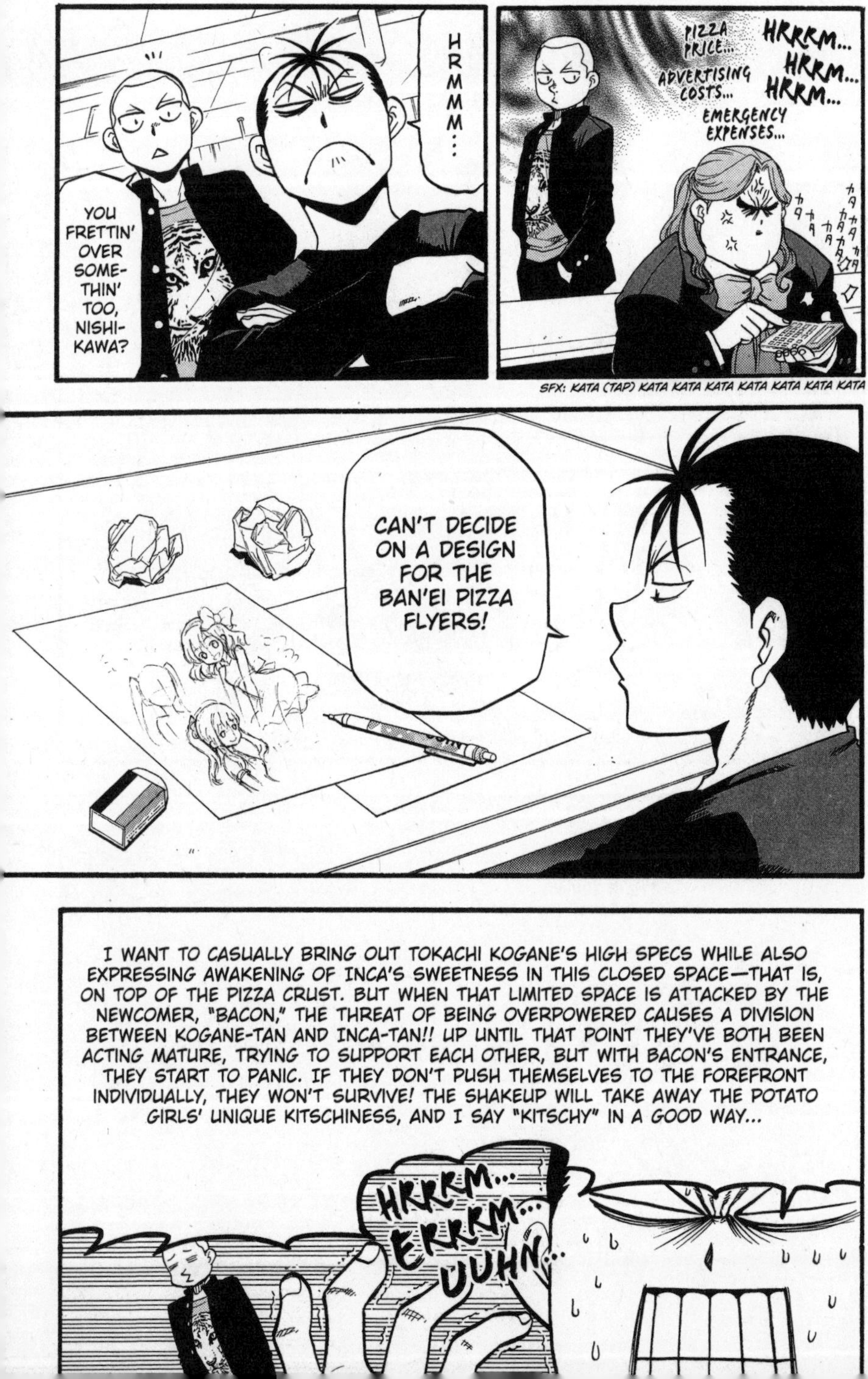
HRRRM... HRRM... HRRM...
PIZZA PRICE...
ADVERTISING COSTS...
EMERGENCY EXPENSES...
SFX: KATA (TAP) KATA KATA KATA KATA KATA KATA KATA
HRMMM...
YOU FRETTIN' OVER SOME-THIN' TOO, NISHI-KAWA?
CAN'T DECIDE ON A DESIGN FOR THE BAN'EI PIZZA FLYERS!
I WANT TO CASUALLY BRING OUT TOKACHI KOGANE'S HIGH SPECS WHILE ALSO EXPRESSING AWAKENING OF INCA'S SWEETNESS IN THIS CLOSED SPACE—THAT IS, ON TOP OF THE PIZZA CRUST. BUT WHEN THAT LIMITED SPACE IS ATTACKED BY THE NEWCOMER, "BACON," THE THREAT OF BEING OVERPOWERED CAUSES A DIVISION BETWEEN KOGANE-TAN AND INCA-TAN!! UP UNTIL THAT POINT THEY'VE BOTH BEEN ACTING MATURE, TRYING TO SUPPORT EACH OTHER, BUT WITH BACON'S ENTRANCE, THEY START TO PANIC. IF THEY DON'T PUSH THEMSELVES TO THE FOREFRONT INDIVIDUALLY, THEY WON'T SURVIVE! THE SHAKEUP WILL TAKE AWAY THE POTATO GIRLS' UNIQUE KITSCHINESS, AND I SAY "KITSCHY" IN A GOOD WAY...
HRRRM... ERRRM... UUHN...

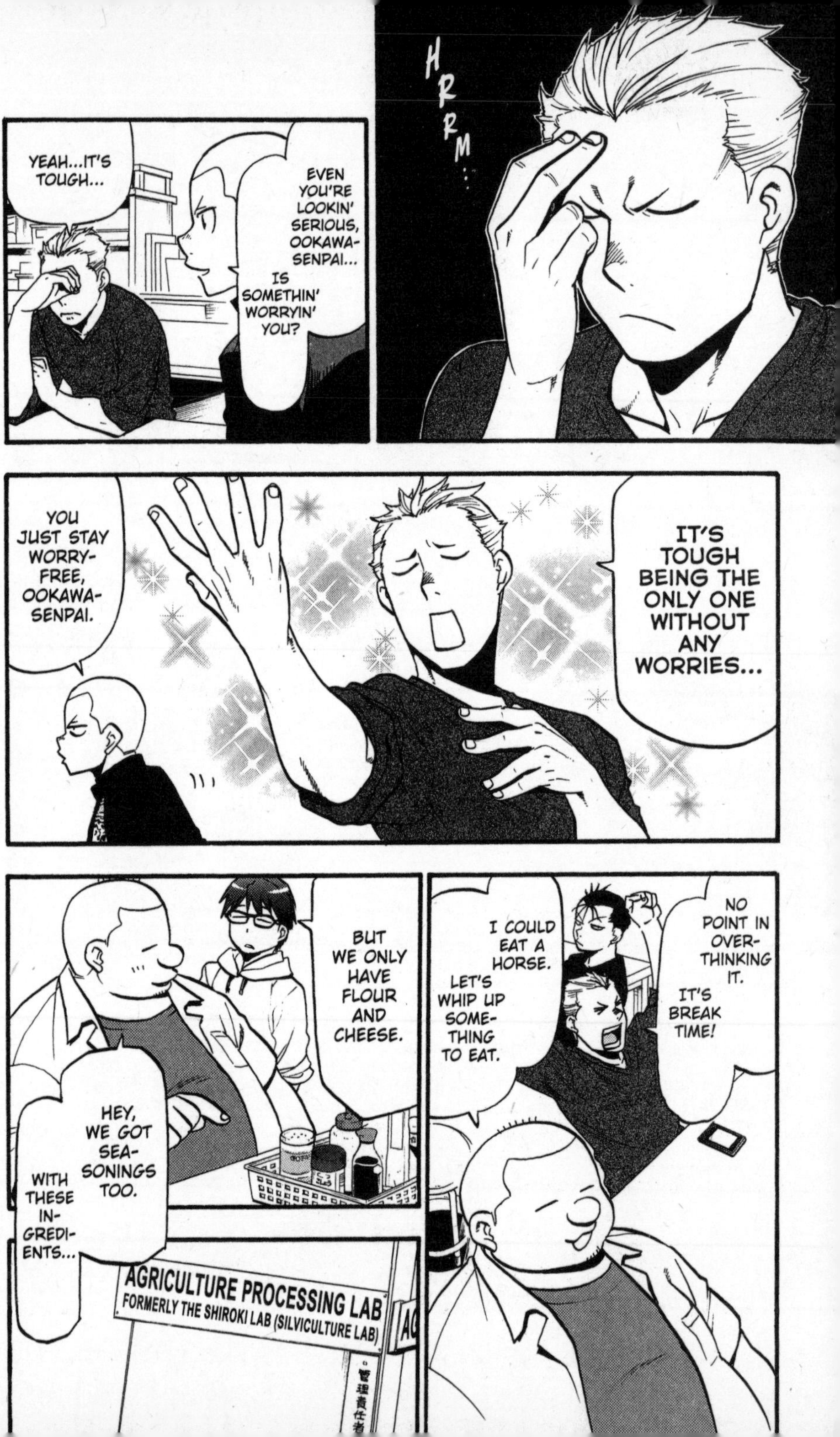
HRRM...
EVEN YOU'RE LOOKIN' SERIOUS, OOKAWA-SENPAI... IS SOMETHIN' WORRYIN' YOU?
YEAH...IT'S TOUGH...
IT'S TOUGH BEING THE ONLY ONE WITHOUT ANY WORRIES...
YOU JUST STAY WORRY-FREE, OOKAWA-SENPAI.
NO POINT IN OVER-THINKING IT. IT'S BREAK TIME!
I COULD EAT A HORSE. LET'S WHIP UP SOME-THING TO EAT.
BUT WE ONLY HAVE FLOUR AND CHEESE.
HEY, WE GOT SEA-SONINGS TOO.
WITH THESE IN-GREDI-ENTS...
AGRICULTURE PROCESSING LAB
FORMERLY THE SHIROKI LAB (SILVICULTURE LAB)
管理責任者

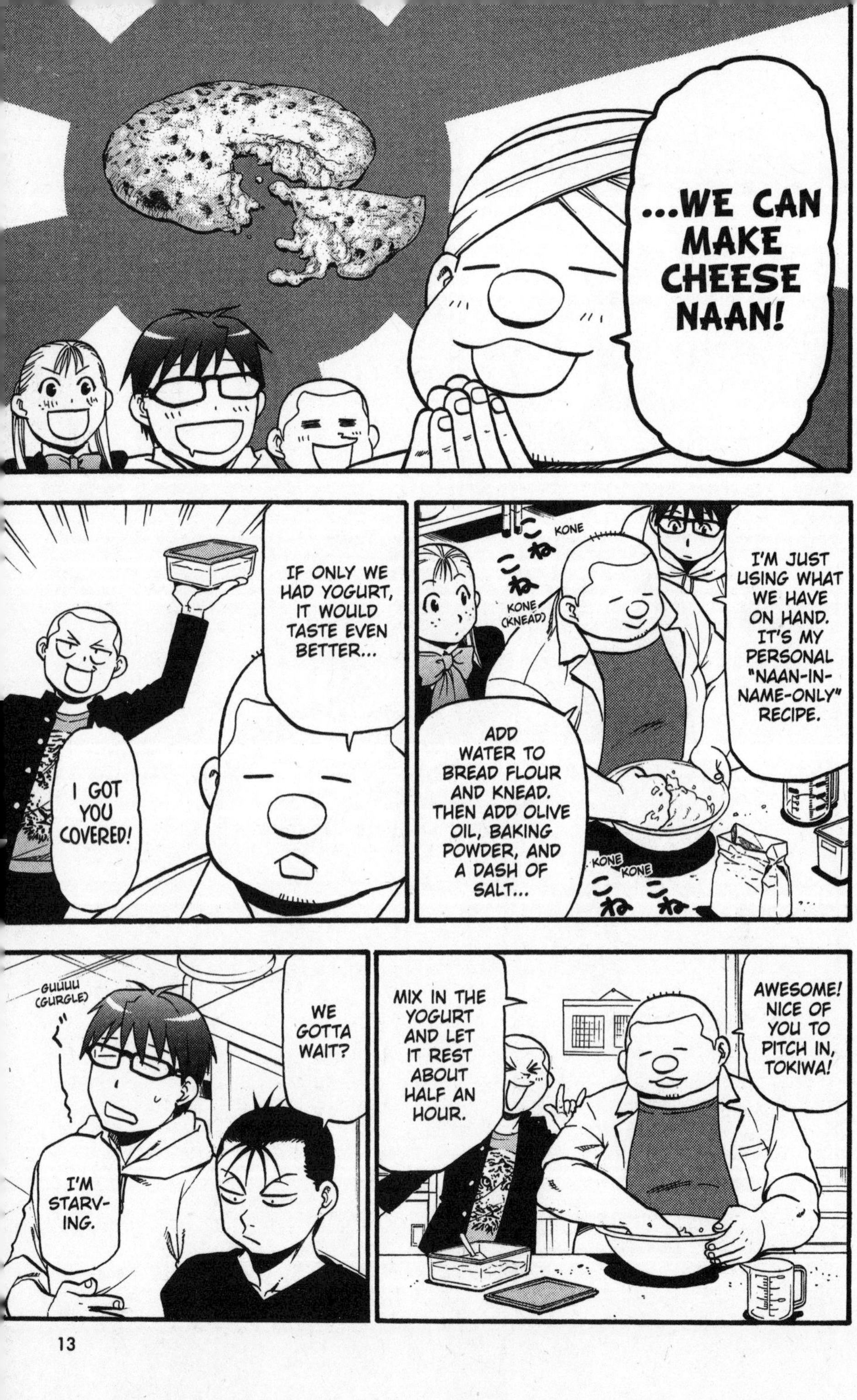
...WE CAN MAKE CHEESE NAAN!
こね こね
KONE
KONE (KNEAD)
I'M JUST USING WHAT WE HAVE ON HAND. IT'S MY PERSONAL "NAAN-IN-NAME-ONLY" RECIPE.
ADD WATER TO BREAD FLOUR AND KNEAD. THEN ADD OLIVE OIL, BAKING POWDER, AND A DASH OF SALT...
こね こね
KONE KONE
IF ONLY WE HAD YOGURT, IT WOULD TASTE EVEN BETTER...
I GOT YOU COVERED!
AWESOME! NICE OF YOU TO PITCH IN, TOKIWA!
MIX IN THE YOGURT AND LET IT REST ABOUT HALF AN HOUR.
WE GOTTA WAIT?
GUUUU (GURGLE)
I'M STARVING.

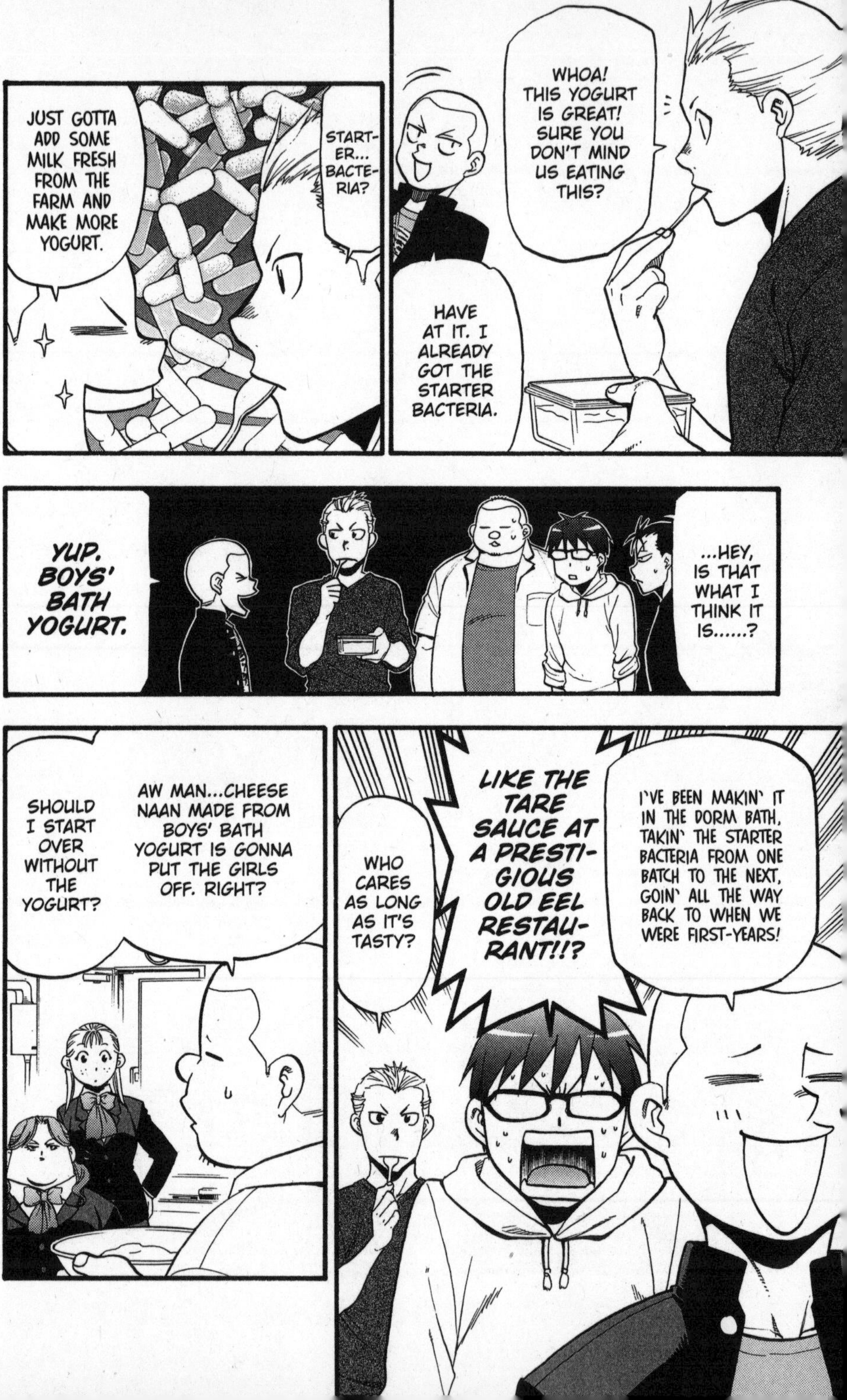
WHOA! THIS YOGURT IS GREAT! SURE YOU DON'T MIND US EATING THIS?
HAVE AT IT. I ALREADY GOT THE STARTER BACTERIA.
STARTER... BACTERIA?
JUST GOTTA ADD SOME MILK FRESH FROM THE FARM AND MAKE MORE YOGURT.
...HEY, IS THAT WHAT I THINK IT IS......?
YUP. BOYS' BATH YOGURT.
I'VE BEEN MAKIN' IT IN THE DORM BATH, TAKIN' THE STARTER BACTERIA FROM ONE BATCH TO THE NEXT, GOIN' ALL THE WAY BACK TO WHEN WE WERE FIRST-YEARS!
LIKE THE TARE SAUCE AT A PRESTIGIOUS OLD EEL RESTAURANT!!?
WHO CARES AS LONG AS IT'S TASTY?
AW MAN...CHEESE NAAN MADE FROM BOYS' BATH YOGURT IS GONNA PUT THE GIRLS OFF. RIGHT?
SHOULD I START OVER WITHOUT THE YOGURT?

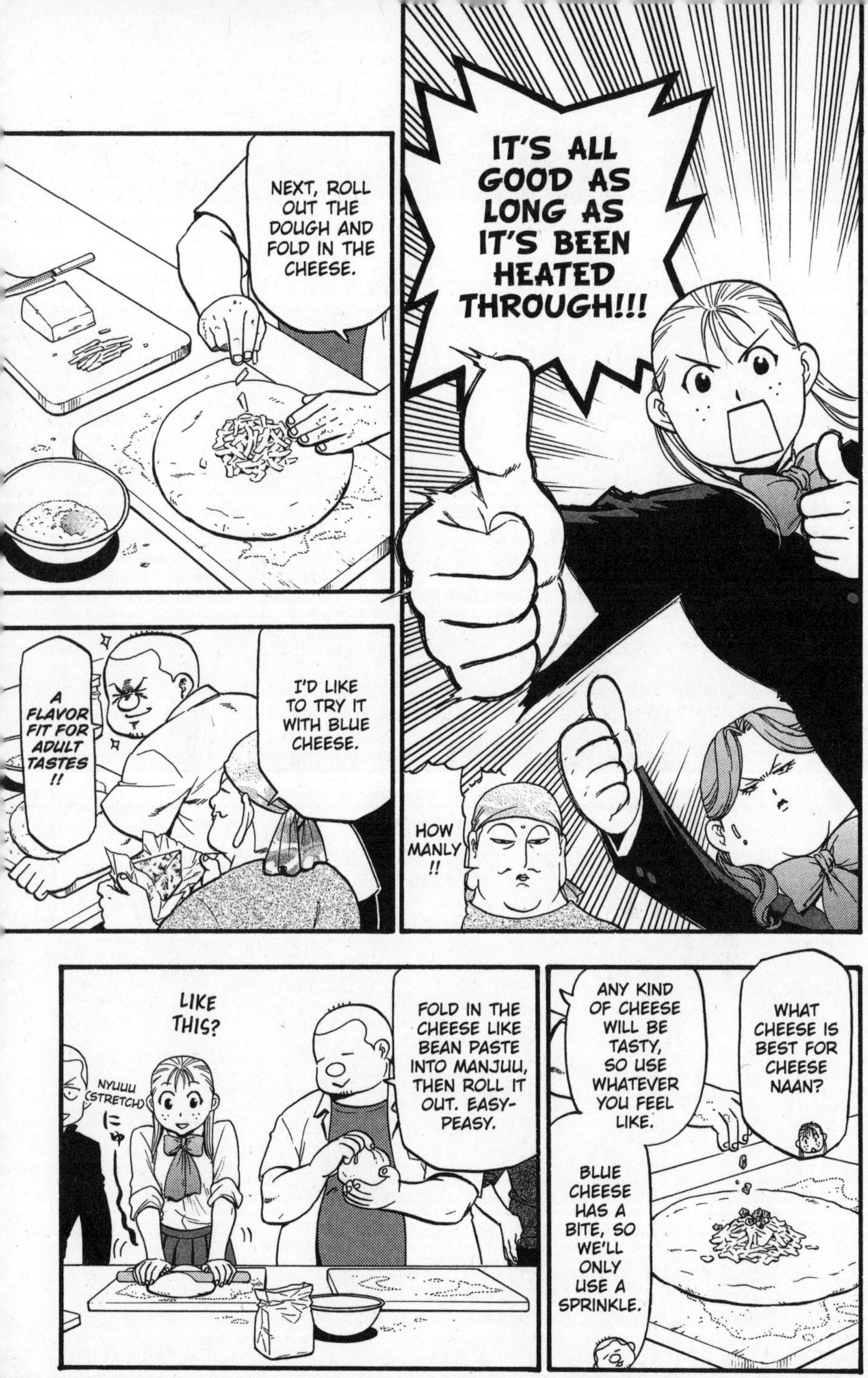
IT'S ALL GOOD AS LONG AS IT'S BEEN HEATED THROUGH!!!
HOW MANLY!!
NEXT, ROLL OUT THE DOUGH AND FOLD IN THE CHEESE.
I'D LIKE TO TRY IT WITH BLUE CHEESE.
A FLAVOR FIT FOR ADULT TASTES!!
WHAT CHEESE IS BEST FOR CHEESE NAAN?
ANY KIND OF CHEESE WILL BE TASTY, SO USE WHATEVER YOU FEEL LIKE.
BLUE CHEESE HAS A BITE, SO WE'LL ONLY USE A SPRINKLE.
FOLD IN THE CHEESE LIKE BEAN PASTE INTO MANJUU, THEN ROLL IT OUT. EASY-PEASY.
LIKE THIS?
NYUUU (STRETCH)
にゅ

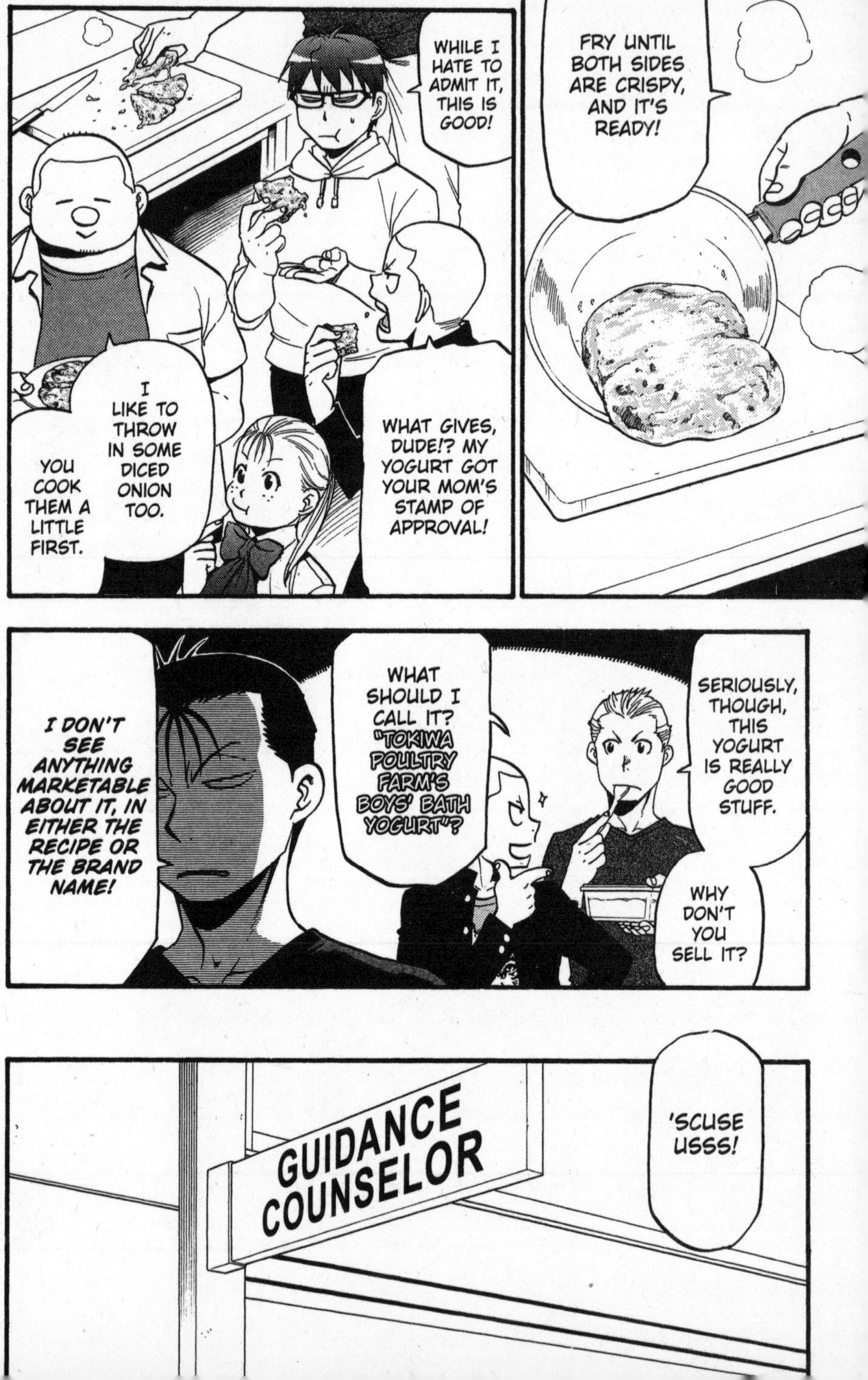
FRY UNTIL BOTH SIDES ARE CRISPY, AND IT'S READY!
WHILE I HATE TO ADMIT IT, THIS IS GOOD!
WHAT GIVES, DUDE!? MY YOGURT GOT YOUR MOM'S STAMP OF APPROVAL!
I LIKE TO THROW IN SOME DICED ONION TOO.
YOU COOK THEM A LITTLE FIRST.
SERIOUSLY, THOUGH, THIS YOGURT IS REALLY GOOD STUFF.
WHY DON'T YOU SELL IT?
WHAT SHOULD I CALL IT? "TOKIWA POULTRY FARM'S BOYS' BATH YOGURT"?
I DON'T SEE ANYTHING MARKETABLE ABOUT IT, IN EITHER THE RECIPE OR THE BRAND NAME!
'SCUSE USSS!
GUIDANCE COUNSELOR

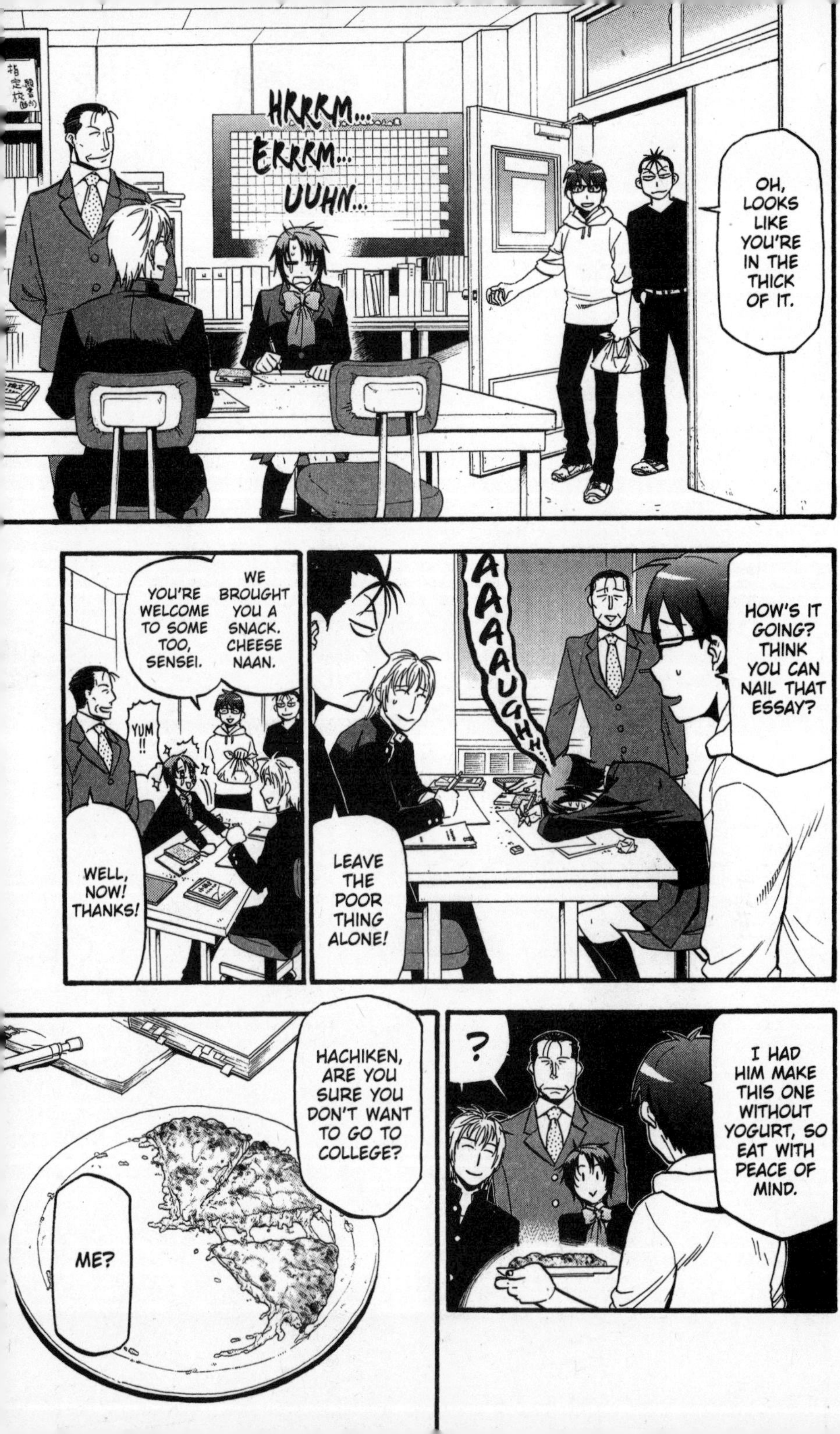
HRRRM... ERRRM... UUHN...
OH, LOOKS LIKE YOU'RE IN THE THICK OF IT.
HOW'S IT GOING? THINK YOU CAN NAIL THAT ESSAY?
AAAAAUGHH!
LEAVE THE POOR THING ALONE!
WE BROUGHT YOU A SNACK. CHEESE NAAN.
YOU'RE WELCOME TO SOME TOO, SENSEI.
YUM!!
WELL, NOW! THANKS!
I HAD HIM MAKE THIS ONE WITHOUT YOGURT, SO EAT WITH PEACE OF MIND.
?
HACHIKEN, ARE YOU SURE YOU DON'T WANT TO GO TO COLLEGE?
ME?

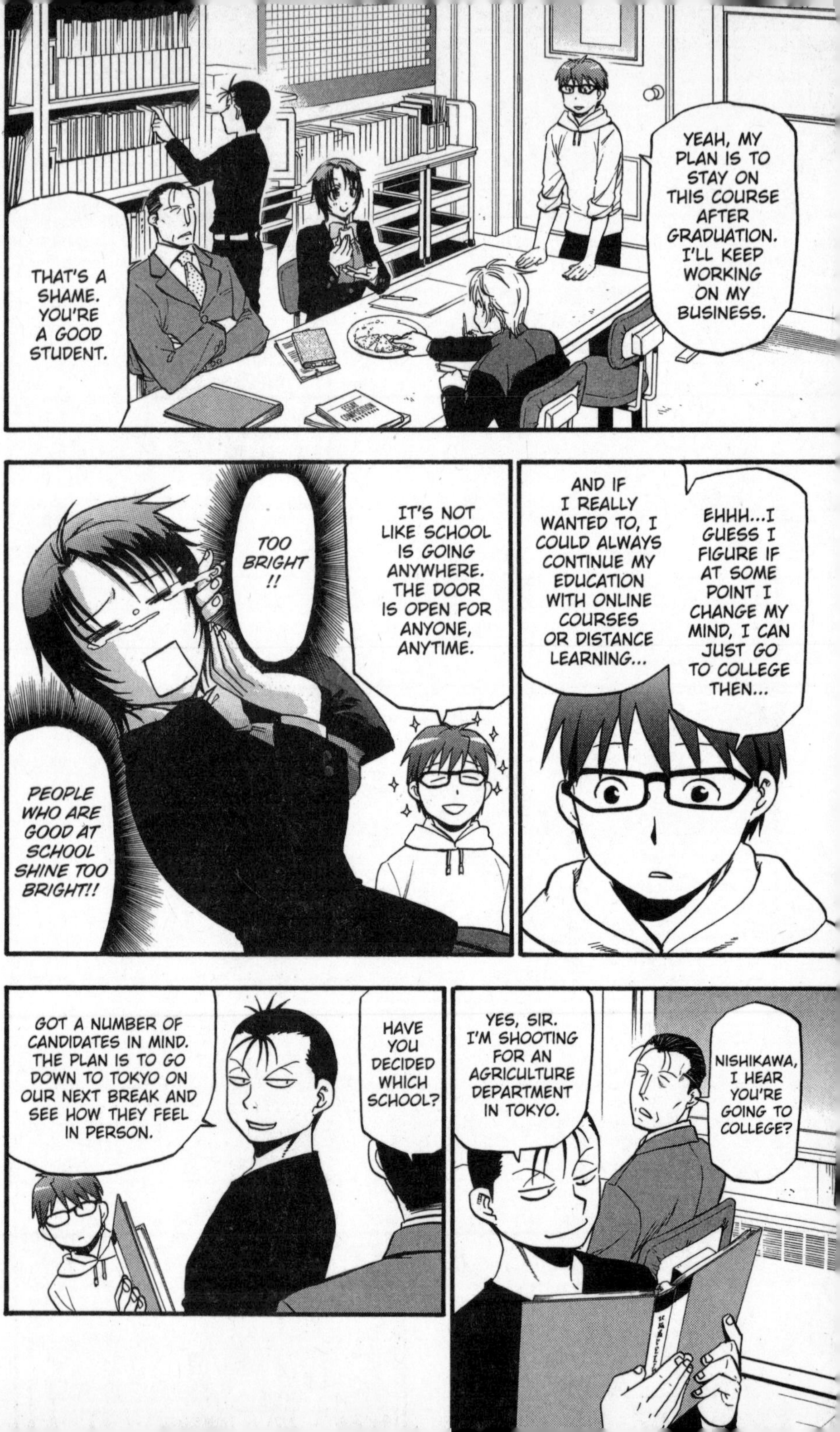
YEAH, MY PLAN IS TO STAY ON THIS COURSE AFTER GRADUATION. I'LL KEEP WORKING ON MY BUSINESS.
THAT'S A SHAME. YOU'RE A GOOD STUDENT.
EHHH...I GUESS I FIGURE IF AT SOME POINT I CHANGE MY MIND, I CAN JUST GO TO COLLEGE THEN...
AND IF I REALLY WANTED TO, I COULD ALWAYS CONTINUE MY EDUCATION WITH ONLINE COURSES OR DISTANCE LEARNING...
IT'S NOT LIKE SCHOOL IS GOING ANYWHERE. THE DOOR IS OPEN FOR ANYONE, ANYTIME.
TOO BRIGHT !!
PEOPLE WHO ARE GOOD AT SCHOOL SHINE TOO BRIGHT!!
NISHIKAWA, I HEAR YOU'RE GOING TO COLLEGE?
YES, SIR. I'M SHOOTING FOR AN AGRICULTURE DEPARTMENT IN TOKYO.
HAVE YOU DECIDED WHICH SCHOOL?
GOT A NUMBER OF CANDIDATES IN MIND. THE PLAN IS TO GO DOWN TO TOKYO ON OUR NEXT BREAK AND SEE HOW THEY FEEL IN PERSON.

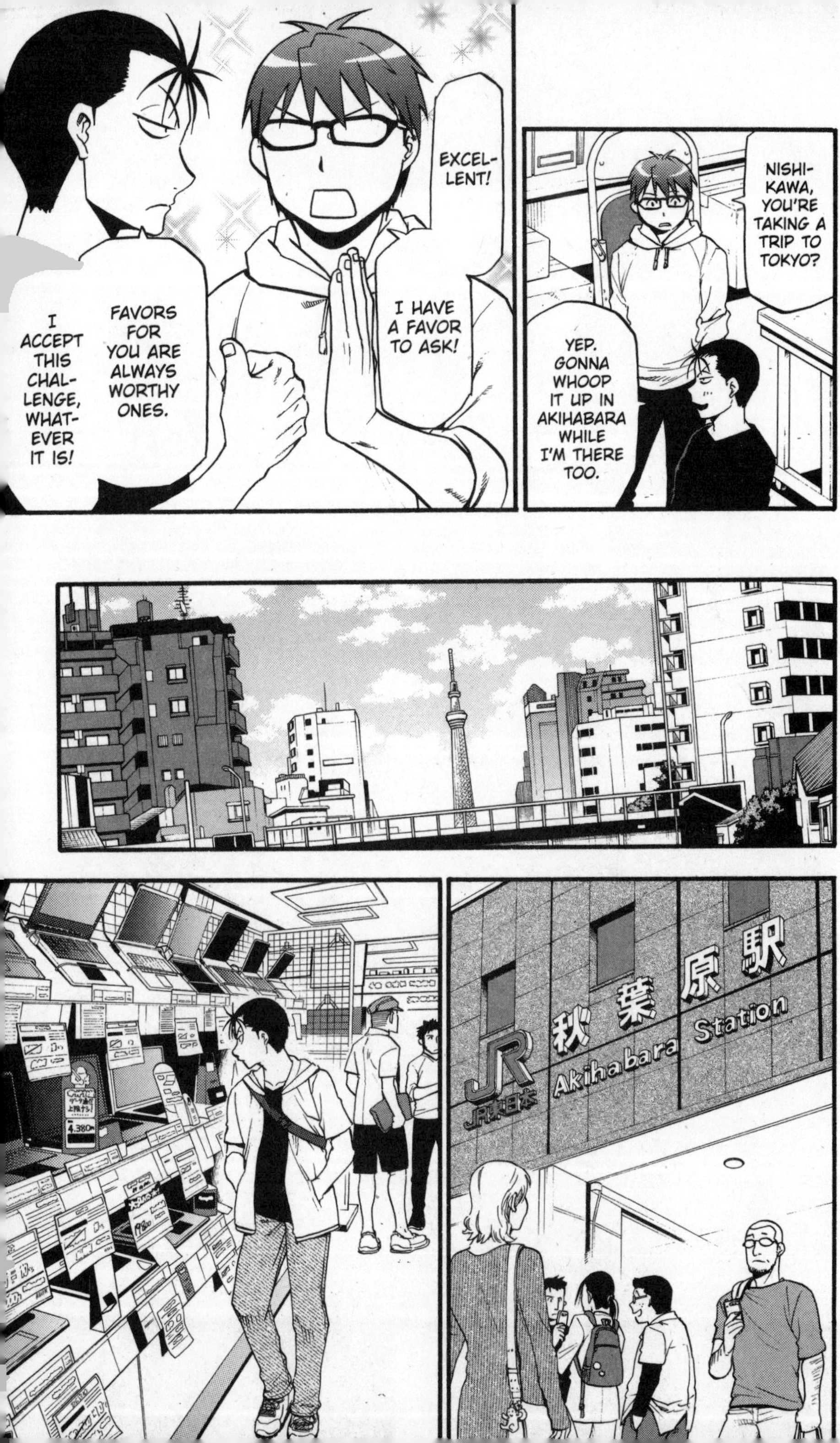
NISHIKAWA, YOU'RE TAKING A TRIP TO TOKYO?
YEP. GONNA WHOOP IT UP IN AKIHABARA WHILE I'M THERE TOO.
EXCELLENT!
I HAVE A FAVOR TO ASK!
FAVORS FOR YOU ARE ALWAYS WORTHY ONES.
I ACCEPT THIS CHALLENGE, WHATEVER IT IS!
JR
秋葉原駅
Akihabara Station
JR東日本

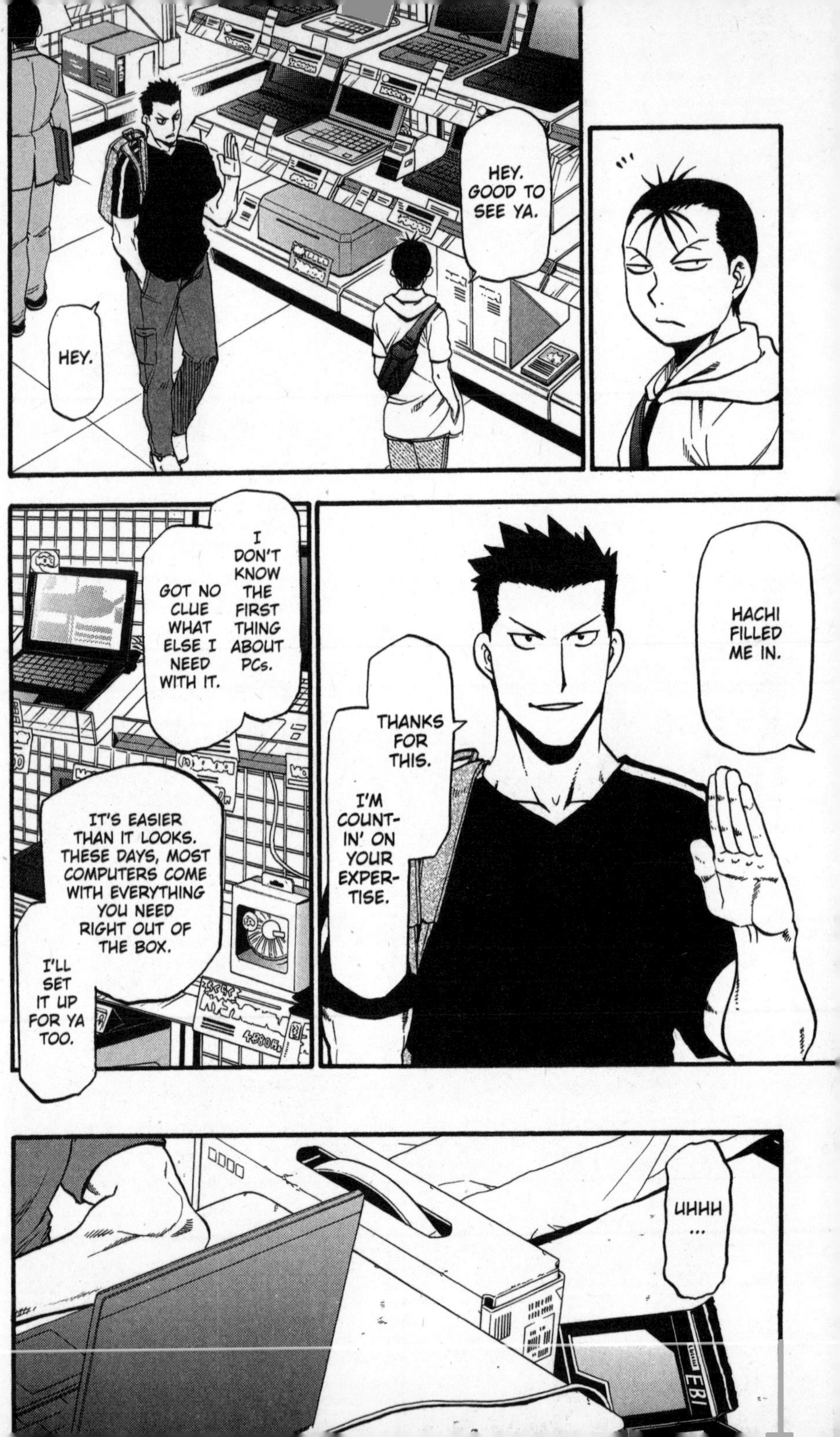
HEY. GOOD TO SEE YA.
HEY.
HACHI FILLED ME IN.
THANKS FOR THIS.
I'M COUNT-IN' ON YOUR EXPER-TISE.
I DON'T KNOW THE FIRST THING ABOUT PCs.
GOT NO CLUE WHAT ELSE I NEED WITH IT.
IT'S EASIER THAN IT LOOKS. THESE DAYS, MOST COMPUTERS COME WITH EVERYTHING YOU NEED RIGHT OUT OF THE BOX.
I'LL SET IT UP FOR YA TOO.
UHHH...
EBI

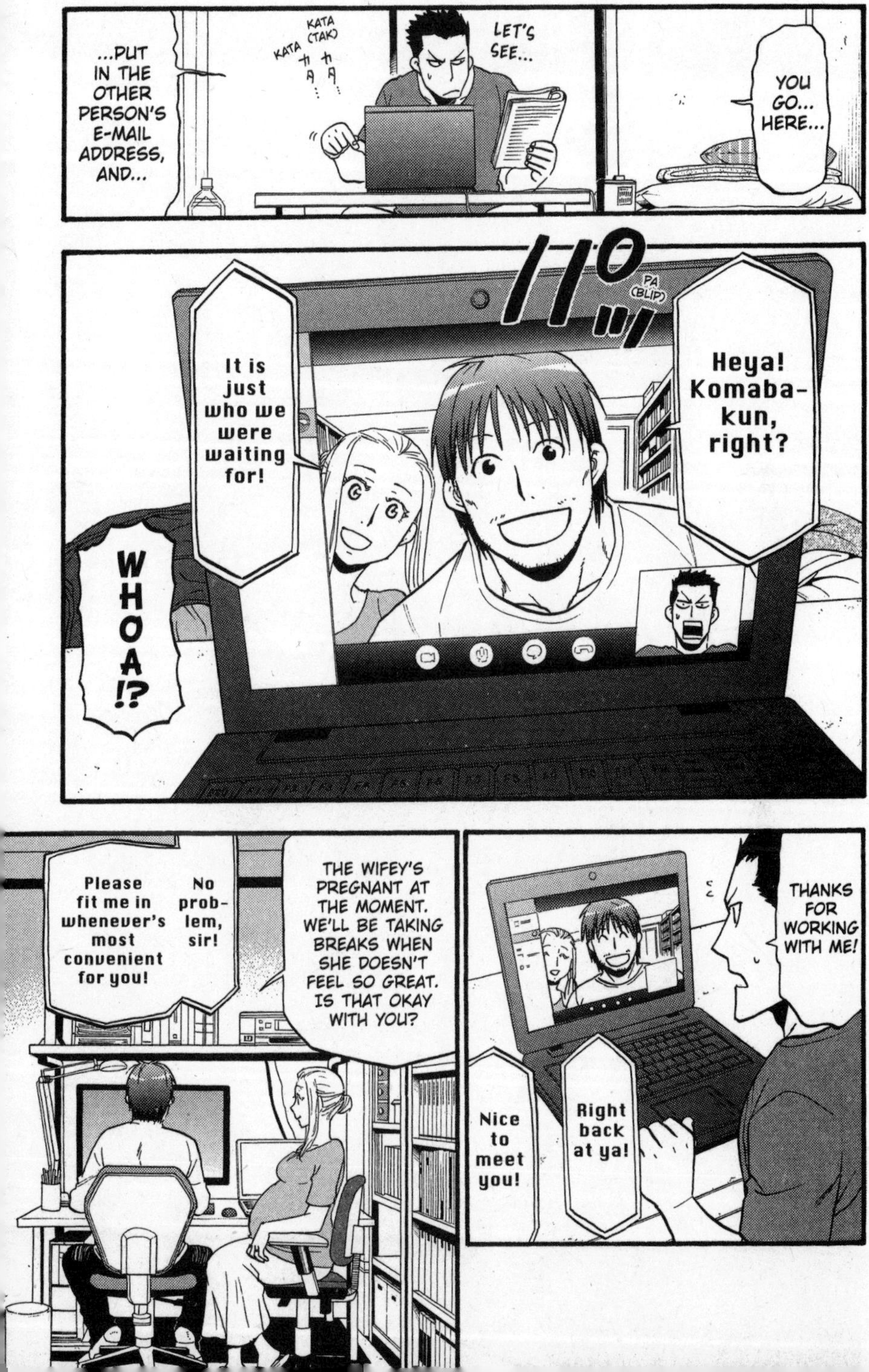
YOU GO... HERE...
LET'S SEE...
KATA (TAK)
KATA
...PUT IN THE OTHER PERSON'S E-MAIL ADDRESS, AND...
PA (BLIP)
Heya! Komaba-kun, right?
It is just who we were waiting for!
WHOA!?
THANKS FOR WORKING WITH ME!
Right back at ya!
Nice to meet you!
THE WIFEY'S PREGNANT AT THE MOMENT. WE'LL BE TAKING BREAKS WHEN SHE DOESN'T FEEL SO GREAT. IS THAT OKAY WITH YOU?
No prob-lem, sir!
Please fit me in whenever's most convenient for you!

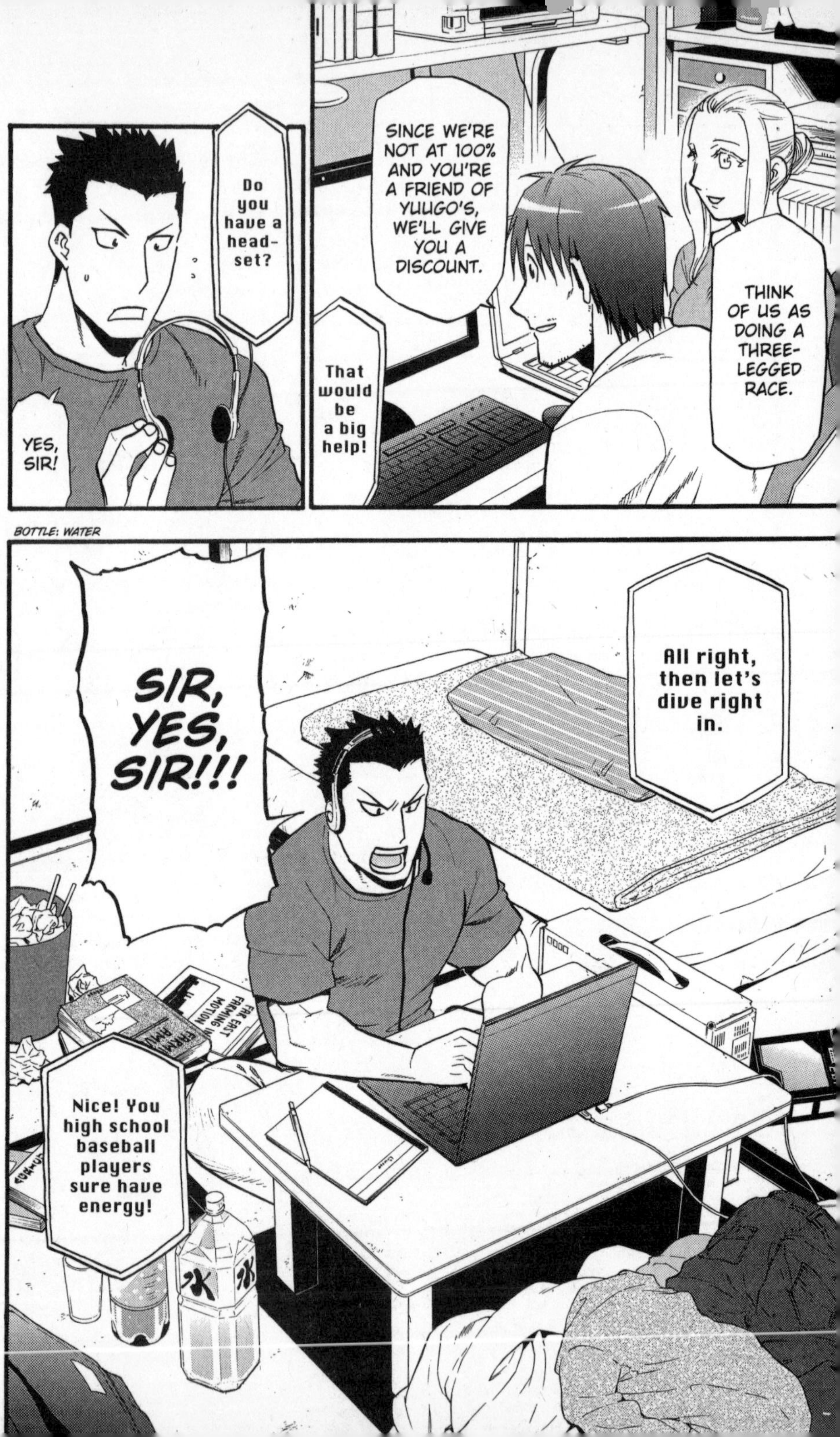
SINCE WE'RE NOT AT 100% AND YOU'RE A FRIEND OF YUUGO'S, WE'LL GIVE YOU A DISCOUNT.
THINK OF US AS DOING A THREE-LEGGED RACE.
That would be a big help!
Do you have a head-set?
YES, SIR!
BOTTLE: WATER
All right, then let's dive right in.
SIR, YES, SIR!!!
Nice! You high school baseball players sure have energy!

Silver Spoon

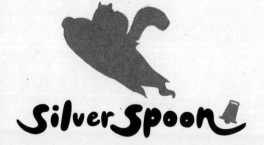

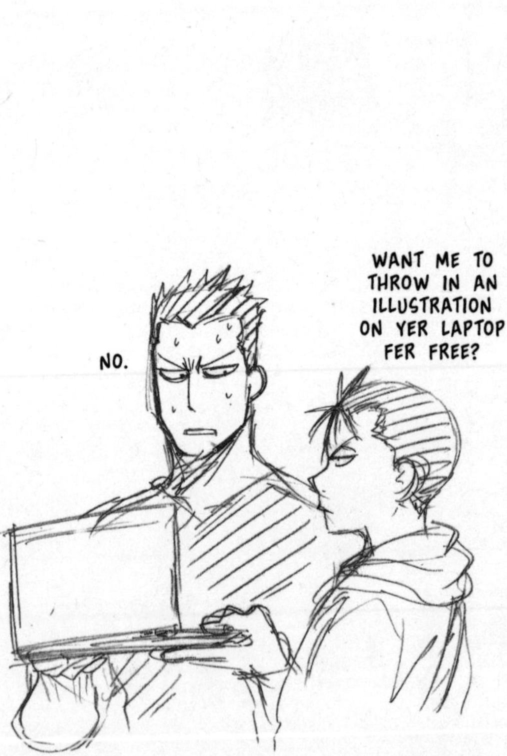
WANT ME TO THROW IN AN ILLUSTRATION ON YER LAPTOP FER FREE?
NO.

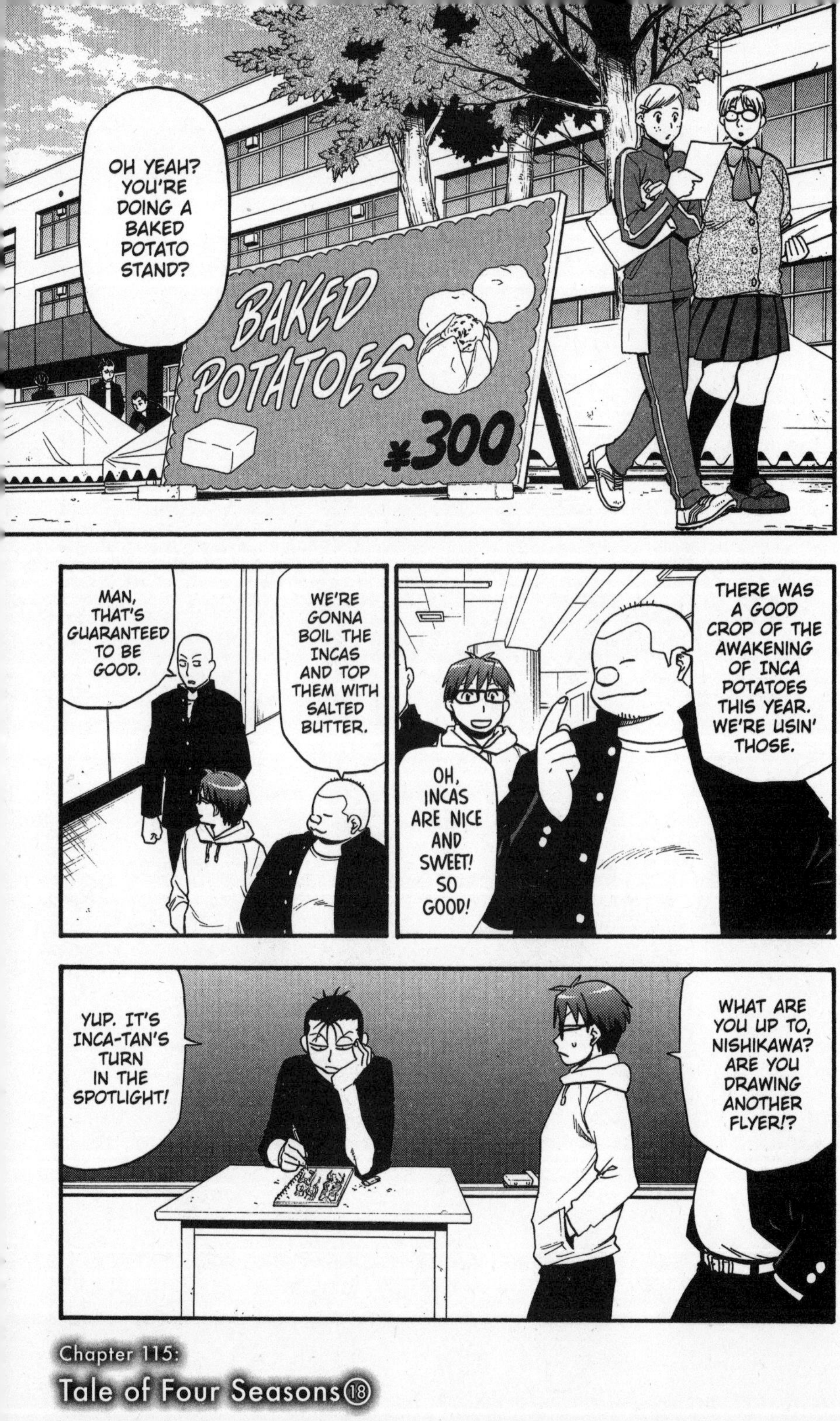
OH YEAH? YOU'RE DOING A BAKED POTATO STAND?
BAKED POTATOES
¥300
THERE WAS A GOOD CROP OF THE AWAKENING OF INCA POTATOES THIS YEAR. WE'RE USIN' THOSE.
OH, INCAS ARE NICE AND SWEET! SO GOOD!
WE'RE GONNA BOIL THE INCAS AND TOP THEM WITH SALTED BUTTER.
MAN, THAT'S GUARANTEED TO BE GOOD.
WHAT ARE YOU UP TO, NISHIKAWA? ARE YOU DRAWING ANOTHER FLYER!?
YUP. IT'S INCA-TAN'S TURN IN THE SPOTLIGHT!

Chapter 115:
Tale of Four Seasons ⑱

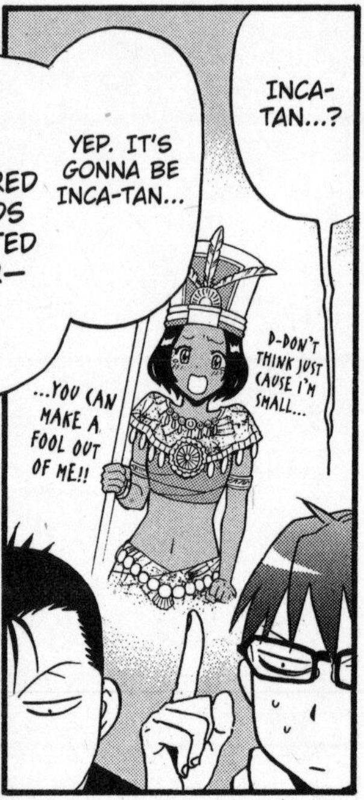
INCA-TAN...?
YEP. IT'S GONNA BE INCA-TAN...
...COVERED IN LOADS OF MELTED BUTTER—
D-DON'T THINK JUST CAUSE I'M SMALL...
...YOU CAN MAKE A FOOL OUT OF ME!!

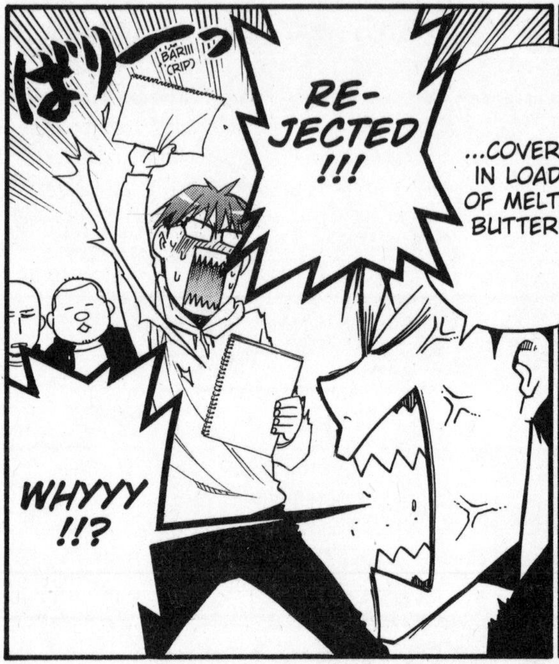
RE-JECTED!!!
ばりーっ
BARIII (RIP)
WHYYY!!?

Chapter 115:

Tale of Four Seasons ⑱

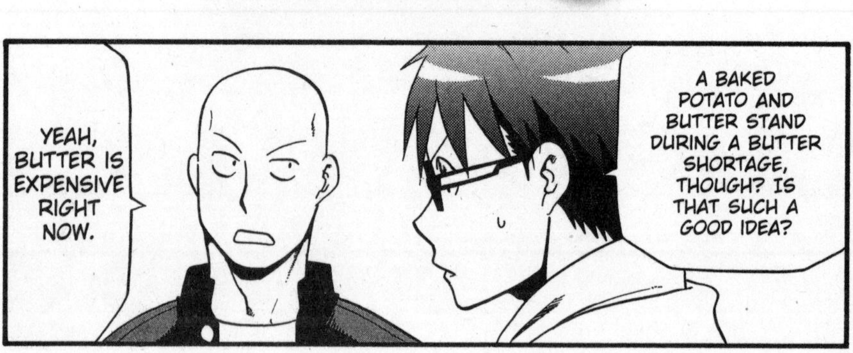
A BAKED POTATO AND BUTTER STAND DURING A BUTTER SHORTAGE, THOUGH? IS THAT SUCH A GOOD IDEA?
YEAH, BUTTER IS EXPENSIVE RIGHT NOW.

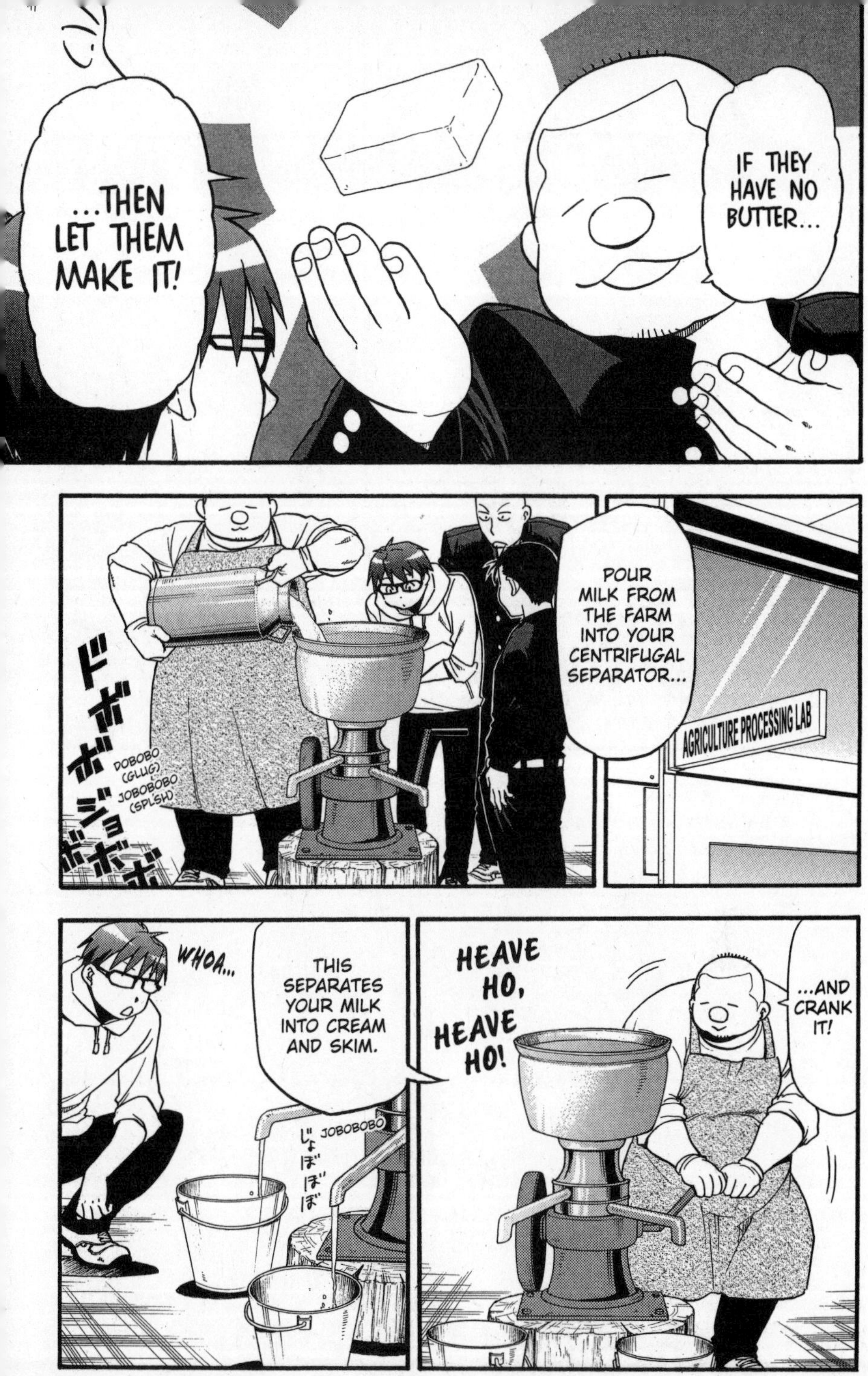
IF THEY HAVE NO BUTTER...
...THEN LET THEM MAKE IT!
POUR MILK FROM THE FARM INTO YOUR CENTRIFUGAL SEPARATOR...
AGRICULTURE PROCESSING LAB
ドボボ
DOBOBO (GLUG)
ジョボボボ
JOBOBOBO (SPLSH)
...AND CRANK IT!
HEAVE HO, HEAVE HO!
THIS SEPARATES YOUR MILK INTO CREAM AND SKIM.
WHOA...
じょぼぼぼ
JOBOBOBO

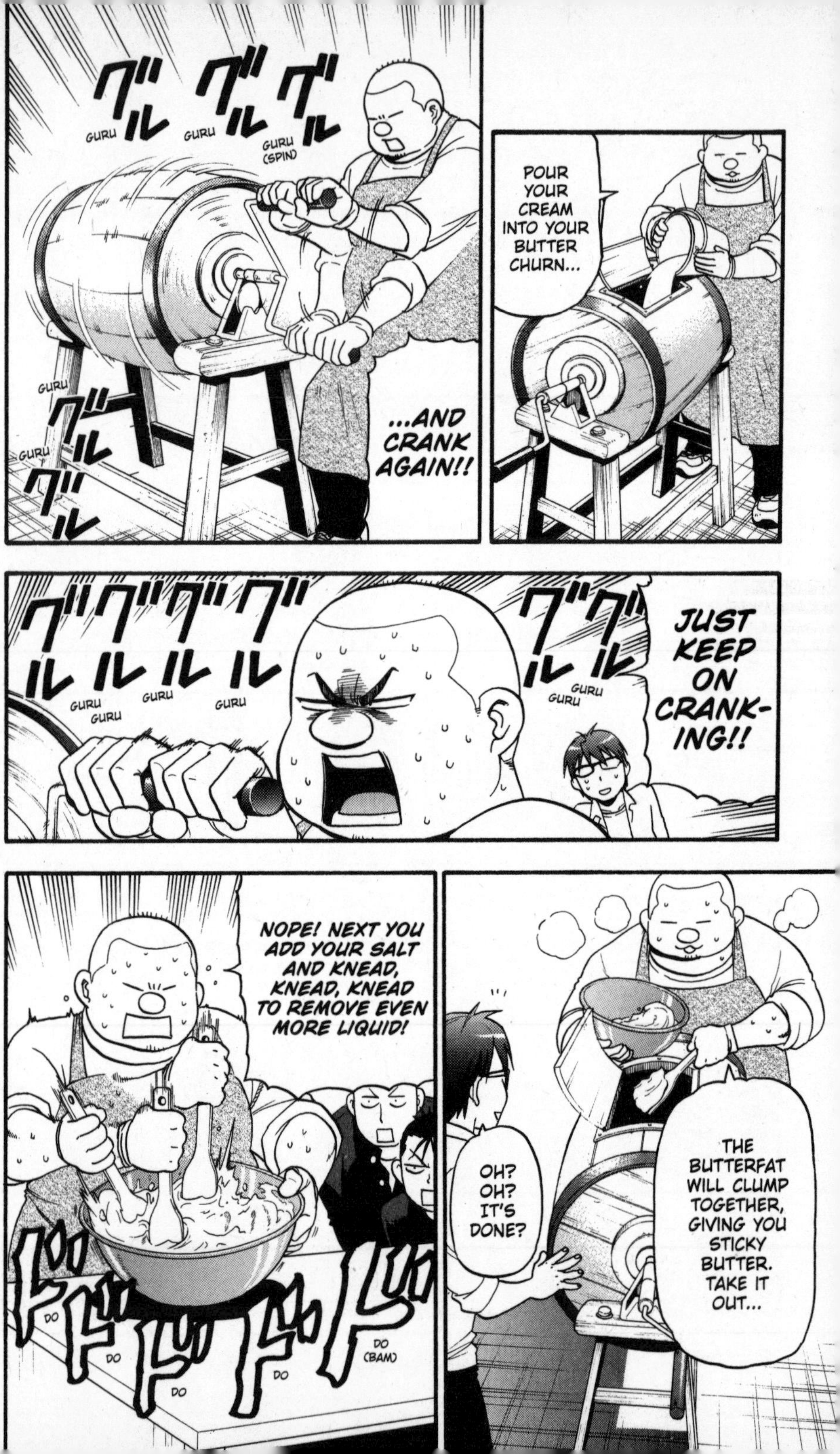
POUR YOUR CREAM INTO YOUR BUTTER CHURN...
GURU
GURU
GURU (SPIN)
...AND CRANK AGAIN!!
GURU
GURU
JUST KEEP ON CRANKING!!
GURU
GURU
GURU
GURU
GURU
GURU
THE BUTTERFAT WILL CLUMP TOGETHER, GIVING YOU STICKY BUTTER. TAKE IT OUT...
OH? OH? IT'S DONE?
NOPE! NEXT YOU ADD YOUR SALT AND KNEAD, KNEAD, KNEAD TO REMOVE EVEN MORE LIQUID!
DO
DO
DO
DO
DO (BAM)

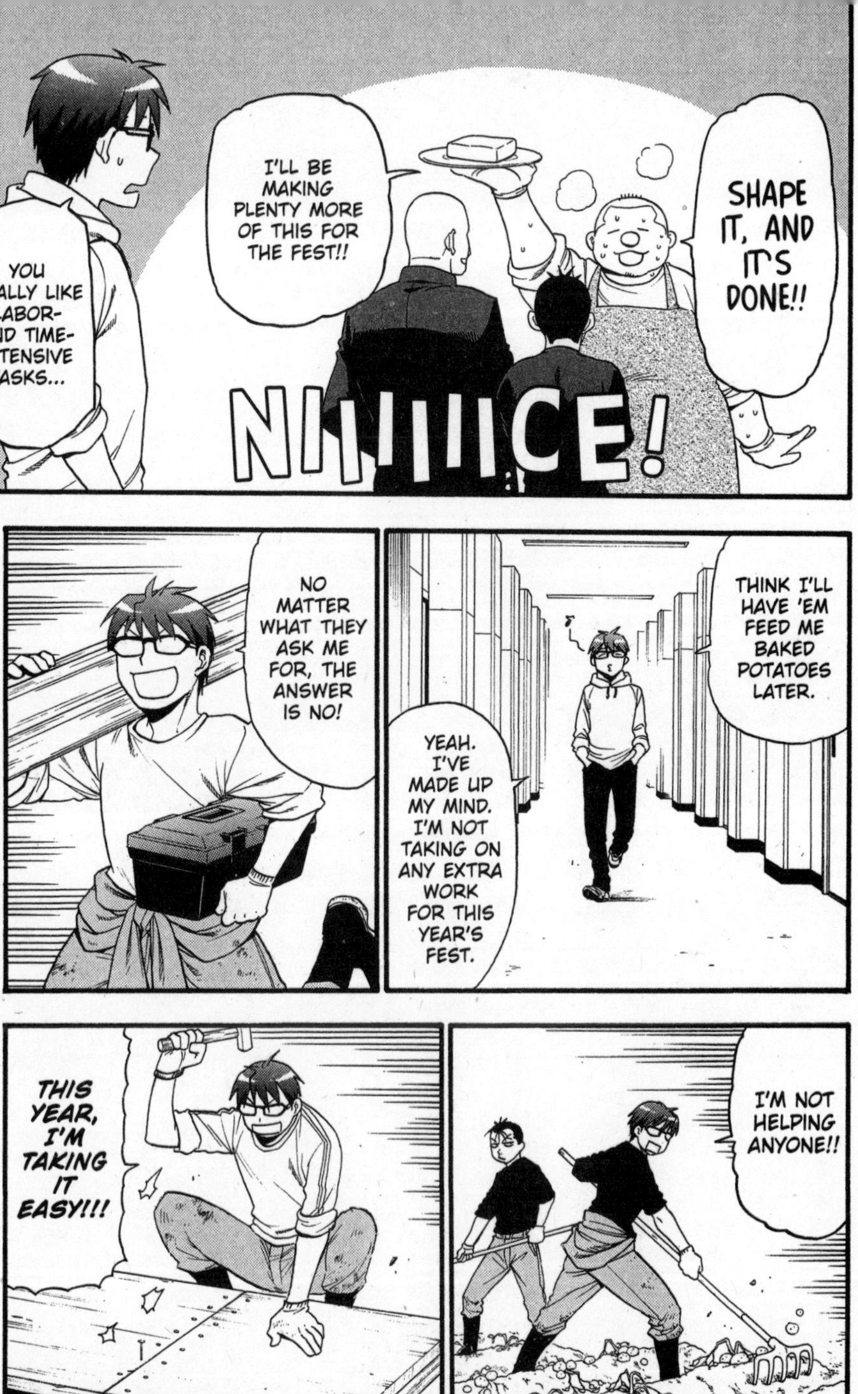
SHAPE IT, AND IT'S DONE!!
I'LL BE MAKING PLENTY MORE OF THIS FOR THE FEST!!
NIIIIICE!
YOU REALLY LIKE LABOR- AND TIME-INTENSIVE TASKS...
THINK I'LL HAVE 'EM FEED ME BAKED POTATOES LATER.
YEAH. I'VE MADE UP MY MIND. I'M NOT TAKING ON ANY EXTRA WORK FOR THIS YEAR'S FEST.
NO MATTER WHAT THEY ASK ME FOR, THE ANSWER IS NO!
I'M NOT HELPING ANYONE!!
THIS YEAR, I'M TAKING IT EASY!!!

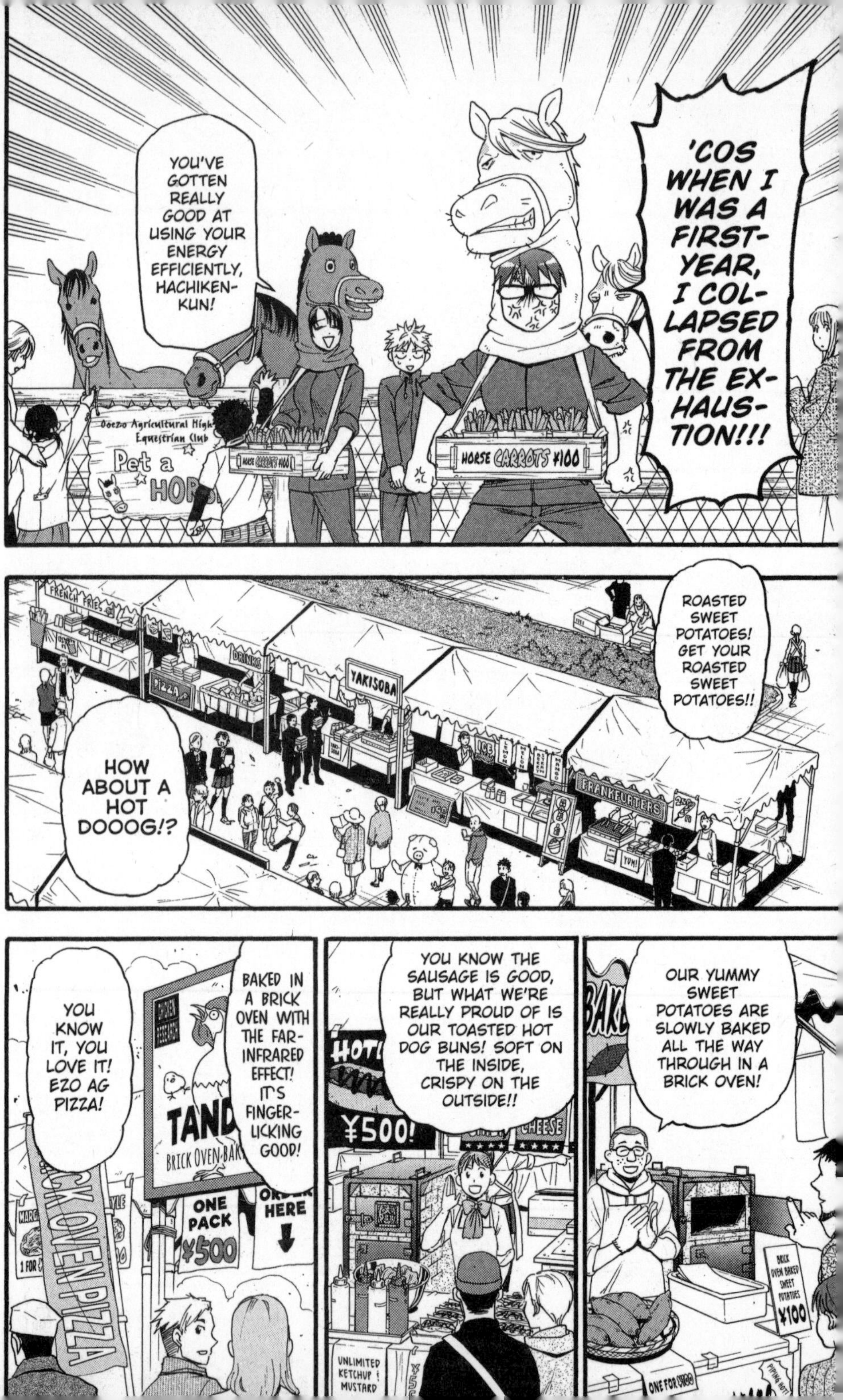
'COS WHEN I WAS A FIRST-YEAR, I COL-LAPSED FROM THE EX-HAUS-TION!!!
YOU'VE GOTTEN REALLY GOOD AT USING YOUR ENERGY EFFICIENTLY, HACHIKEN-KUN!
HORSE CARROTS ¥100
Oezo Agricultural High Equestrian Club
Pet a HORS
ROASTED SWEET POTATOES! GET YOUR ROASTED SWEET POTATOES!!
HOW ABOUT A HOT DOOOG!?
FRENCH FRIES
DRINKS
PIZZA
YAKISOBA
ICE
FRANKFURTERS
OUR YUMMY SWEET POTATOES ARE SLOWLY BAKED ALL THE WAY THROUGH IN A BRICK OVEN!
BRICK OVEN BAKED SWEET POTATOES ¥100
YOU KNOW THE SAUSAGE IS GOOD, BUT WHAT WE'RE REALLY PROUD OF IS OUR TOASTED HOT DOG BUNS! SOFT ON THE INSIDE, CRISPY ON THE OUTSIDE!!
¥500!
CHEESE
UNLIMITED KETCHUP & MUSTARD
BAKED IN A BRICK OVEN WITH THE FAR-INFRARED EFFECT! IT'S FINGER-LICKING GOOD!
YOU KNOW IT, YOU LOVE IT! EZO AG PIZZA!
TAND
BRICK OVEN BAK
ONE PACK ¥500
ORDER HERE

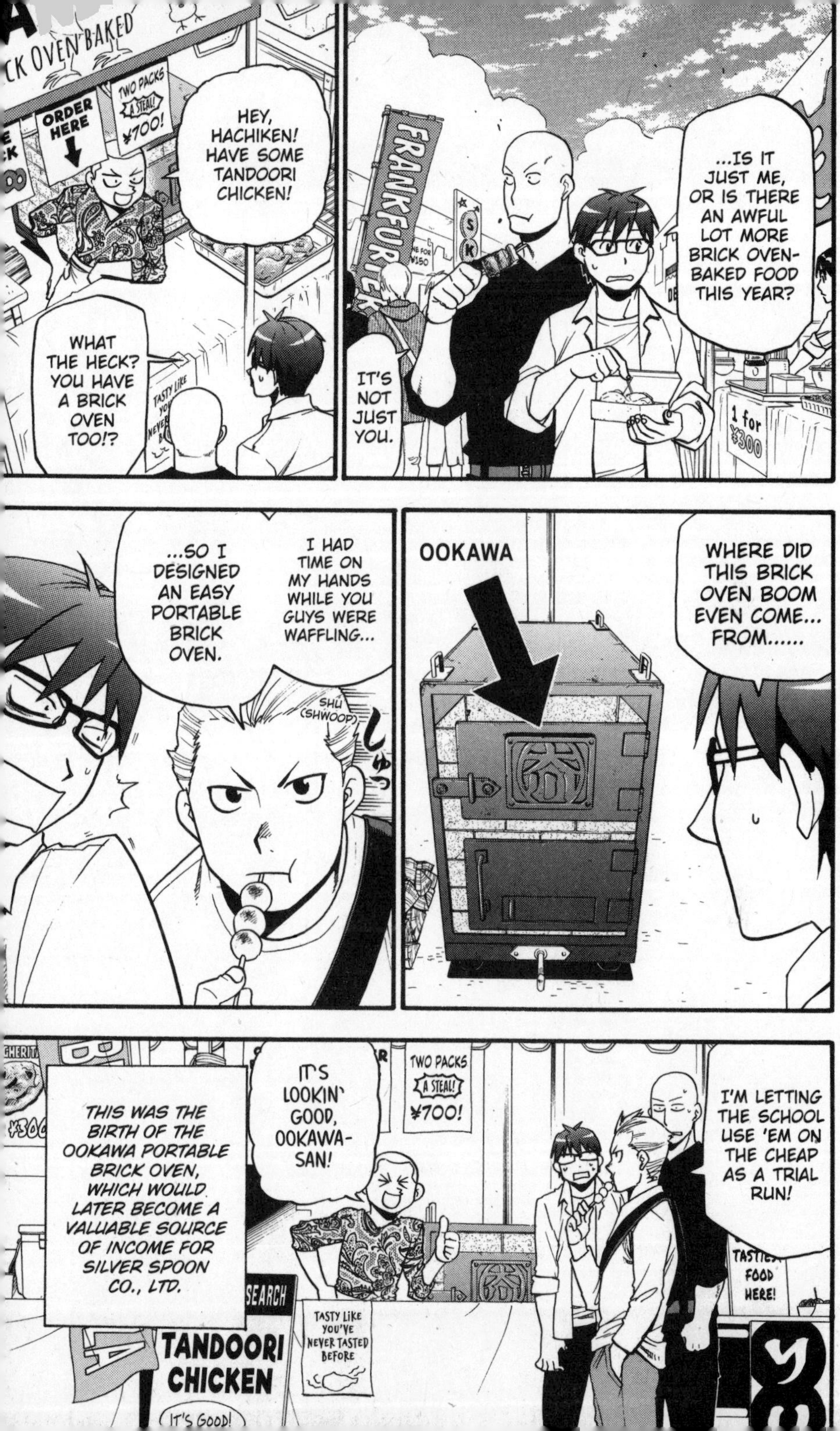
...IS IT JUST ME, OR IS THERE AN AWFUL LOT MORE BRICK OVEN-BAKED FOOD THIS YEAR?
IT'S NOT JUST YOU.
FRANKFURTER
1 for ¥300
CK OVEN BAKED
ORDER HERE
TWO PACKS A STEAL! ¥700!
HEY, HACHIKEN! HAVE SOME TANDOORI CHICKEN!
WHAT THE HECK? YOU HAVE A BRICK OVEN TOO!?
WHERE DID THIS BRICK OVEN BOOM EVEN COME... FROM......
OOKAWA
I HAD TIME ON MY HANDS WHILE YOU GUYS WERE WAFFLING...
...SO I DESIGNED AN EASY PORTABLE BRICK OVEN.
SHU (SHWOOP)
I'M LETTING THE SCHOOL USE 'EM ON THE CHEAP AS A TRIAL RUN!
TASTIEST FOOD HERE!
TWO PACKS A STEAL! ¥700!
IT'S LOOKIN' GOOD, OOKAWA-SAN!
THIS WAS THE BIRTH OF THE OOKAWA PORTABLE BRICK OVEN, WHICH WOULD LATER BECOME A VALUABLE SOURCE OF INCOME FOR SILVER SPOON CO., LTD.
SEARCH
TANDOORI CHICKEN
IT'S GOOD!
TASTY LIKE YOU'VE NEVER TASTED BEFORE

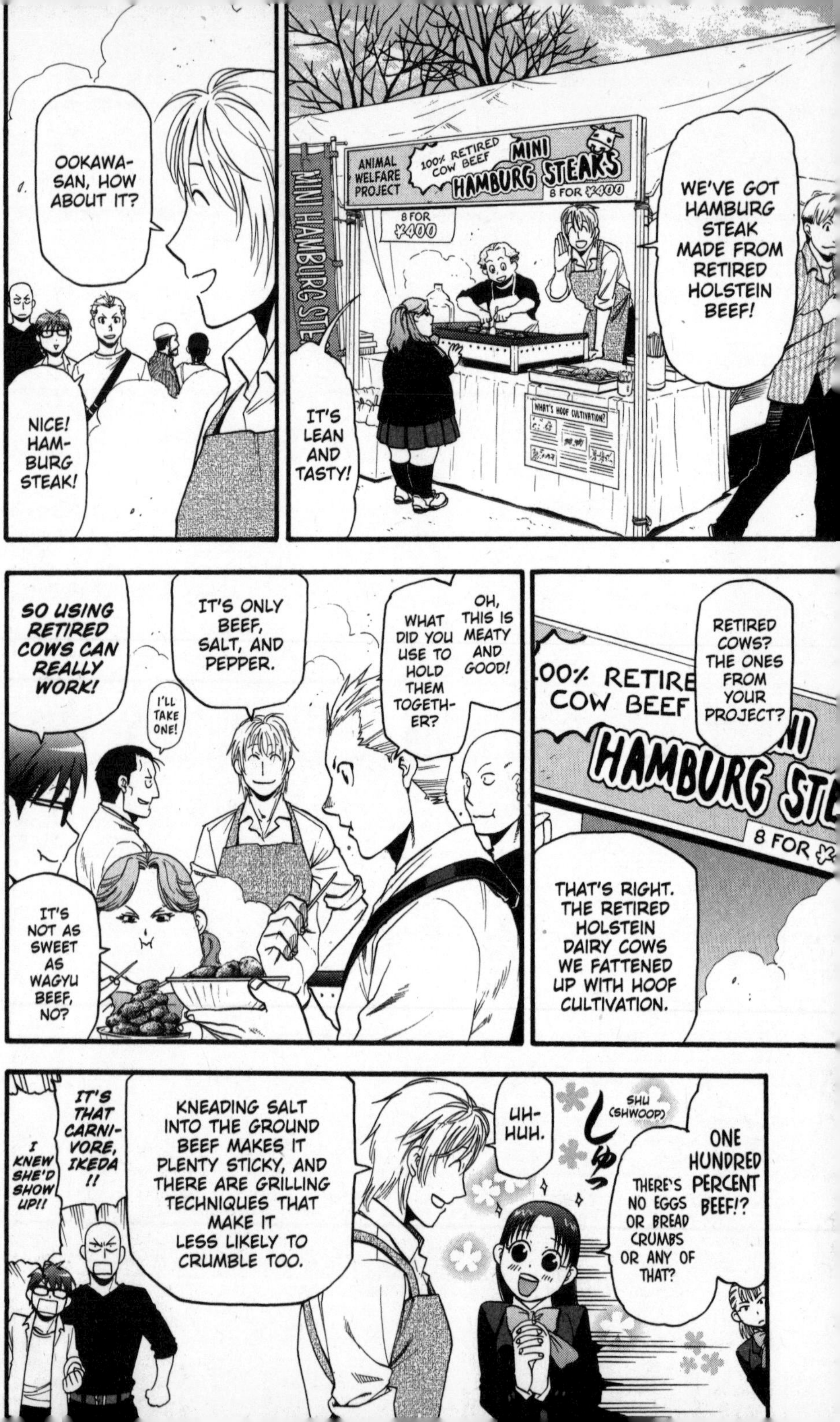

ANIMAL WELFARE PROJECT
100% RETIRED COW BEEF
MINI HAMBURG STEAKS
8 FOR ¥400
8 FOR ¥400
MINI HAMBURG STE
WHAT'S HOOF CULTIVATION?
WE'VE GOT HAMBURG STEAK MADE FROM RETIRED HOLSTEIN BEEF!
IT'S LEAN AND TASTY!
OOKAWA-SAN, HOW ABOUT IT?
NICE! HAMBURG STEAK!
100% RETIRE COW BEEF
HAMBURG STE
8 FOR
RETIRED COWS? THE ONES FROM YOUR PROJECT?
THAT'S RIGHT. THE RETIRED HOLSTEIN DAIRY COWS WE FATTENED UP WITH HOOF CULTIVATION.
OH, THIS IS MEATY AND GOOD!
WHAT DID YOU USE TO HOLD THEM TOGETHER?
IT'S ONLY BEEF, SALT, AND PEPPER.
I'LL TAKE ONE!
SO USING RETIRED COWS CAN REALLY WORK!
IT'S NOT AS SWEET AS WAGYU BEEF, NO?
SHU (SHWOOP)
ONE HUNDRED PERCENT BEEF!?
THERE'S NO EGGS OR BREAD CRUMBS OR ANY OF THAT?
UH-HUH.
KNEADING SALT INTO THE GROUND BEEF MAKES IT PLENTY STICKY, AND THERE ARE GRILLING TECHNIQUES THAT MAKE IT LESS LIKELY TO CRUMBLE TOO.
IT'S THAT CARNIVORE, IKEDA!!
I KNEW SHE'D SHOW UP!!

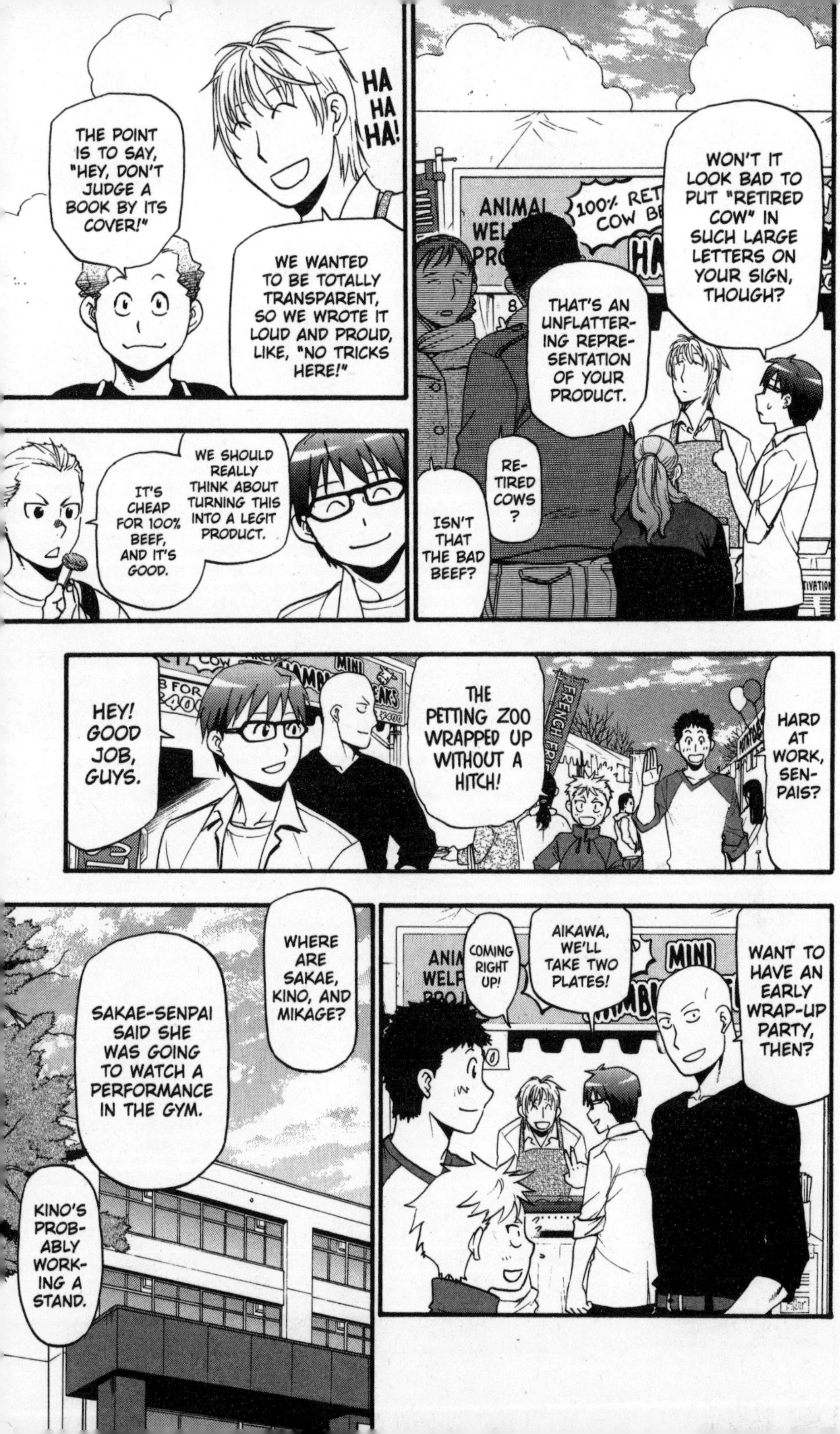
WON'T IT LOOK BAD TO PUT "RETIRED COW" IN SUCH LARGE LETTERS ON YOUR SIGN, THOUGH?
THAT'S AN UNFLATTERING REPRESENTATION OF YOUR PRODUCT.
RETIRED COWS?
ISN'T THAT THE BAD BEEF?
HA HA HA!
WE WANTED TO BE TOTALLY TRANSPARENT, SO WE WROTE IT LOUD AND PROUD, LIKE, "NO TRICKS HERE!"
THE POINT IS TO SAY, "HEY, DON'T JUDGE A BOOK BY ITS COVER!"
IT'S CHEAP FOR 100% BEEF, AND IT'S GOOD.
WE SHOULD REALLY THINK ABOUT TURNING THIS INTO A LEGIT PRODUCT.
HARD AT WORK, SENPAIS?
THE PETTING ZOO WRAPPED UP WITHOUT A HITCH!
HEY! GOOD JOB, GUYS.
WANT TO HAVE AN EARLY WRAP-UP PARTY, THEN?
AIKAWA, WE'LL TAKE TWO PLATES!
COMING RIGHT UP!
WHERE ARE SAKAE, KINO, AND MIKAGE?
SAKAE-SENPAI SAID SHE WAS GOING TO WATCH A PERFORMANCE IN THE GYM.
KINO'S PROBABLY WORKING A STAND.

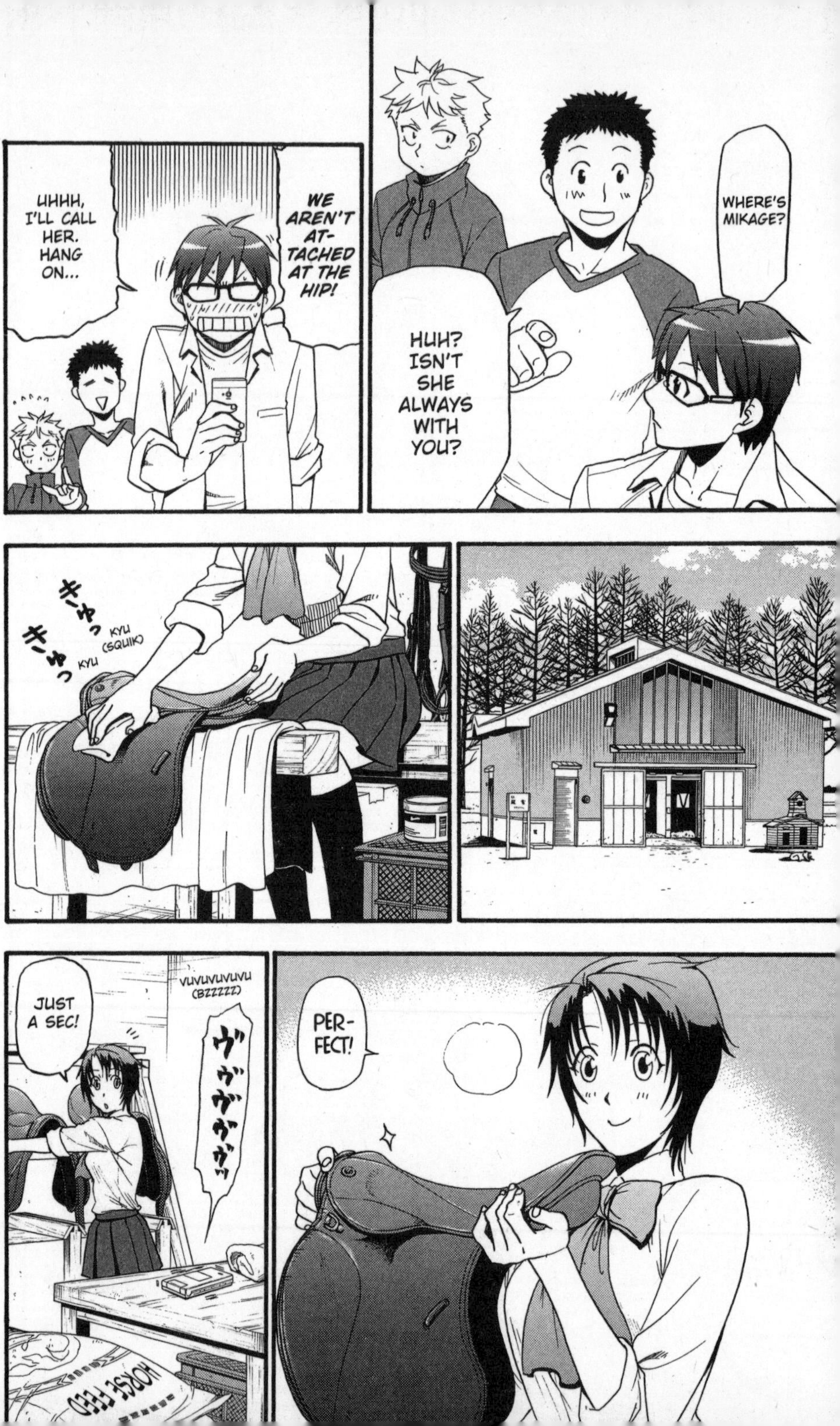
WHERE'S MIKAGE?
HUH? ISN'T SHE ALWAYS WITH YOU?
WE AREN'T AT-TACHED AT THE HIP!
UHHH, I'LL CALL HER. HANG ON...
きゅっ KYU (SQUIK)
きゅっ KYU
PER-FECT!
ヴヴヴヴヴッ VUVUVUVUVU (BZZZZZ)
JUST A SEC!
HORSE FEED

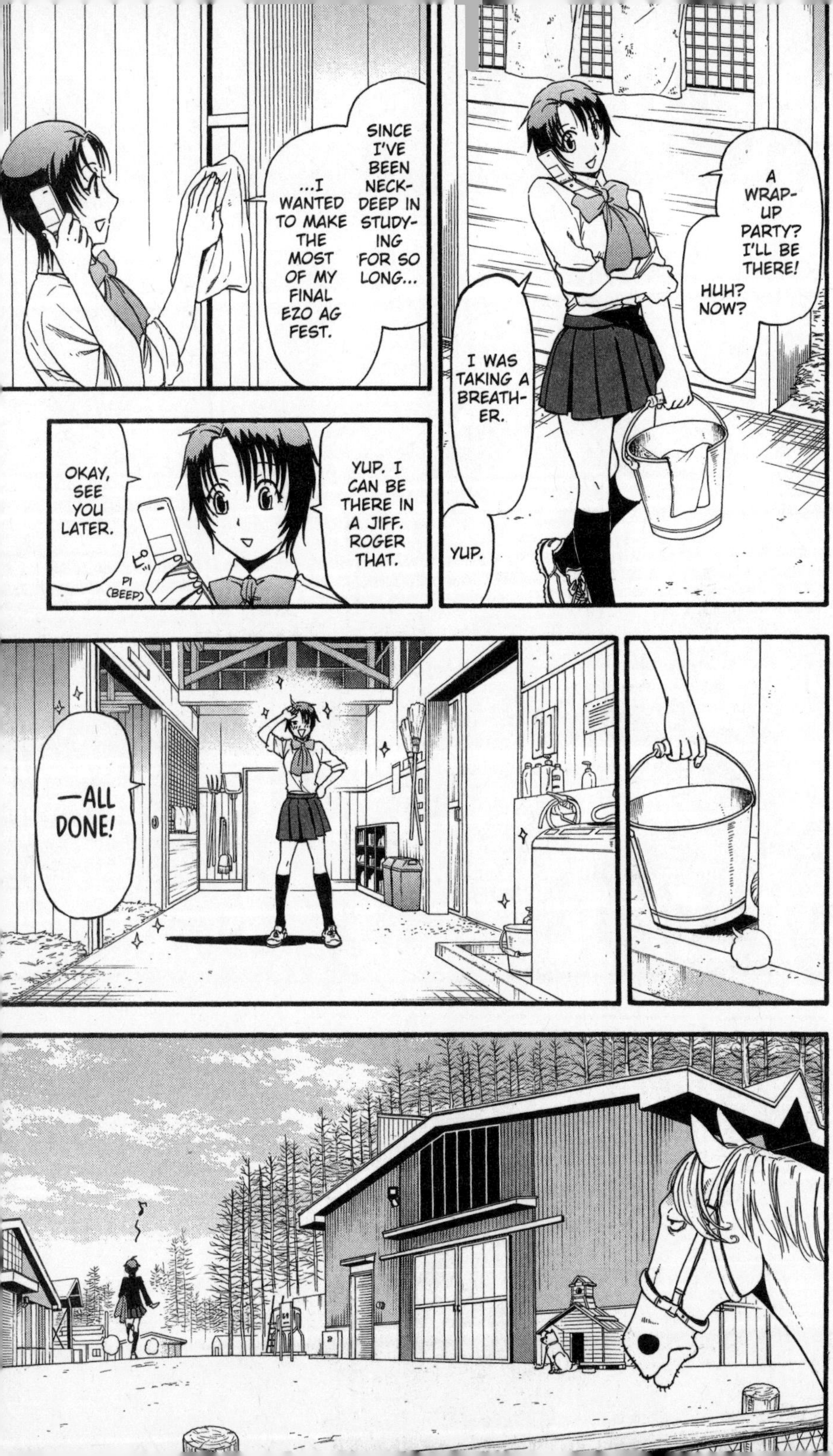
A WRAP-UP PARTY? I'LL BE THERE!
HUH? NOW?
I WAS TAKING A BREATHER.
YUP.
SINCE I'VE BEEN NECK-DEEP IN STUDYING FOR SO LONG...
...I WANTED TO MAKE THE MOST OF MY FINAL EZO AG FEST.
YUP. I CAN BE THERE IN A JIFF. ROGER THAT.
OKAY, SEE YOU LATER.
PI (BEEP)
—ALL DONE!

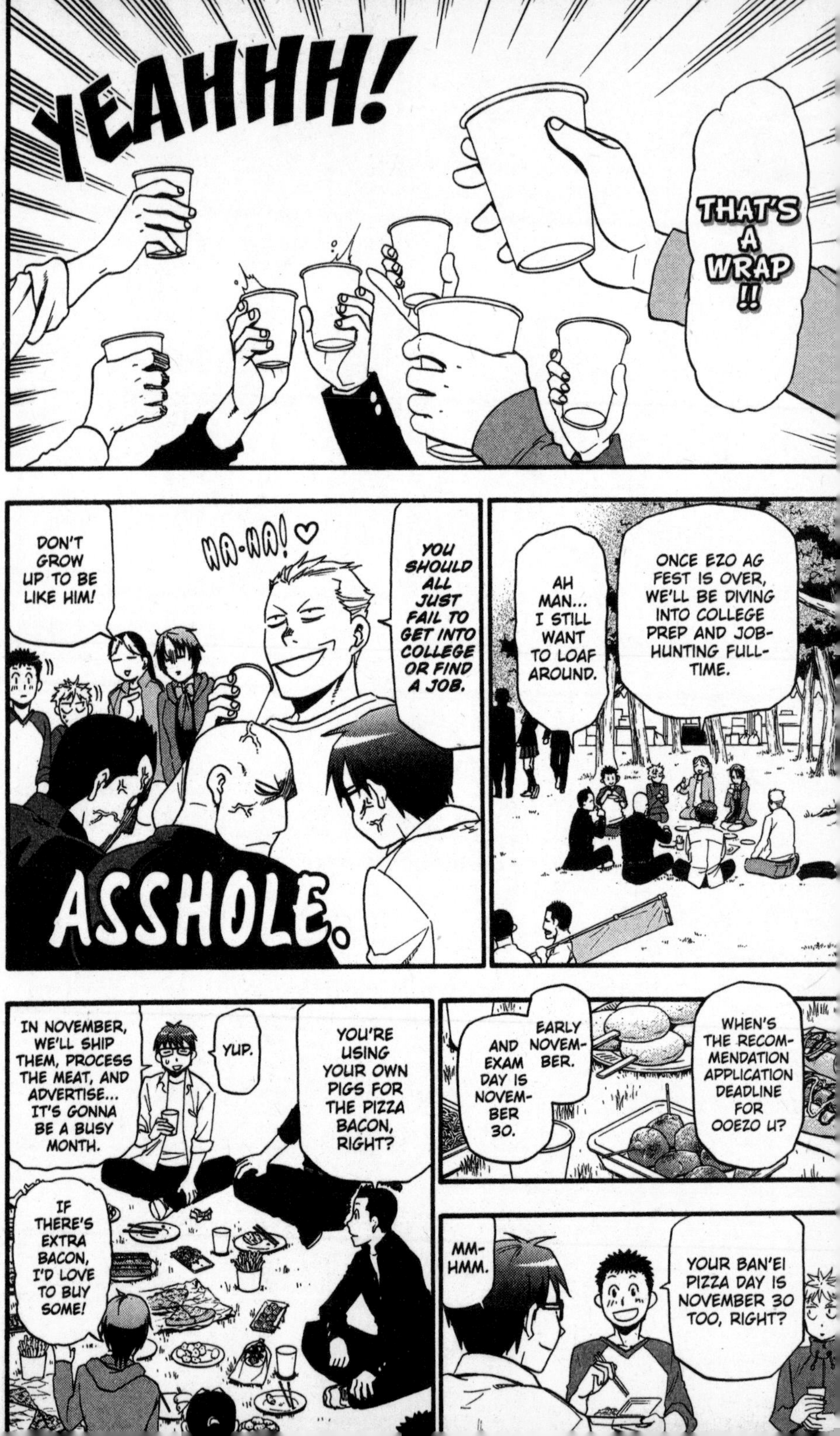
THAT'S A WRAP!!
YEAHHH!
ONCE EZO AG FEST IS OVER, WE'LL BE DIVING INTO COLLEGE PREP AND JOB-HUNTING FULL-TIME.
AH MAN... I STILL WANT TO LOAF AROUND.
YOU SHOULD ALL JUST FAIL TO GET INTO COLLEGE OR FIND A JOB.
HA-HA! ♡
DON'T GROW UP TO BE LIKE HIM!
ASSHOLE.
WHEN'S THE RECOMMENDATION APPLICATION DEADLINE FOR OOEZO U?
EARLY NOVEMBER.
AND EXAM DAY IS NOVEMBER 30.
YOUR BAN'EI PIZZA DAY IS NOVEMBER 30 TOO, RIGHT?
MM-HMM.
YOU'RE USING YOUR OWN PIGS FOR THE PIZZA BACON, RIGHT?
YUP.
IN NOVEMBER, WE'LL SHIP THEM, PROCESS THE MEAT, AND ADVERTISE... IT'S GONNA BE A BUSY MONTH.
IF THERE'S EXTRA BACON, I'D LOVE TO BUY SOME!

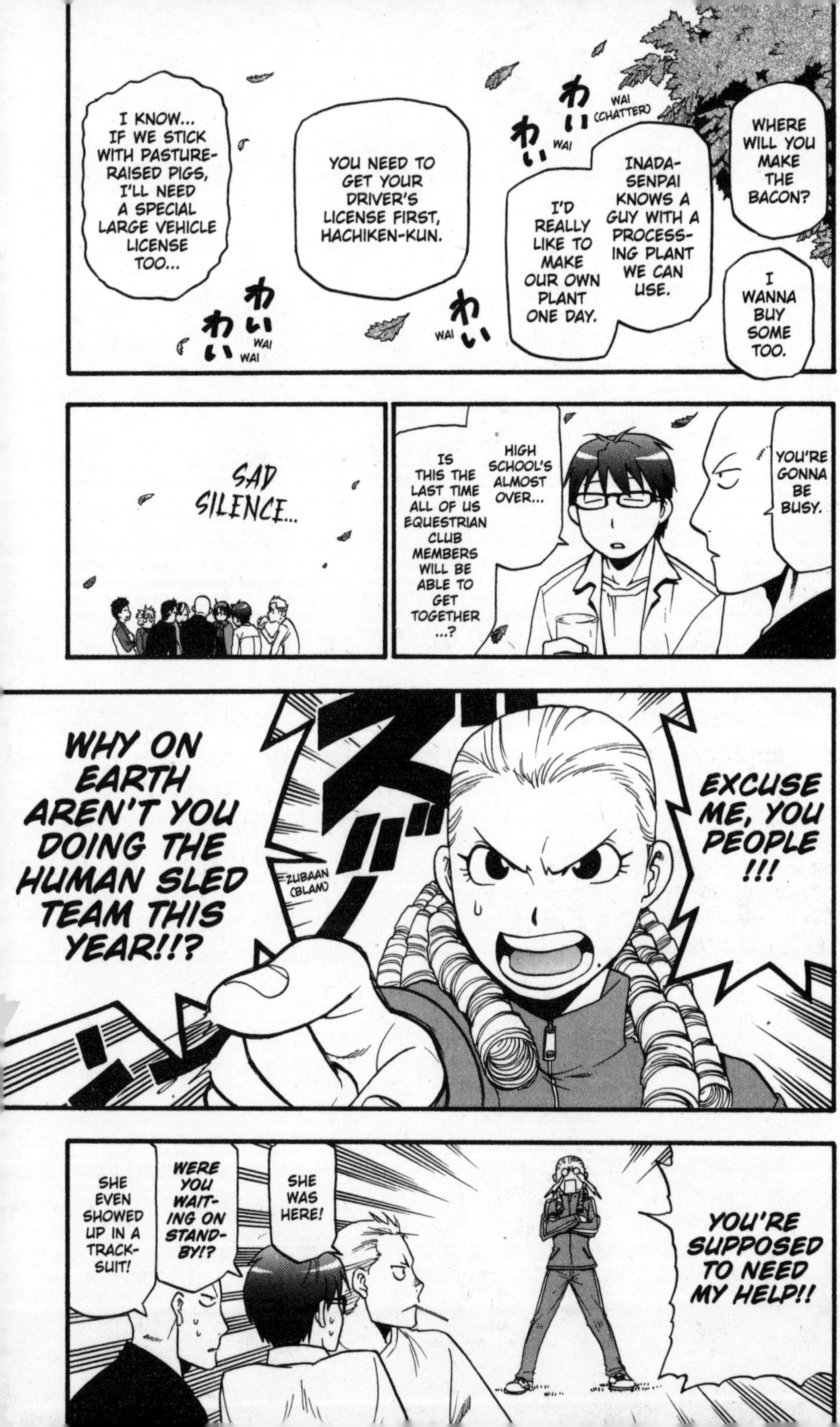
WHERE WILL YOU MAKE THE BACON?
I WANNA BUY SOME TOO.
INADA-SENPAI KNOWS A GUY WITH A PROCESSING PLANT WE CAN USE.
I'D REALLY LIKE TO MAKE OUR OWN PLANT ONE DAY.
わい WAI (CHATTER)
わい WAI
わい WAI
YOU NEED TO GET YOUR DRIVER'S LICENSE FIRST, HACHIKEN-KUN.
I KNOW... IF WE STICK WITH PASTURE-RAISED PIGS, I'LL NEED A SPECIAL LARGE VEHICLE LICENSE TOO...
わい WAI
わい WAI
YOU'RE GONNA BE BUSY.
HIGH SCHOOL'S ALMOST OVER...
IS THIS THE LAST TIME ALL OF US EQUESTRIAN CLUB MEMBERS WILL BE ABLE TO GET TOGETHER ...?
SAD SILENCE...
EXCUSE ME, YOU PEOPLE!!!
ZUBAAN (BLAM)
WHY ON EARTH AREN'T YOU DOING THE HUMAN SLED TEAM THIS YEAR!!?
YOU'RE SUPPOSED TO NEED MY HELP!!
SHE WAS HERE!
WERE YOU WAITING ON STANDBY!?
SHE EVEN SHOWED UP IN A TRACKSUIT!

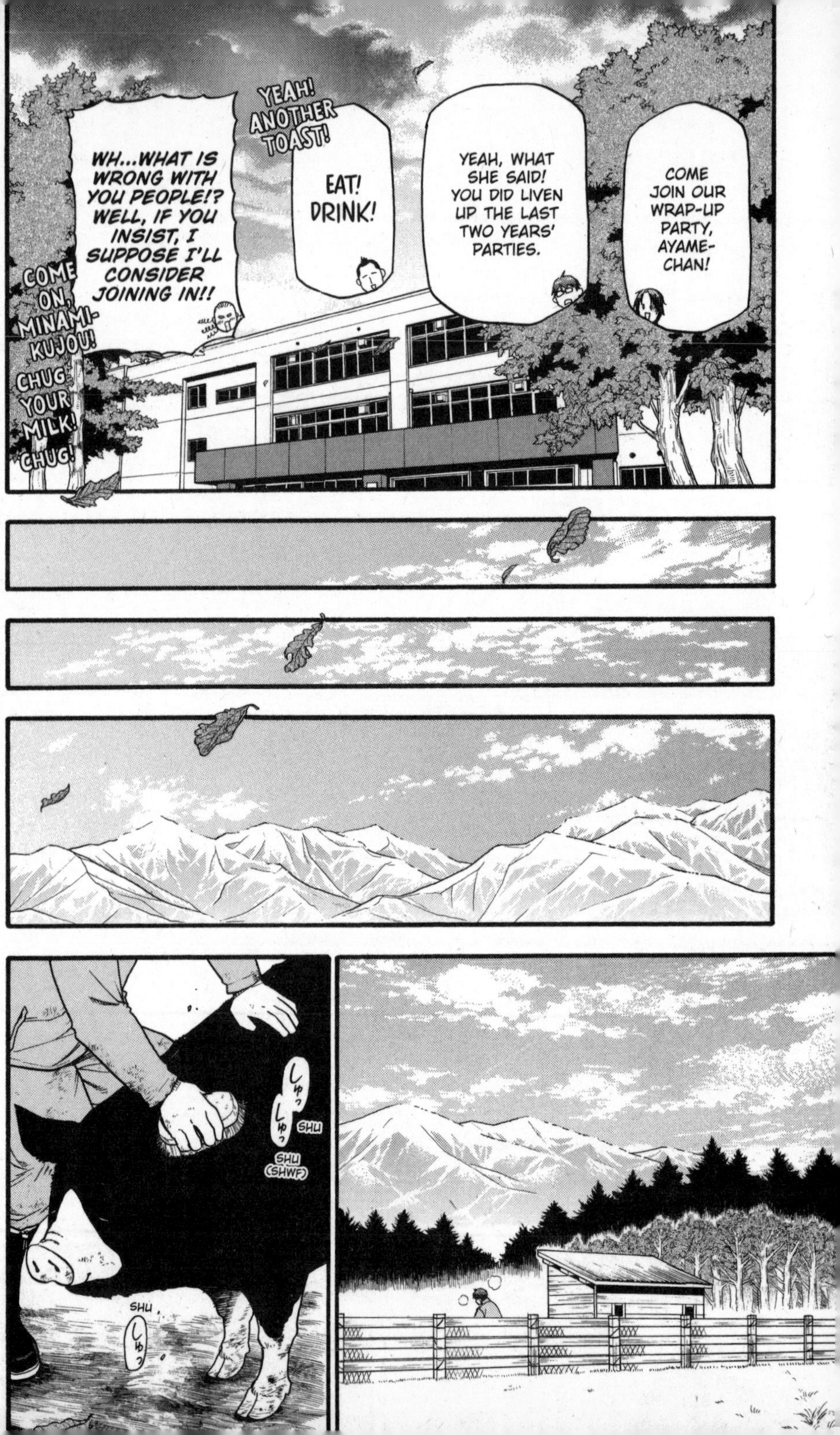
COME JOIN OUR WRAP-UP PARTY, AYAME-CHAN!
YEAH, WHAT SHE SAID! YOU DID LIVEN UP THE LAST TWO YEARS' PARTIES.
EAT! DRINK!
YEAH! ANOTHER TOAST!
WH...WHAT IS WRONG WITH YOU PEOPLE!? WELL, IF YOU INSIST, I SUPPOSE I'LL CONSIDER JOINING IN!!
COME ON, MINAMI-KUJOU! CHUG YOUR MILK! CHUG!
しゅっ しゅっ
SHU
SHU (SHWF)
SHU
しゅっ

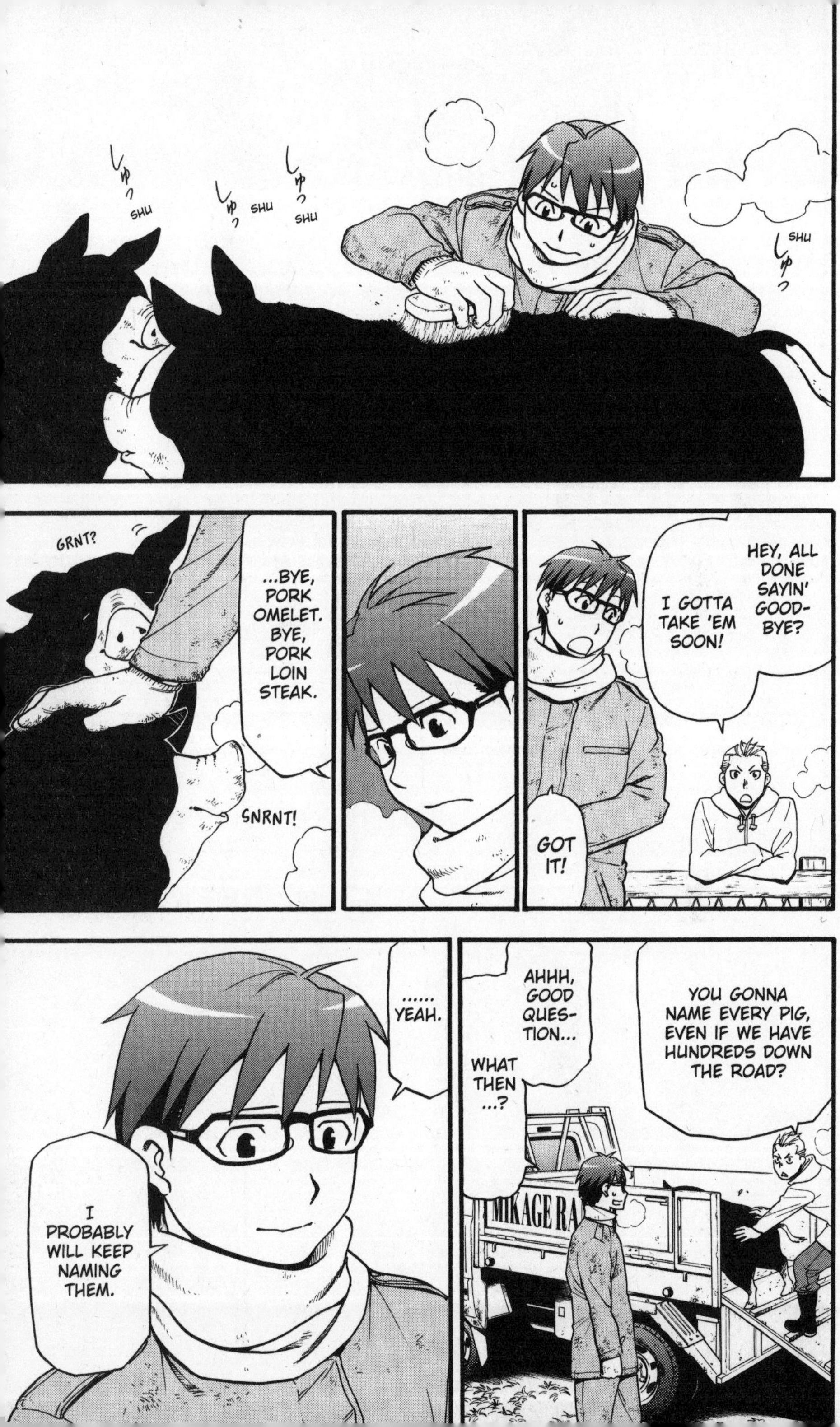

しゅっ SHU
しゅっ SHU
しゅっ SHU
しゅっ SHU
HEY, ALL DONE SAYIN' GOOD-BYE?
I GOTTA TAKE 'EM SOON!
GOT IT!
...BYE, PORK OMELET. BYE, PORK LOIN STEAK.
GRNT?
SNRNT!
YOU GONNA NAME EVERY PIG, EVEN IF WE HAVE HUNDREDS DOWN THE ROAD?
AHHH, GOOD QUES-TION...
WHAT THEN ...?
MIKAGE RA
...... YEAH.
I PROBABLY WILL KEEP NAMING THEM.

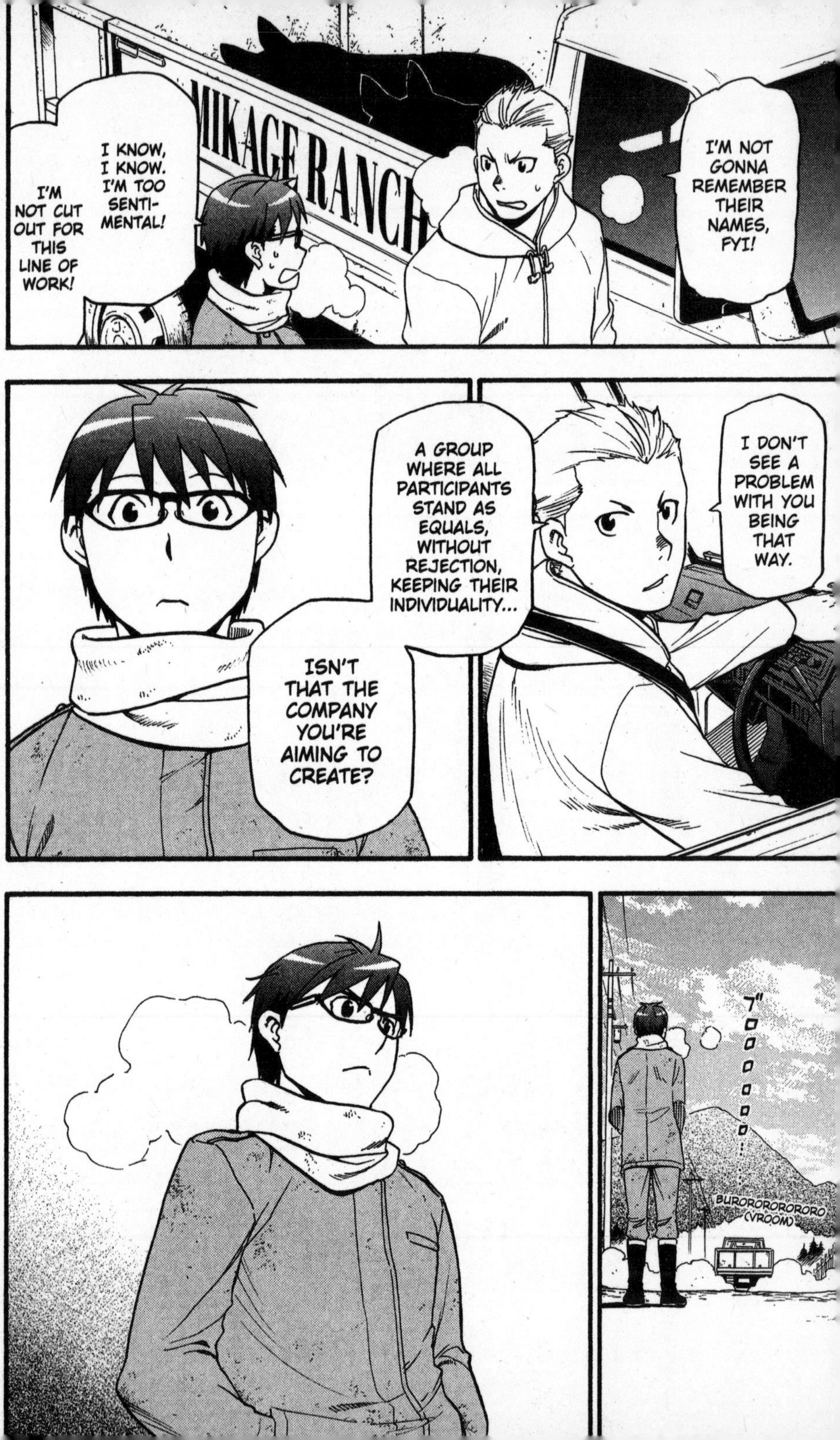
MIKAGE RANCH
I'M NOT GONNA REMEMBER THEIR NAMES, FYI!
I KNOW, I KNOW. I'M TOO SENTI-MENTAL!
I'M NOT CUT OUT FOR THIS LINE OF WORK!
I DON'T SEE A PROBLEM WITH YOU BEING THAT WAY.
A GROUP WHERE ALL PARTICIPANTS STAND AS EQUALS, WITHOUT REJECTION, KEEPING THEIR INDIVIDUALITY...
ISN'T THAT THE COMPANY YOU'RE AIMING TO CREATE?
BURORORORORORO (VROOM)

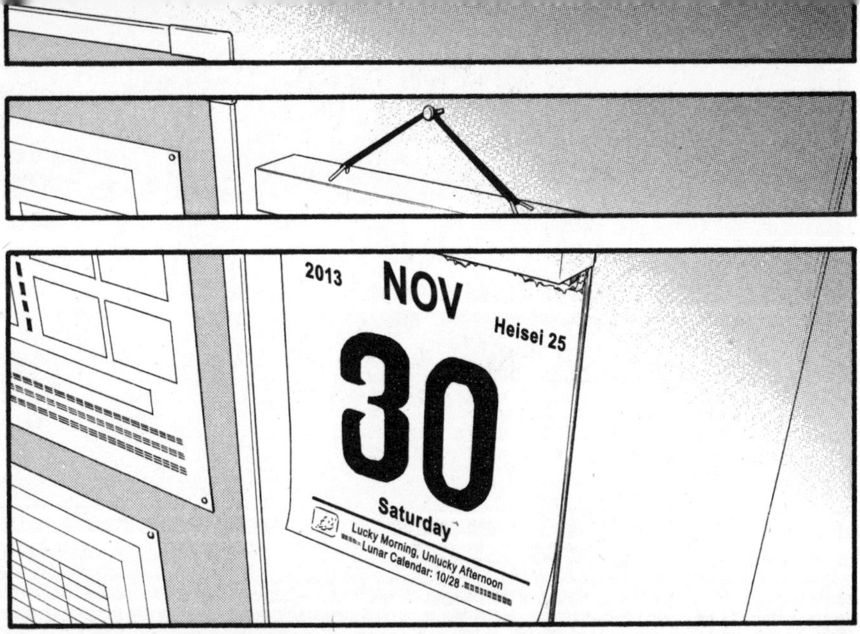
2013
NOV
Heisei 25
30
Saturday
Lucky Morning, Unlucky Afternoon
Lunar Calendar: 10/28

SIGN: BAN'EI

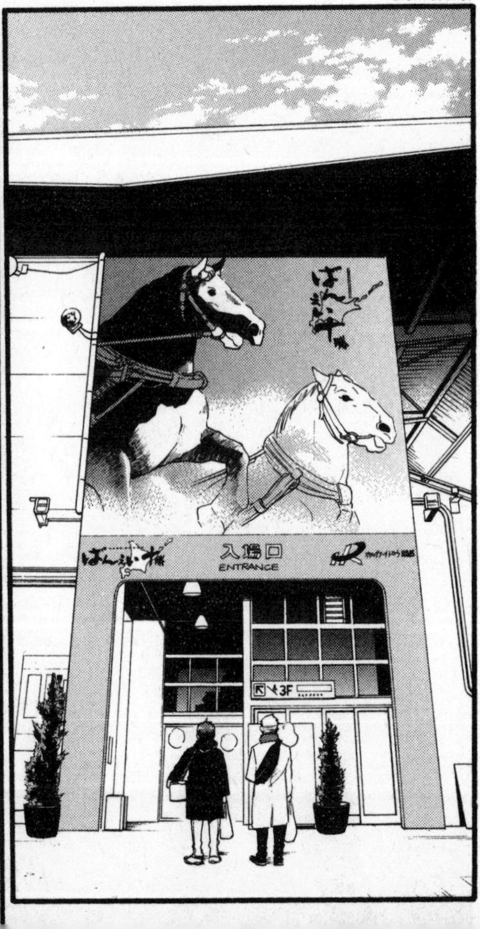
入場口
ENTRANCE
3F

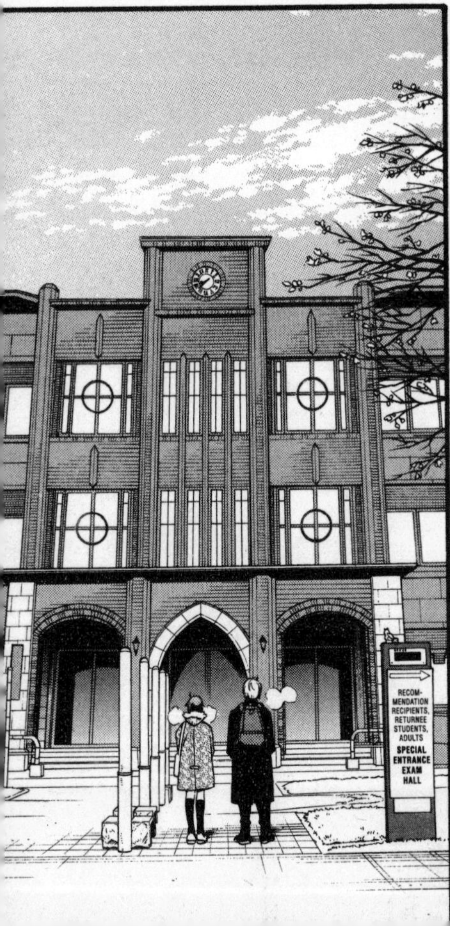
RECOMMENDATION RECIPIENTS, RETURNEE STUDENTS, ADULTS
SPECIAL ENTRANCE EXAM HALL

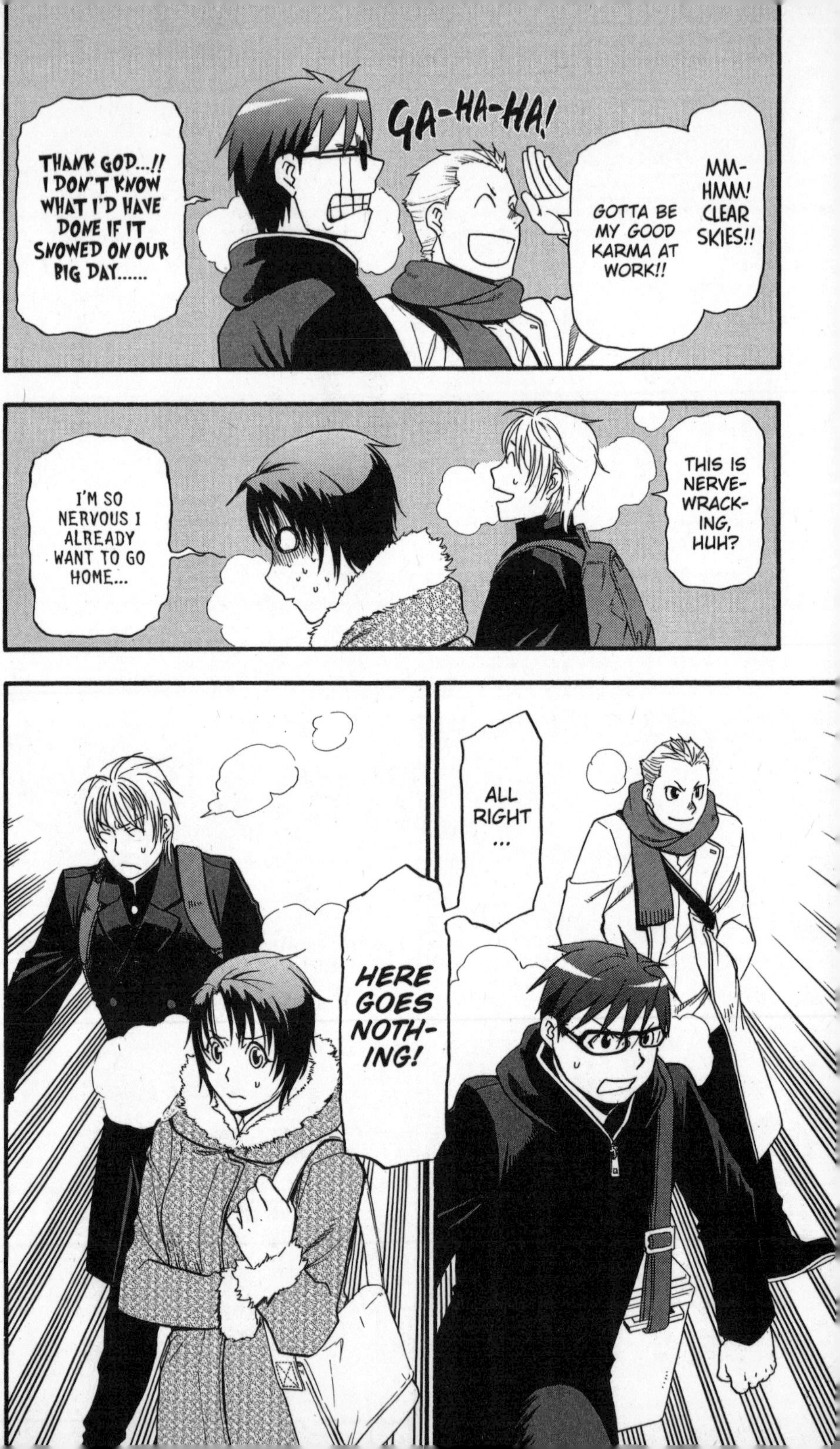
MM-HMM! CLEAR SKIES!!
GOTTA BE MY GOOD KARMA AT WORK!!
GA-HA-HA!
THANK GOD...!! I DON'T KNOW WHAT I'D HAVE DONE IF IT SNOWED ON OUR BIG DAY......
THIS IS NERVE-WRACKING, HUH?
I'M SO NERVOUS I ALREADY WANT TO GO HOME...
ALL RIGHT ...
HERE GOES NOTHING!

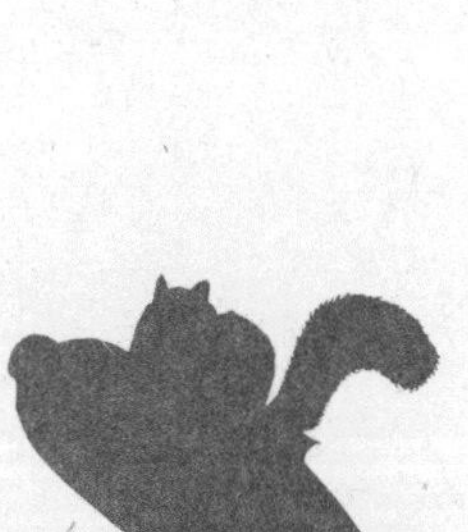

Silver Spoon

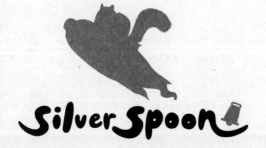

Chapter 116: Tale of Four Seasons ⑲

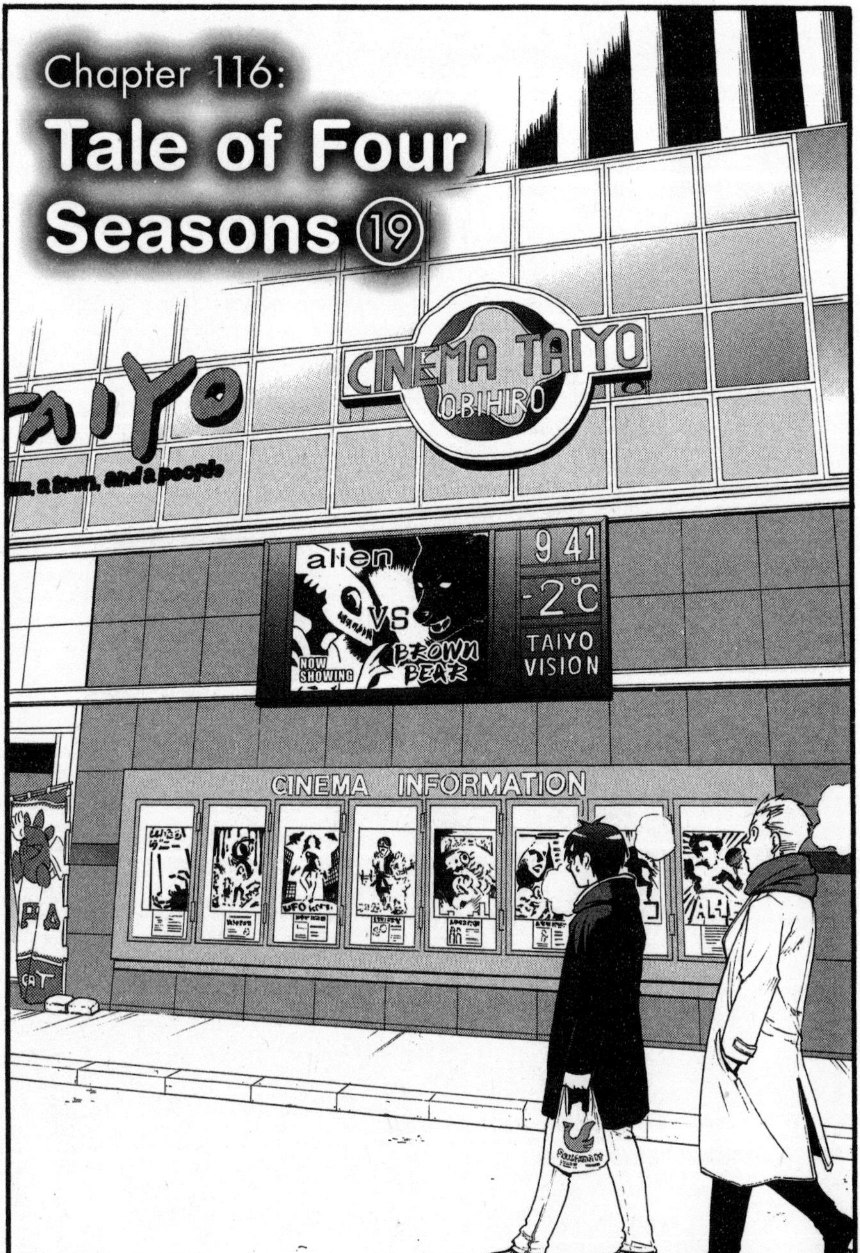

TAIYO
CINEMA TAIYO
OBIHIRO
alien VS BROWN BEAR
NOW SHOWING
9 41
-2°C
TAIYO VISION
CINEMA INFORMATION

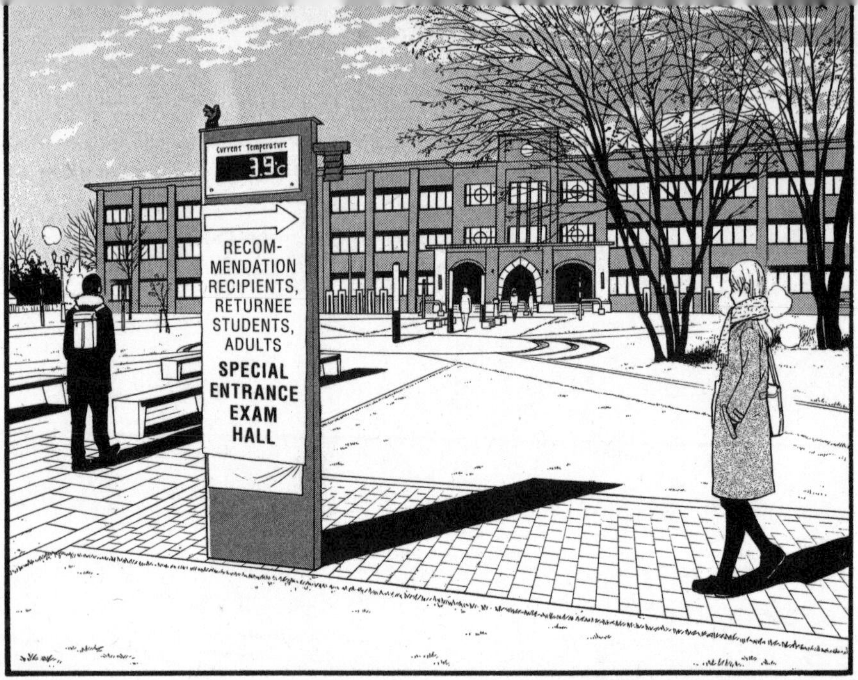
Current Temperature
3.9°C
RECOM-MENDATION RECIPIENTS, RETURNEE STUDENTS, ADULTS
SPECIAL ENTRANCE EXAM HALL

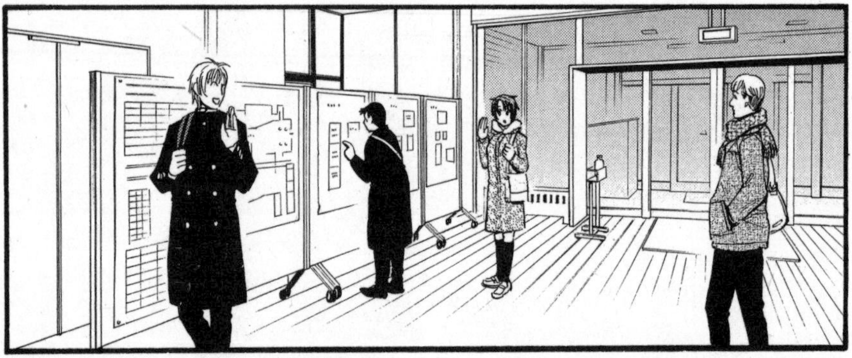

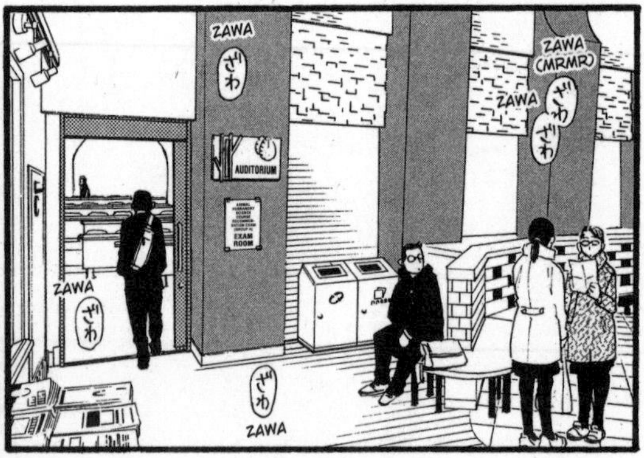
ZAWA
ざわ
ZAWA (MRMR)
ZAWA
ざわ
ざわ
AUDITORIUM
EXAM ROOM
ZAWA
ざわ
ざわ
ZAWA

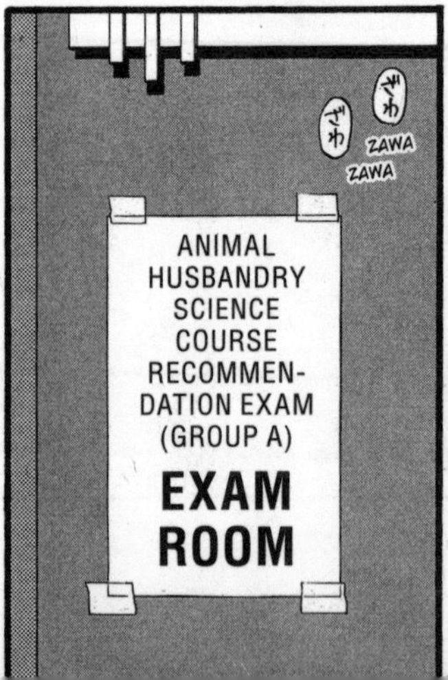
ざわ
ざわ
ZAWA
ZAWA
ANIMAL HUSBANDRY SCIENCE COURSE RECOMMEN-DATION EXAM (GROUP A)
EXAM ROOM

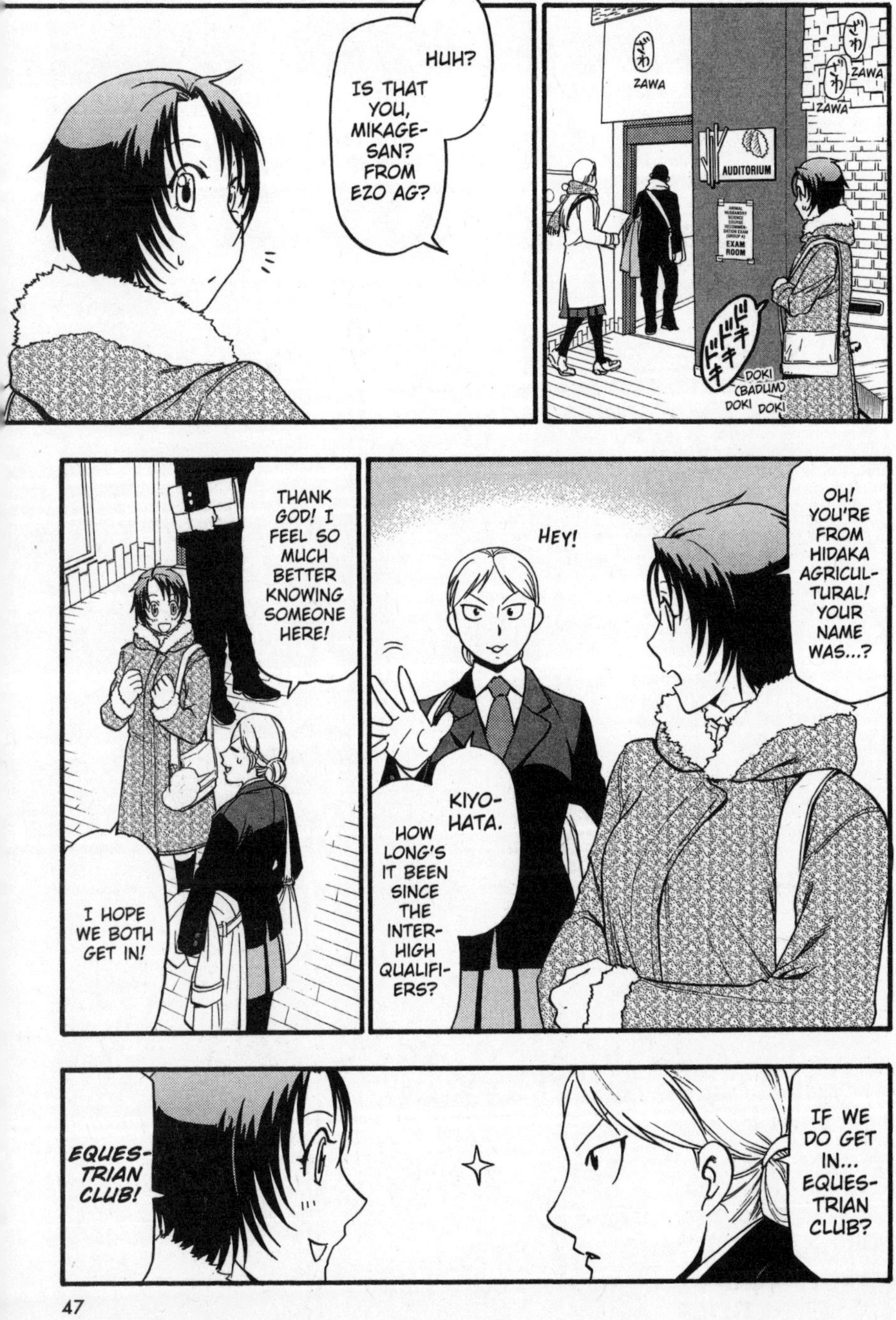

ざわ
ZAWA
ざわ
ZAWA
ざわ
ZAWA
AUDITORIUM
ANIMAL HUSBANDRY SCIENCE COURSE RECOMMENDATION EXAM (GROUP A) EXAM ROOM
ドキドキ
DOKI (BADUM) DOKI DOKI
HUH? IS THAT YOU, MIKAGE-SAN? FROM EZO AG?
OH! YOU'RE FROM HIDAKA AGRICULTURAL! YOUR NAME WAS...?
HEY!
KIYO-HATA. HOW LONG'S IT BEEN SINCE THE INTER-HIGH QUALIFIERS?
THANK GOD! I FEEL SO MUCH BETTER KNOWING SOMEONE HERE!
I HOPE WE BOTH GET IN!
IF WE DO GET IN... EQUES-TRIAN CLUB?
EQUES-TRIAN CLUB!

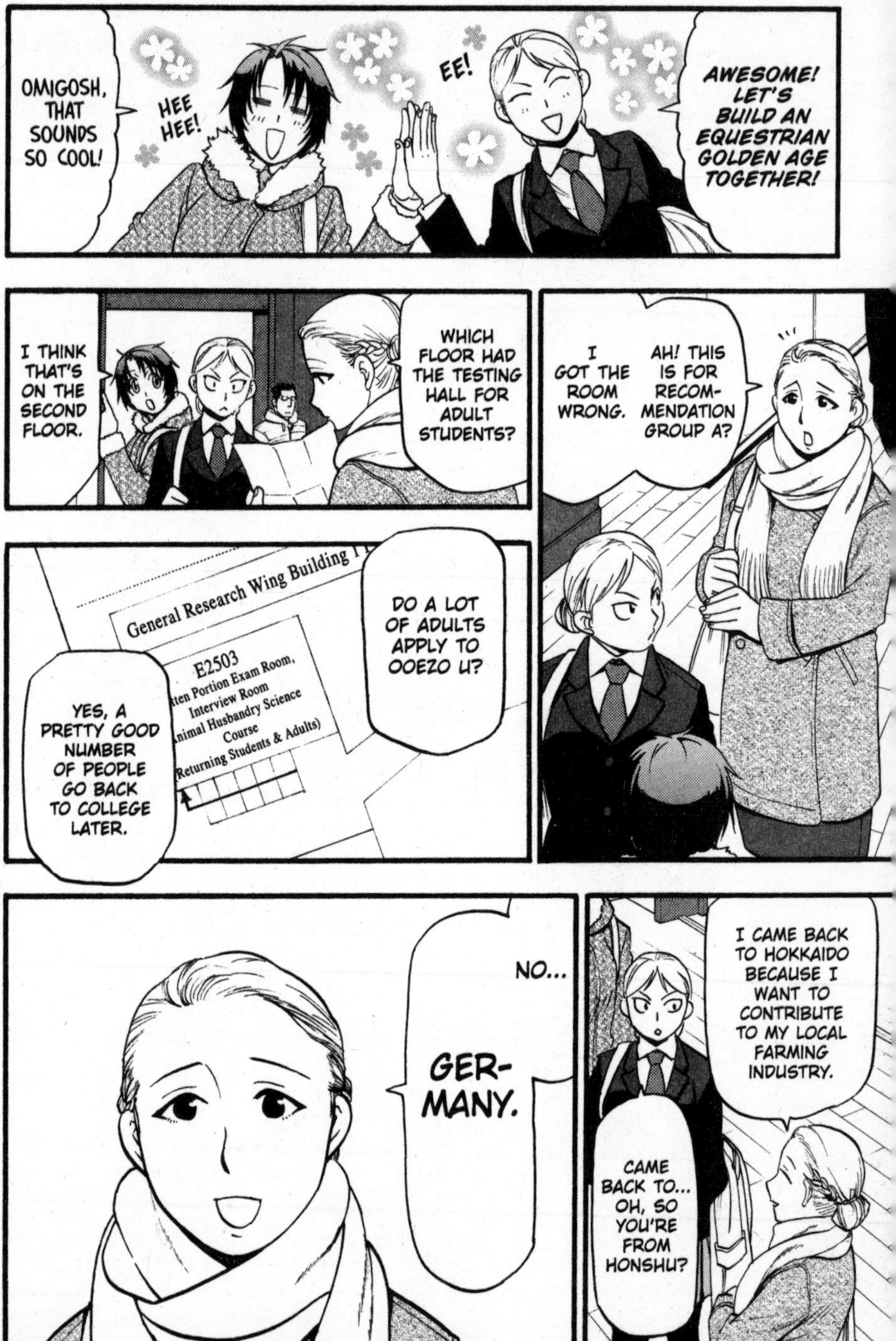
AWESOME! LET'S BUILD AN EQUESTRIAN GOLDEN AGE TOGETHER!
EE!
HEE HEE!
OMIGOSH, THAT SOUNDS SO COOL!
AH! THIS IS FOR RECOM-MENDATION GROUP A?
I GOT THE ROOM WRONG.
WHICH FLOOR HAD THE TESTING HALL FOR ADULT STUDENTS?
I THINK THAT'S ON THE SECOND FLOOR.
DO A LOT OF ADULTS APPLY TO OOEZO U?
General Research Wing Building
E2503
Interview Room
Course
YES, A PRETTY GOOD NUMBER OF PEOPLE GO BACK TO COLLEGE LATER.
I CAME BACK TO HOKKAIDO BECAUSE I WANT TO CONTRIBUTE TO MY LOCAL FARMING INDUSTRY.
CAME BACK TO... OH, SO YOU'RE FROM HONSHU?
NO...
GER-MANY.

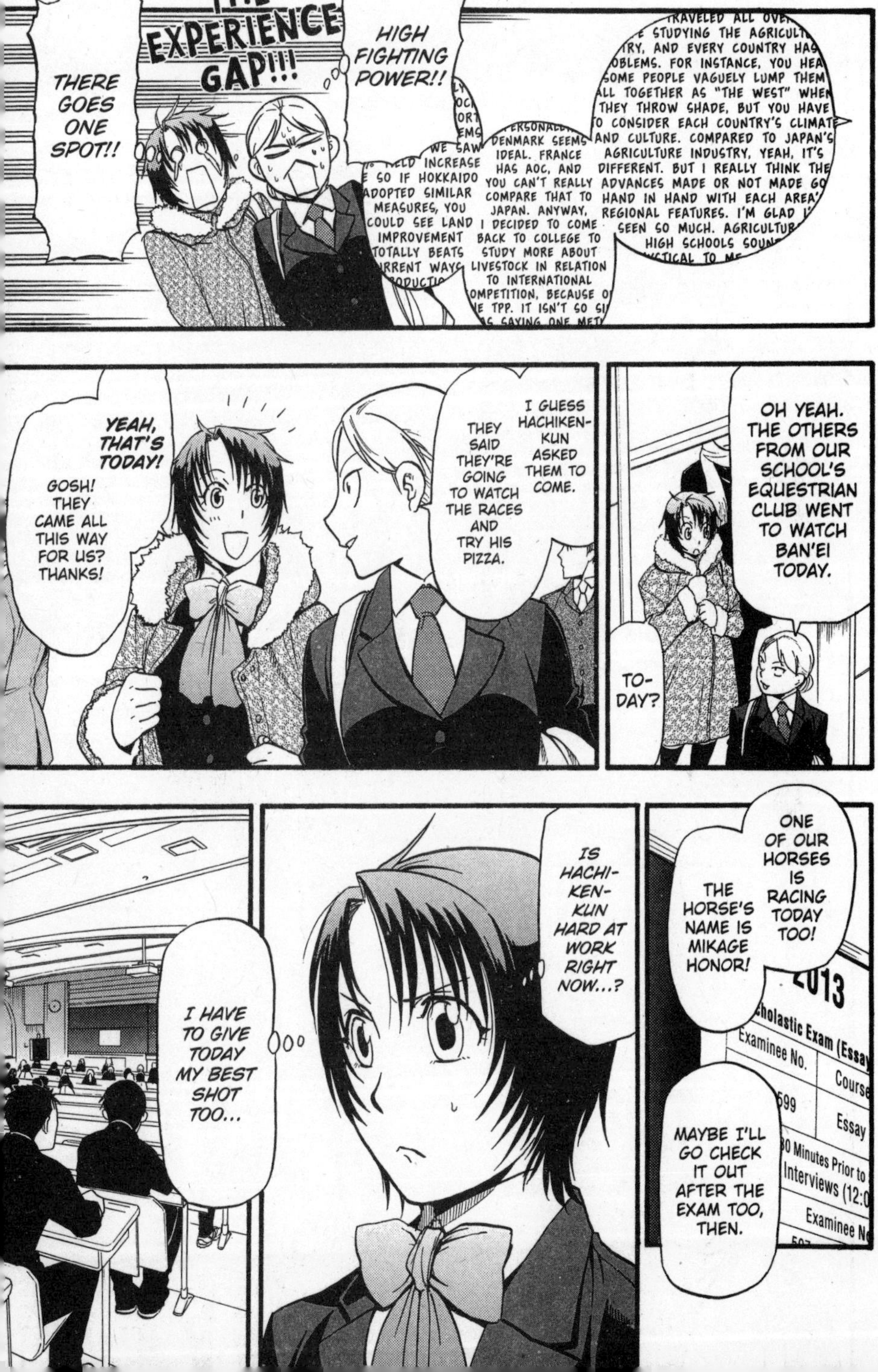
TRAVELED ALL OVE
STUDYING THE AGRICULT
TRY, AND EVERY COUNTRY HAS
OBLEMS. FOR INSTANCE, YOU HEA
SOME PEOPLE VAGUELY LUMP THEM
ALL TOGETHER AS "THE WEST" WHEN
THEY THROW SHADE, BUT YOU HAVE
TO CONSIDER EACH COUNTRY'S CLIMATE
AND CULTURE. COMPARED TO JAPAN'S
AGRICULTURE INDUSTRY, YEAH, IT'S
DIFFERENT. BUT I REALLY THINK THE
ADVANCES MADE OR NOT MADE GO
HAND IN HAND WITH EACH AREA'
REGIONAL FEATURES. I'M GLAD I'
SEEN SO MUCH. AGRICULTU
HIGH SCHOOLS SOUN
DENMARK SEEMS IDEAL. FRANCE HAS AOC, AND YOU CAN'T REALLY COMPARE THAT TO JAPAN. ANYWAY, I DECIDED TO COME BACK TO COLLEGE TO STUDY MORE ABOUT LIVESTOCK IN RELATION TO INTERNATIONAL COMPETITION, BECAUSE OF THE TPP. IT ISN'T SO SI
WE SAW ELD INCREASE E SO IF HOKKAIDO ADOPTED SIMILAR MEASURES, YOU COULD SEE LAND IMPROVEMENT TOTALLY BEATS RRENT WAYS
HIGH FIGHTING POWER!!
THE EXPERIENCE GAP!!!
THERE GOES ONE SPOT!!
OH YEAH. THE OTHERS FROM OUR SCHOOL'S EQUESTRIAN CLUB WENT TO WATCH BAN'EI TODAY.
TO-DAY?
I GUESS HACHIKEN-KUN ASKED THEM TO COME.
THEY SAID THEY'RE GOING TO WATCH THE RACES AND TRY HIS PIZZA.
YEAH, THAT'S TODAY!
GOSH! THEY CAME ALL THIS WAY FOR US? THANKS!
ONE OF OUR HORSES IS RACING TODAY TOO!
THE HORSE'S NAME IS MIKAGE HONOR!
2013
cholastic Exam (Essay
Examinee No.
Course
599
Essay
30 Minutes Prior to
Interviews (12:0
Examinee N
MAYBE I'LL GO CHECK IT OUT AFTER THE EXAM TOO, THEN.
IS HACHIKEN-KUN HARD AT WORK RIGHT NOW...?
I HAVE TO GIVE TODAY MY BEST SHOT TOO...

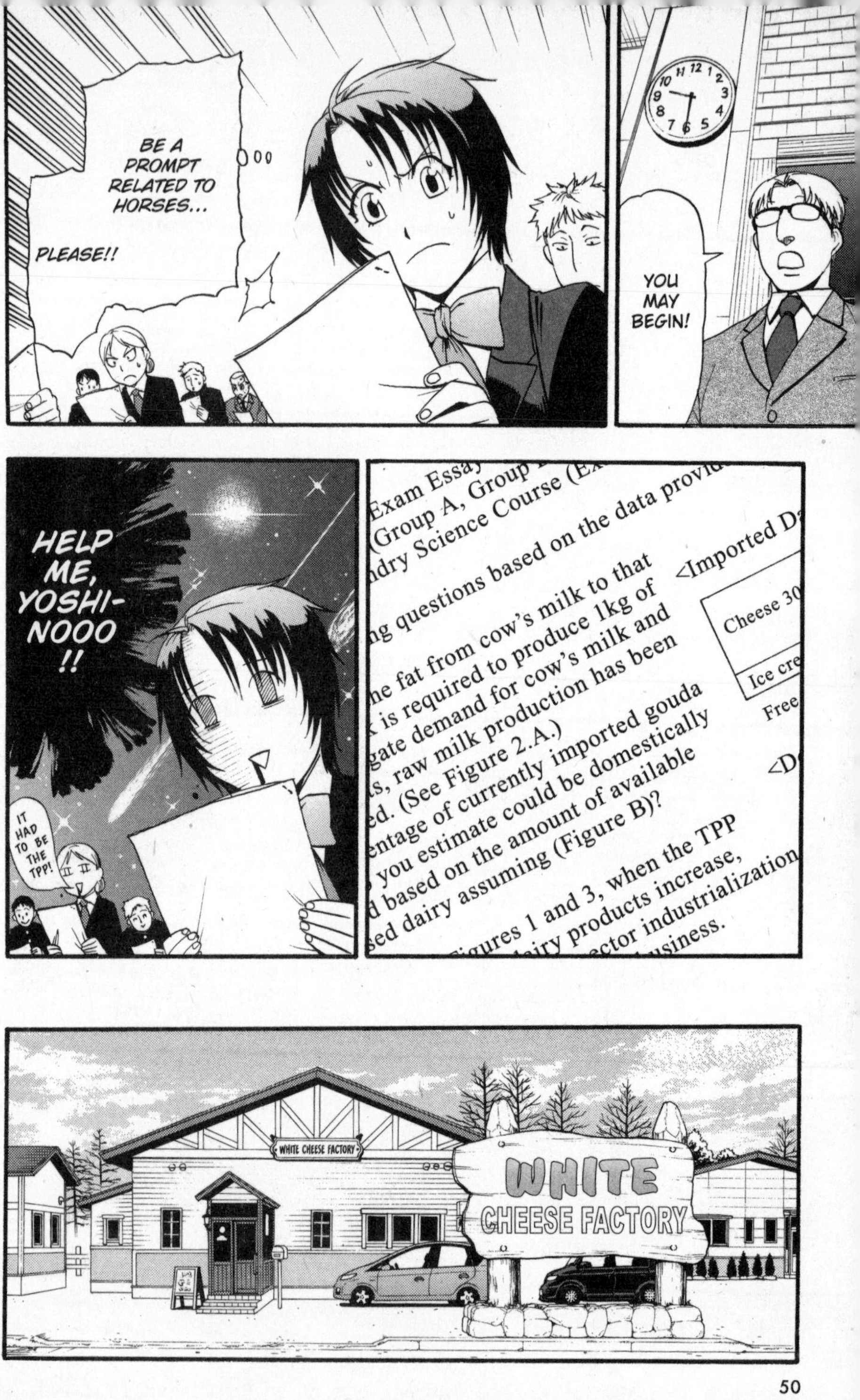
YOU MAY BEGIN!
BE A PROMPT RELATED TO HORSES...
PLEASE!!
Exam Essay
(Group A, Group
ndry Science Course (Ex
questions based on the data provid
g questions based on the data provi
<Imported D
he fat from cow's milk to that
k is required to produce 1kg of
gate demand for cow's milk and
s, raw milk production has been
ed. (See Figure 2.A.)
entage of currently imported gouda
you estimate could be domestically
d based on the amount of available
sed dairy assuming (Figure B)?
Figures 1 and 3, when the TPP
dairy products increase,
ector industrialization
usiness.
Cheese 30
Ice cre
Free
<D
HELP ME, YOSHI-NOOO!!
IT HAD TO BE THE TPP!
WHITE CHEESE FACTORY
WHITE CHEESE FACTORY

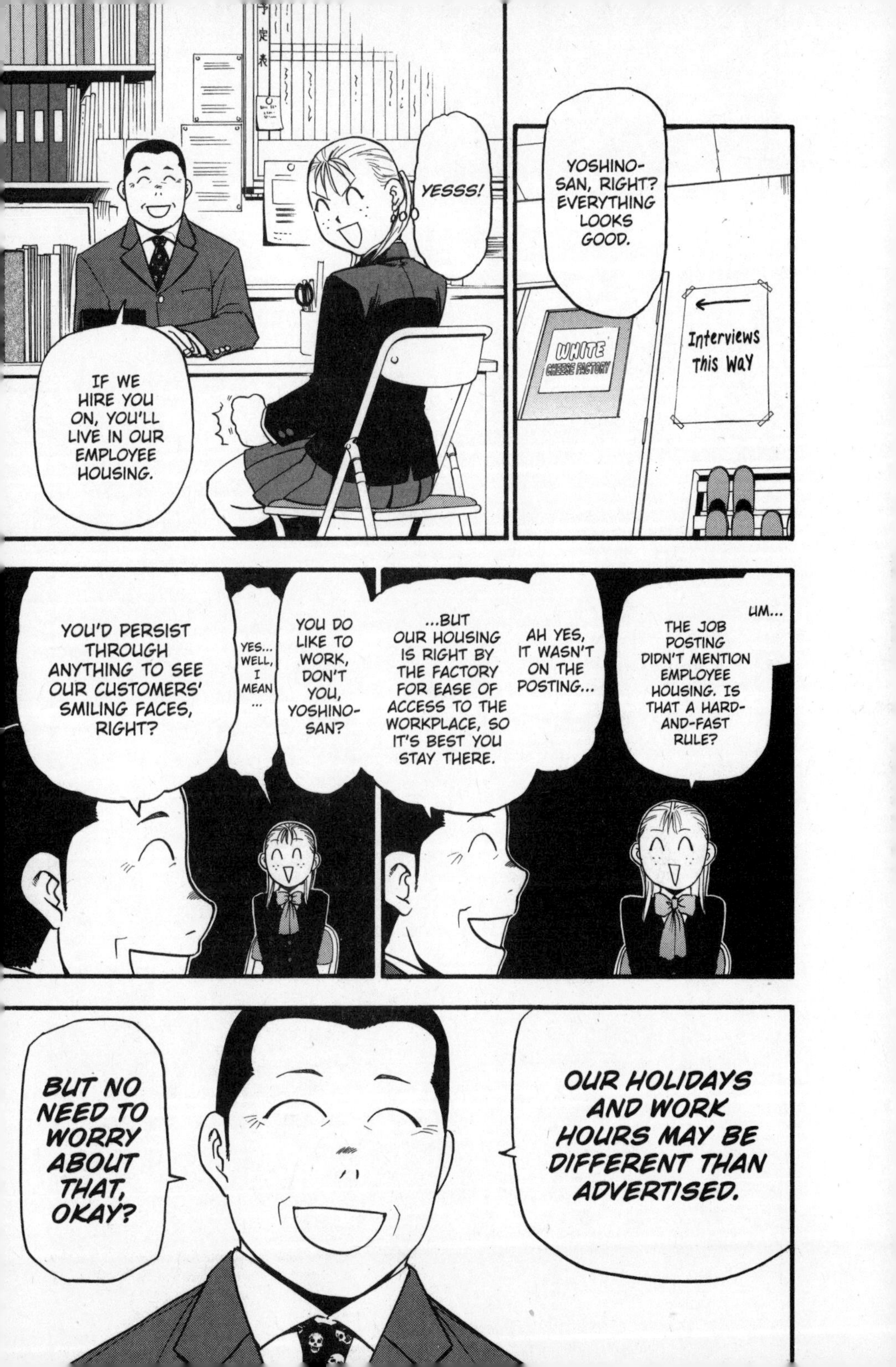
YOSHINO-SAN, RIGHT? EVERYTHING LOOKS GOOD.
WHITE CHEESE FACTORY
Interviews This Way
YESSS!
IF WE HIRE YOU ON, YOU'LL LIVE IN OUR EMPLOYEE HOUSING.
UM...
THE JOB POSTING DIDN'T MENTION EMPLOYEE HOUSING. IS THAT A HARD-AND-FAST RULE?
AH YES, IT WASN'T ON THE POSTING...
...BUT OUR HOUSING IS RIGHT BY THE FACTORY FOR EASE OF ACCESS TO THE WORKPLACE, SO IT'S BEST YOU STAY THERE.
YOU DO LIKE TO WORK, DON'T YOU, YOSHINO-SAN?
YES... WELL, I MEAN...
YOU'D PERSIST THROUGH ANYTHING TO SEE OUR CUSTOMERS' SMILING FACES, RIGHT?
OUR HOLIDAYS AND WORK HOURS MAY BE DIFFERENT THAN ADVERTISED.
BUT NO NEED TO WORRY ABOUT THAT, OKAY?

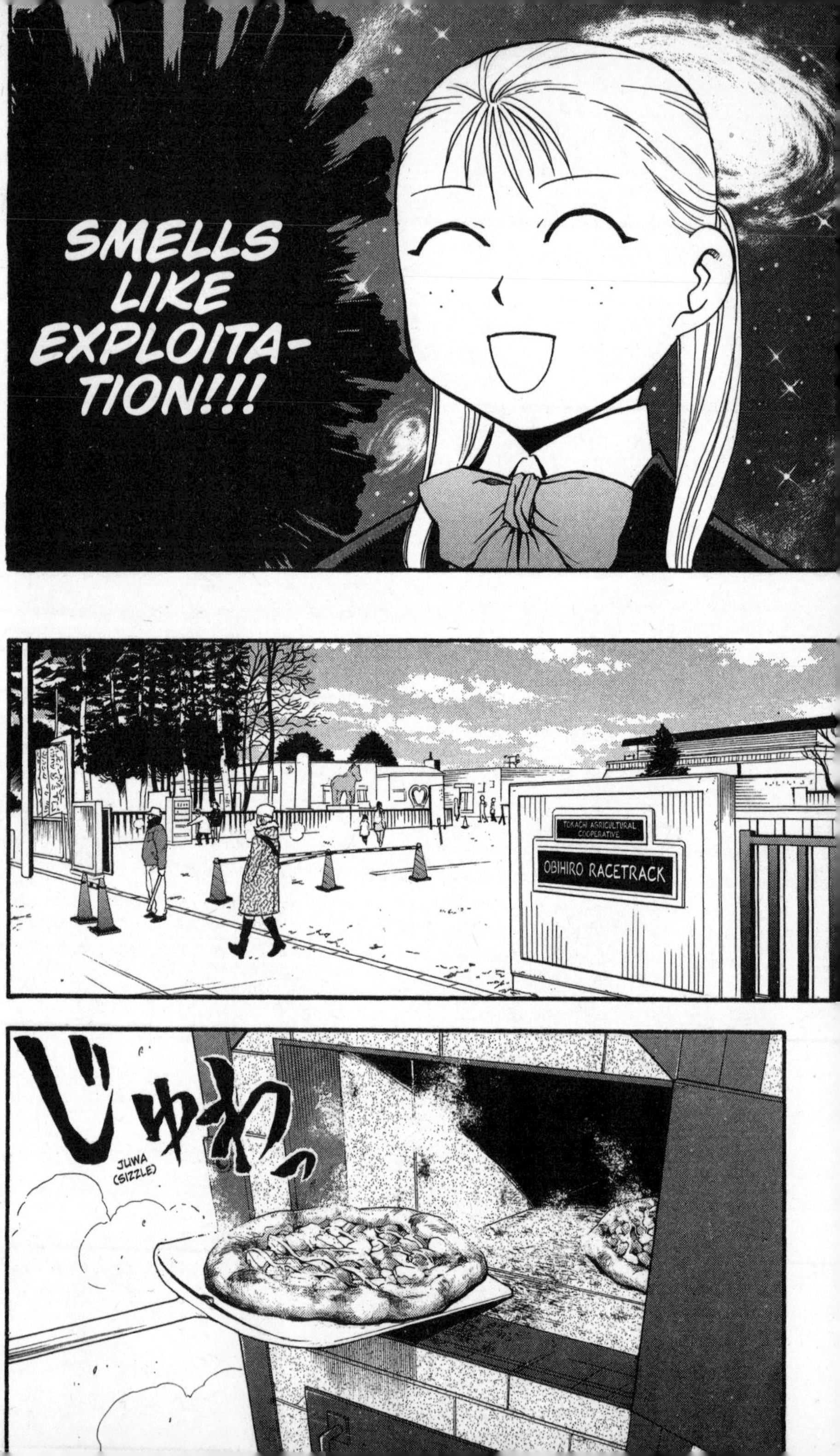
SMELLS LIKE EXPLOITATION!!!
TOKACHI AGRICULTURAL COOPERATIVE
OBIHIRO RACETRACK
じゅわっ
JUWA (SIZZLE)

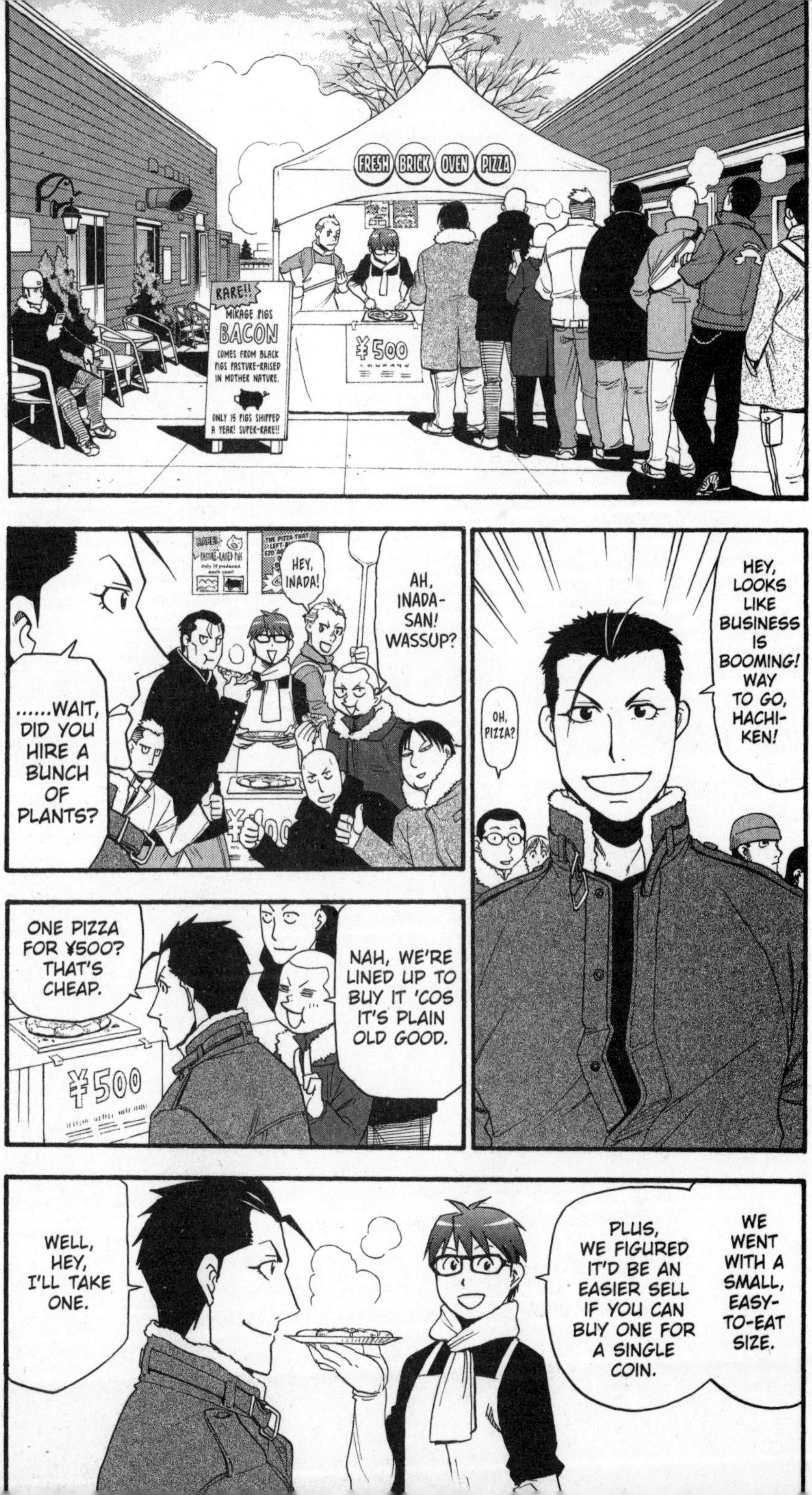
FRESH BRICK OVEN PIZZA
RARE!! MIKAGE PIGS BACON COMES FROM BLACK PIGS PASTURE-RAISED IN MOTHER NATURE. ONLY 15 PIGS SHIPPED A YEAR! SUPER-RARE!!
¥500
HEY, LOOKS LIKE BUSINESS IS BOOMING! WAY TO GO, HACHI-KEN!
OH, PIZZA?
AH, INADA-SAN! WASSUP?
HEY, INADA!
......WAIT, DID YOU HIRE A BUNCH OF PLANTS?
ONE PIZZA FOR ¥500? THAT'S CHEAP.
NAH, WE'RE LINED UP TO BUY IT 'COS IT'S PLAIN OLD GOOD.
¥500
WE WENT WITH A SMALL, EASY-TO-EAT SIZE.
PLUS, WE FIGURED IT'D BE AN EASIER SELL IF YOU CAN BUY ONE FOR A SINGLE COIN.
WELL, HEY, I'LL TAKE ONE.

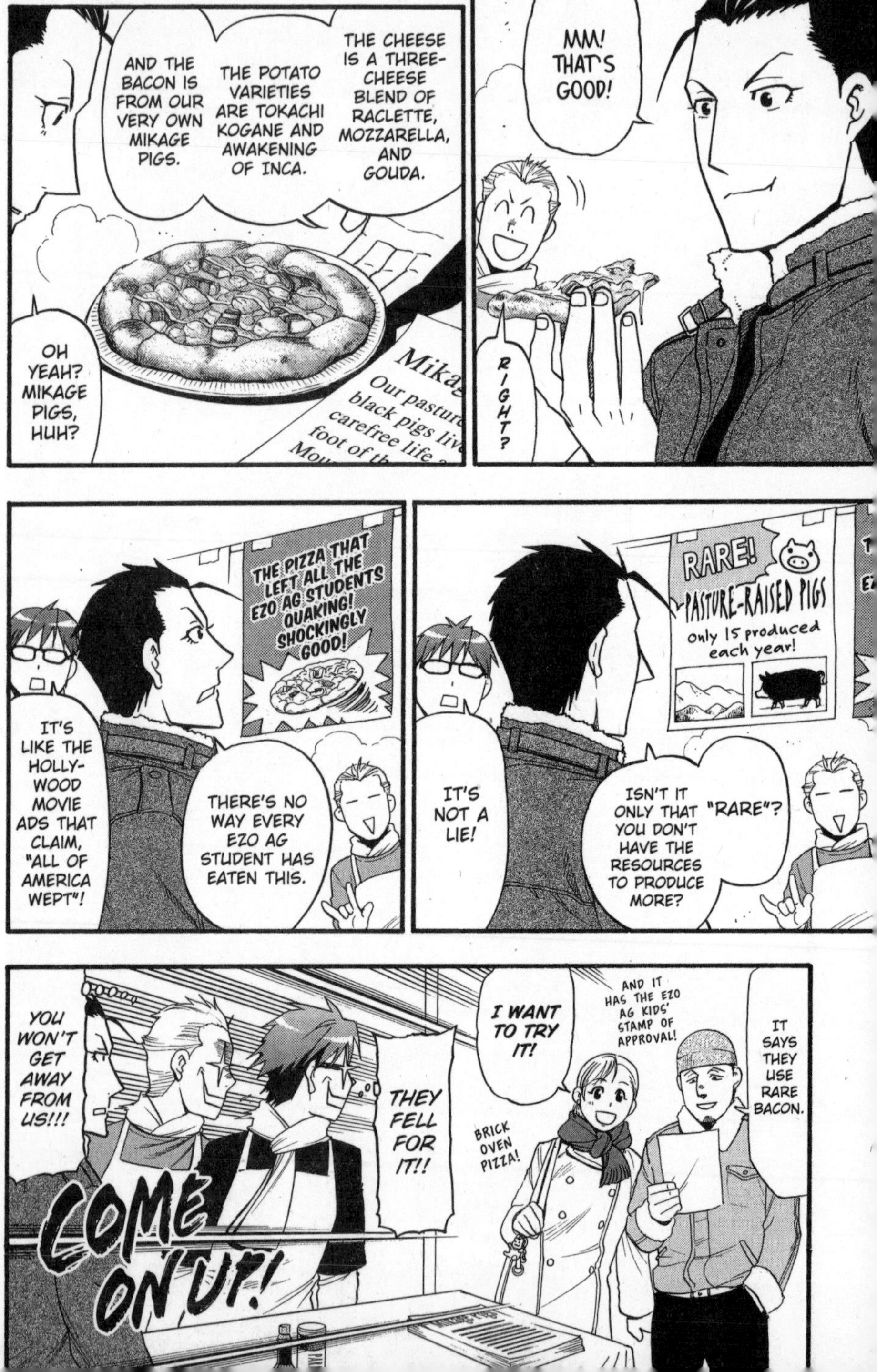
MM! THAT'S GOOD!
RIGHT?
THE CHEESE IS A THREE-CHEESE BLEND OF RACLETTE, MOZZARELLA, AND GOUDA.
THE POTATO VARIETIES ARE TOKACHI KOGANE AND AWAKENING OF INCA.
AND THE BACON IS FROM OUR VERY OWN MIKAGE PIGS.
Our pasture black pigs live carefree life foot of the
OH YEAH? MIKAGE PIGS, HUH?
RARE!
PASTURE-RAISED PIGS
Only 15 produced each year!
ISN'T IT ONLY THAT YOU DON'T HAVE THE RESOURCES TO PRODUCE MORE?
"RARE"?
IT'S NOT A LIE!
THE PIZZA THAT LEFT ALL THE EZO AG STUDENTS QUAKING! SHOCKINGLY GOOD!
THERE'S NO WAY EVERY EZO AG STUDENT HAS EATEN THIS.
IT'S LIKE THE HOLLYWOOD MOVIE ADS THAT CLAIM, "ALL OF AMERICA WEPT"!
IT SAYS THEY USE RARE BACON.
AND IT HAS THE EZO AG KIDS' STAMP OF APPROVAL!
I WANT TO TRY IT!
BRICK OVEN PIZZA!
THEY FELL FOR IT!!
YOU WON'T GET AWAY FROM US!!!
COME ON UP!

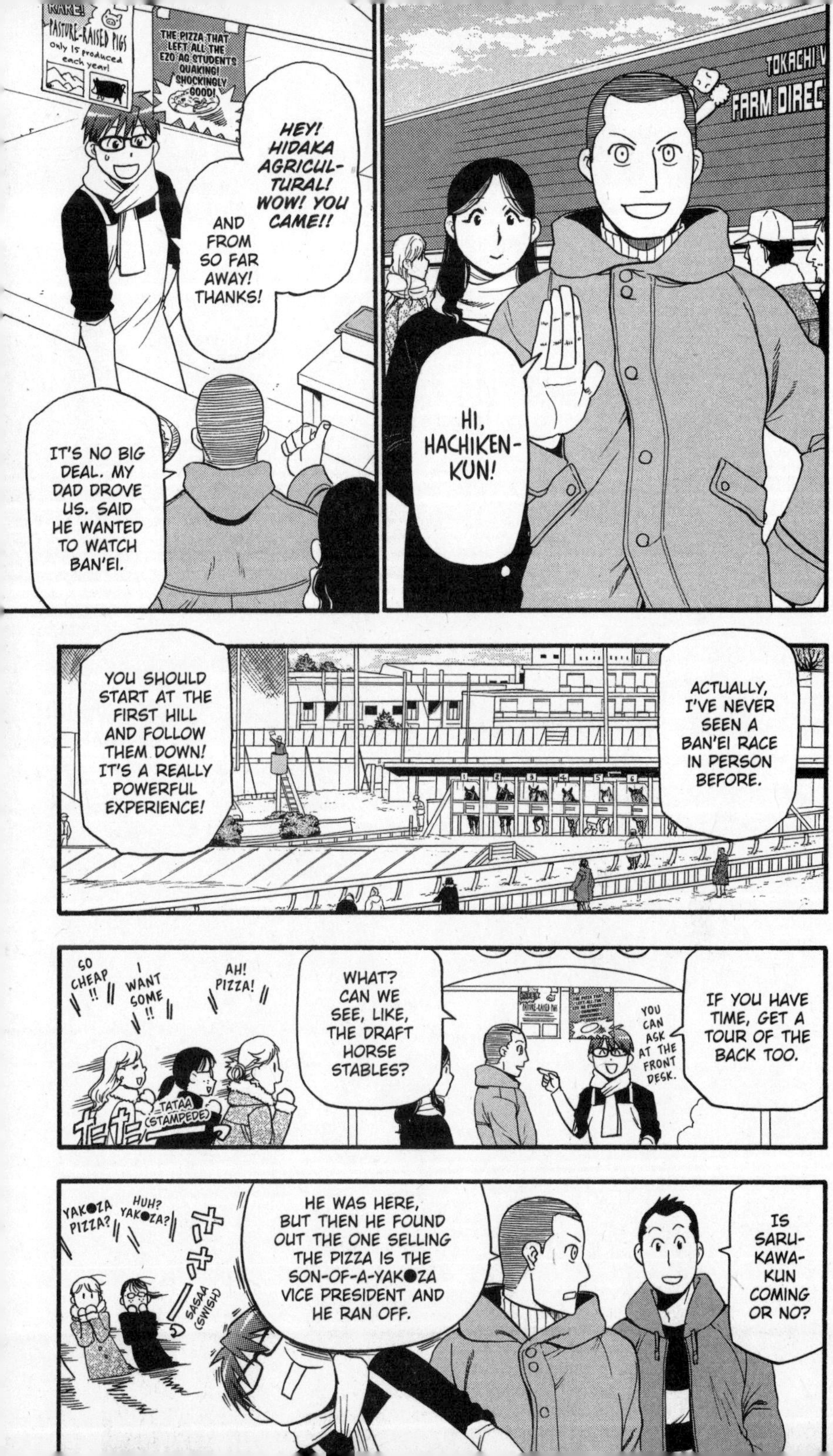
TOKACHI V
FARM DIREC
HI, HACHIKEN-KUN!
RARE! PASTURE-RAISED PIGS
Only 15 produced each year!
THE PIZZA THAT LEFT ALL THE EZO AG STUDENTS QUAKING! SHOCKINGLY GOOD!
HEY! HIDAKA AGRICULTURAL! WOW! YOU CAME!!
AND FROM SO FAR AWAY! THANKS!
IT'S NO BIG DEAL. MY DAD DROVE US. SAID HE WANTED TO WATCH BAN'EI.
ACTUALLY, I'VE NEVER SEEN A BAN'EI RACE IN PERSON BEFORE.
YOU SHOULD START AT THE FIRST HILL AND FOLLOW THEM DOWN! IT'S A REALLY POWERFUL EXPERIENCE!
IF YOU HAVE TIME, GET A TOUR OF THE BACK TOO.
YOU CAN ASK AT THE FRONT DESK.
WHAT? CAN WE SEE, LIKE, THE DRAFT HORSE STABLES?
AH! PIZZA!
I WANT SOME!!
SO CHEAP!!
TATAA (STAMPEDE)
IS SARU-KAWA-KUN COMING OR NO?
HE WAS HERE, BUT THEN HE FOUND OUT THE ONE SELLING THE PIZZA IS THE SON-OF-A-YAK●ZA VICE PRESIDENT AND HE RAN OFF.
HUH? YAK●ZA?
YAK●ZA PIZZA?
SASAA (SWISH)

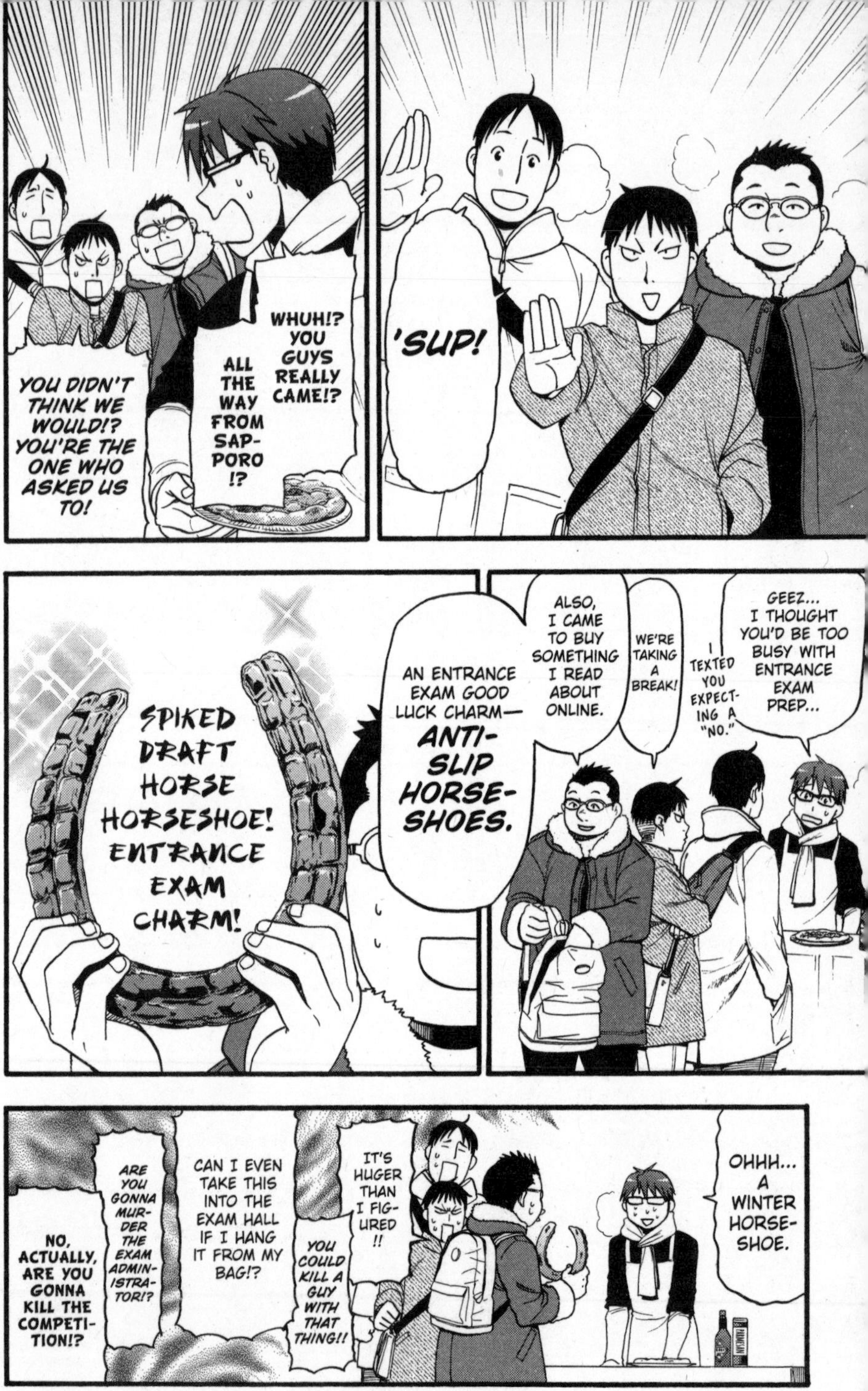
'SUP!
WHUH!? YOU GUYS REALLY CAME!?
ALL THE WAY FROM SAPPORO!?
YOU DIDN'T THINK WE WOULD!? YOU'RE THE ONE WHO ASKED US TO!
GEEZ... I THOUGHT YOU'D BE TOO BUSY WITH ENTRANCE EXAM PREP...
I TEXTED YOU EXPECTING A "NO."
WE'RE TAKING A BREAK!
ALSO, I CAME TO BUY SOMETHING I READ ABOUT ONLINE.
AN ENTRANCE EXAM GOOD LUCK CHARM—ANTI-SLIP HORSESHOES.
SPIKED DRAFT HORSE HORSESHOE! ENTRANCE EXAM CHARM!
OHHH... A WINTER HORSESHOE.
IT'S HUGER THAN I FIGURED!!
YOU COULD KILL A GUY WITH THAT THING!!
CAN I EVEN TAKE THIS INTO THE EXAM HALL IF I HANG IT FROM MY BAG!?
ARE YOU GONNA MURDER THE EXAM ADMINISTRATOR!?
NO, ACTUALLY, ARE YOU GONNA KILL THE COMPETITION!?

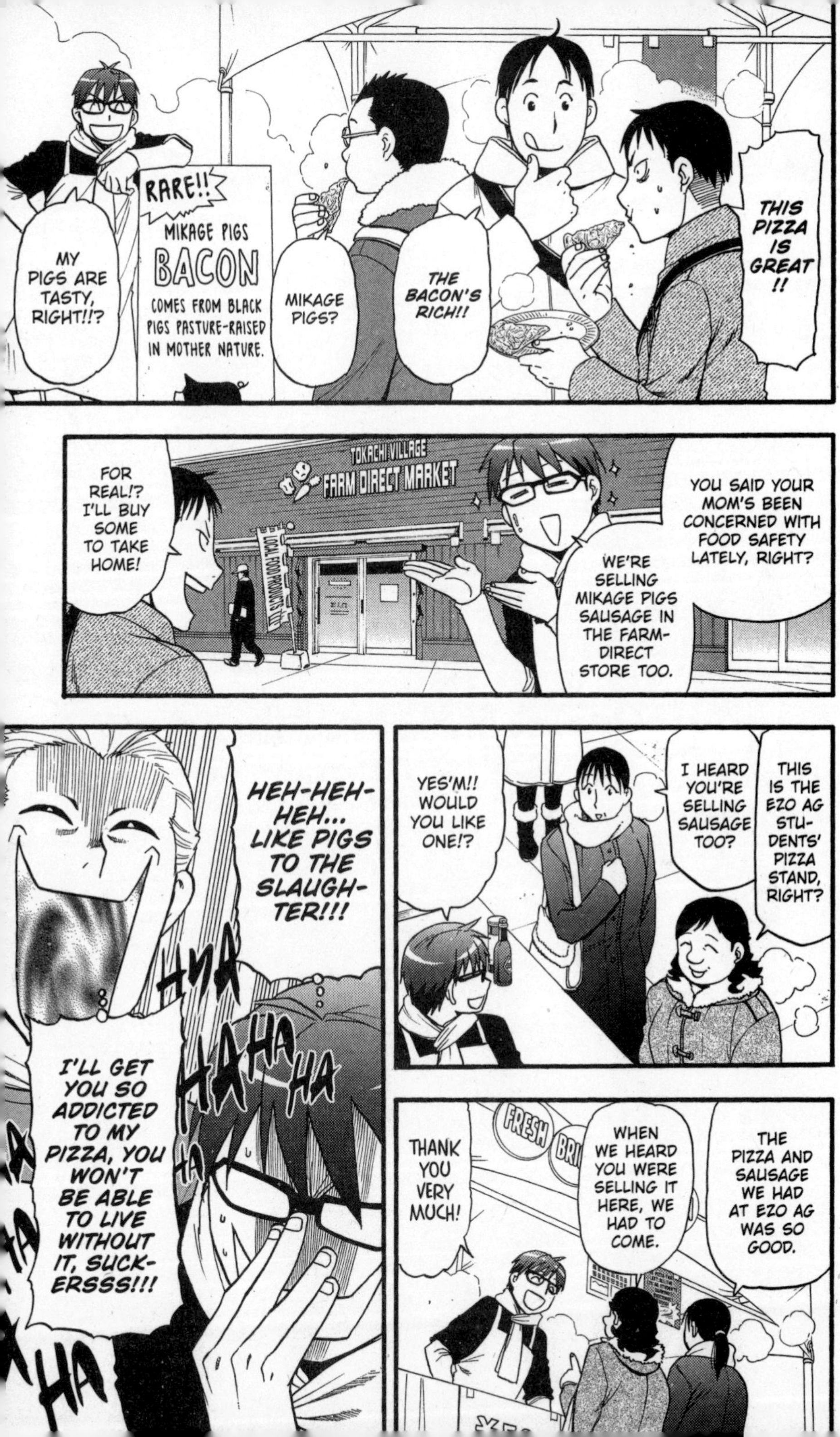
THIS PIZZA IS GREAT!!
THE BACON'S RICH!!
MIKAGE PIGS?
RARE!!
MIKAGE PIGS BACON COMES FROM BLACK PIGS PASTURE-RAISED IN MOTHER NATURE.
MY PIGS ARE TASTY, RIGHT!!?
YOU SAID YOUR MOM'S BEEN CONCERNED WITH FOOD SAFETY LATELY, RIGHT?
WE'RE SELLING MIKAGE PIGS SAUSAGE IN THE FARM-DIRECT STORE TOO.
TOKACHI VILLAGE
FARM DIRECT MARKET
LOCAL FOOD PRODUCTS
FOR REAL!? I'LL BUY SOME TO TAKE HOME!
THIS IS THE EZO AG STU-DENTS' PIZZA STAND, RIGHT?
I HEARD YOU'RE SELLING SAUSAGE TOO?
YES'M!! WOULD YOU LIKE ONE!?
THE PIZZA AND SAUSAGE WE HAD AT EZO AG WAS SO GOOD.
WHEN WE HEARD YOU WERE SELLING IT HERE, WE HAD TO COME.
FRESH
THANK YOU VERY MUCH!
HEH-HEH-HEH... LIKE PIGS TO THE SLAUGH-TER!!!
HA HA HA HA HA HA HA HA
I'LL GET YOU SO ADDICTED TO MY PIZZA, YOU WON'T BE ABLE TO LIVE WITHOUT IT, SUCK-ERSSS!!!

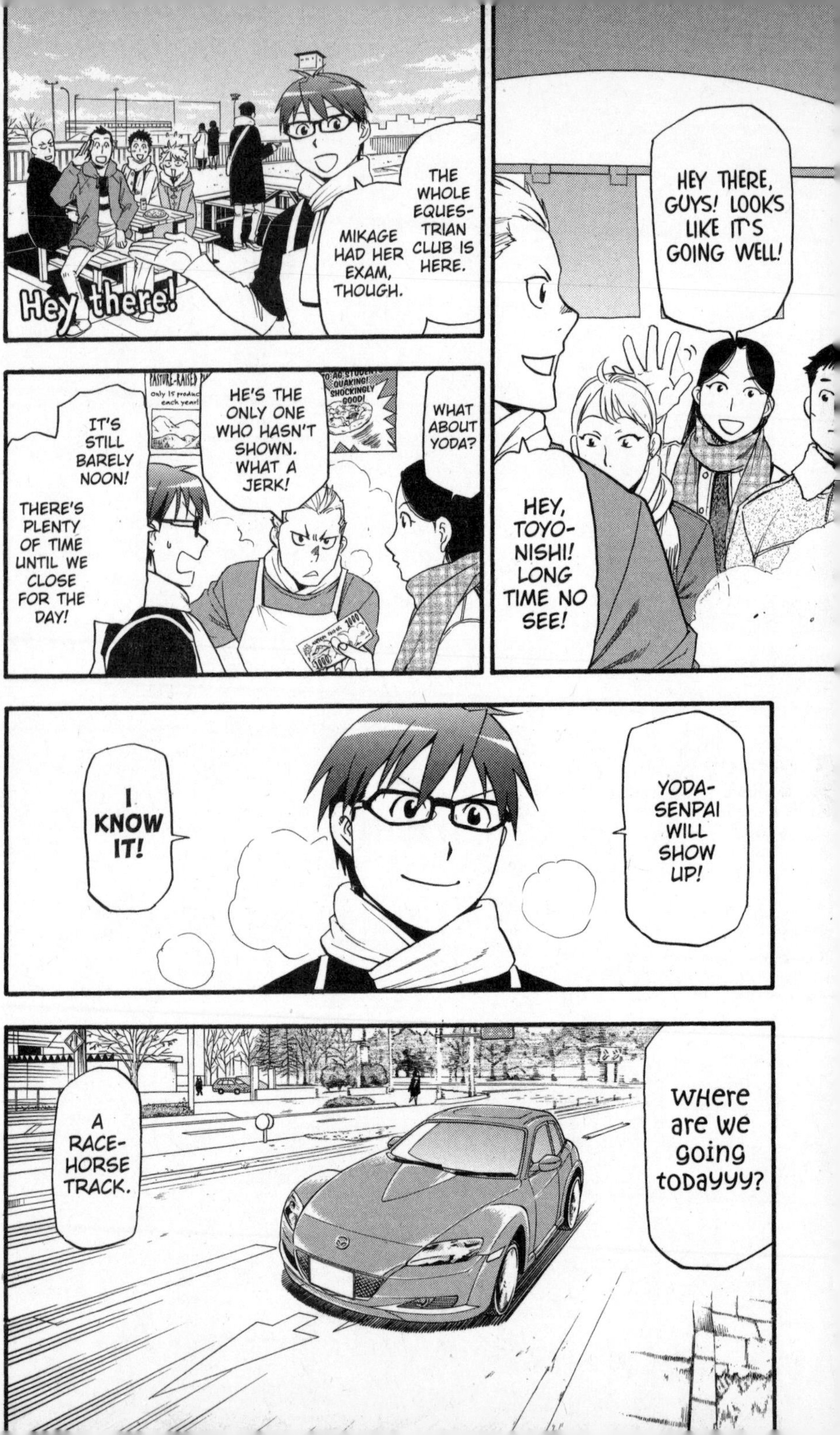
HEY THERE, GUYS! LOOKS LIKE IT'S GOING WELL!
HEY, TOYO-NISHI! LONG TIME NO SEE!
THE WHOLE EQUES-TRIAN CLUB IS HERE.
MIKAGE HAD HER EXAM, THOUGH.
Hey there!
WHAT ABOUT YODA?
HE'S THE ONLY ONE WHO HASN'T SHOWN. WHAT A JERK!
QUAKING! SHOCKINGLY GOOD!
IT'S STILL BARELY NOON!
THERE'S PLENTY OF TIME UNTIL WE CLOSE FOR THE DAY!
YODA-SENPAI WILL SHOW UP!
I KNOW IT!
Where are we going todayyy?
A RACE-HORSE TRACK.

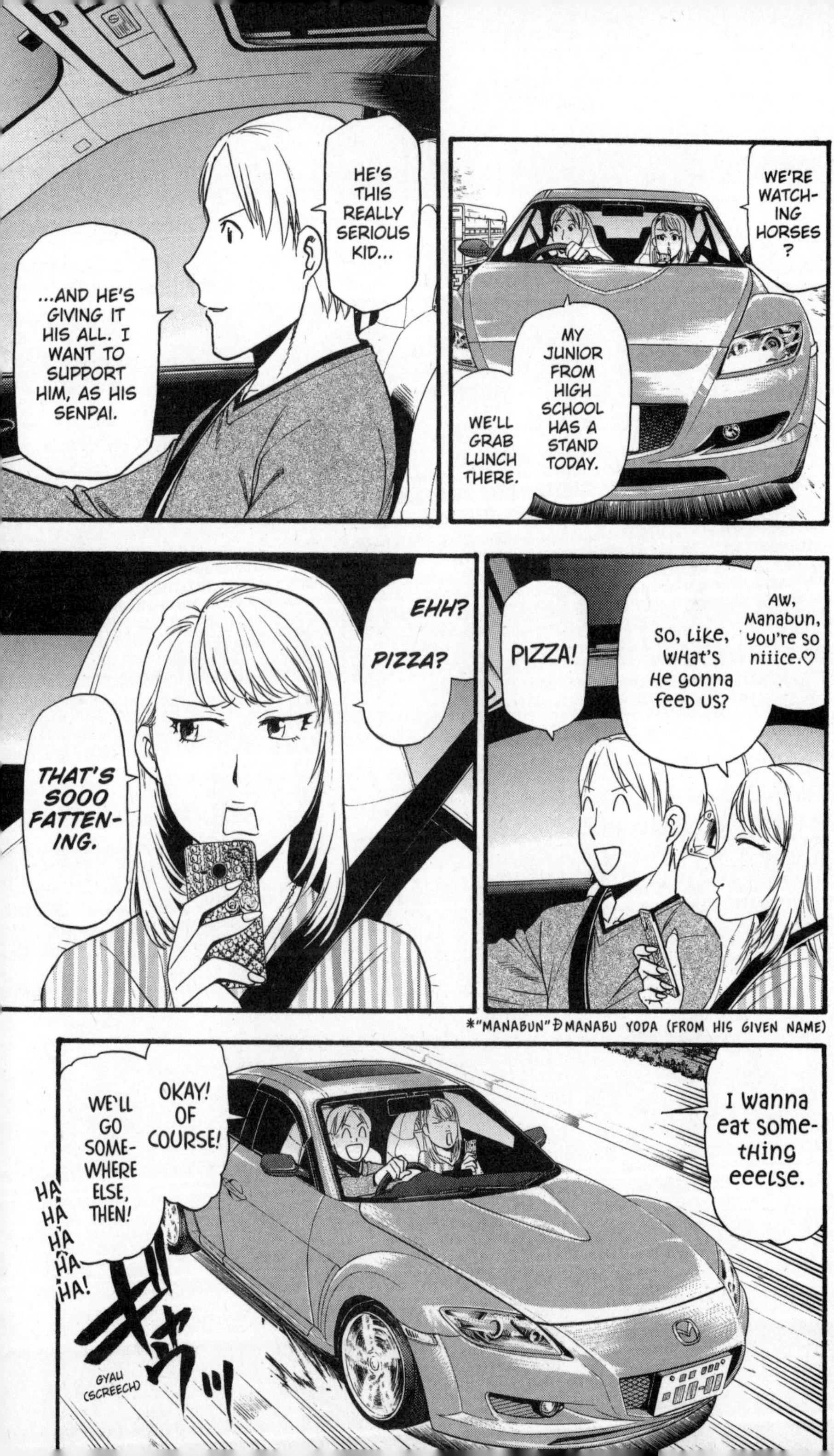
WE'RE WATCHING HORSES?
MY JUNIOR FROM HIGH SCHOOL HAS A STAND TODAY.
WE'LL GRAB LUNCH THERE.
HE'S THIS REALLY SERIOUS KID...
...AND HE'S GIVING IT HIS ALL. I WANT TO SUPPORT HIM, AS HIS SENPAI.
AW, Manabun, you're so niiice.♡
So, like, what's he gonna feed us?
PIZZA!
EHH?
PIZZA?
THAT'S SOOO FATTENING.
*"MANABUN" Đ MANABU YODA (FROM HIS GIVEN NAME)
I wanna eat something eeelse.
OKAY! OF COURSE!
WE'LL GO SOMEWHERE ELSE, THEN!
HA HA HA HA HA!
GYAU (SCREECH)

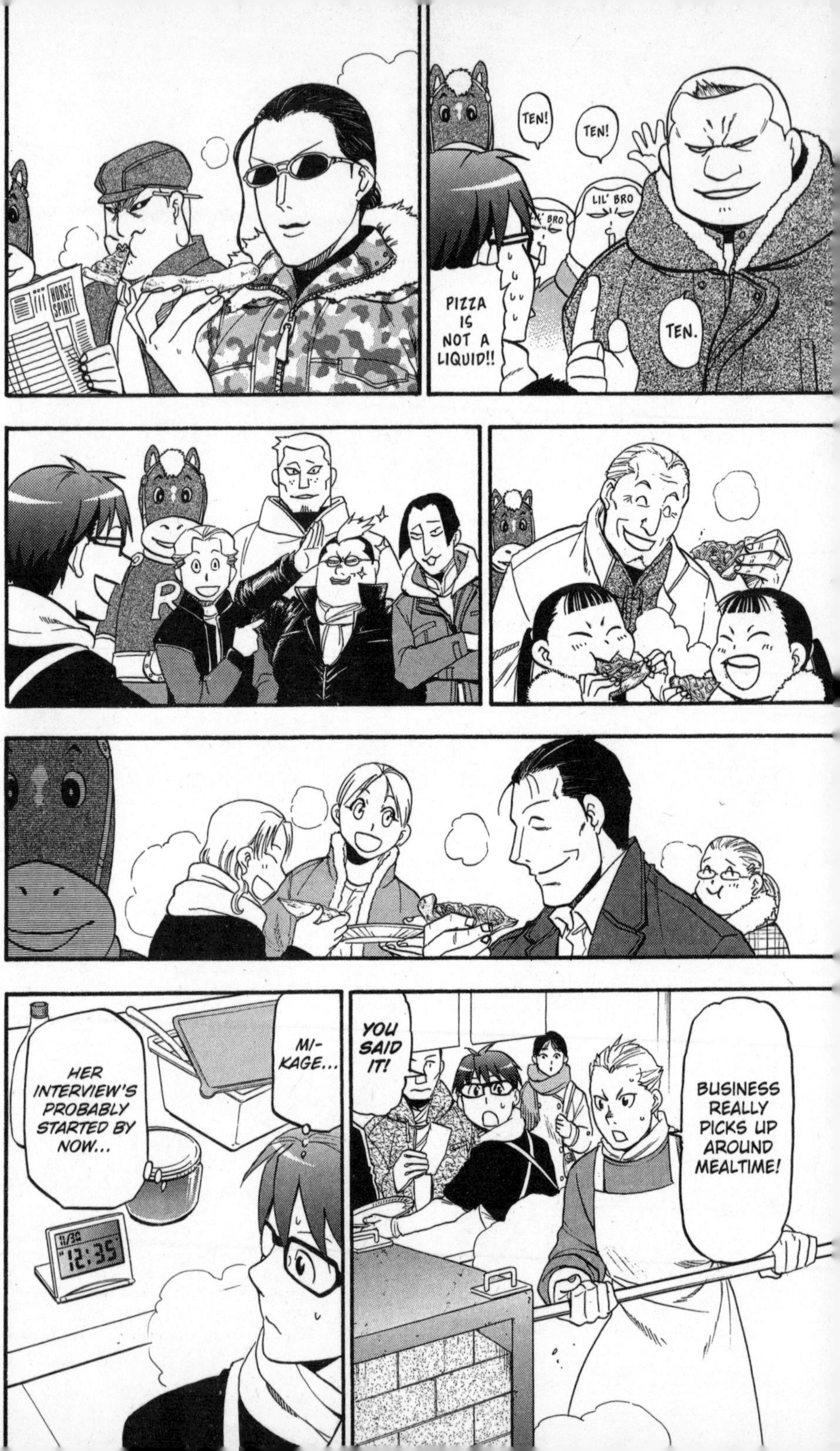
TEN!
TEN!
LIL' BRO
TEN.
PIZZA IS NOT A LIQUID!!
HORSE SPIRIT
BUSINESS REALLY PICKS UP AROUND MEALTIME!
YOU SAID IT!
MI-KAGE...
HER INTERVIEW'S PROBABLY STARTED BY NOW...
12:35

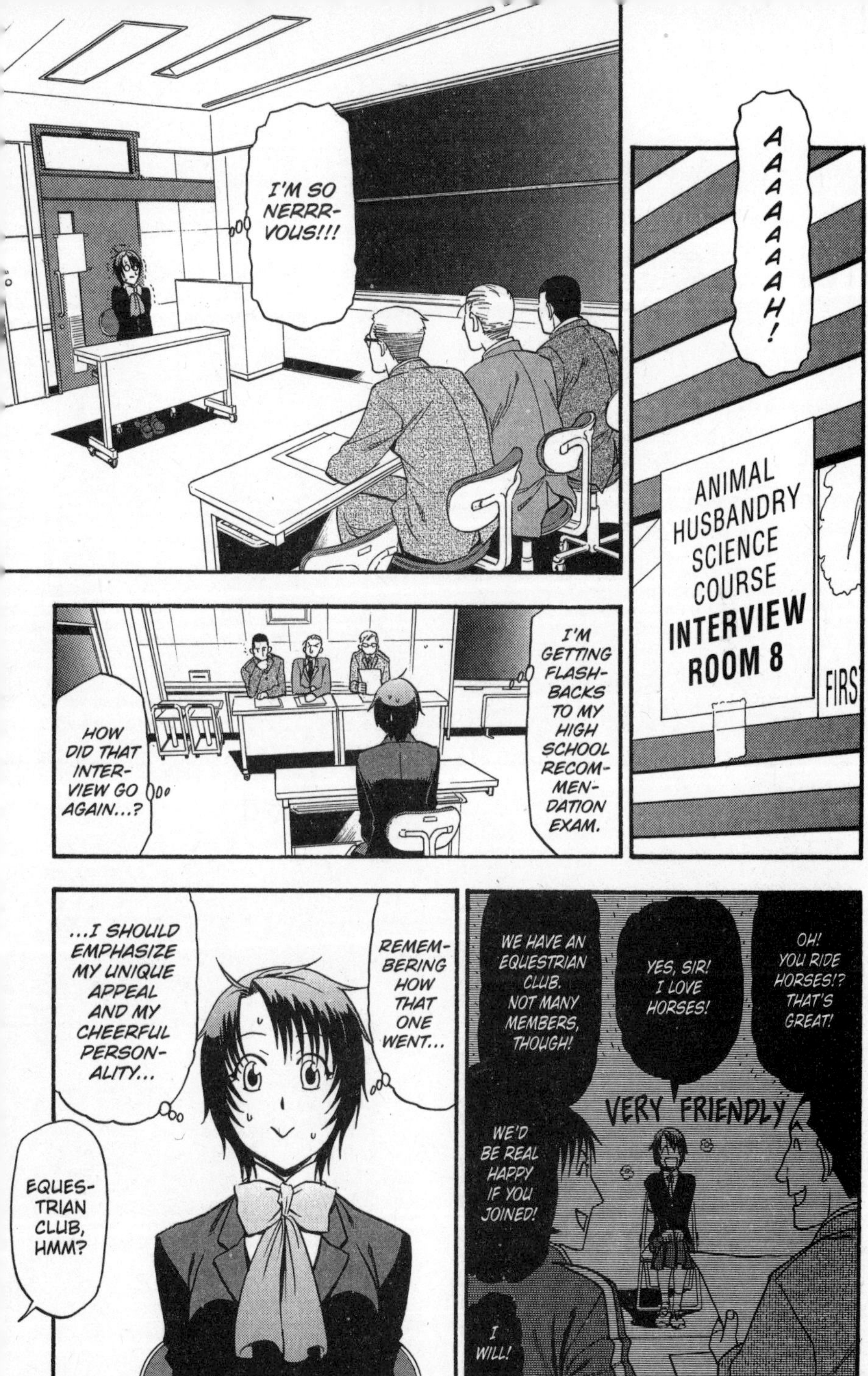
AAAAAAAH!
ANIMAL HUSBANDRY SCIENCE COURSE
INTERVIEW ROOM 8
FIRST
I'M SO NERRR-VOUS!!!
I'M GETTING FLASH-BACKS TO MY HIGH SCHOOL RECOMMEN-DATION EXAM.
HOW DID THAT INTER-VIEW GO AGAIN...?
OH! YOU RIDE HORSES!? THAT'S GREAT!
YES, SIR! I LOVE HORSES!
WE HAVE AN EQUESTRIAN CLUB. NOT MANY MEMBERS, THOUGH!
VERY FRIENDLY
WE'D BE REAL HAPPY IF YOU JOINED!
I WILL!
REMEM-BERING HOW THAT ONE WENT...
...I SHOULD EMPHASIZE MY UNIQUE APPEAL AND MY CHEERFUL PERSON-ALITY...
EQUES-TRIAN CLUB, HMM?

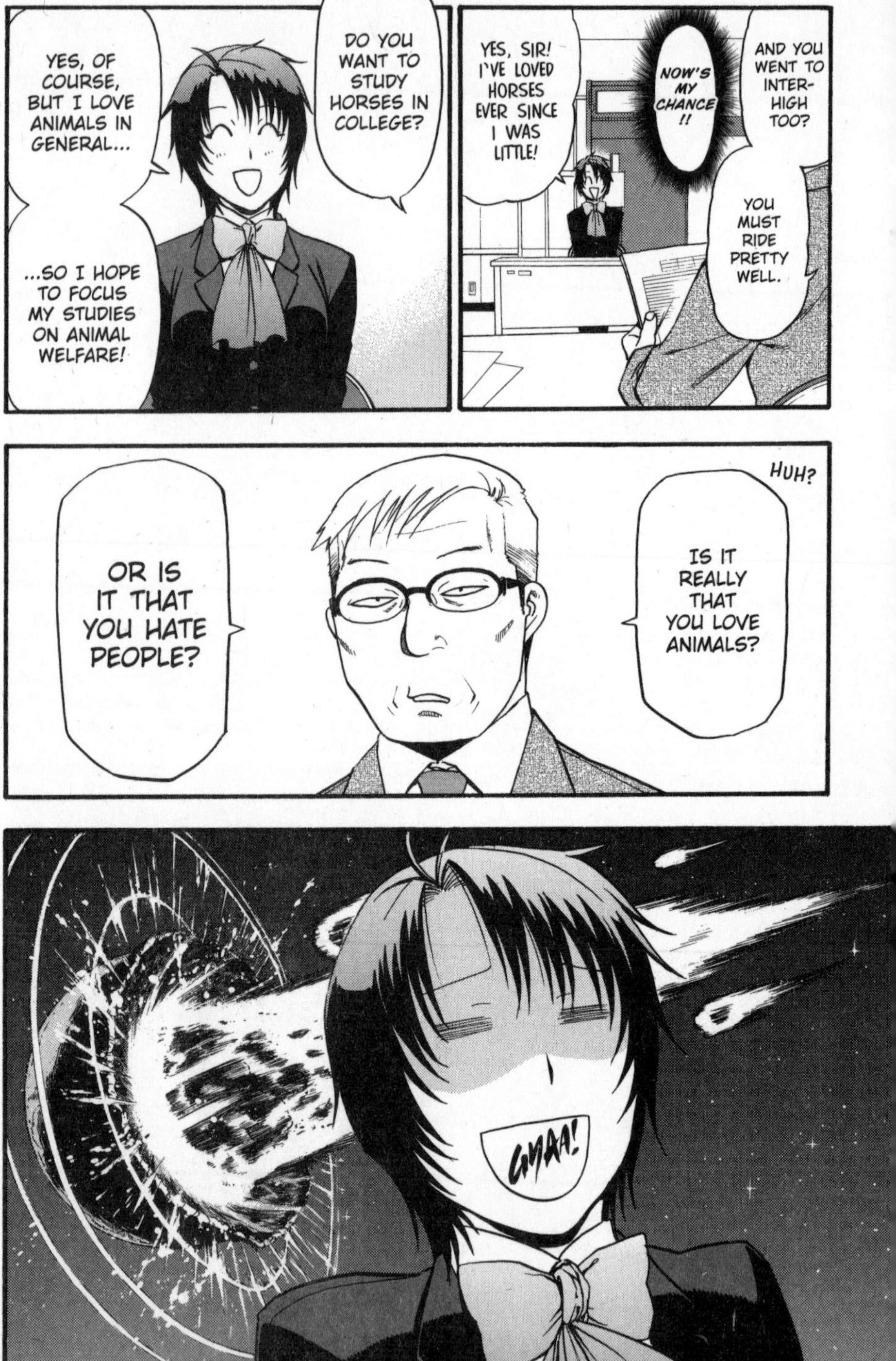
AND YOU WENT TO INTER-HIGH TOO?
YOU MUST RIDE PRETTY WELL.
NOW'S MY CHANCE!!
YES, SIR! I'VE LOVED HORSES EVER SINCE I WAS LITTLE!
DO YOU WANT TO STUDY HORSES IN COLLEGE?
YES, OF COURSE, BUT I LOVE ANIMALS IN GENERAL...
...SO I HOPE TO FOCUS MY STUDIES ON ANIMAL WELFARE!
HUH?
IS IT REALLY THAT YOU LOVE ANIMALS?
OR IS IT THAT YOU HATE PEOPLE?
GWAA!

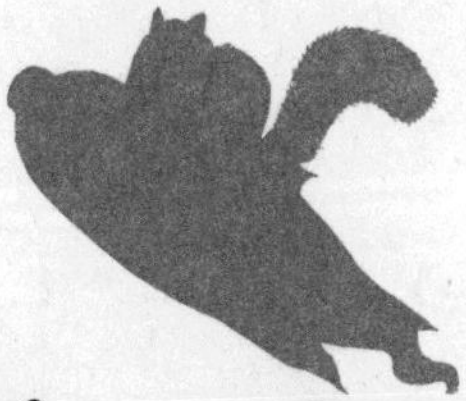

Silver Spoon

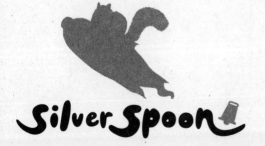

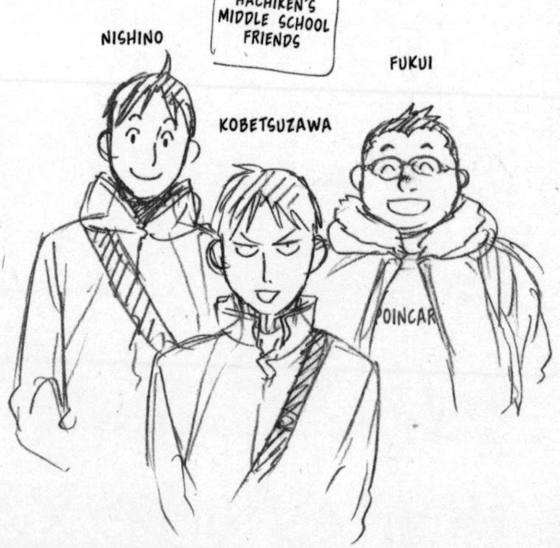
HACHIKEN'S MIDDLE SCHOOL FRIENDS
NISHINO
KOBETSUZAWA
FUKUI
POINCAR

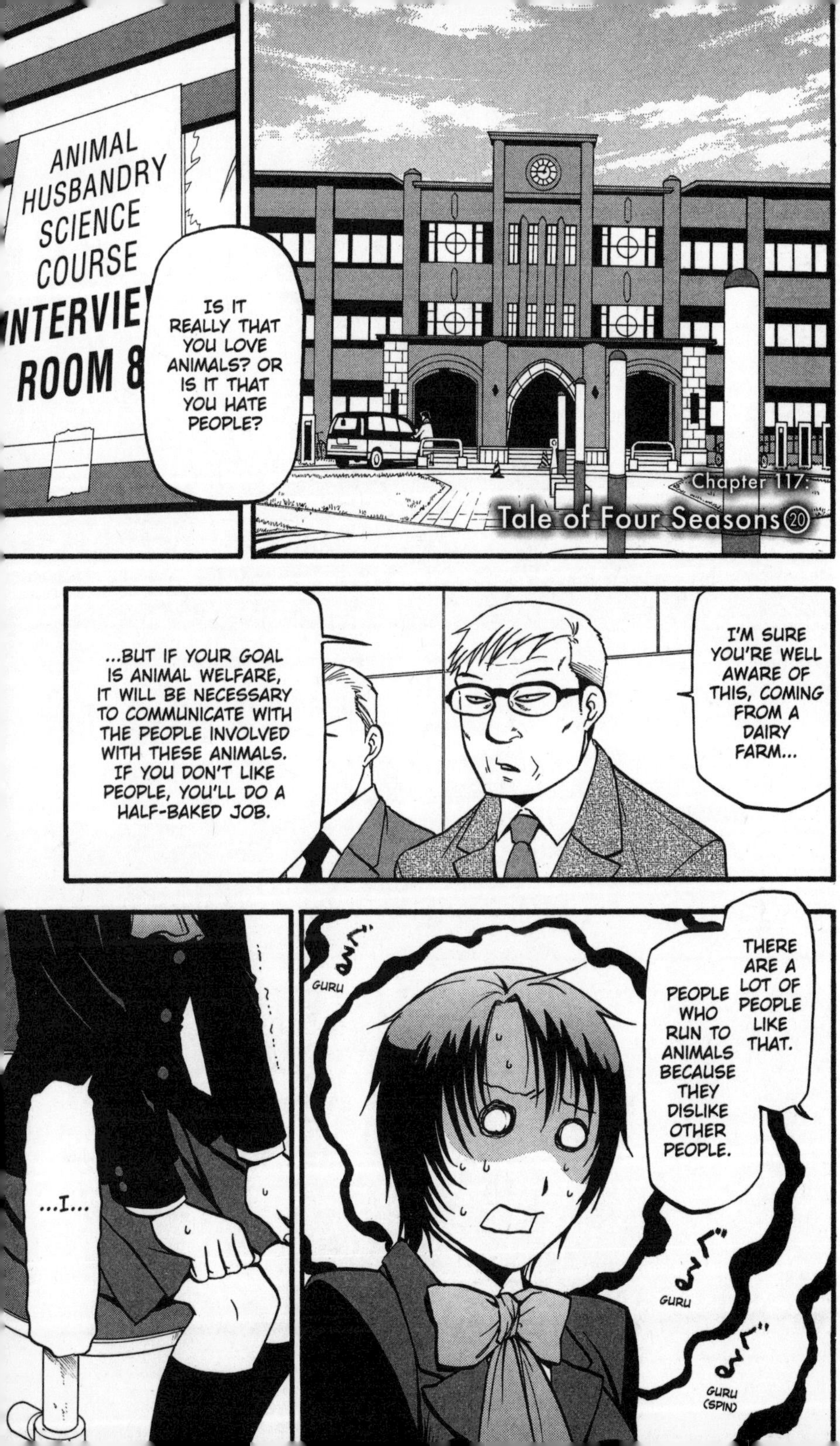

Chapter 117:
Tale of Four Seasons ⑳
IS IT REALLY THAT YOU LOVE ANIMALS? OR IS IT THAT YOU HATE PEOPLE?
ANIMAL HUSBANDRY SCIENCE COURSE
INTERVIE
ROOM 8
I'M SURE YOU'RE WELL AWARE OF THIS, COMING FROM A DAIRY FARM...
...BUT IF YOUR GOAL IS ANIMAL WELFARE, IT WILL BE NECESSARY TO COMMUNICATE WITH THE PEOPLE INVOLVED WITH THESE ANIMALS. IF YOU DON'T LIKE PEOPLE, YOU'LL DO A HALF-BAKED JOB.
THERE ARE A LOT OF PEOPLE LIKE THAT.
PEOPLE WHO RUN TO ANIMALS BECAUSE THEY DISLIKE OTHER PEOPLE.
GURU
GURU
GURU (SPIN)
...I...

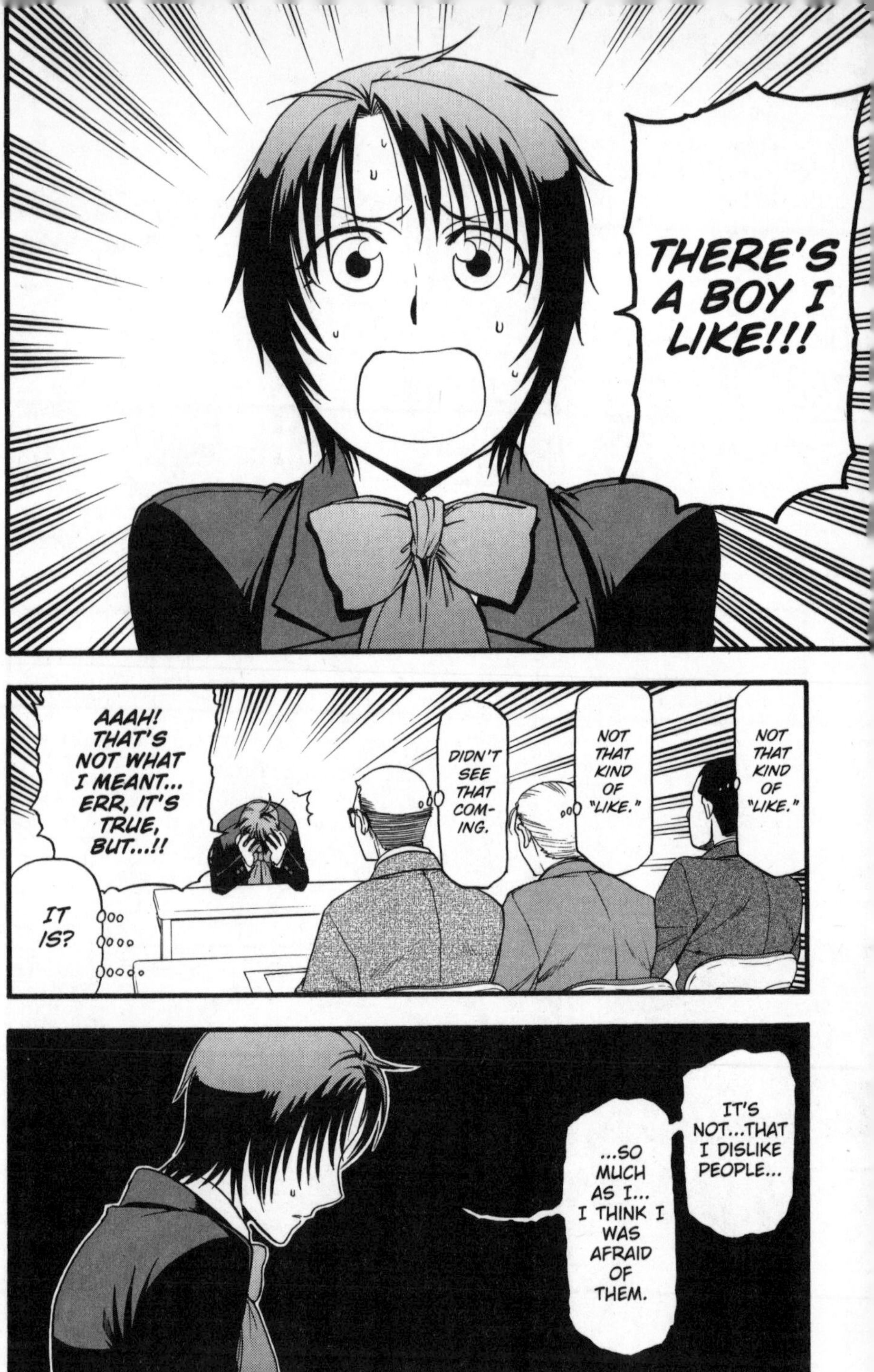
THERE'S A BOY I LIKE!!!
NOT THAT KIND OF "LIKE."
NOT THAT KIND OF "LIKE."
DIDN'T SEE THAT COMING.
AAAH! THAT'S NOT WHAT I MEANT... ERR, IT'S TRUE, BUT...!!
IT IS?
IT'S NOT...THAT I DISLIKE PEOPLE...
...SO MUCH AS I... I THINK I WAS AFRAID OF THEM.

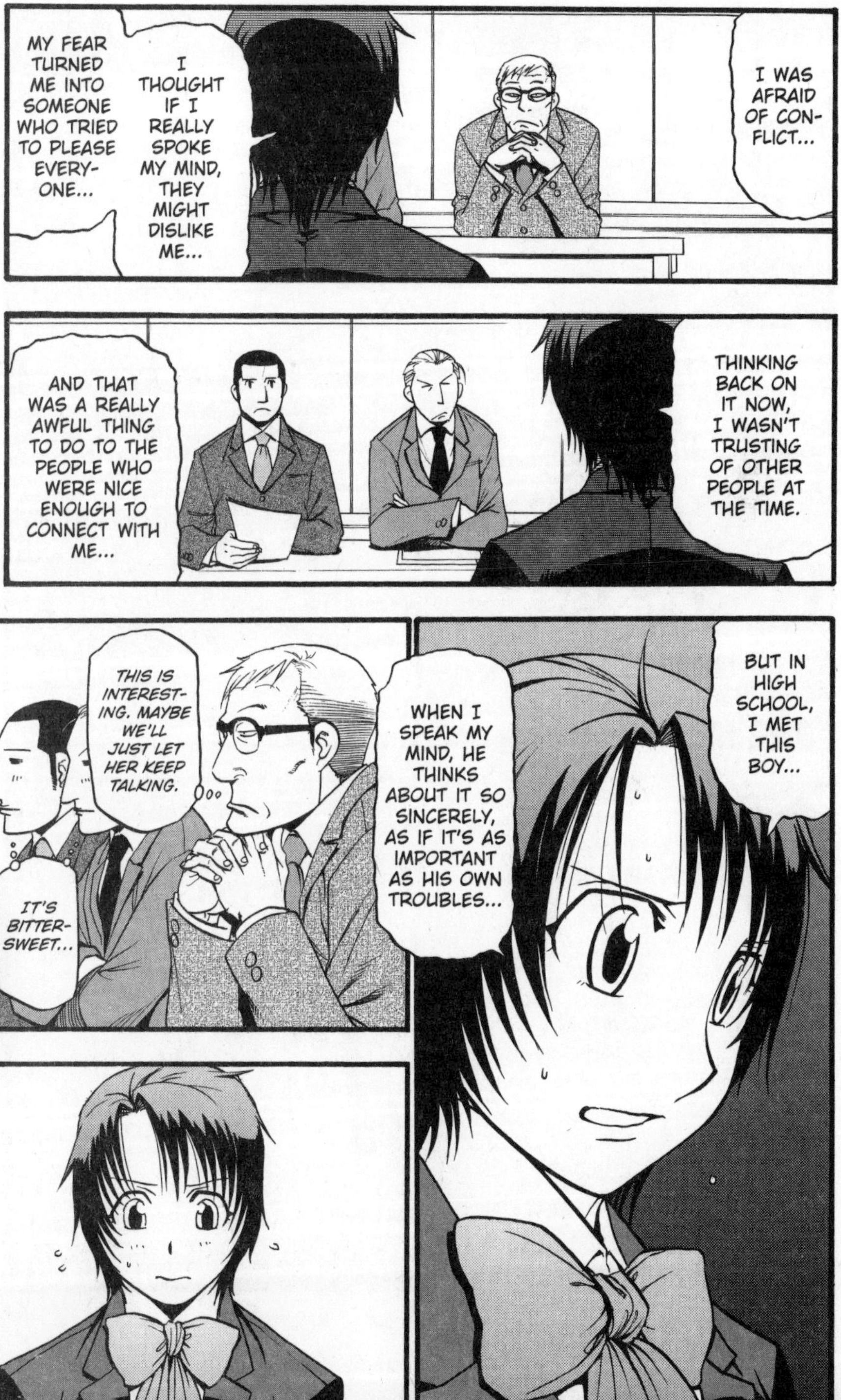

I WAS AFRAID OF CON-FLICT...
I THOUGHT IF I REALLY SPOKE MY MIND, THEY MIGHT DISLIKE ME...
MY FEAR TURNED ME INTO SOMEONE WHO TRIED TO PLEASE EVERY-ONE...
THINKING BACK ON IT NOW, I WASN'T TRUSTING OF OTHER PEOPLE AT THE TIME.
AND THAT WAS A REALLY AWFUL THING TO DO TO THE PEOPLE WHO WERE NICE ENOUGH TO CONNECT WITH ME...
BUT IN HIGH SCHOOL, I MET THIS BOY...
WHEN I SPEAK MY MIND, HE THINKS ABOUT IT SO SINCERELY, AS IF IT'S AS IMPORTANT AS HIS OWN TROUBLES...
THIS IS INTEREST-ING. MAYBE WE'LL JUST LET HER KEEP TALKING.
IT'S BITTER-SWEET...

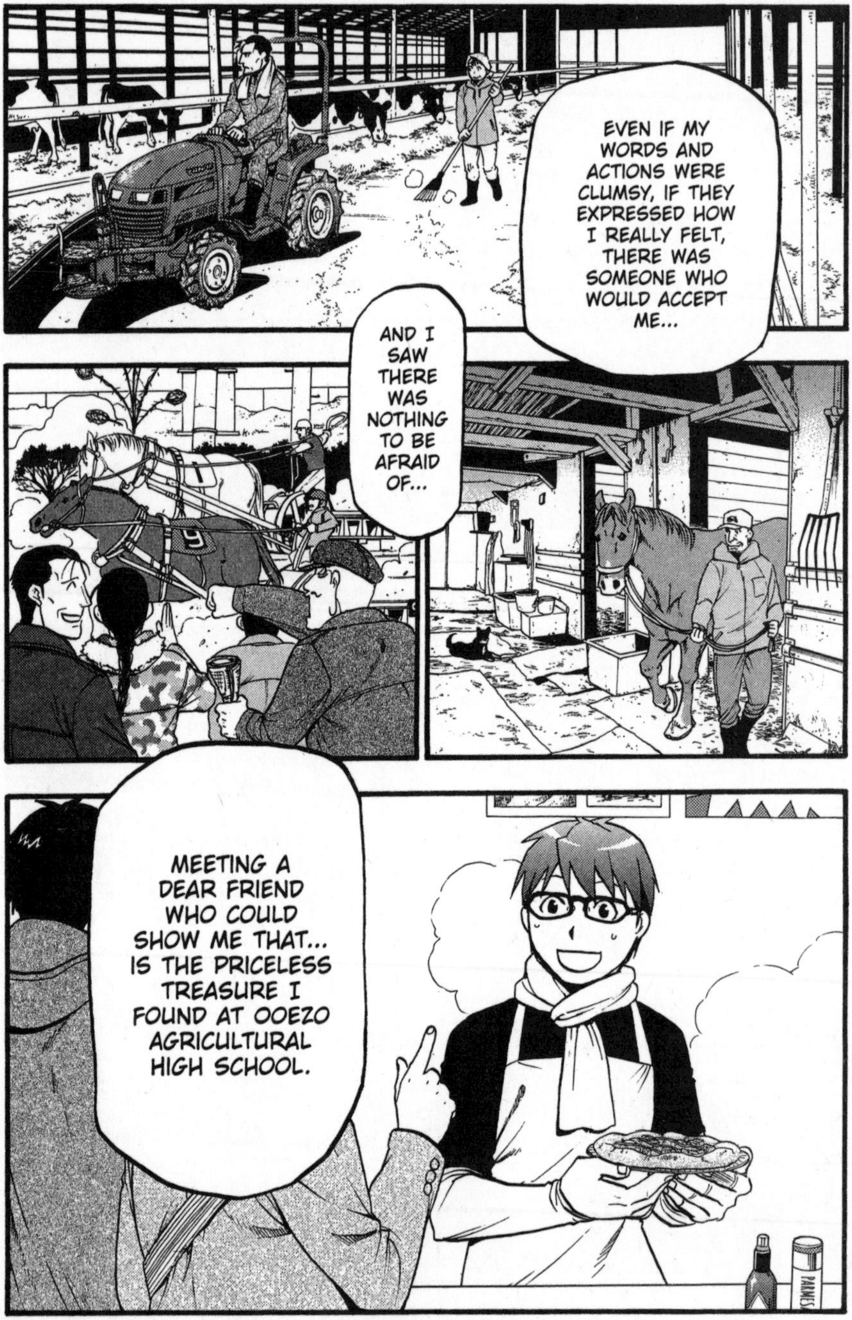
EVEN IF MY WORDS AND ACTIONS WERE CLUMSY, IF THEY EXPRESSED HOW I REALLY FELT, THERE WAS SOMEONE WHO WOULD ACCEPT ME...
AND I SAW THERE WAS NOTHING TO BE AFRAID OF...
MEETING A DEAR FRIEND WHO COULD SHOW ME THAT... IS THE PRICELESS TREASURE I FOUND AT OOEZO AGRICULTURAL HIGH SCHOOL.

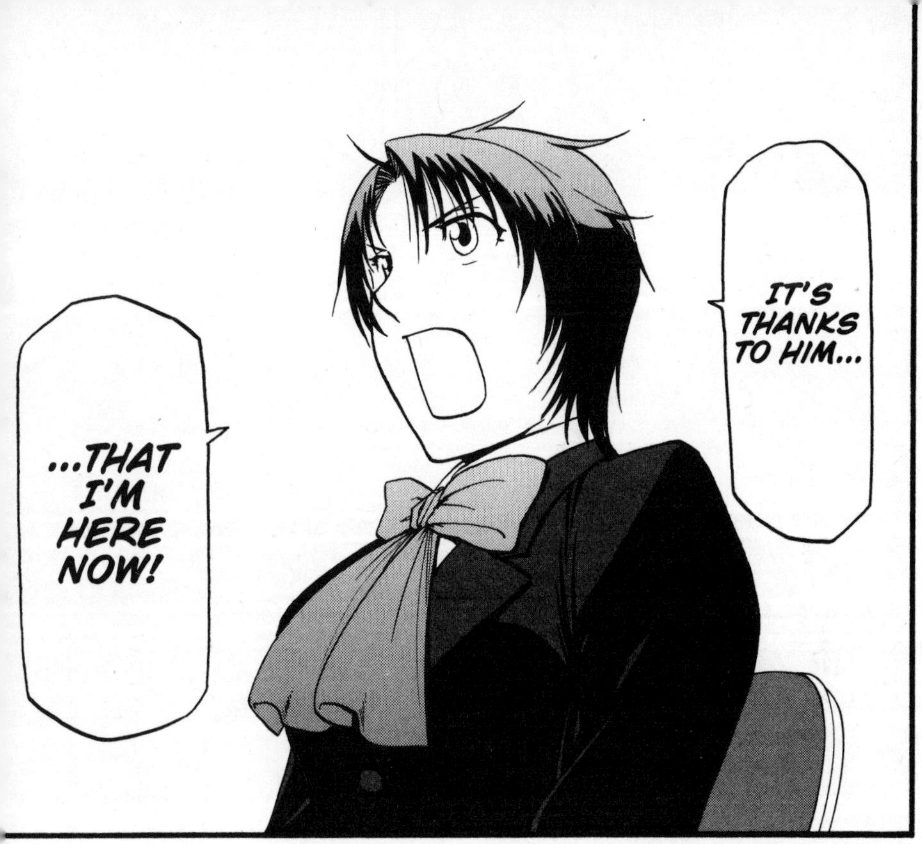
IT'S THANKS TO HIM...
...THAT I'M HERE NOW!

Chapter 117: Tale of Four Seasons ⑳

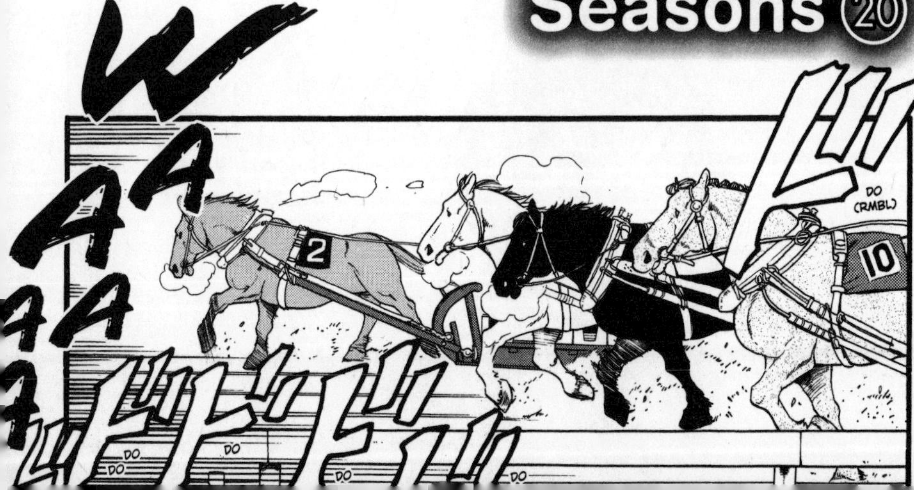
DO (RMBL)
WAAAA
DO
DO
DO
DO
DO

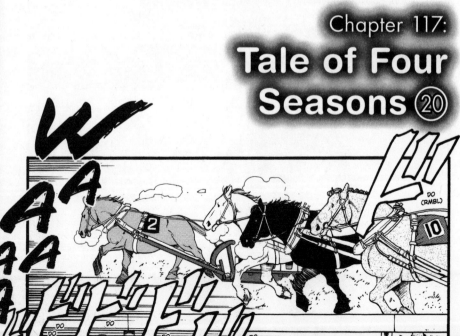

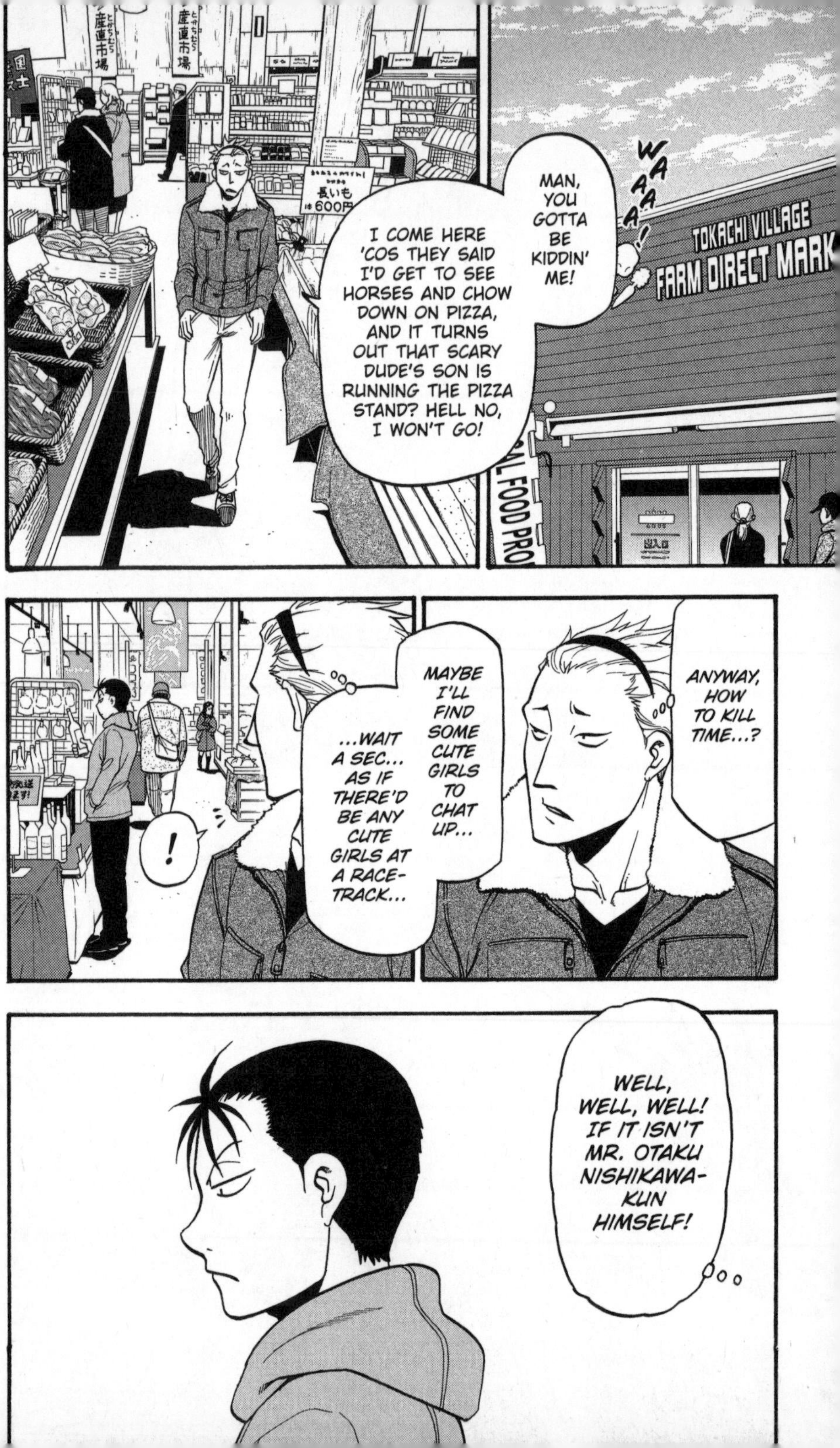
TOKACHI VILLAGE
FARM DIRECT MARK
WAAAA!
MAN, YOU GOTTA BE KIDDIN' ME!
産直市場
産直市場
長いも
I COME HERE 'COS THEY SAID I'D GET TO SEE HORSES AND CHOW DOWN ON PIZZA, AND IT TURNS OUT THAT SCARY DUDE'S SON IS RUNNING THE PIZZA STAND? HELL NO, I WON'T GO!
ANYWAY, HOW TO KILL TIME...?
MAYBE I'LL FIND SOME CUTE GIRLS TO CHAT UP...
...WAIT A SEC... AS IF THERE'D BE ANY CUTE GIRLS AT A RACE-TRACK...
!
WELL, WELL, WELL! IF IT ISN'T MR. OTAKU NISHIKAWA-KUN HIMSELF!

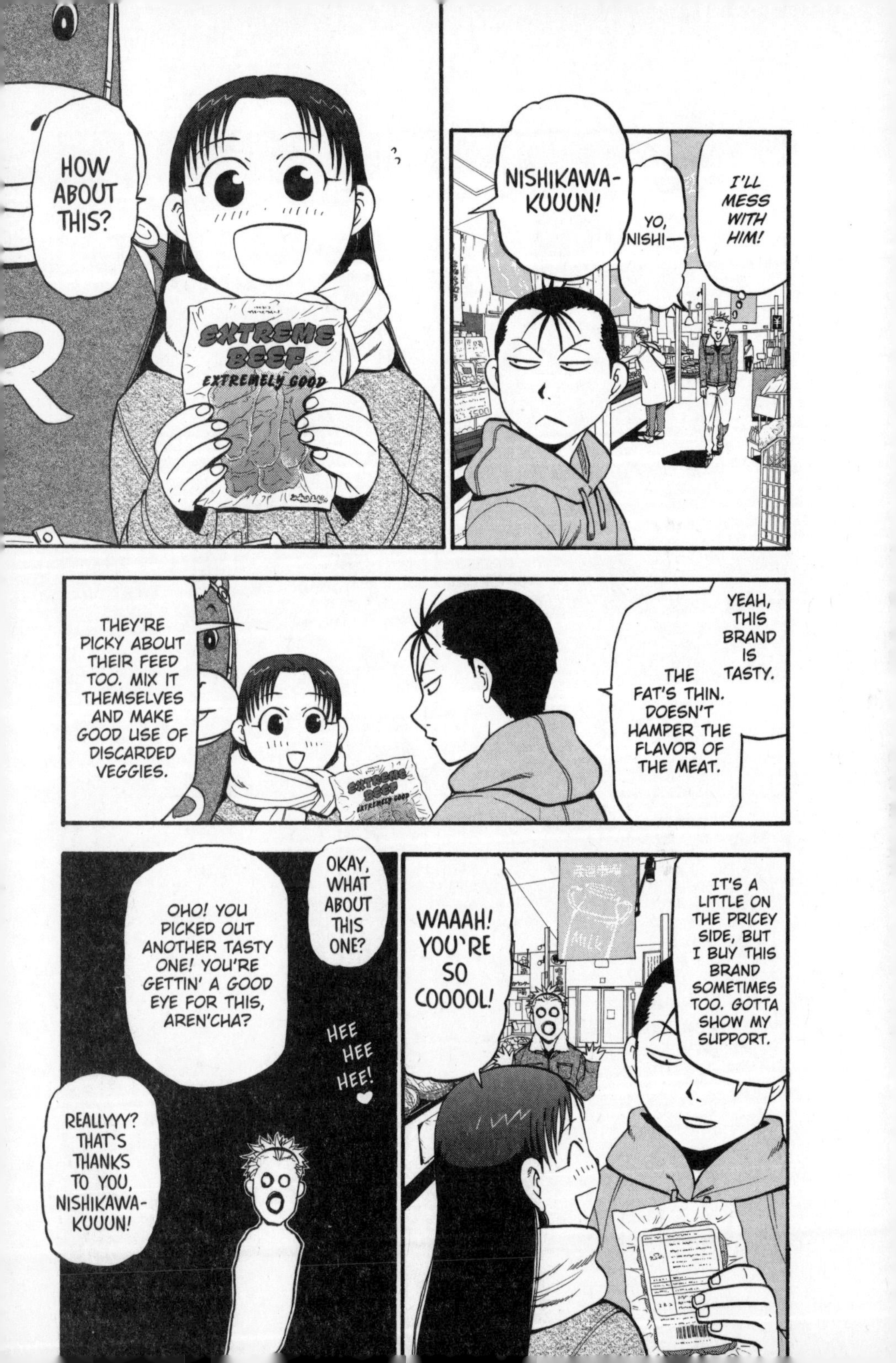
NISHIKAWA-KUUUN!
YO, NISHI—
I'LL MESS WITH HIM!
HOW ABOUT THIS?
EXTREME BEEF
EXTREMELY GOOD
YEAH, THIS BRAND IS TASTY.
THE FAT'S THIN. DOESN'T HAMPER THE FLAVOR OF THE MEAT.
THEY'RE PICKY ABOUT THEIR FEED TOO. MIX IT THEMSELVES AND MAKE GOOD USE OF DISCARDED VEGGIES.
IT'S A LITTLE ON THE PRICEY SIDE, BUT I BUY THIS BRAND SOMETIMES TOO. GOTTA SHOW MY SUPPORT.
WAAAH! YOU'RE SO COOOOL!
OKAY, WHAT ABOUT THIS ONE?
OHO! YOU PICKED OUT ANOTHER TASTY ONE! YOU'RE GETTIN' A GOOD EYE FOR THIS, AREN'CHA?
HEE HEE HEE!
REALLYYY? THAT'S THANKS TO YOU, NISHIKAWA-KUUUN!

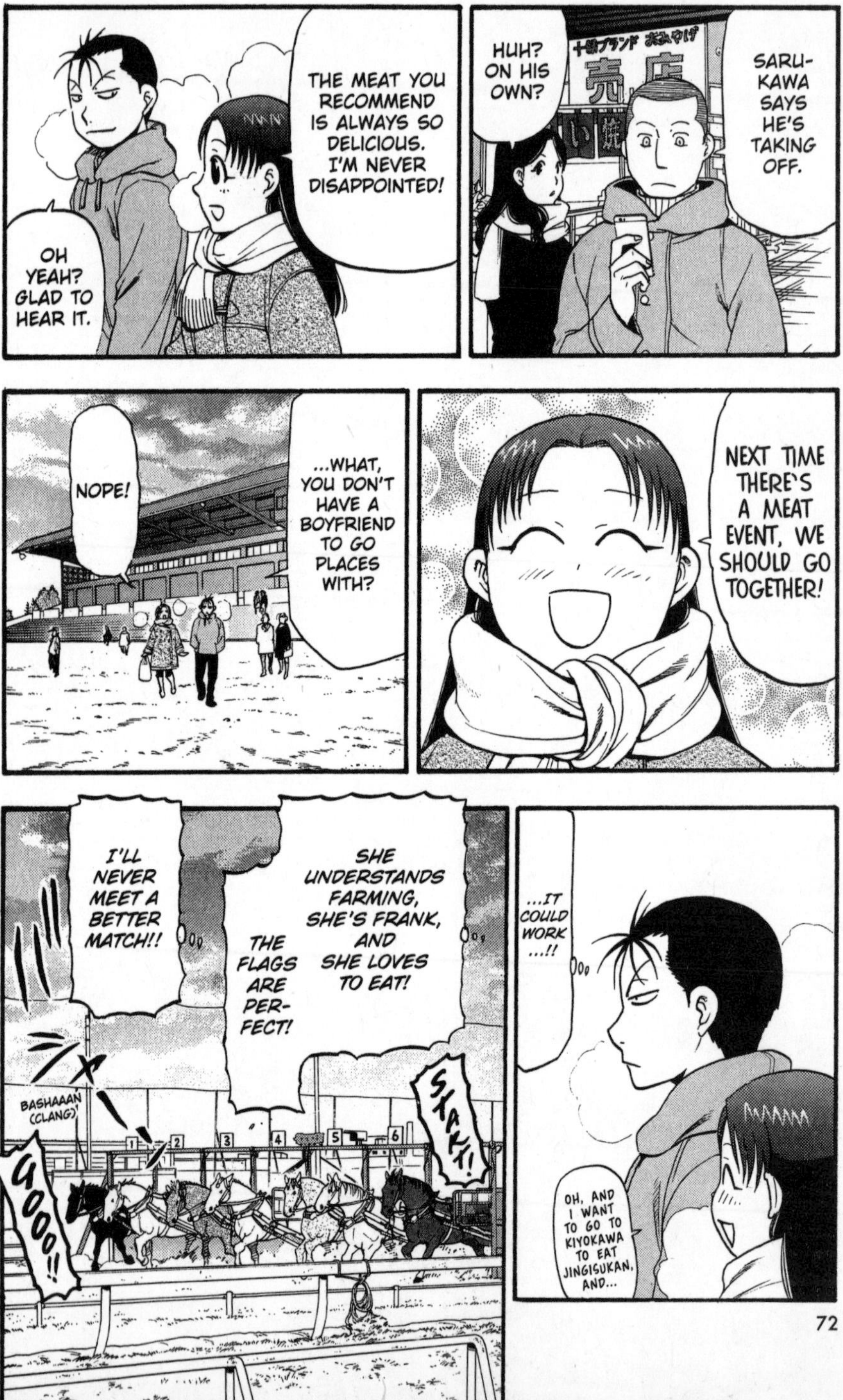

SARU-KAWA SAYS HE'S TAKING OFF.
十勝ブランド おみやげ
売店
HUH? ON HIS OWN?
THE MEAT YOU RECOMMEND IS ALWAYS SO DELICIOUS. I'M NEVER DISAPPOINTED!
OH YEAH? GLAD TO HEAR IT.
NEXT TIME THERE'S A MEAT EVENT, WE SHOULD GO TOGETHER!
...WHAT, YOU DON'T HAVE A BOYFRIEND TO GO PLACES WITH?
NOPE!
...IT COULD WORK ...!!
OH, AND I WANT TO GO TO KIYOKAWA TO EAT JINGISUKAN, AND...
SHE UNDERSTANDS FARMING, SHE'S FRANK, AND SHE LOVES TO EAT!
THE FLAGS ARE PER-FECT!
I'LL NEVER MEET A BETTER MATCH!!
START!
BASHAAAN (CLANG)
GOOO!!

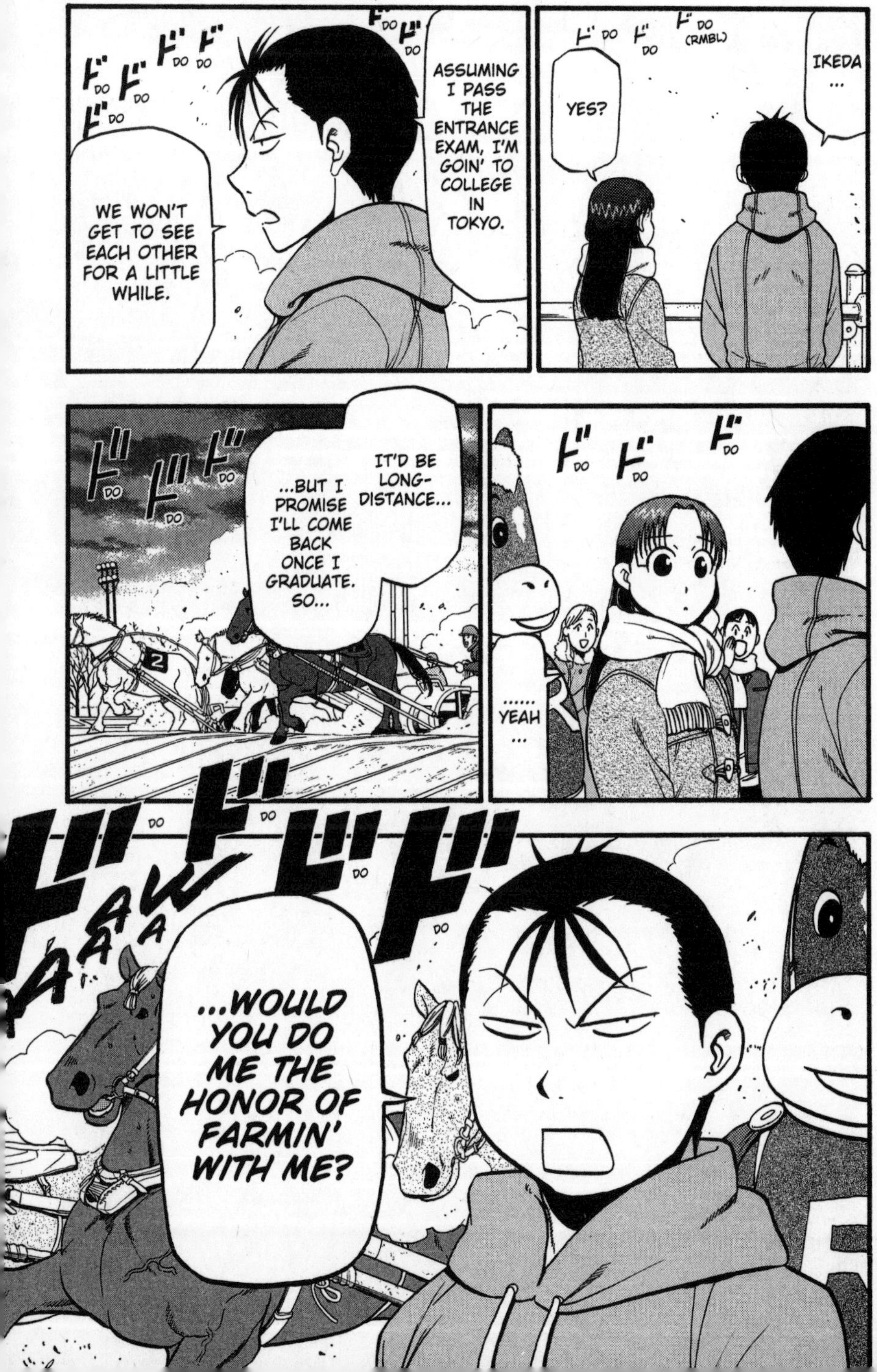
ド DO ド DO ド DO (RMBL)
IKEDA ...
YES?
ド DO ド DO ド DO ド DO ド DO ド DO ド DO
ASSUMING I PASS THE ENTRANCE EXAM, I'M GOIN' TO COLLEGE IN TOKYO.
WE WON'T GET TO SEE EACH OTHER FOR A LITTLE WHILE.
ド DO ド DO ド DO
...... YEAH ...
ド DO ド DO ド DO
IT'D BE LONG-DISTANCE...
...BUT I PROMISE I'LL COME BACK ONCE I GRADUATE. SO...
ド DO ド DO ド DO ド DO ド DO
WAAAA
...WOULD YOU DO ME THE HONOR OF FARMIN' WITH ME?

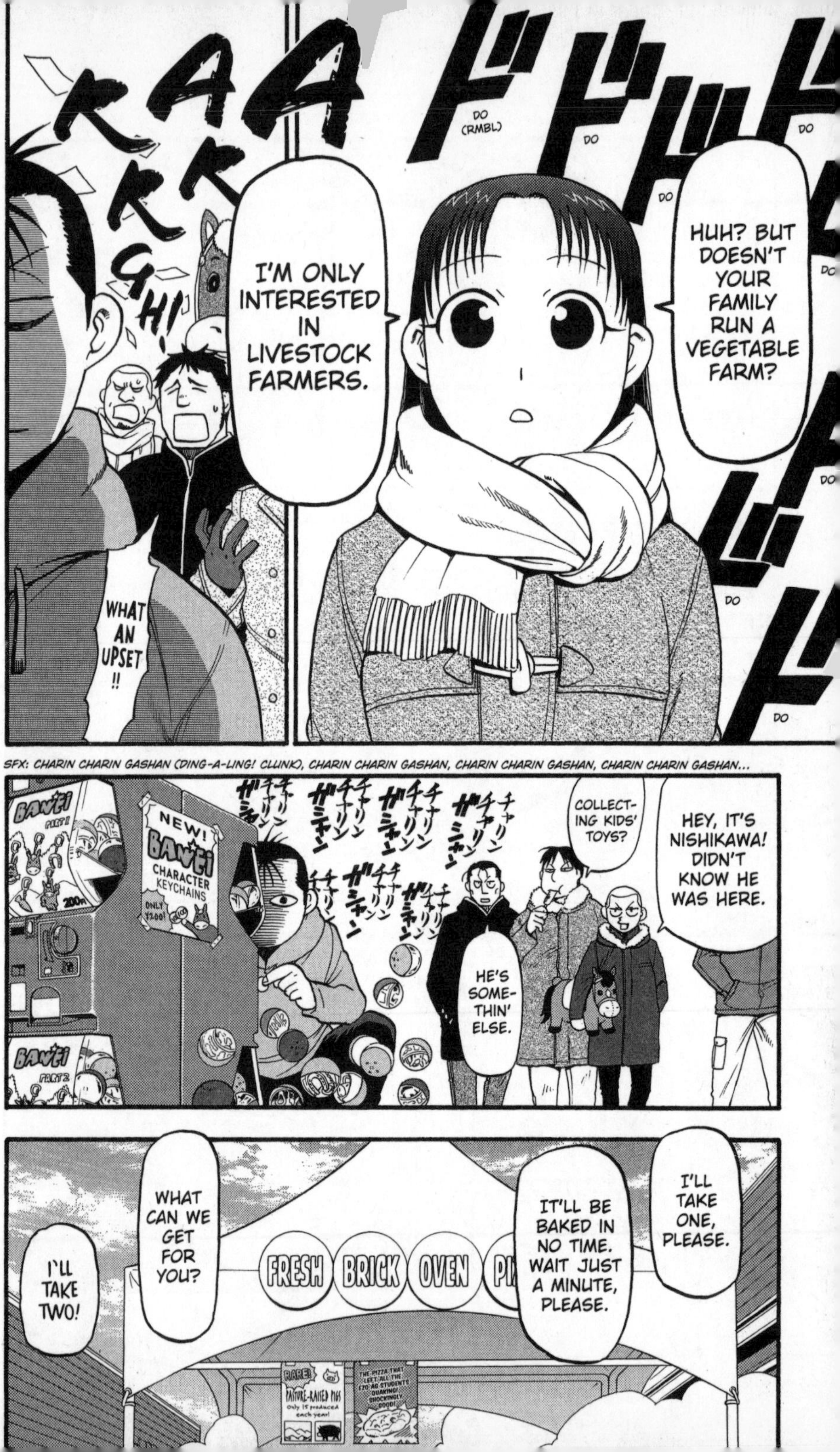
DO (RMBL)
DO
DO
DO
DO
DO
DO
DO
HUH? BUT DOESN'T YOUR FAMILY RUN A VEGETABLE FARM?
I'M ONLY INTERESTED IN LIVESTOCK FARMERS.
KAAAA RRRGH!
WHAT AN UPSET!!
SFX: CHARIN CHARIN GASHAN (DING-A-LING! CLUNK), CHARIN CHARIN GASHAN, CHARIN CHARIN GASHAN, CHARIN CHARIN GASHAN...
HEY, IT'S NISHIKAWA! DIDN'T KNOW HE WAS HERE.
COLLECTING KIDS' TOYS?
HE'S SOMETHIN' ELSE.
NEW! BANEI CHARACTER KEYCHAINS ONLY ¥200!
BANEI PART 1
BANEI PART 2
I'LL TAKE ONE, PLEASE.
IT'LL BE BAKED IN NO TIME. WAIT JUST A MINUTE, PLEASE.
FRESH BRICK OVEN PI
WHAT CAN WE GET FOR YOU?
I'LL TAKE TWO!
RARE! PASTURE-RAISED PIGS Only 15 produced each year!
THE PIZZA THAT LEFT ALL THE EZO AG STUDENTS QUAKING! SHOCKINGLY GOOD!

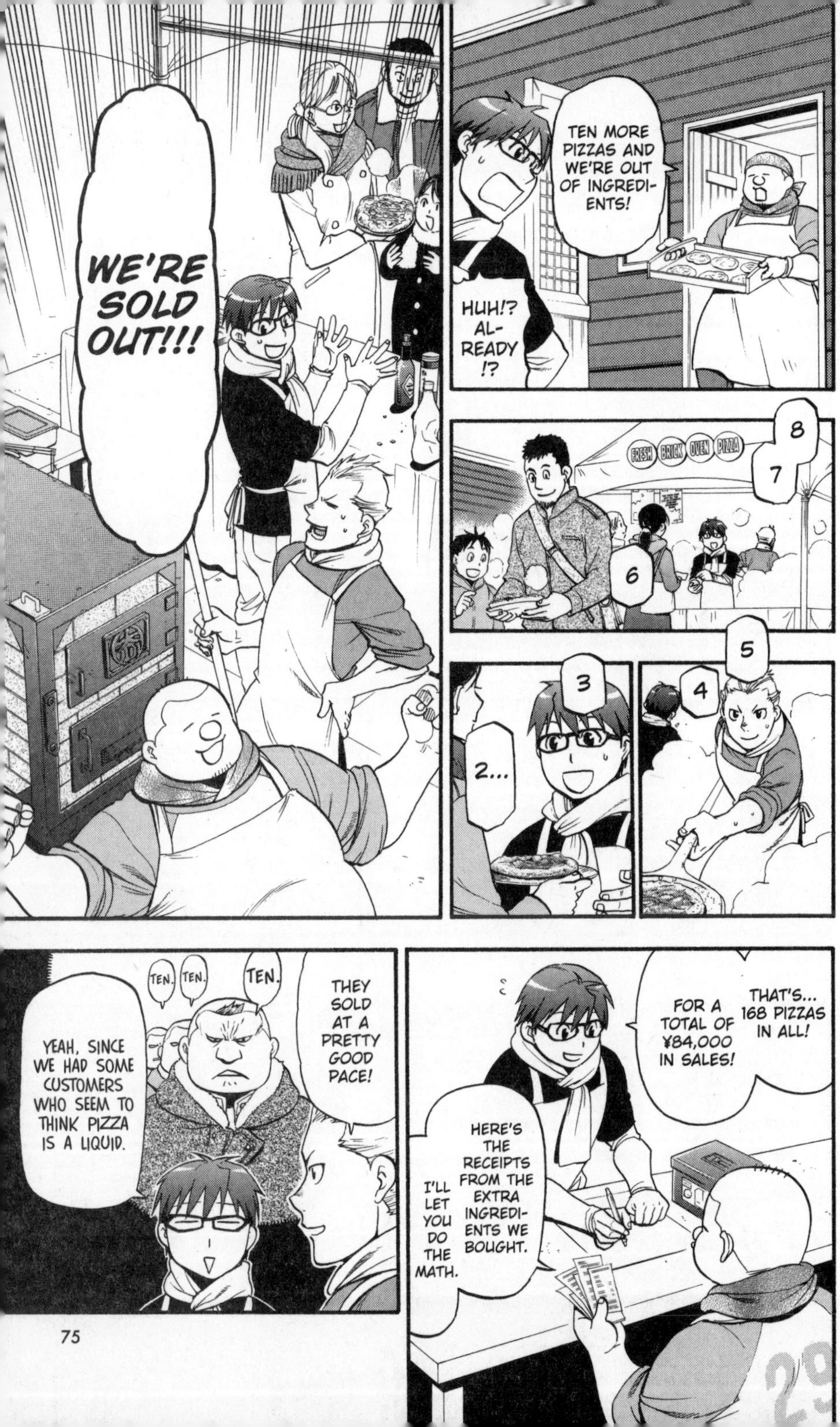
TEN MORE PIZZAS AND WE'RE OUT OF INGREDI-ENTS!
HUH!? AL-READY!?
FRESH BRICK OVEN PIZZA
8
7
6
5
4
3
2...
WE'RE SOLD OUT!!!
THAT'S... 168 PIZZAS IN ALL!
FOR A TOTAL OF ¥84,000 IN SALES!
HERE'S THE RECEIPTS FROM THE EXTRA INGREDI-ENTS WE BOUGHT.
I'LL LET YOU DO THE MATH.
TEN.
TEN.
TEN.
THEY SOLD AT A PRETTY GOOD PACE!
YEAH, SINCE WE HAD SOME CUSTOMERS WHO SEEM TO THINK PIZZA IS A LIQUID.

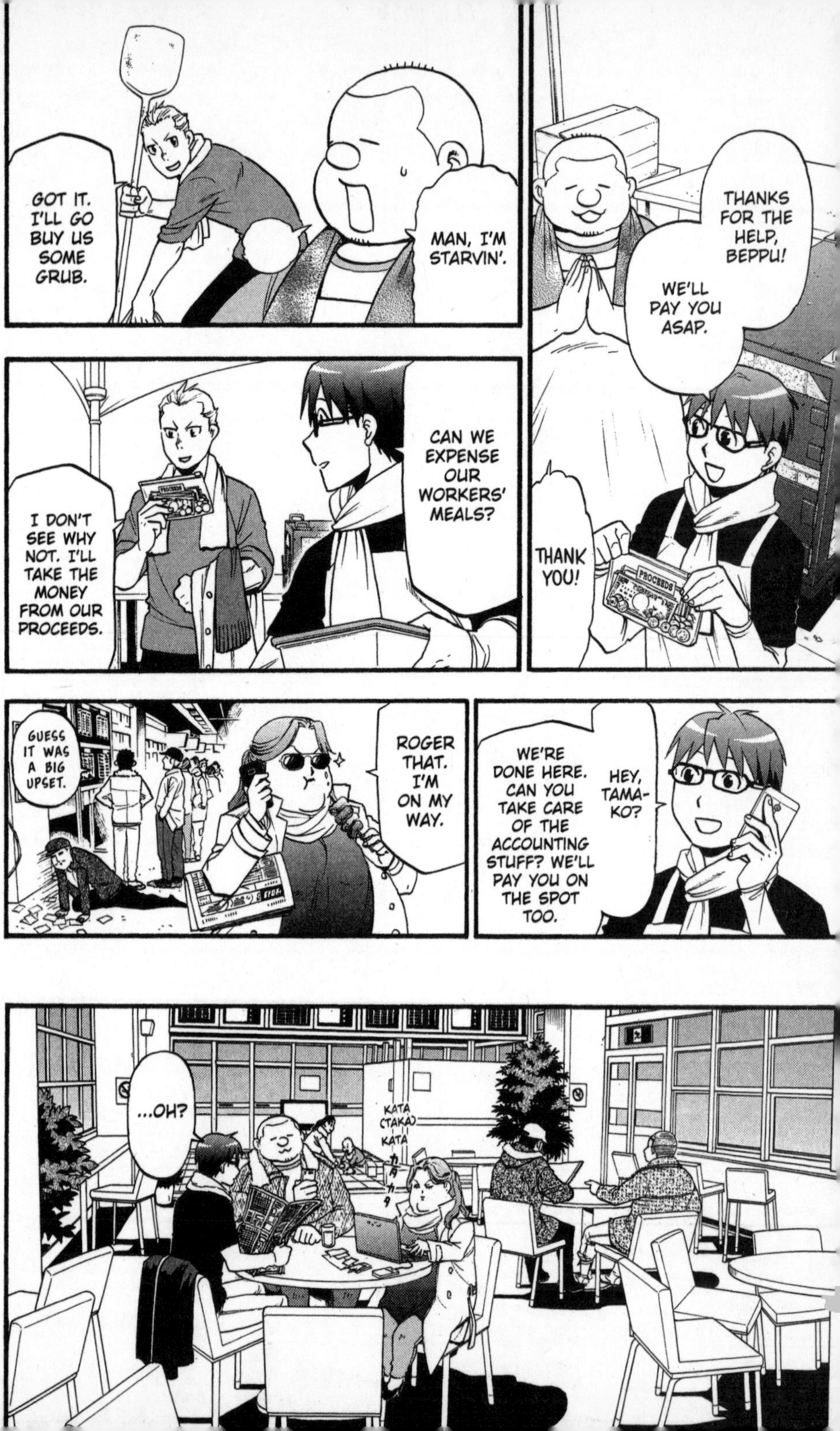
THANKS FOR THE HELP, BEPPU!
WE'LL PAY YOU ASAP.
THANK YOU!
MAN, I'M STARVIN'.
GOT IT. I'LL GO BUY US SOME GRUB.
CAN WE EXPENSE OUR WORKERS' MEALS?
I DON'T SEE WHY NOT. I'LL TAKE THE MONEY FROM OUR PROCEEDS.
HEY, TAMA-KO?
WE'RE DONE HERE. CAN YOU TAKE CARE OF THE ACCOUNTING STUFF? WE'LL PAY YOU ON THE SPOT TOO.
ROGER THAT. I'M ON MY WAY.
GUESS IT WAS A BIG UPSET.
KATA (TAKA) KATA
...OH?

1 White	⋮ ▲ ⋮	**Tokana**	
2 Black	▲ △ ⋮ △ ○	**Mikage Honor**	
3 Red	△ △ △ ○ ○ ◎	**Seaside Park**	

MIKAGE HONOR IS RACING!

YOU'RE ¥1,804 IN THE RED!!!

HOWWW!!?

MIKAGE... HOPE HER INTERVIEW WENT WELL...

TSUTAAAN (TAKK)

AC-COUNT-ING COMPLETE!

KEEP YOUR COSTS DOWN TO 30% OF YOUR SELLING PRICE!!

AND I WANT TO FEED PEOPLE GOOD FOOD!!

B-BUT WE HAD TO ADVERTISE, OR NO ONE WOULD COME! AND STOKING THE OVEN IS CRUCIAL!!

EXTRA INGRE-DIENT COSTS: OVER BUDGET!!

COMMUNI-CATIONS AND ADVER-TISING COSTS: OVER BUDGET!!

FUEL COSTS: OVER BUDGET!!

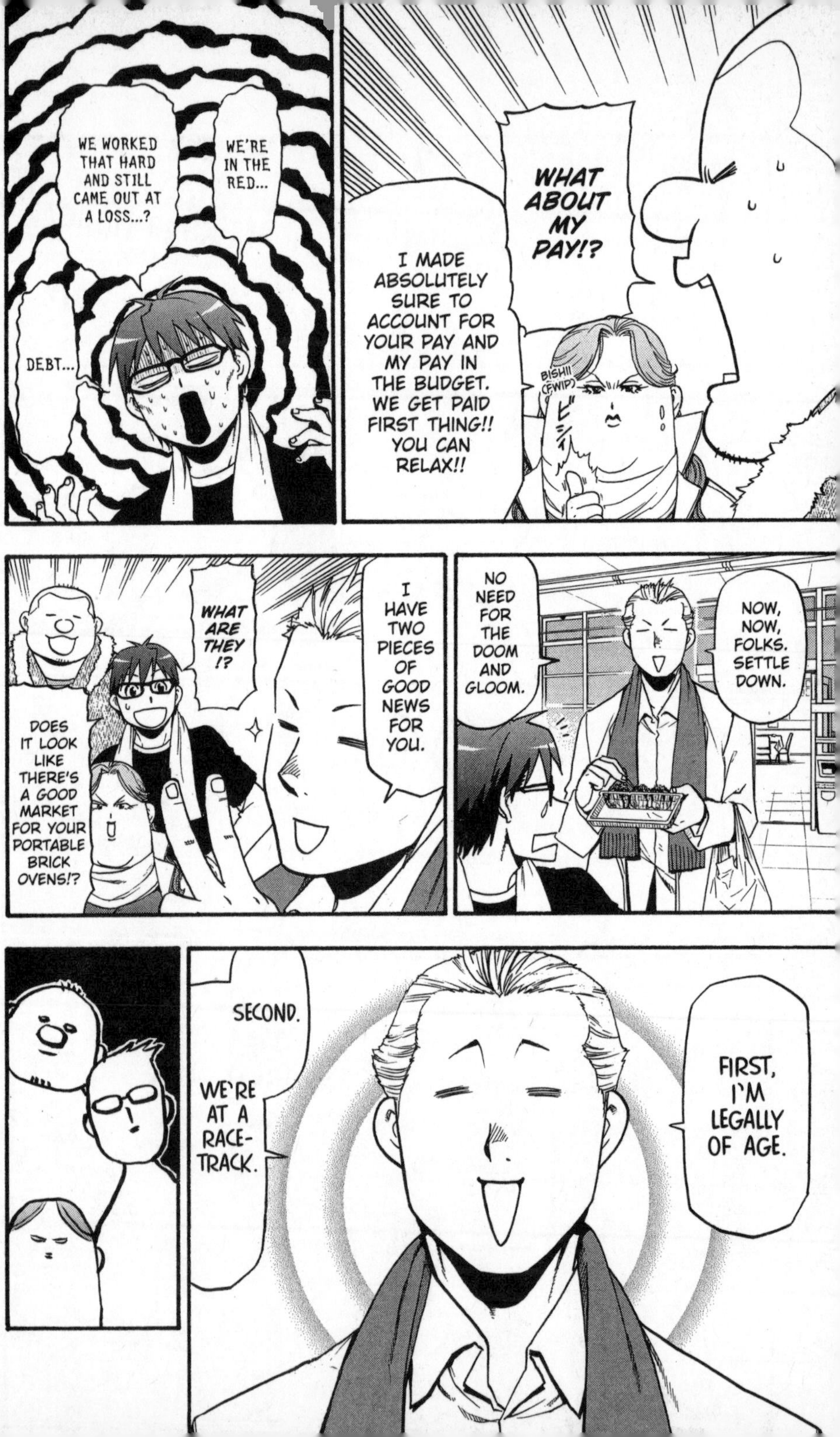
WHAT ABOUT MY PAY!?
I MADE ABSOLUTELY SURE TO ACCOUNT FOR YOUR PAY AND MY PAY IN THE BUDGET. WE GET PAID FIRST THING!! YOU CAN RELAX!!
BISHI (FWIP)
WE'RE IN THE RED...
WE WORKED THAT HARD AND STILL CAME OUT AT A LOSS...?
DEBT...
NOW, NOW, FOLKS. SETTLE DOWN.
NO NEED FOR THE DOOM AND GLOOM.
I HAVE TWO PIECES OF GOOD NEWS FOR YOU.
WHAT ARE THEY!?
DOES IT LOOK LIKE THERE'S A GOOD MARKET FOR YOUR PORTABLE BRICK OVENS!?
FIRST, I'M LEGALLY OF AGE.
SECOND.
WE'RE AT A RACE-TRACK.

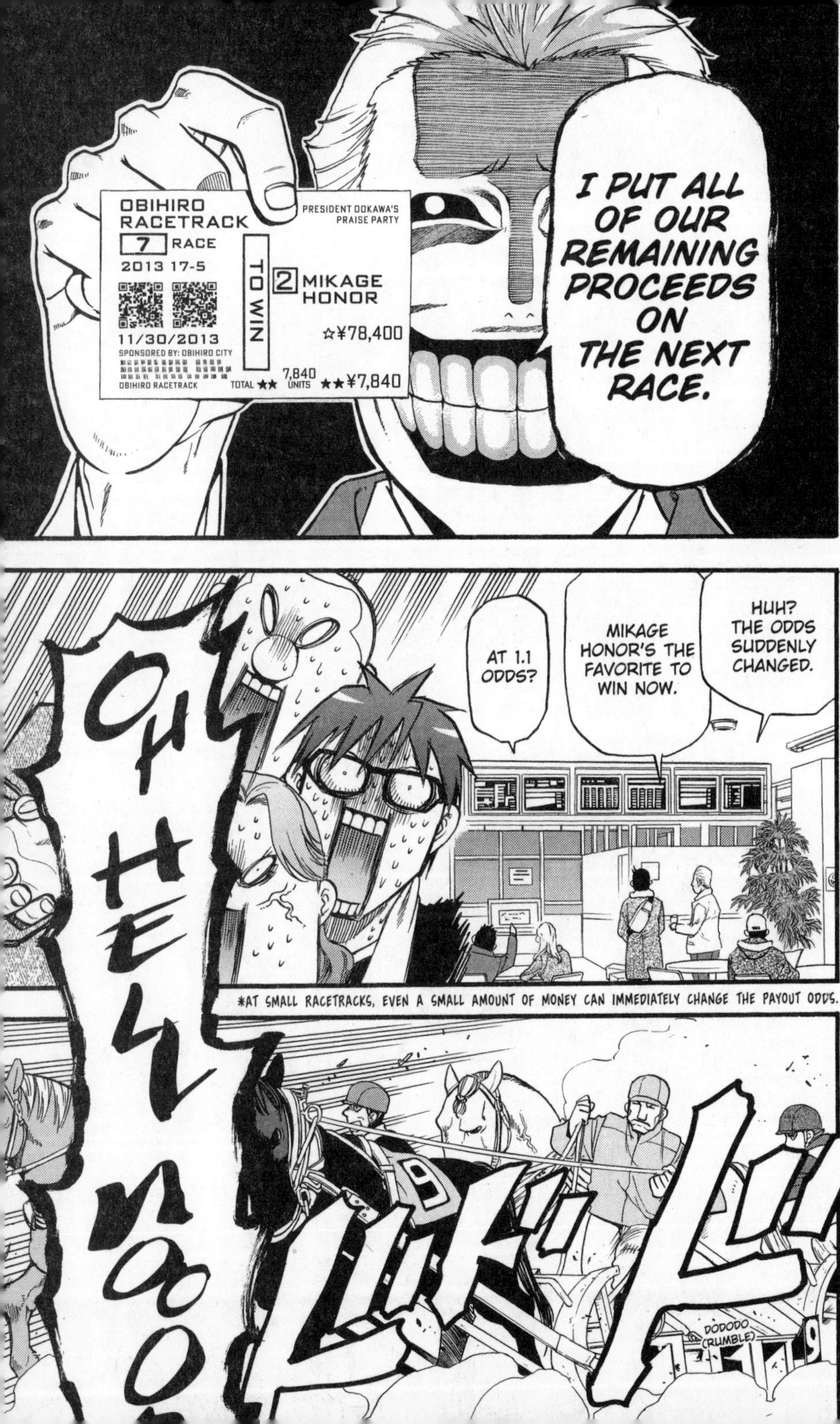
OBIHIRO RACETRACK
7 RACE
2013 17-5
11/30/2013
SPONSORED BY: OBIHIRO CITY
OBIHIRO RACETRACK
TO WIN
PRESIDENT OOKAWA'S PRAISE PARTY
2 MIKAGE HONOR
☆¥78,400
TOTAL ★★ 7,840 UNITS ★★¥7,840
I PUT ALL OF OUR REMAINING PROCEEDS ON THE NEXT RACE.
HUH? THE ODDS SUDDENLY CHANGED.
MIKAGE HONOR'S THE FAVORITE TO WIN NOW.
AT 1.1 ODDS?
OH HELL NOOO
*AT SMALL RACETRACKS, EVEN A SMALL AMOUNT OF MONEY CAN IMMEDIATELY CHANGE THE PAYOUT ODDS.
DODODO (RUMBLE)

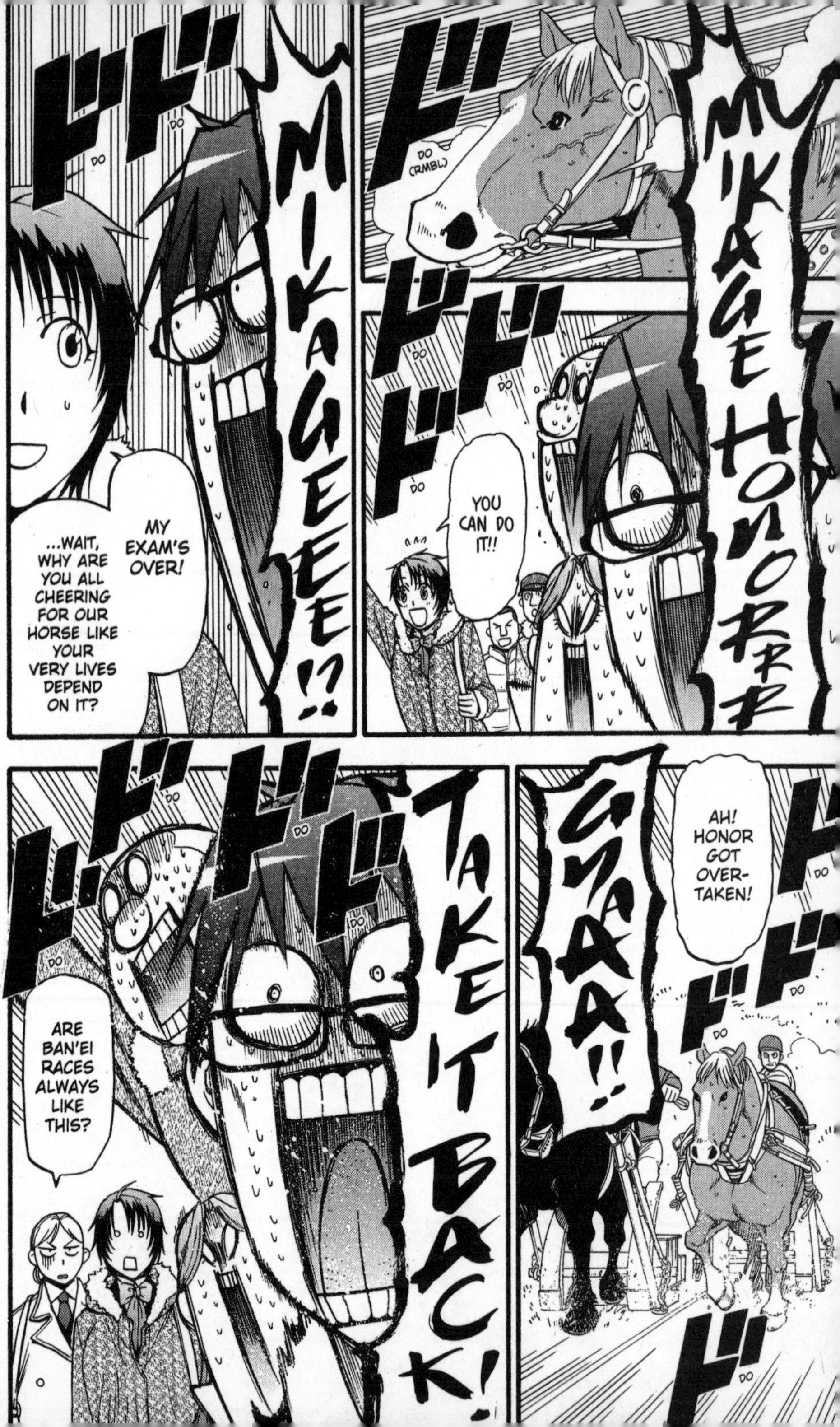
MIKAGE HONORRRR
DO (RMBL)
YOU CAN DO IT!!
MIKAGEEEE!!?
MY EXAM'S OVER!
...WAIT, WHY ARE YOU ALL CHEERING FOR OUR HORSE LIKE YOUR VERY LIVES DEPEND ON IT?
AH! HONOR GOT OVER-TAKEN!
GYAAAA!!
TAKE IT BACK!
ARE BAN'EI RACES ALWAYS LIKE THIS?

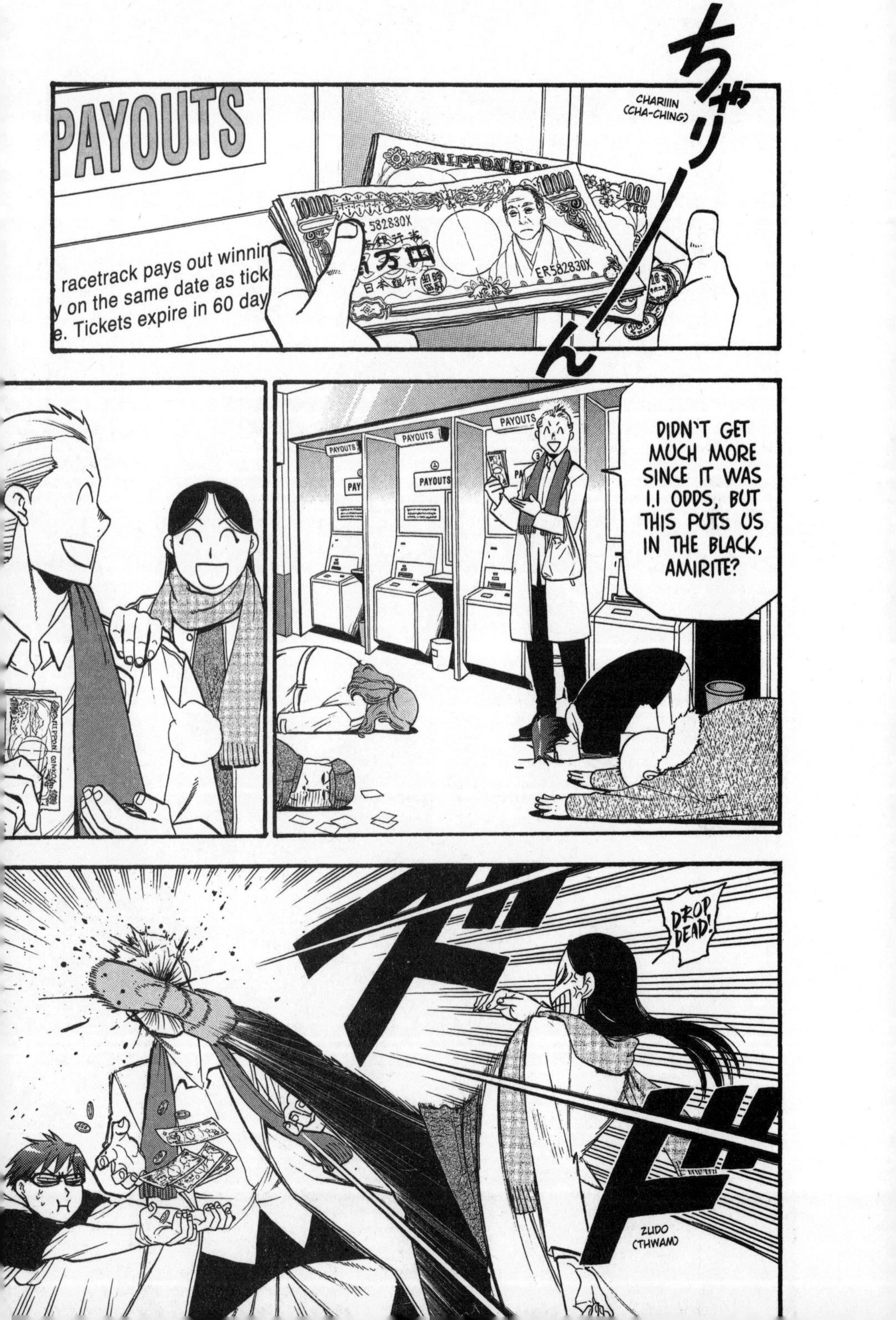
PAYOUTS
racetrack pays out winnin
y on the same date as tick
e. Tickets expire in 60 day
ちゃりーん
CHARIIIN (CHA-CHING)
PAYOUTS
DIDN'T GET MUCH MORE SINCE IT WAS 1.1 ODDS, BUT THIS PUTS US IN THE BLACK, AMIRITE?
DROP DEAD!
ZUDO (THWAM)

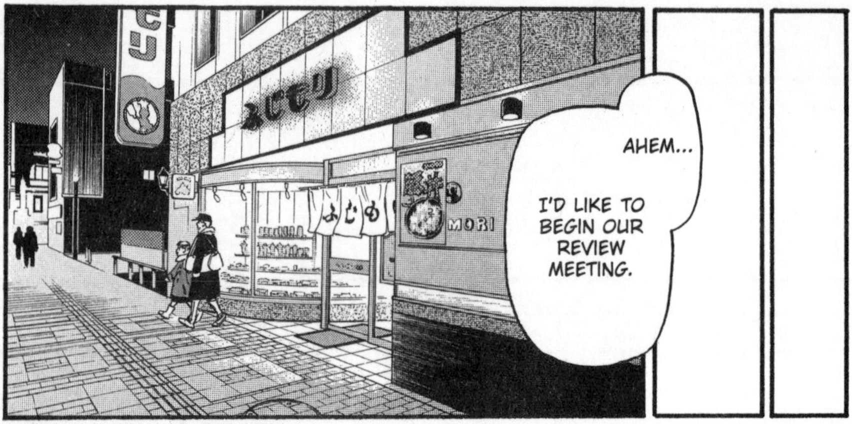
AHEM...
I'D LIKE TO BEGIN OUR REVIEW MEETING.

RESTAURANT: FUJIMORI / SIGN: PORK BOWLS

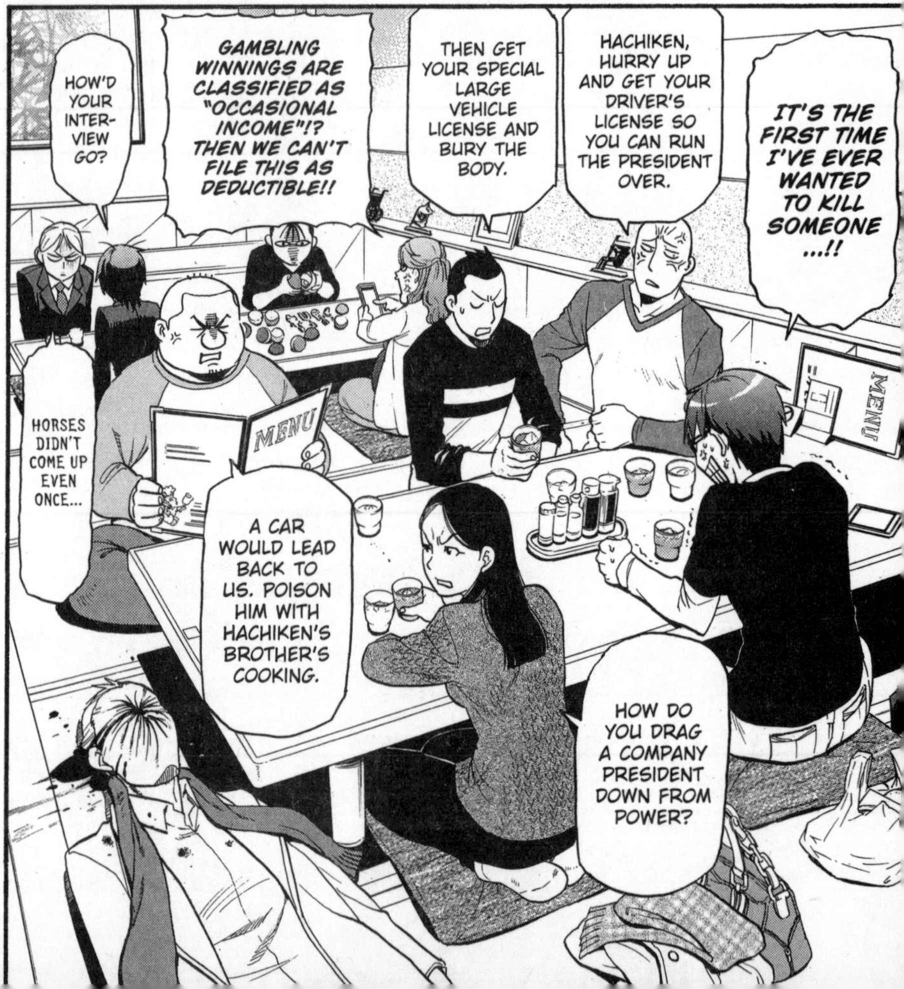
IT'S THE FIRST TIME I'VE EVER WANTED TO KILL SOMEONE ...!!
HACHIKEN, HURRY UP AND GET YOUR DRIVER'S LICENSE SO YOU CAN RUN THE PRESIDENT OVER.
THEN GET YOUR SPECIAL LARGE VEHICLE LICENSE AND BURY THE BODY.
GAMBLING WINNINGS ARE CLASSIFIED AS "OCCASIONAL INCOME"!? THEN WE CAN'T FILE THIS AS DEDUCTIBLE!!
HOW'D YOUR INTER-VIEW GO?
HOW DO YOU DRAG A COMPANY PRESIDENT DOWN FROM POWER?
A CAR WOULD LEAD BACK TO US. POISON HIM WITH HACHIKEN'S BROTHER'S COOKING.
HORSES DIDN'T COME UP EVEN ONCE...

Silver Spoon

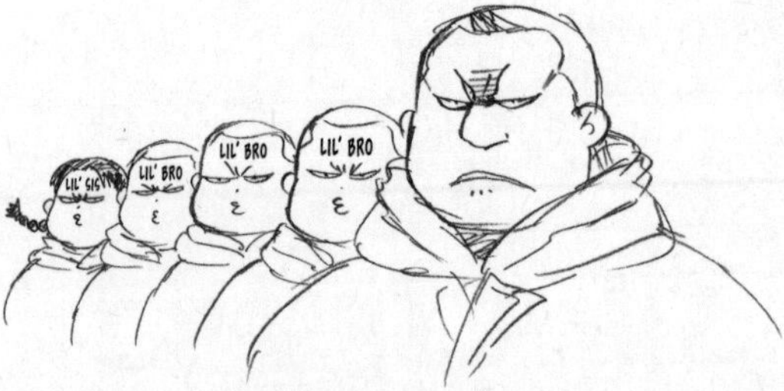
LIL' SIS
LIL' BRO
LIL' BRO
LIL' BRO

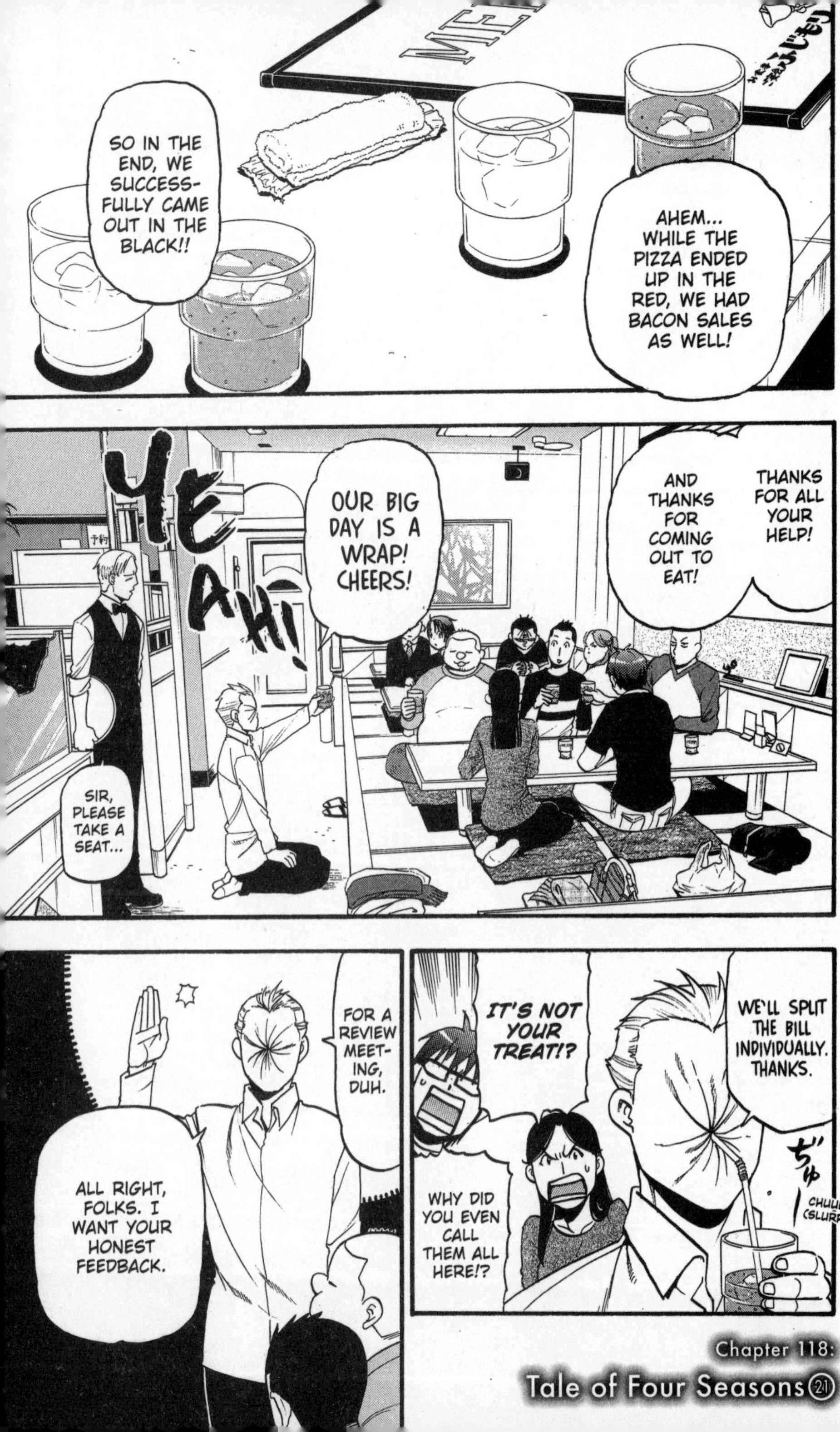
AHEM... WHILE THE PIZZA ENDED UP IN THE RED, WE HAD BACON SALES AS WELL!
SO IN THE END, WE SUCCESS-FULLY CAME OUT IN THE BLACK!!
THANKS FOR ALL YOUR HELP!
AND THANKS FOR COMING OUT TO EAT!
OUR BIG DAY IS A WRAP! CHEERS!
YEAH!
SIR, PLEASE TAKE A SEAT...
WE'LL SPLIT THE BILL INDIVIDUALLY. THANKS.
ちゅ
CHUUU (SLURP)
IT'S NOT YOUR TREAT!?
WHY DID YOU EVEN CALL THEM ALL HERE!?
FOR A REVIEW MEET-ING, DUH.
ALL RIGHT, FOLKS. I WANT YOUR HONEST FEEDBACK.

Chapter 118: Tale of Four Seasons㉑

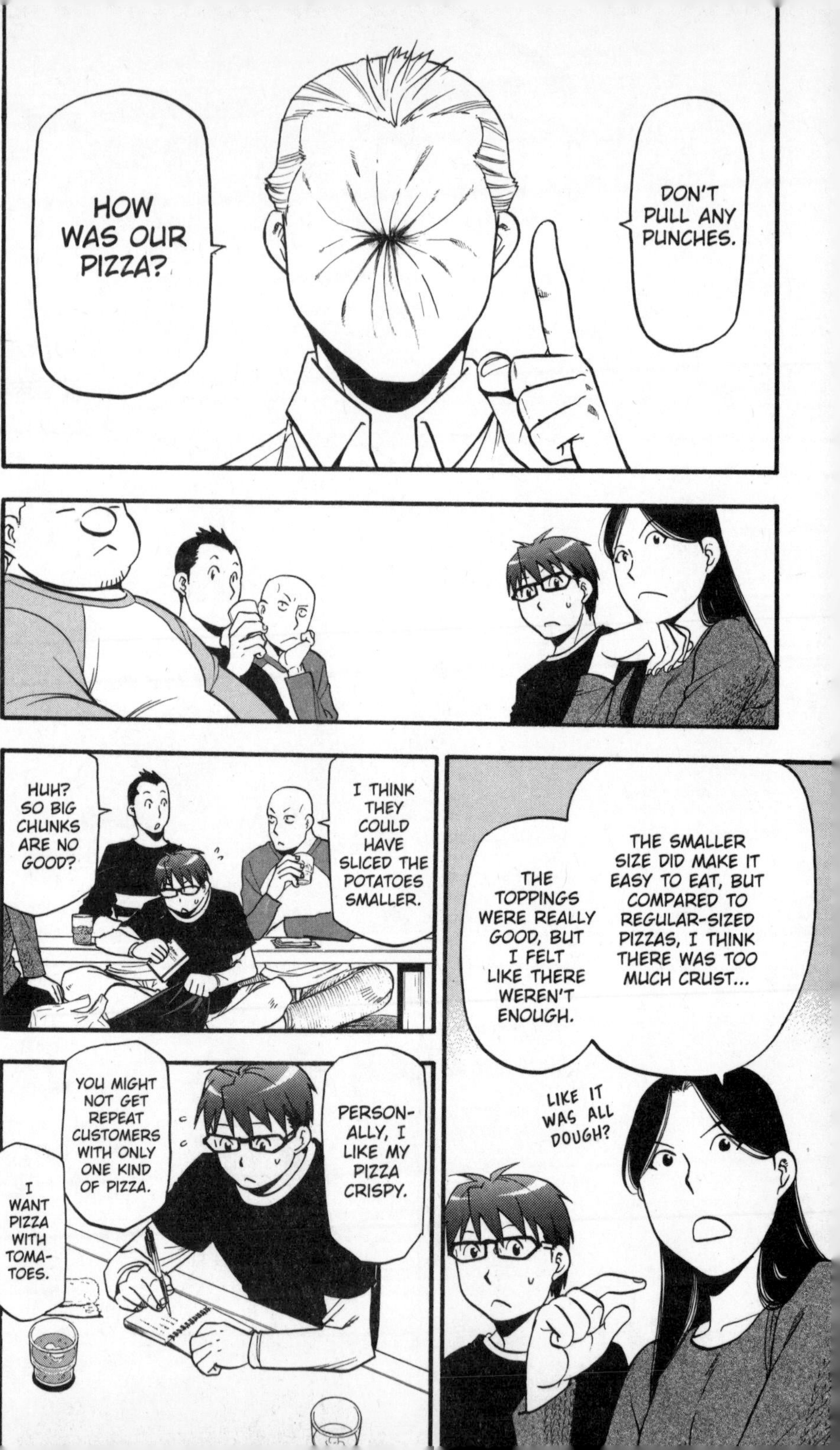
DON'T PULL ANY PUNCHES.
HOW WAS OUR PIZZA?
THE SMALLER SIZE DID MAKE IT EASY TO EAT, BUT COMPARED TO REGULAR-SIZED PIZZAS, I THINK THERE WAS TOO MUCH CRUST...
THE TOPPINGS WERE REALLY GOOD, BUT I FELT LIKE THERE WEREN'T ENOUGH.
LIKE IT WAS ALL DOUGH?
I THINK THEY COULD HAVE SLICED THE POTATOES SMALLER.
HUH? SO BIG CHUNKS ARE NO GOOD?
PERSON-ALLY, I LIKE MY PIZZA CRISPY.
YOU MIGHT NOT GET REPEAT CUSTOMERS WITH ONLY ONE KIND OF PIZZA.
I WANT PIZZA WITH TOMA-TOES.

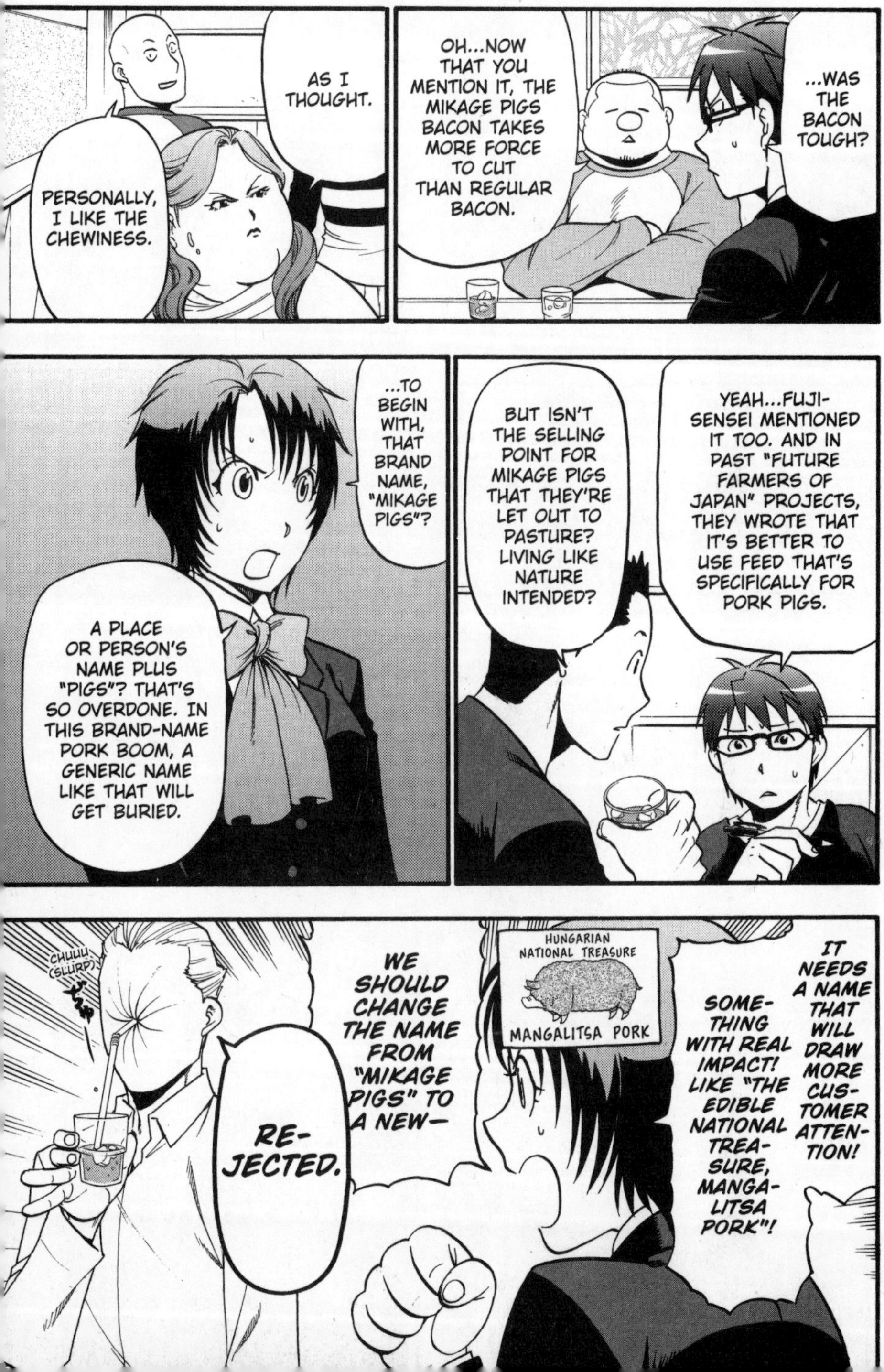
...WAS THE BACON TOUGH?
OH...NOW THAT YOU MENTION IT, THE MIKAGE PIGS BACON TAKES MORE FORCE TO CUT THAN REGULAR BACON.
AS I THOUGHT.
PERSONALLY, I LIKE THE CHEWINESS.
YEAH...FUJI-SENSEI MENTIONED IT TOO. AND IN PAST "FUTURE FARMERS OF JAPAN" PROJECTS, THEY WROTE THAT IT'S BETTER TO USE FEED THAT'S SPECIFICALLY FOR PORK PIGS.
BUT ISN'T THE SELLING POINT FOR MIKAGE PIGS THAT THEY'RE LET OUT TO PASTURE? LIVING LIKE NATURE INTENDED?
...TO BEGIN WITH, THAT BRAND NAME, "MIKAGE PIGS"?
A PLACE OR PERSON'S NAME PLUS "PIGS"? THAT'S SO OVERDONE. IN THIS BRAND-NAME PORK BOOM, A GENERIC NAME LIKE THAT WILL GET BURIED.
IT NEEDS A NAME THAT WILL DRAW MORE CUSTOMER ATTENTION!
SOMETHING WITH REAL IMPACT! LIKE "THE EDIBLE NATIONAL TREASURE, MANGALITSA PORK"!
HUNGARIAN NATIONAL TREASURE
MANGALITSA PORK
WE SHOULD CHANGE THE NAME FROM "MIKAGE PIGS" TO A NEW—
REJECTED.
CHUUU (SLURP)

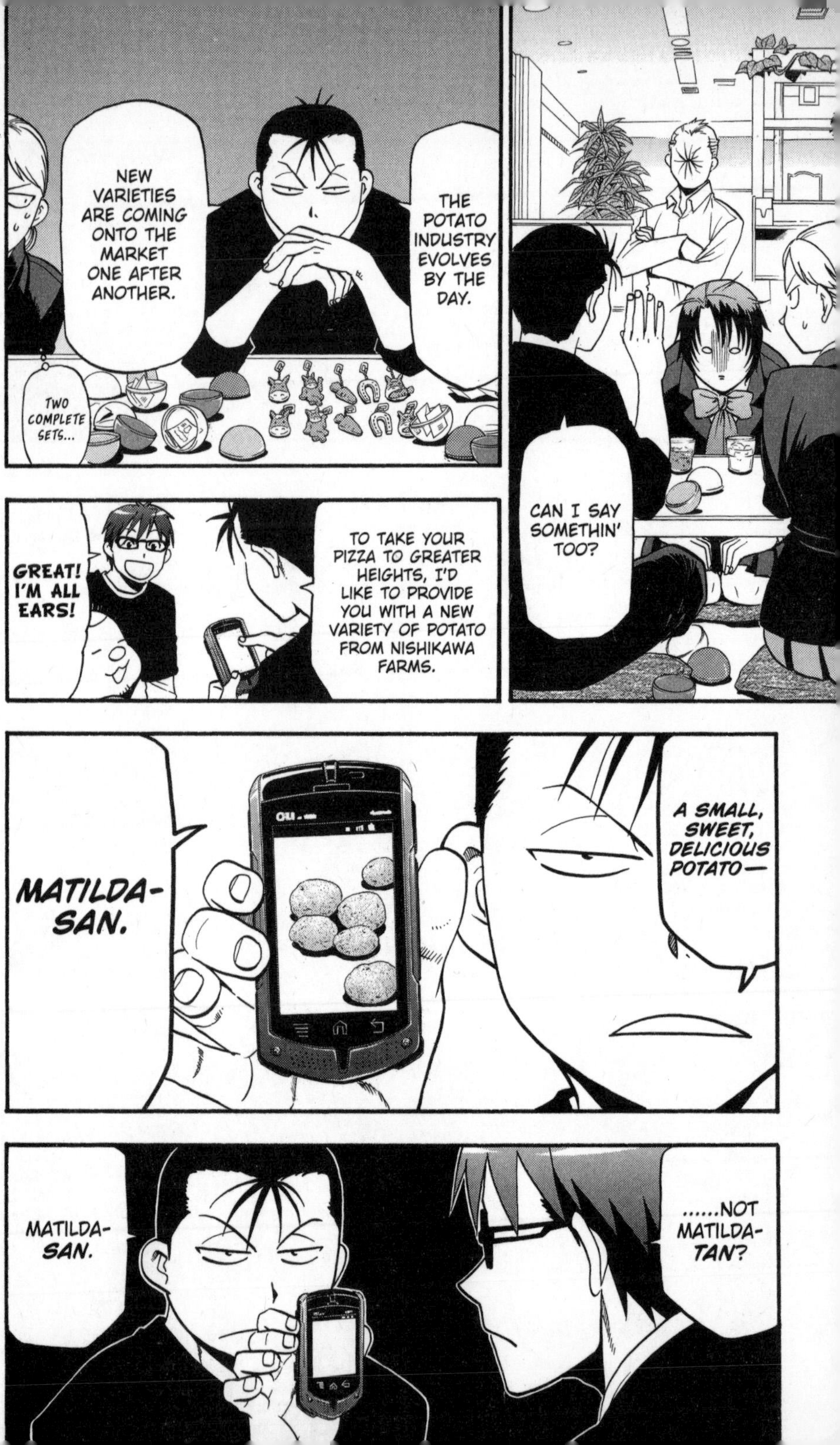
CAN I SAY SOMETHIN' TOO?
THE POTATO INDUSTRY EVOLVES BY THE DAY.
NEW VARIETIES ARE COMING ONTO THE MARKET ONE AFTER ANOTHER.
TWO COMPLETE SETS...
TO TAKE YOUR PIZZA TO GREATER HEIGHTS, I'D LIKE TO PROVIDE YOU WITH A NEW VARIETY OF POTATO FROM NISHIKAWA FARMS.
GREAT! I'M ALL EARS!
A SMALL, SWEET, DELICIOUS POTATO—
MATILDA-SAN.
......NOT MATILDA-TAN?
MATILDA-SAN.

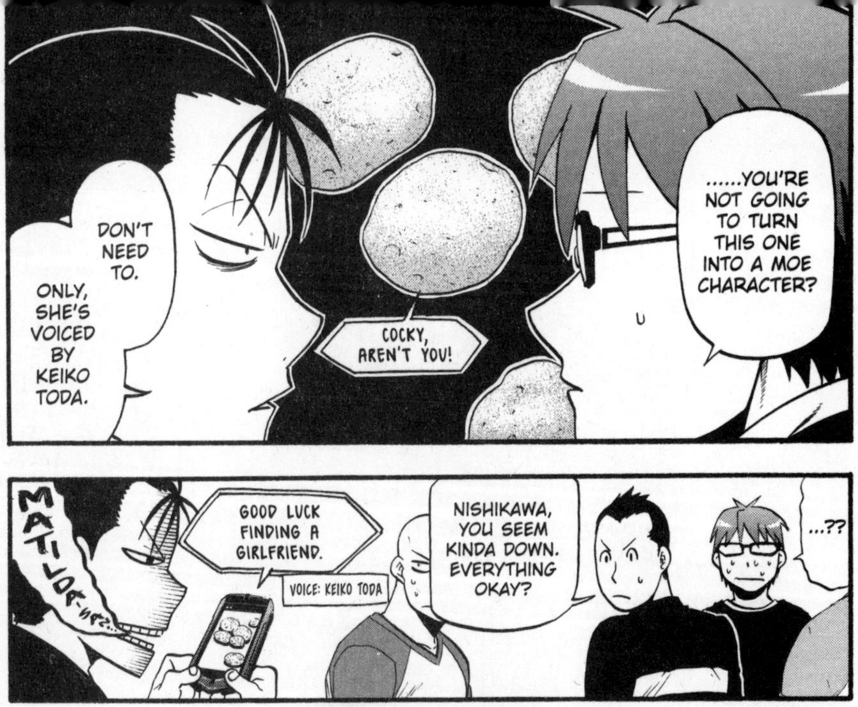
......YOU'RE NOT GOING TO TURN THIS ONE INTO A MOE CHARACTER?
COCKY, AREN'T YOU!
DON'T NEED TO.
ONLY, SHE'S VOICED BY KEIKO TODA.
...??
NISHIKAWA, YOU SEEM KINDA DOWN. EVERYTHING OKAY?
GOOD LUCK FINDING A GIRLFRIEND.
VOICE: KEIKO TODA
MATILDA

Chapter 118:
Tale of Four Seasons ㉑

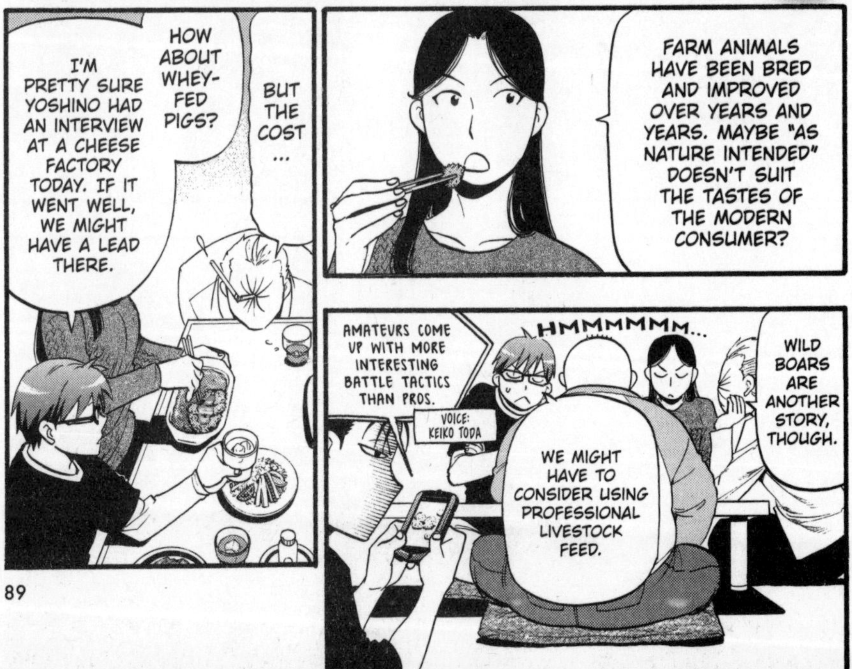
FARM ANIMALS HAVE BEEN BRED AND IMPROVED OVER YEARS AND YEARS. MAYBE "AS NATURE INTENDED" DOESN'T SUIT THE TASTES OF THE MODERN CONSUMER?
WILD BOARS ARE ANOTHER STORY, THOUGH.
HMMMMMM...
WE MIGHT HAVE TO CONSIDER USING PROFESSIONAL LIVESTOCK FEED.
AMATEURS COME UP WITH MORE INTERESTING BATTLE TACTICS THAN PROS.
VOICE: KEIKO TODA
BUT THE COST ...
HOW ABOUT WHEY-FED PIGS?
I'M PRETTY SURE YOSHINO HAD AN INTERVIEW AT A CHEESE FACTORY TODAY. IF IT WENT WELL, WE MIGHT HAVE A LEAD THERE.

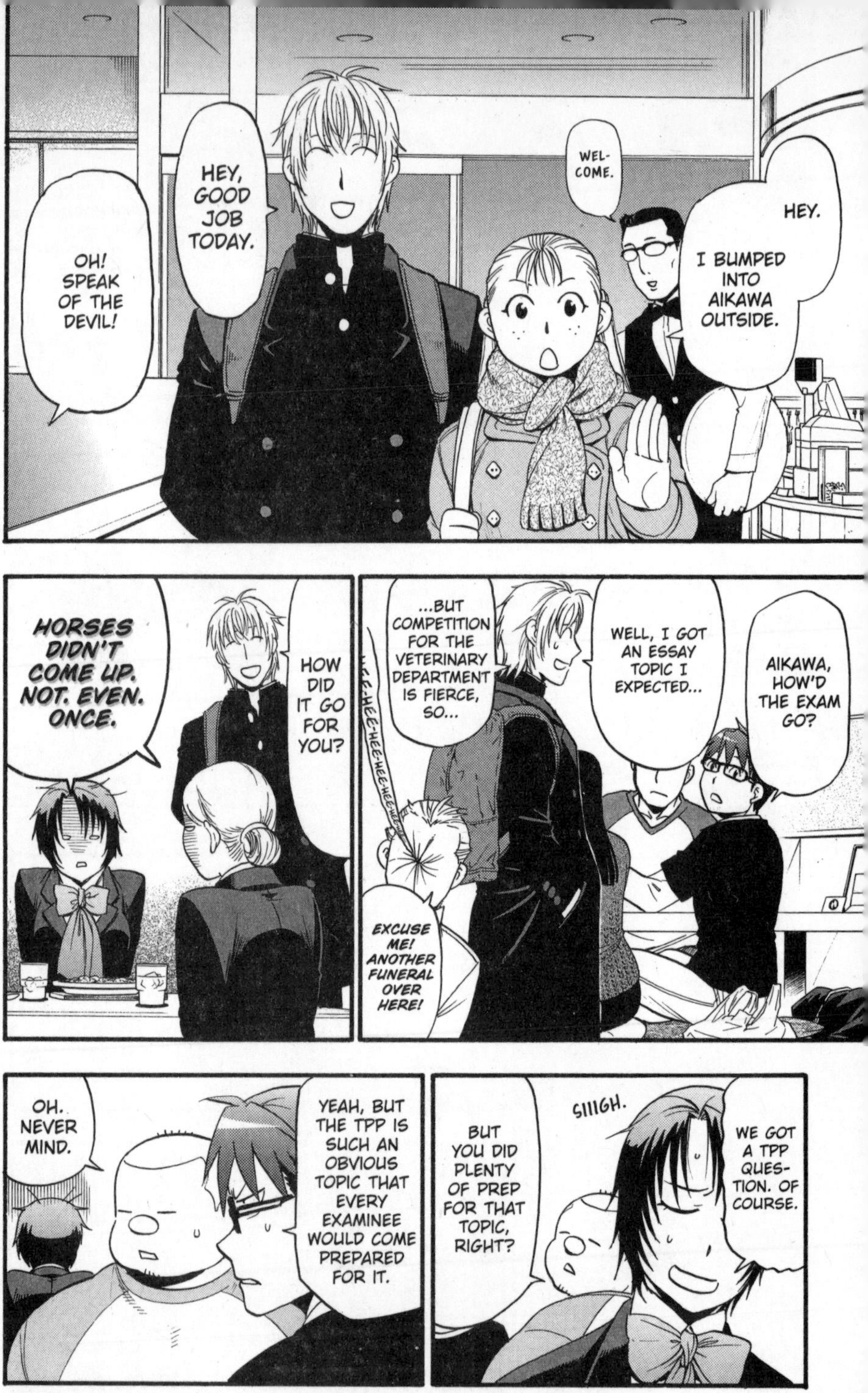
HEY.
I BUMPED INTO AIKAWA OUTSIDE.
WEL-COME.
HEY, GOOD JOB TODAY.
OH! SPEAK OF THE DEVIL!
AIKAWA, HOW'D THE EXAM GO?
WELL, I GOT AN ESSAY TOPIC I EXPECTED...
...BUT COMPETITION FOR THE VETERINARY DEPARTMENT IS FIERCE, SO...
EXCUSE ME! ANOTHER FUNERAL OVER HERE!
HOW DID IT GO FOR YOU?
HORSES DIDN'T COME UP. NOT. EVEN. ONCE.
WE GOT A TPP QUES-TION. OF COURSE.
SIIIGH.
BUT YOU DID PLENTY OF PREP FOR THAT TOPIC, RIGHT?
YEAH, BUT THE TPP IS SUCH AN OBVIOUS TOPIC THAT EVERY EXAMINEE WOULD COME PREPARED FOR IT.
OH. NEVER MIND.

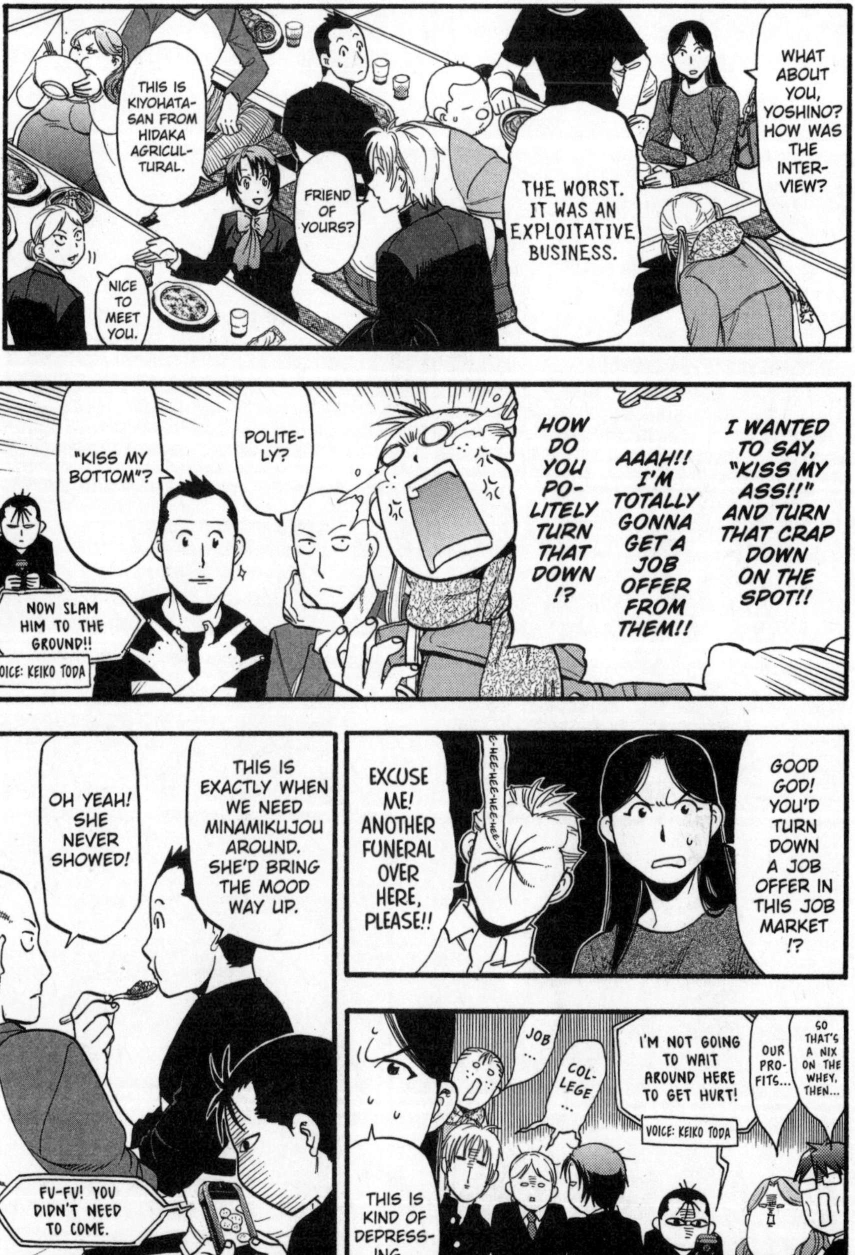
WHAT ABOUT YOU, YOSHINO? HOW WAS THE INTERVIEW?
THE WORST. IT WAS AN EXPLOITATIVE BUSINESS.
FRIEND OF YOURS?
THIS IS KIYOHATA-SAN FROM HIDAKA AGRICULTURAL.
NICE TO MEET YOU.
I WANTED TO SAY, "KISS MY ASS!!" AND TURN THAT CRAP DOWN ON THE SPOT!!
AAAH!! I'M TOTALLY GONNA GET A JOB OFFER FROM THEM!!
HOW DO YOU POLITELY TURN THAT DOWN!?
POLITELY?
"KISS MY BOTTOM"?
NOW SLAM HIM TO THE GROUND!!
VOICE: KEIKO TODA
GOOD GOD! YOU'D TURN DOWN A JOB OFFER IN THIS JOB MARKET!?
HEE-HEE-HEE-HEE...
EXCUSE ME! ANOTHER FUNERAL OVER HERE, PLEASE!!
SO THAT'S A NIX ON THE WHEY, THEN...
OUR PROFITS...
I'M NOT GOING TO WAIT AROUND HERE TO GET HURT!
VOICE: KEIKO TODA
COLLEGE...
JOB...
THIS IS KIND OF DEPRESSING...
THIS IS EXACTLY WHEN WE NEED MINAMIKUJOU AROUND. SHE'D BRING THE MOOD WAY UP.
OH YEAH! SHE NEVER SHOWED!
FU-FU! YOU DIDN'T NEED TO COME.
VOICE: KEIKO TODA

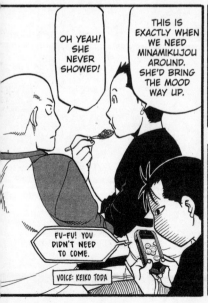

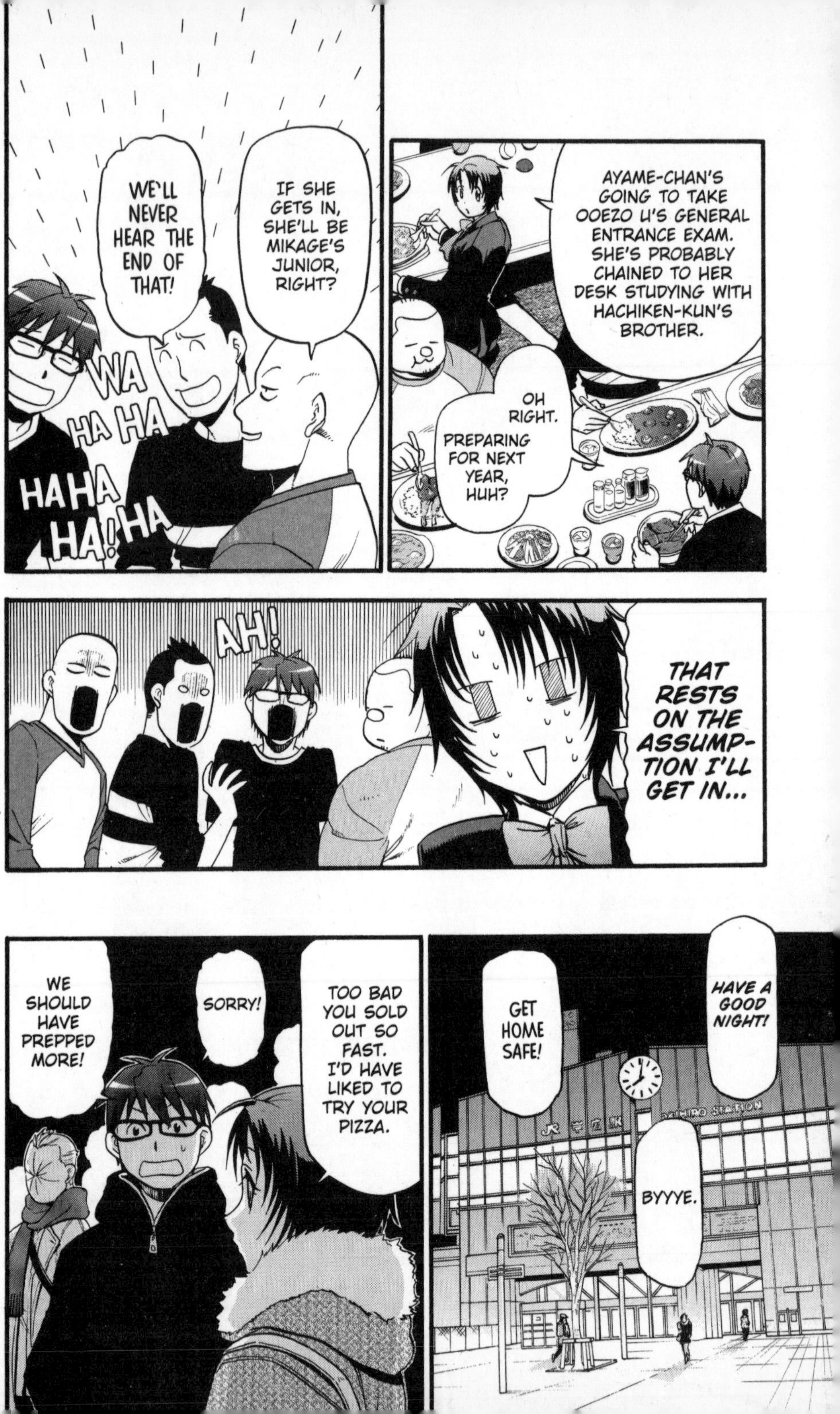
AYAME-CHAN'S GOING TO TAKE OOEZO U'S GENERAL ENTRANCE EXAM. SHE'S PROBABLY CHAINED TO HER DESK STUDYING WITH HACHIKEN-KUN'S BROTHER.
OH RIGHT. PREPARING FOR NEXT YEAR, HUH?
IF SHE GETS IN, SHE'LL BE MIKAGE'S JUNIOR, RIGHT?
WE'LL NEVER HEAR THE END OF THAT!
WA HA HA
HAHA HA! HA
AH!
THAT RESTS ON THE ASSUMPTION I'LL GET IN...
HAVE A GOOD NIGHT!
GET HOME SAFE!
BYYYE.
TOO BAD YOU SOLD OUT SO FAST. I'D HAVE LIKED TO TRY YOUR PIZZA.
SORRY!
WE SHOULD HAVE PREPPED MORE!

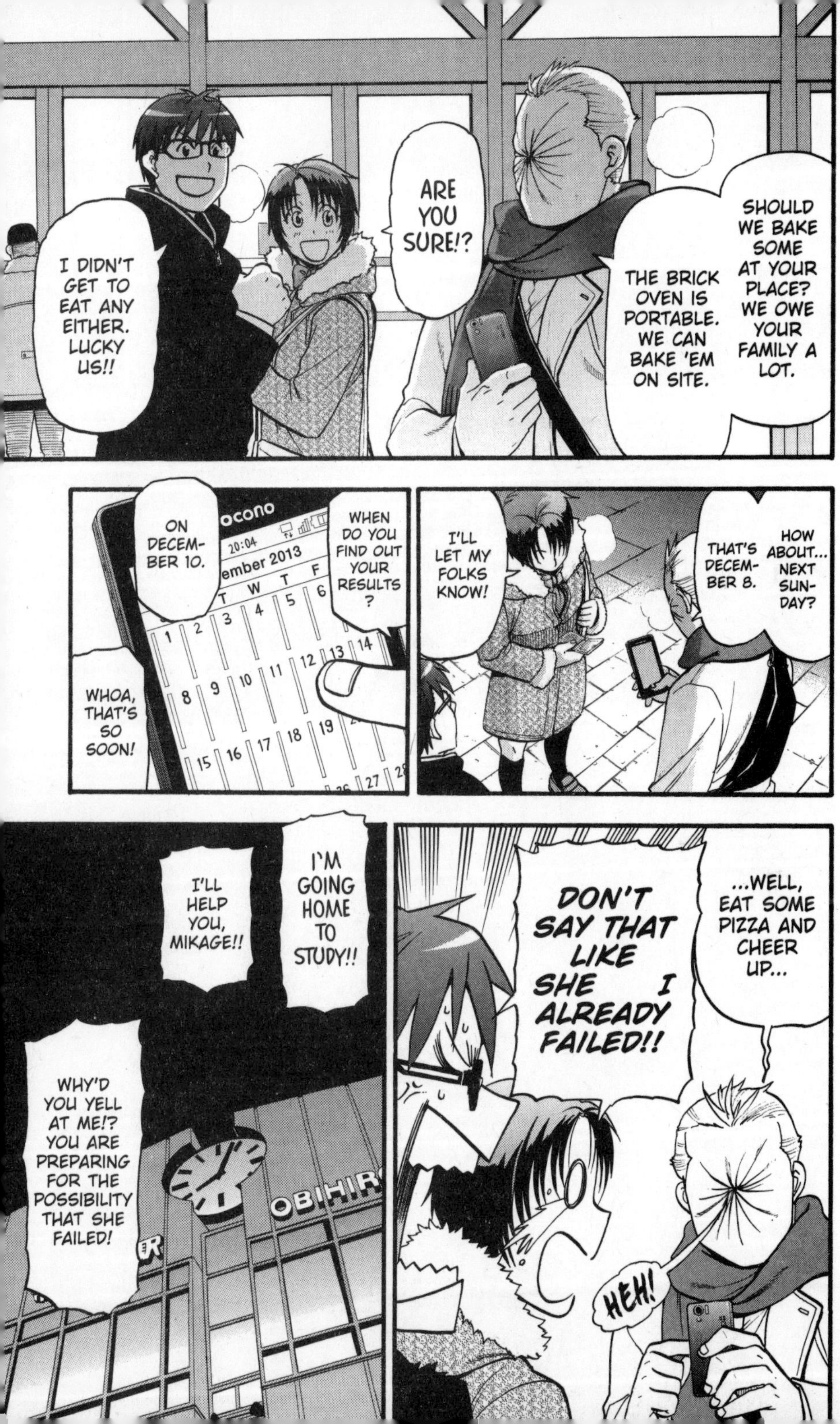
SHOULD WE BAKE SOME AT YOUR PLACE? WE OWE YOUR FAMILY A LOT.
THE BRICK OVEN IS PORTABLE. WE CAN BAKE 'EM ON SITE.
ARE YOU SURE!?
I DIDN'T GET TO EAT ANY EITHER. LUCKY US!!
HOW ABOUT... NEXT SUNDAY?
THAT'S DECEMBER 8.
I'LL LET MY FOLKS KNOW!
WHEN DO YOU FIND OUT YOUR RESULTS?
ON DECEMBER 10.
WHOA, THAT'S SO SOON!
...WELL, EAT SOME PIZZA AND CHEER UP...
DON'T SAY THAT LIKE SHE I ALREADY FAILED!!
HEH!
I'M GOING HOME TO STUDY!!
I'LL HELP YOU, MIKAGE!!
WHY'D YOU YELL AT ME!? YOU ARE PREPARING FOR THE POSSIBILITY THAT SHE FAILED!
OBIHIR

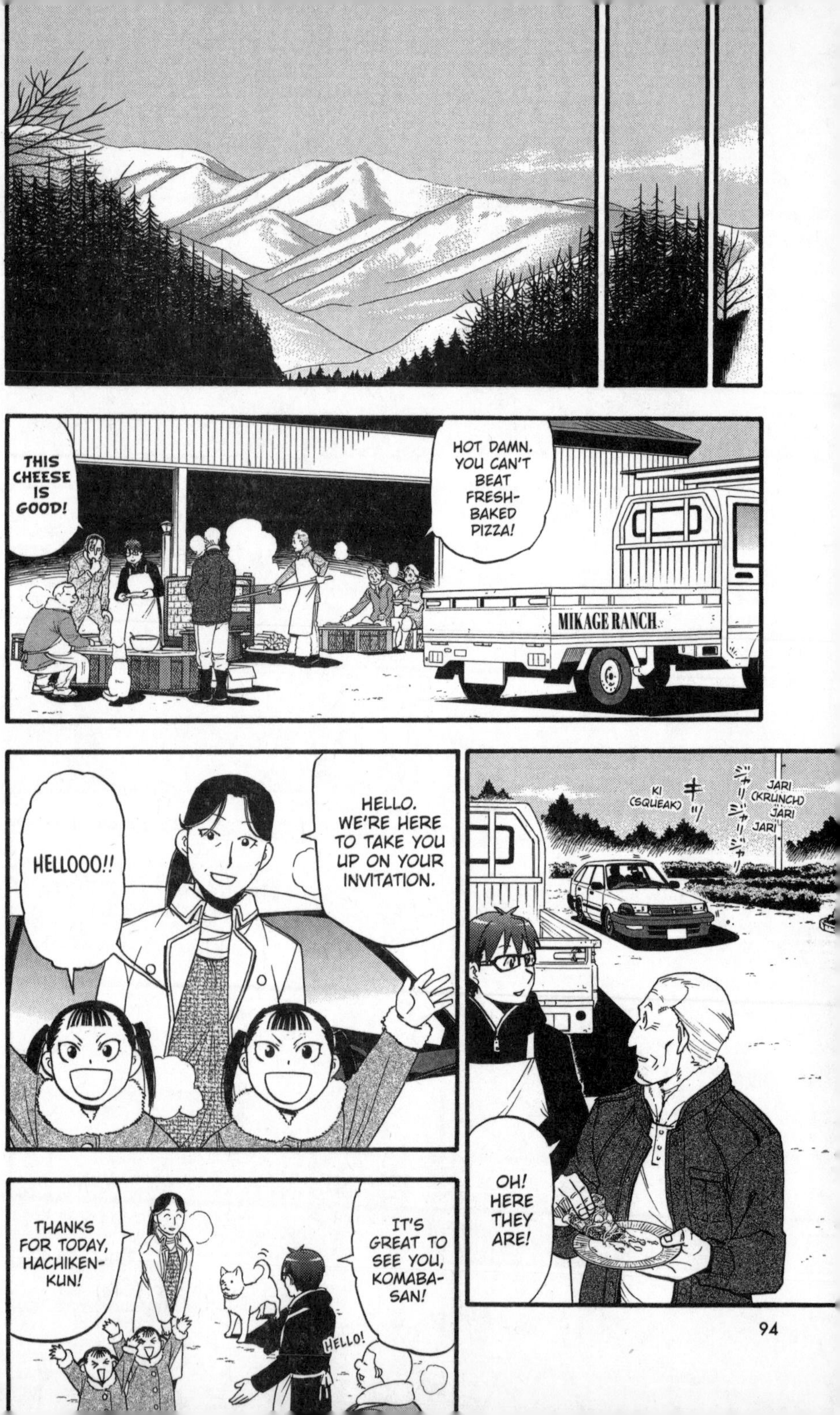
HOT DAMN. YOU CAN'T BEAT FRESH-BAKED PIZZA!
THIS CHEESE IS GOOD!
MIKAGE RANCH
ジャリジャリジャリ
JARI (KRUNCH) JARI JARI
キッ
KI (SQUEAK)
OH! HERE THEY ARE!
HELLO. WE'RE HERE TO TAKE YOU UP ON YOUR INVITATION.
HELLOOO!!
IT'S GREAT TO SEE YOU, KOMABA-SAN!
HELLO!
THANKS FOR TODAY, HACHIKEN-KUN!

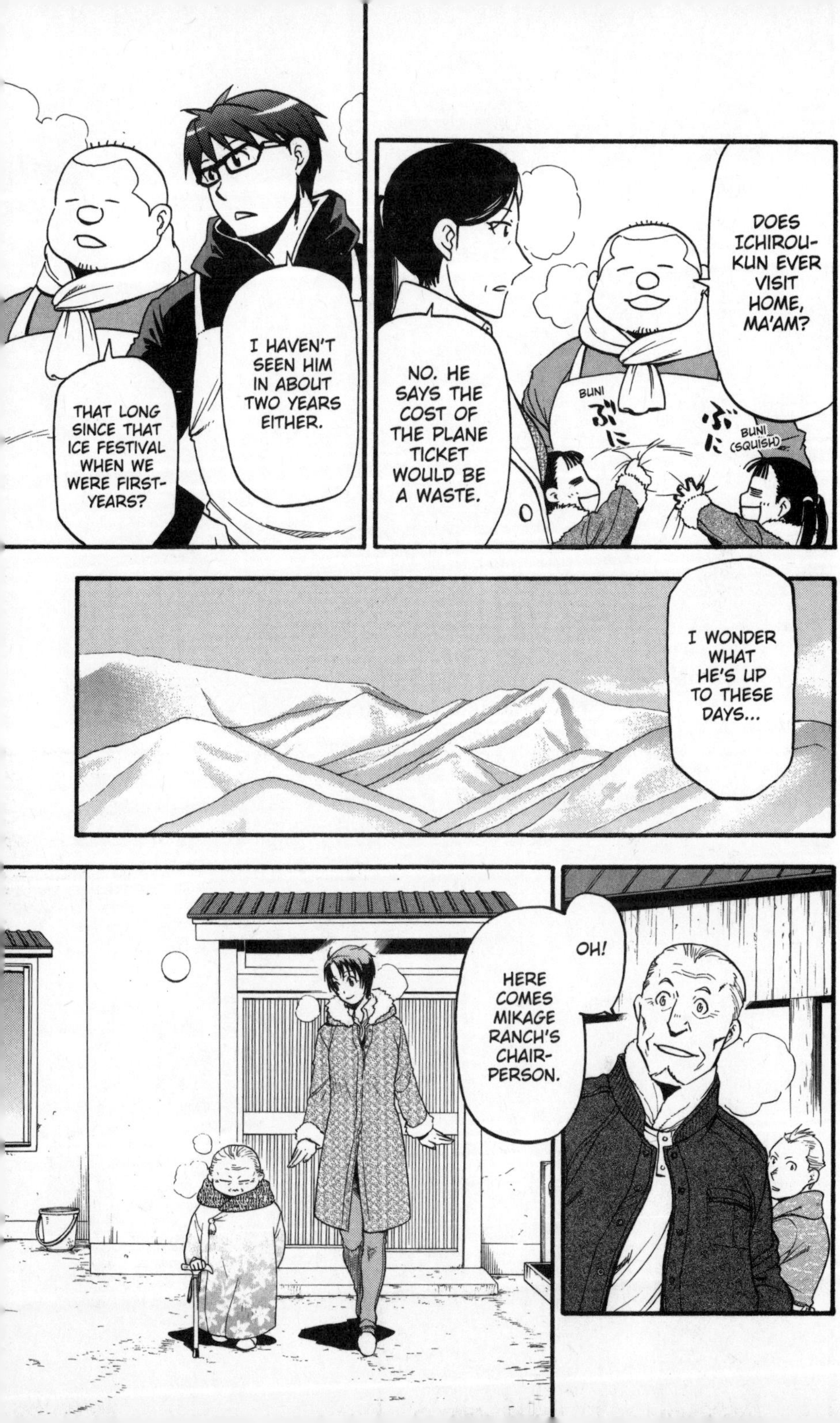
DOES ICHIROU-KUN EVER VISIT HOME, MA'AM?
ぶに
BUNI (SQUISH)
BUNI
ぶに
NO. HE SAYS THE COST OF THE PLANE TICKET WOULD BE A WASTE.
I HAVEN'T SEEN HIM IN ABOUT TWO YEARS EITHER.
THAT LONG SINCE THAT ICE FESTIVAL WHEN WE WERE FIRST-YEARS?
I WONDER WHAT HE'S UP TO THESE DAYS...
OH!
HERE COMES MIKAGE RANCH'S CHAIR-PERSON.

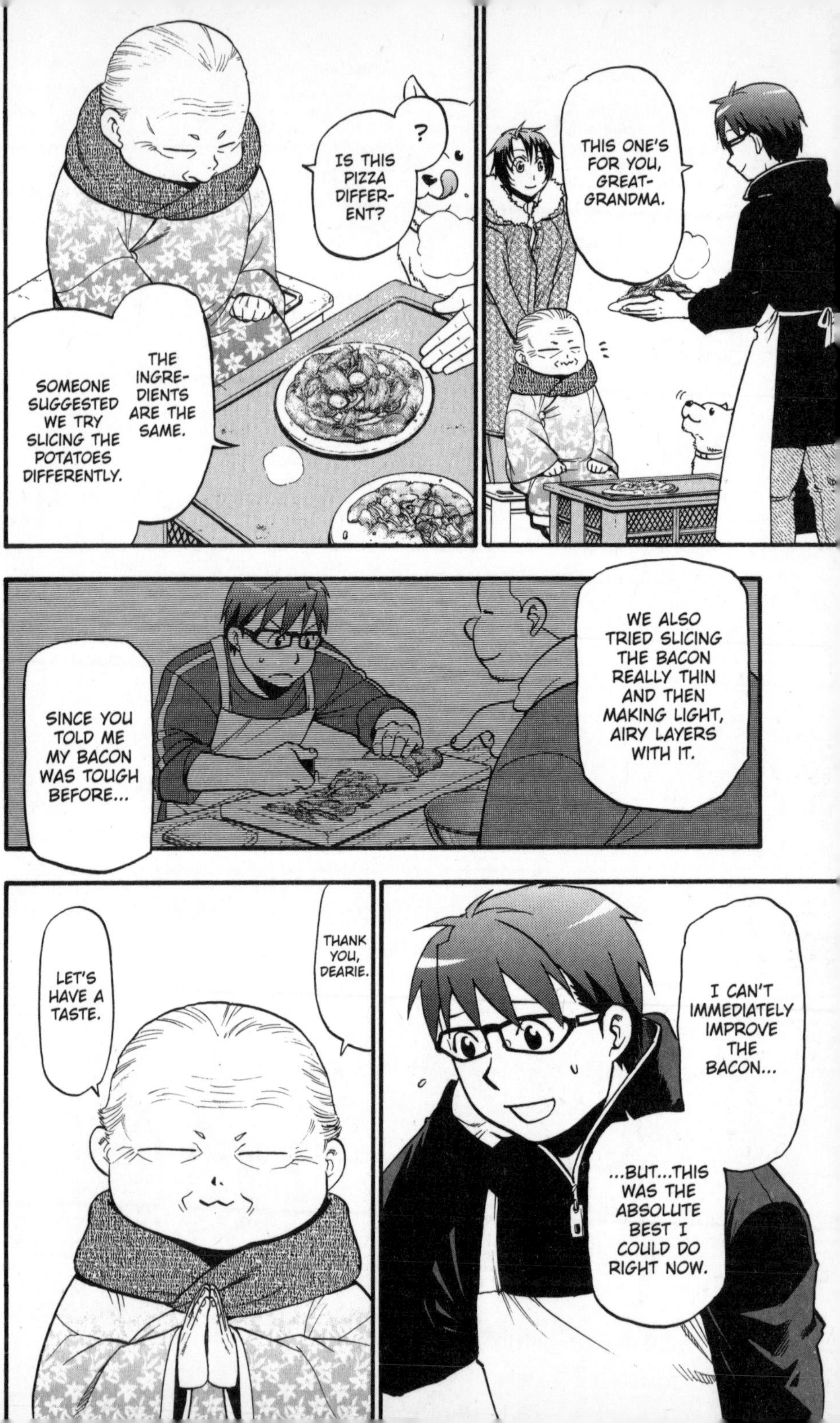
THIS ONE'S FOR YOU, GREAT-GRANDMA.
?
IS THIS PIZZA DIFFERENT?
THE INGRE-DIENTS ARE THE SAME.
SOMEONE SUGGESTED WE TRY SLICING THE POTATOES DIFFERENTLY.
WE ALSO TRIED SLICING THE BACON REALLY THIN AND THEN MAKING LIGHT, AIRY LAYERS WITH IT.
SINCE YOU TOLD ME MY BACON WAS TOUGH BEFORE...
I CAN'T IMMEDIATELY IMPROVE THE BACON...
...BUT...THIS WAS THE ABSOLUTE BEST I COULD DO RIGHT NOW.
THANK YOU, DEARIE.
LET'S HAVE A TASTE.

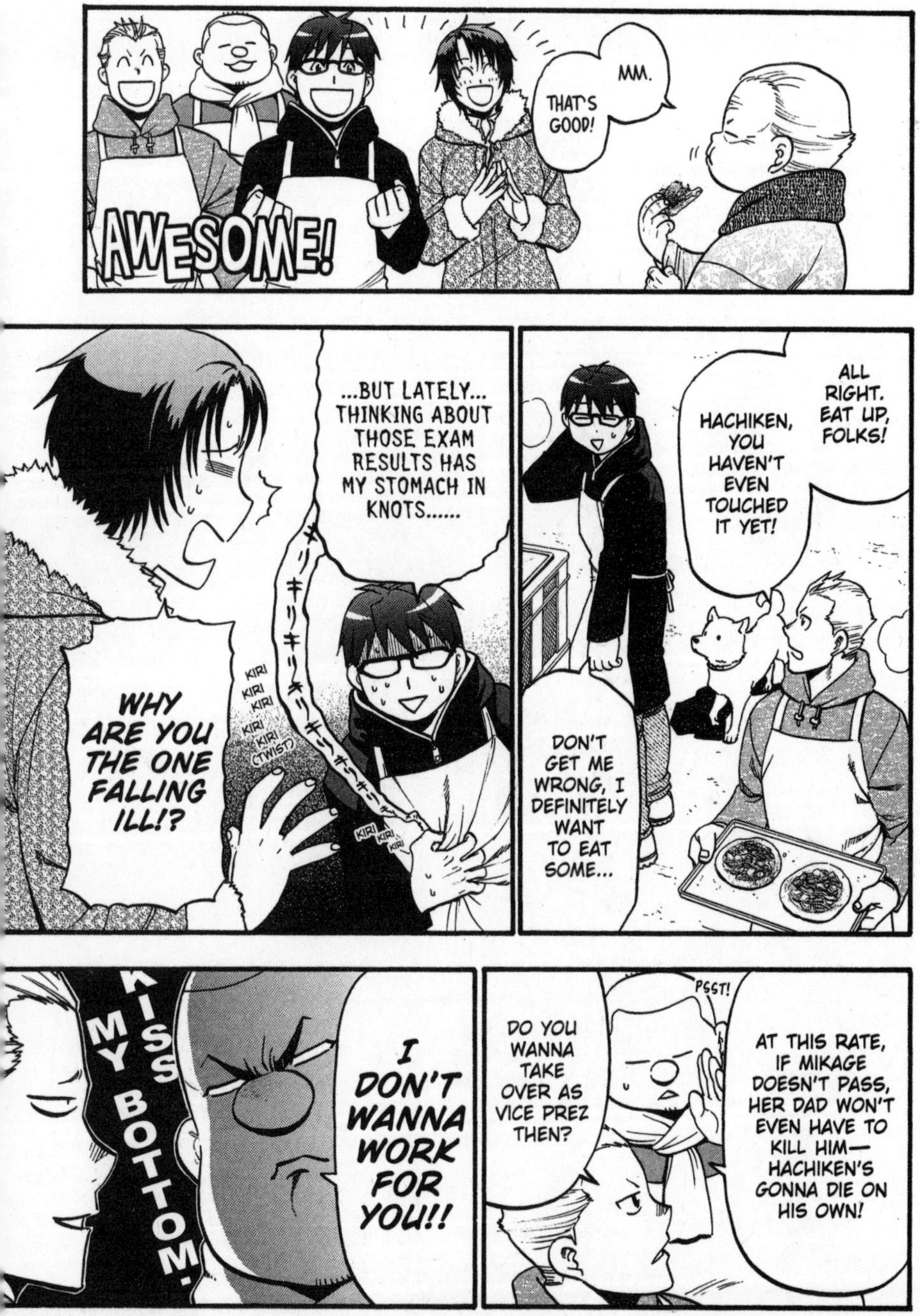
MM.
THAT'S GOOD!
AWESOME!
ALL RIGHT. EAT UP, FOLKS!
HACHIKEN, YOU HAVEN'T EVEN TOUCHED IT YET!
DON'T GET ME WRONG, I DEFINITELY WANT TO EAT SOME...
...BUT LATELY... THINKING ABOUT THOSE EXAM RESULTS HAS MY STOMACH IN KNOTS......
KIRI KIRI KIRI KIRI KIRI (TWIST)
KIRI KIRI KIRI
WHY ARE YOU THE ONE FALLING ILL!?
PSST!
AT THIS RATE, IF MIKAGE DOESN'T PASS, HER DAD WON'T EVEN HAVE TO KILL HIM—HACHIKEN'S GONNA DIE ON HIS OWN!
DO YOU WANNA TAKE OVER AS VICE PREZ THEN?
I DON'T WANNA WORK FOR YOU!!
KISS MY BOTTOM.

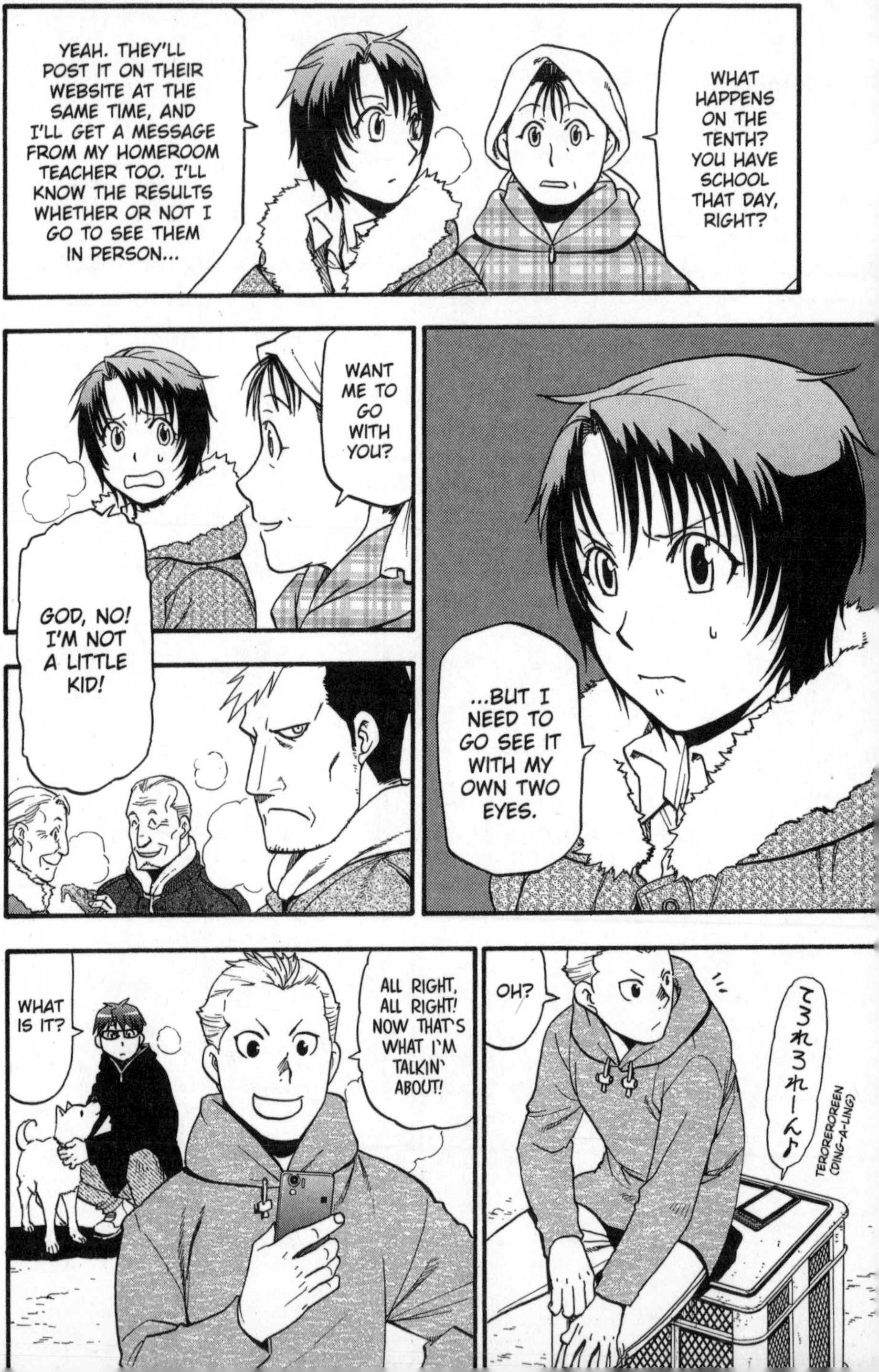
WHAT HAPPENS ON THE TENTH? YOU HAVE SCHOOL THAT DAY, RIGHT?
YEAH. THEY'LL POST IT ON THEIR WEBSITE AT THE SAME TIME, AND I'LL GET A MESSAGE FROM MY HOMEROOM TEACHER TOO. I'LL KNOW THE RESULTS WHETHER OR NOT I GO TO SEE THEM IN PERSON...
...BUT I NEED TO GO SEE IT WITH MY OWN TWO EYES.
WANT ME TO GO WITH YOU?
GOD, NO! I'M NOT A LITTLE KID!
てろれろれーん♪
TERORERORREEN (DING-A-LING)
OH?
ALL RIGHT, ALL RIGHT! NOW THAT'S WHAT I'M TALKIN' ABOUT!
WHAT IS IT?

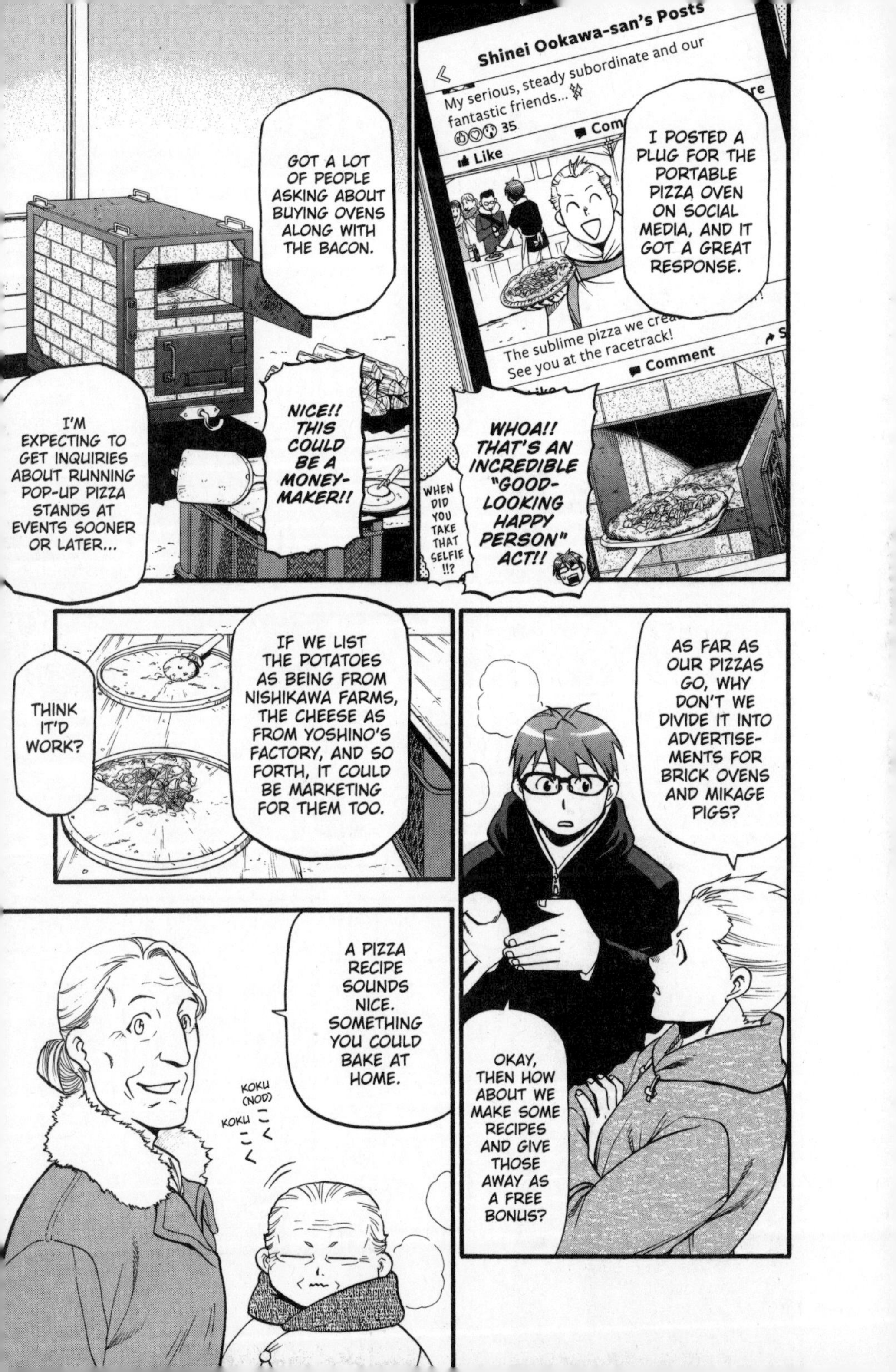
Shinei Ookawa-san's Posts
My serious, steady subordinate and our fantastic friends...
35
Like
See you at the racetrack!
Comment
I POSTED A PLUG FOR THE PORTABLE PIZZA OVEN ON SOCIAL MEDIA, AND IT GOT A GREAT RESPONSE.
WHOA!! THAT'S AN INCREDIBLE "GOOD-LOOKING HAPPY PERSON" ACT!!
WHEN DID YOU TAKE THAT SELFIE!!?
GOT A LOT OF PEOPLE ASKING ABOUT BUYING OVENS ALONG WITH THE BACON.
NICE!! THIS COULD BE A MONEY-MAKER!!
I'M EXPECTING TO GET INQUIRIES ABOUT RUNNING POP-UP PIZZA STANDS AT EVENTS SOONER OR LATER...
AS FAR AS OUR PIZZAS GO, WHY DON'T WE DIVIDE IT INTO ADVERTISE-MENTS FOR BRICK OVENS AND MIKAGE PIGS?
OKAY, THEN HOW ABOUT WE MAKE SOME RECIPES AND GIVE THOSE AWAY AS A FREE BONUS?
IF WE LIST THE POTATOES AS BEING FROM NISHIKAWA FARMS, THE CHEESE AS FROM YOSHINO'S FACTORY, AND SO FORTH, IT COULD BE MARKETING FOR THEM TOO.
THINK IT'D WORK?
A PIZZA RECIPE SOUNDS NICE. SOMETHING YOU COULD BAKE AT HOME.
KOKU (NOD)
こく
KOKU
こく

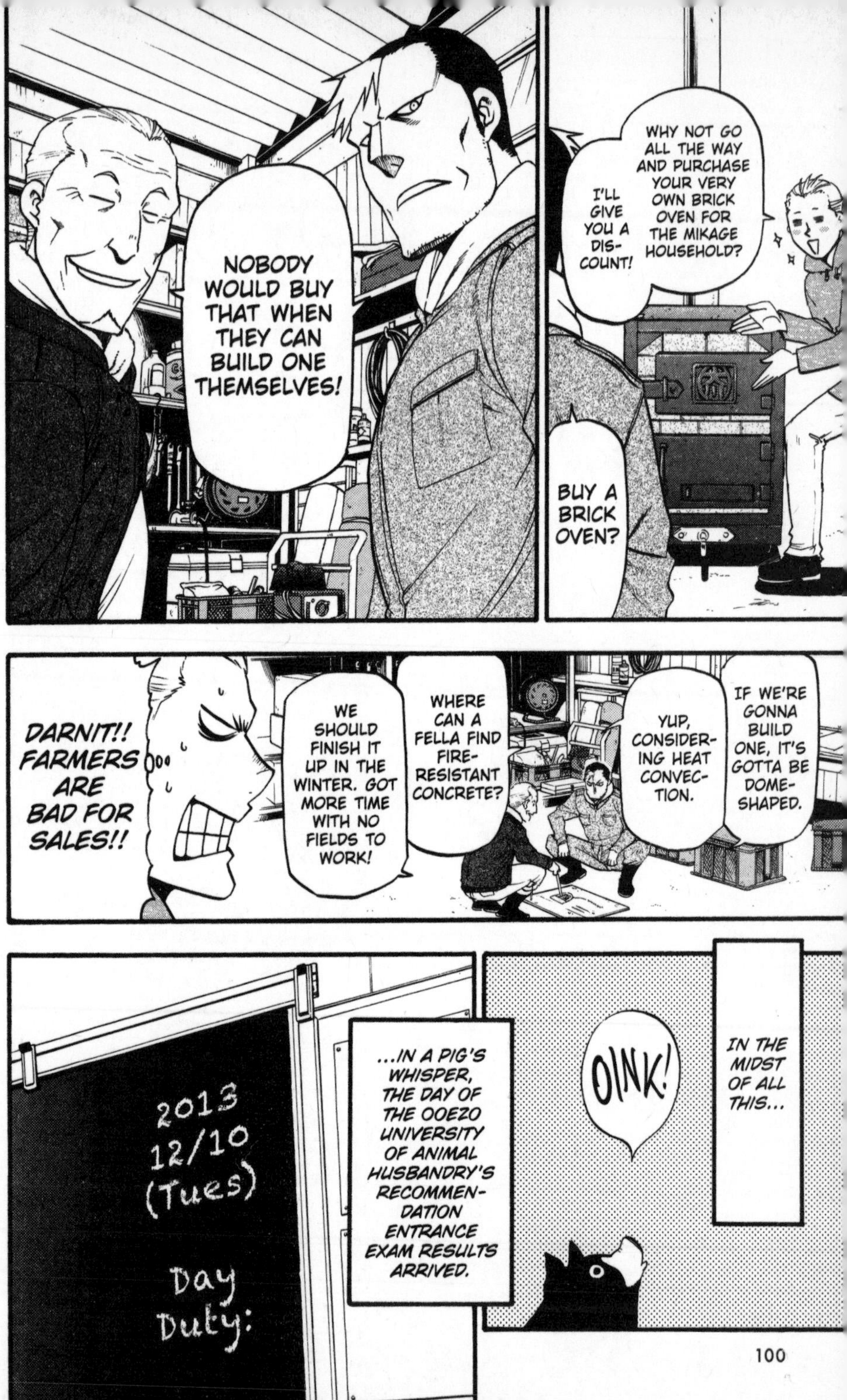
WHY NOT GO ALL THE WAY AND PURCHASE YOUR VERY OWN BRICK OVEN FOR THE MIKAGE HOUSEHOLD?
I'LL GIVE YOU A DIS-COUNT!
BUY A BRICK OVEN?
NOBODY WOULD BUY THAT WHEN THEY CAN BUILD ONE THEMSELVES!
IF WE'RE GONNA BUILD ONE, IT'S GOTTA BE DOME-SHAPED.
YUP, CONSIDER-ING HEAT CONVEC-TION.
WHERE CAN A FELLA FIND FIRE-RESISTANT CONCRETE?
WE SHOULD FINISH IT UP IN THE WINTER. GOT MORE TIME WITH NO FIELDS TO WORK!
DARNIT!! FARMERS ARE BAD FOR SALES!!
IN THE MIDST OF ALL THIS...
OINK!
...IN A PIG'S WHISPER, THE DAY OF THE OOEZO UNIVERSITY OF ANIMAL HUSBANDRY'S RECOMMEN-DATION ENTRANCE EXAM RESULTS ARRIVED.
2013 12/10 (Tues)
Day Duty:

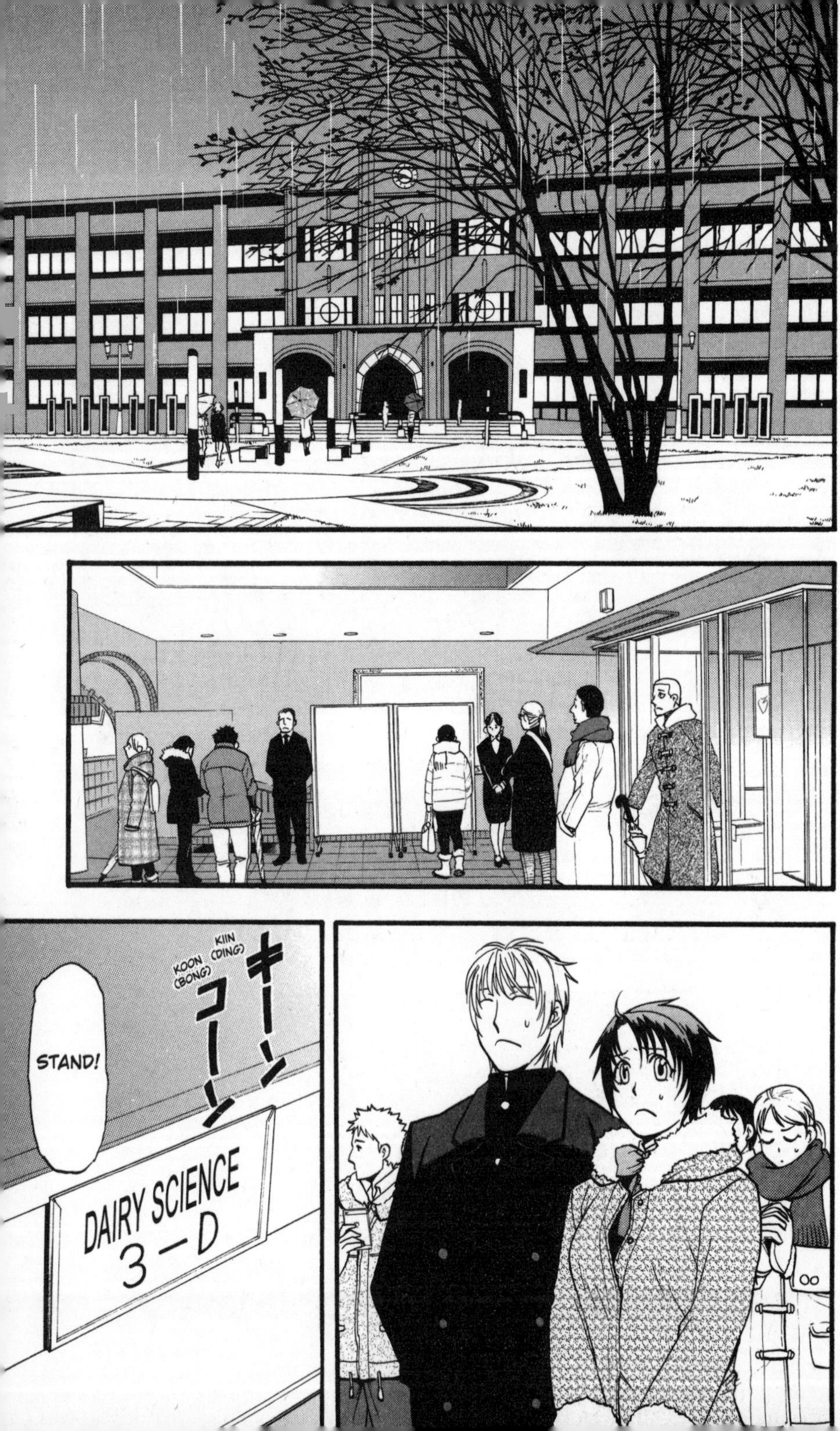

KIIN (DING)
KOON (BONG)
STAND!
DAIRY SCIENCE 3 – D

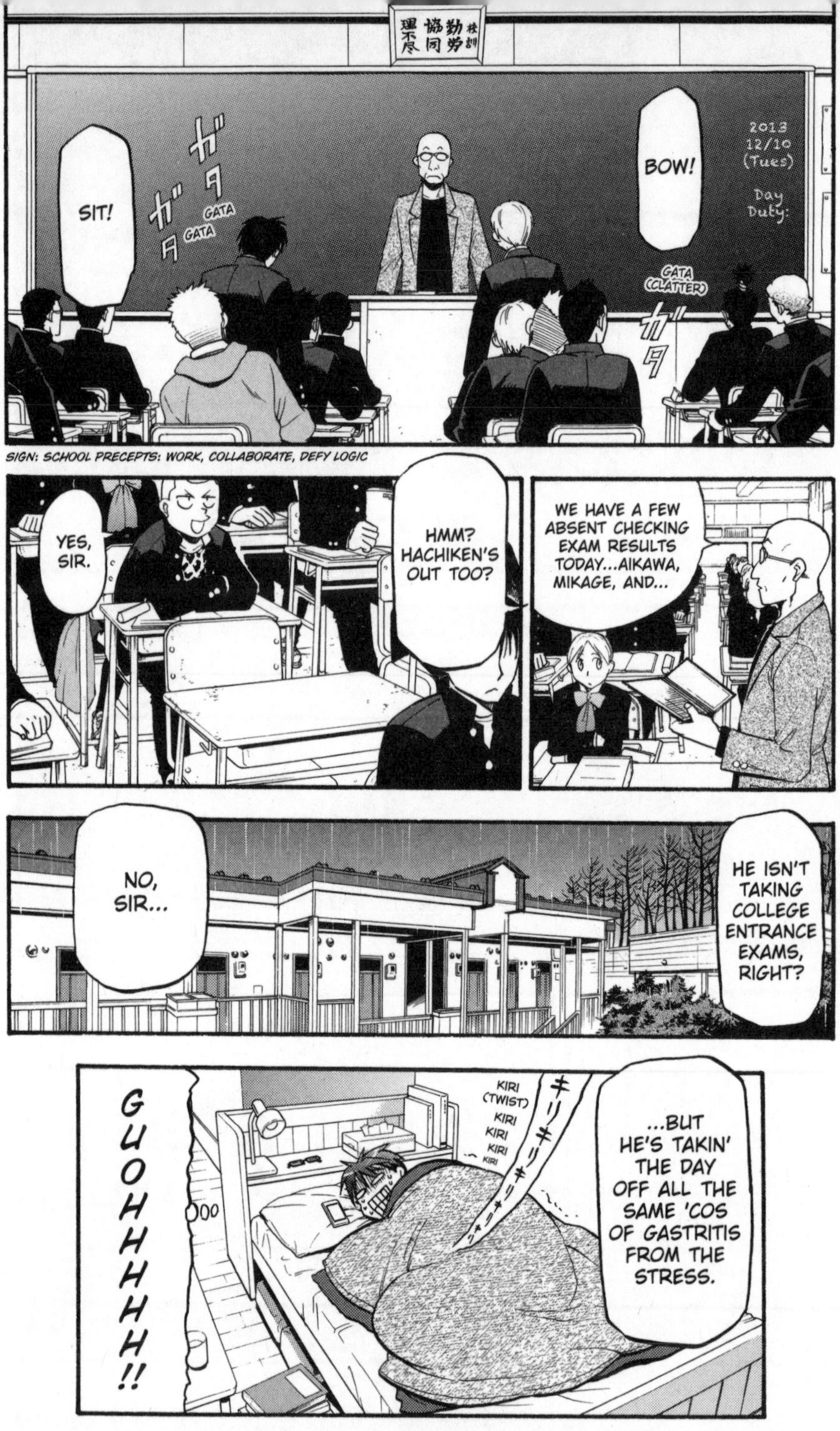
校訓
勤労
協同
理不尽
2013 12/10 (Tues) Day Duty:
BOW!
GATA (CLATTER)
ガタ
SIT!
ガタ
ガタ
GATA
GATA
SIGN: SCHOOL PRECEPTS: WORK, COLLABORATE, DEFY LOGIC
WE HAVE A FEW ABSENT CHECKING EXAM RESULTS TODAY...AIKAWA, MIKAGE, AND...
HMM? HACHIKEN'S OUT TOO?
YES, SIR.
HE ISN'T TAKING COLLEGE ENTRANCE EXAMS, RIGHT?
NO, SIR...
...BUT HE'S TAKIN' THE DAY OFF ALL THE SAME 'COS OF GASTRITIS FROM THE STRESS.
キリキリキリキリ
KIRI (TWIST) KIRI KIRI KIRI KIRI
GUOHHHHHH!!

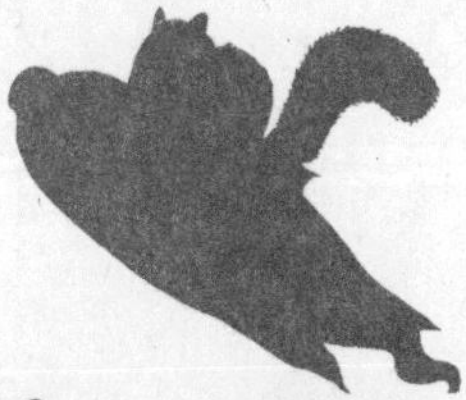

Silver Spoon

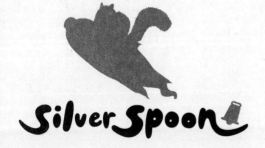

Chapter 119:

Tale of Four Seasons ㉒

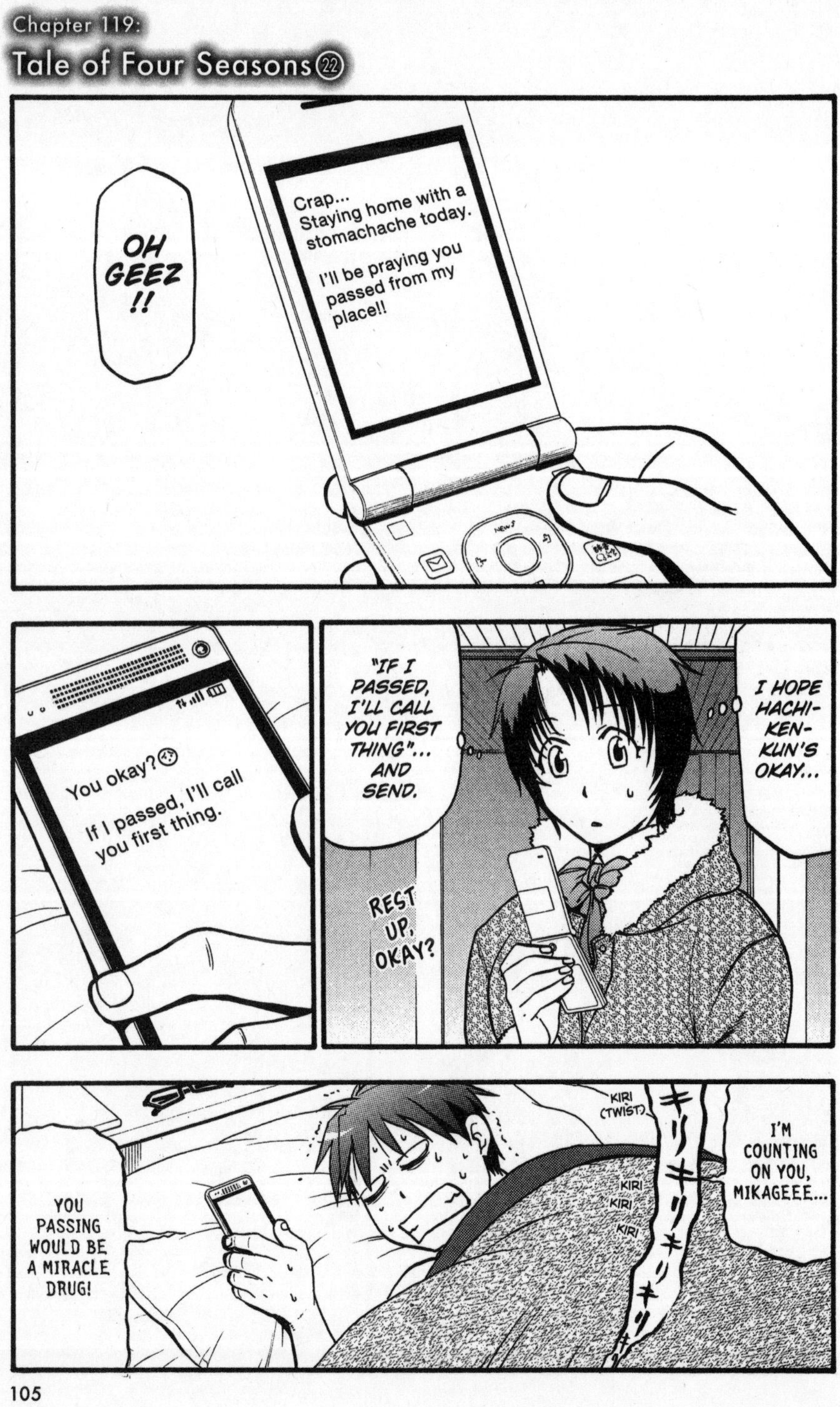
Crap...
Staying home with a stomachache today.
I'll be praying you passed from my place!!
OH GEEZ !!
I HOPE HACHI-KEN-KUN'S OKAY...
"IF I PASSED, I'LL CALL YOU FIRST THING"... AND SEND.
REST UP, OKAY?
You okay?
If I passed, I'll call you first thing.
KIRI (TWIST)
I'M COUNTING ON YOU, MIKAGEEE...
KIRI
KIRI
KIRI
YOU PASSING WOULD BE A MIRACLE DRUG!

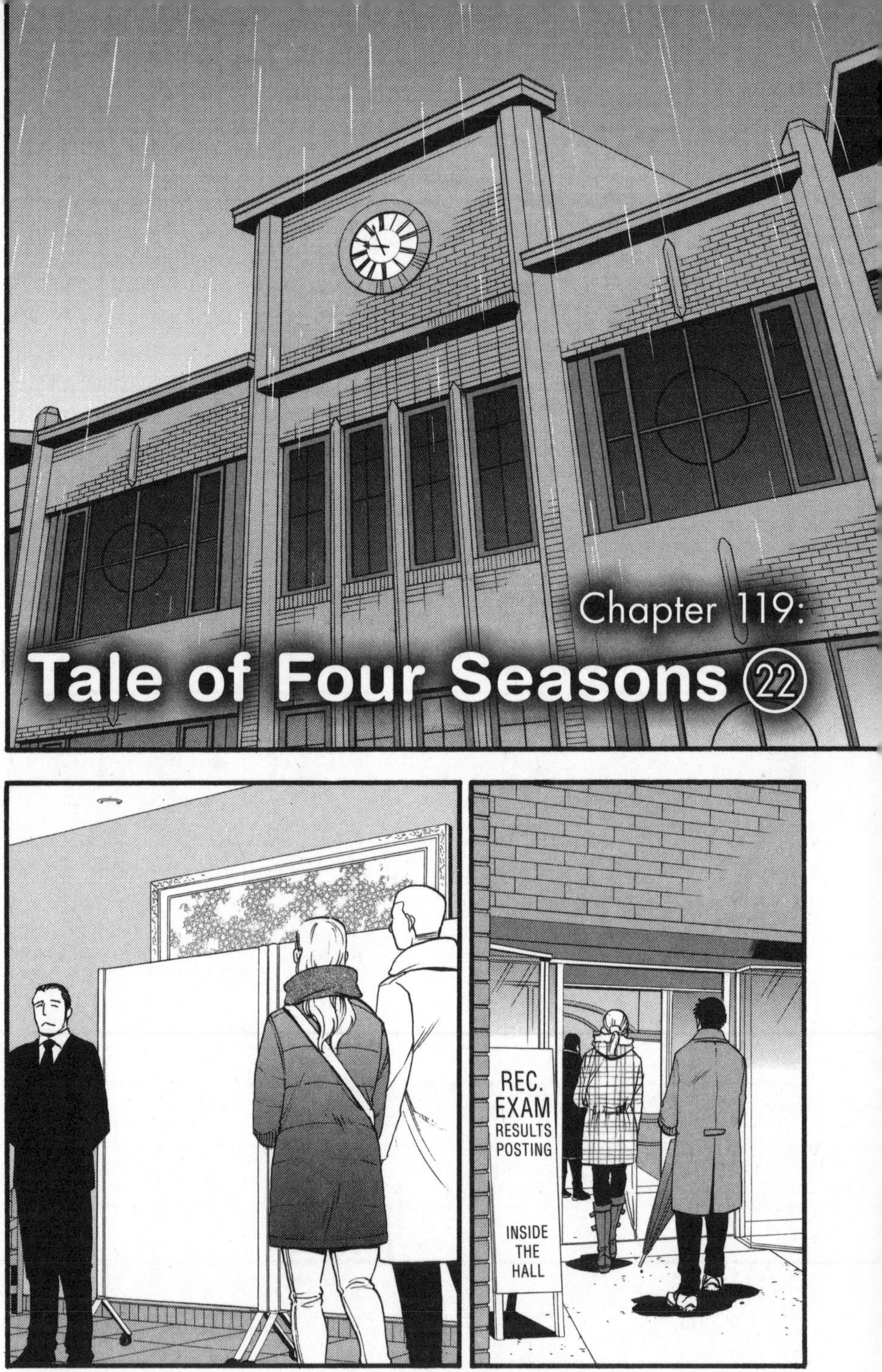
Chapter 119:
Tale of Four Seasons ㉒
REC. EXAM RESULTS POSTING
INSIDE THE HALL

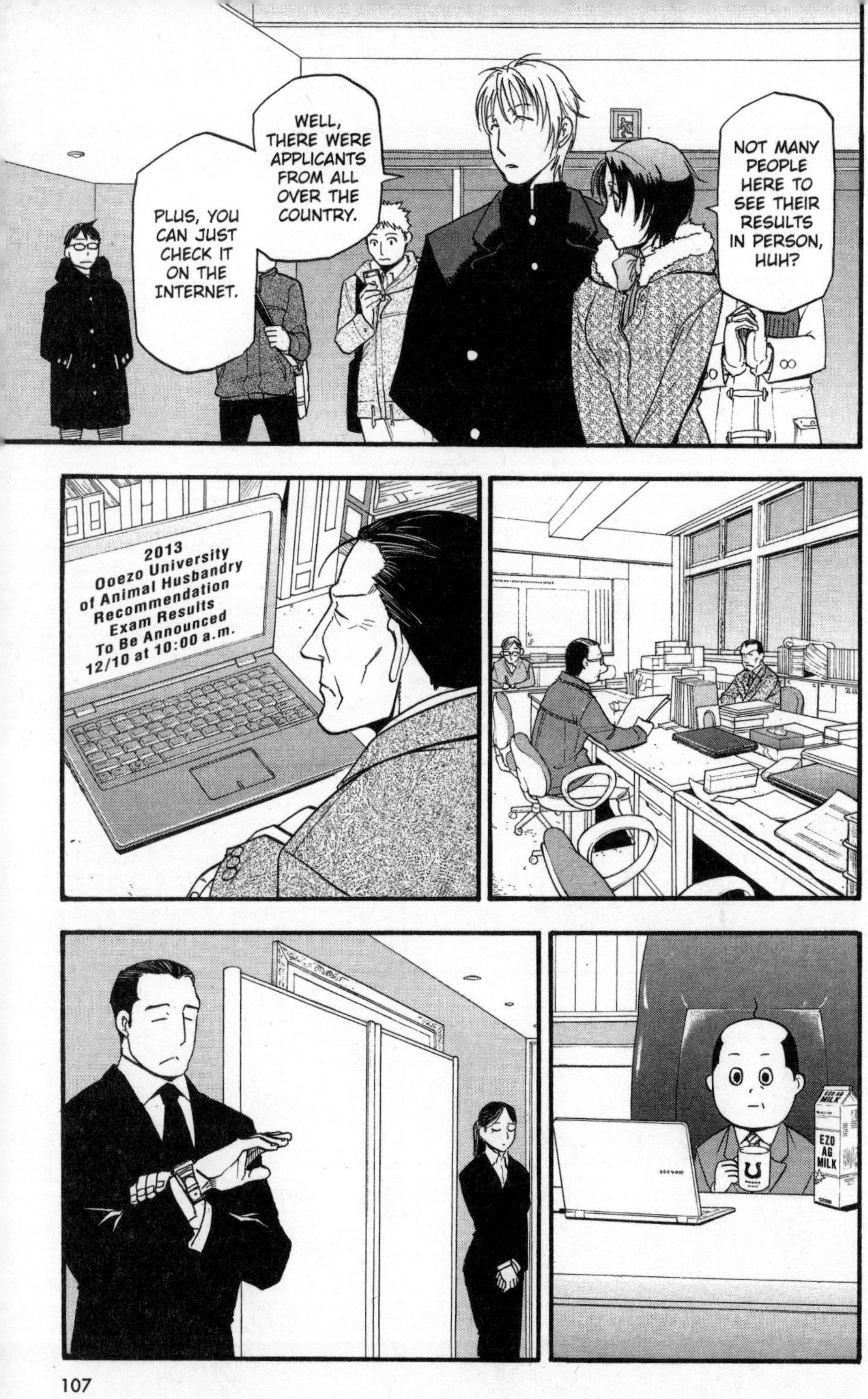
NOT MANY PEOPLE HERE TO SEE THEIR RESULTS IN PERSON, HUH?
WELL, THERE WERE APPLICANTS FROM ALL OVER THE COUNTRY.
PLUS, YOU CAN JUST CHECK IT ON THE INTERNET.
2013 Ooezo University of Animal Husbandry Recommendation Exam Results To Be Announced 12/10 at 10:00 a.m.
EZO AG MILK

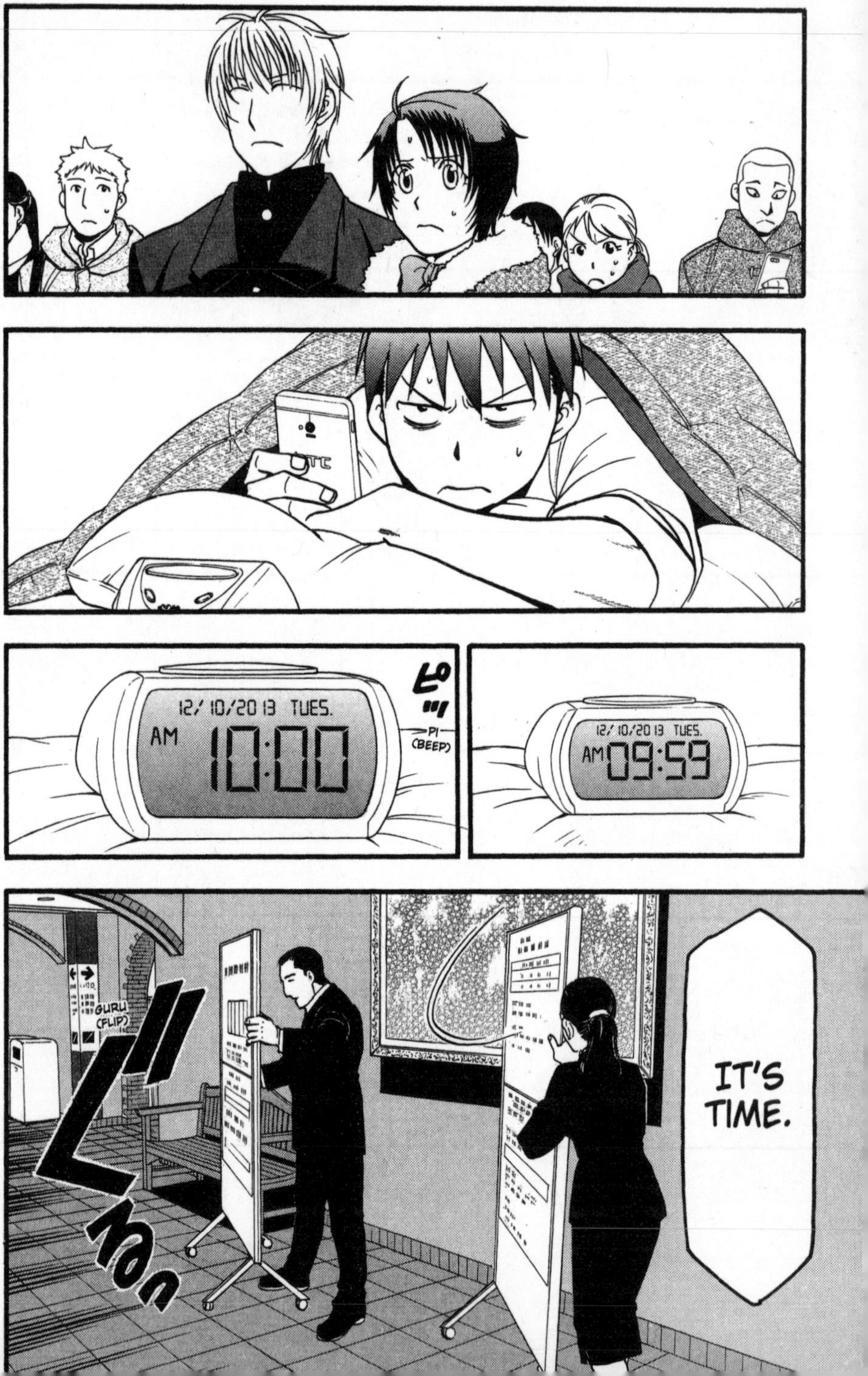

12/10/2013 TUES.
AM 09:59
ピッ
PI (BEEP)
12/10/2013 TUES.
AM 10:00
IT'S TIME.
GURU (FLIP)

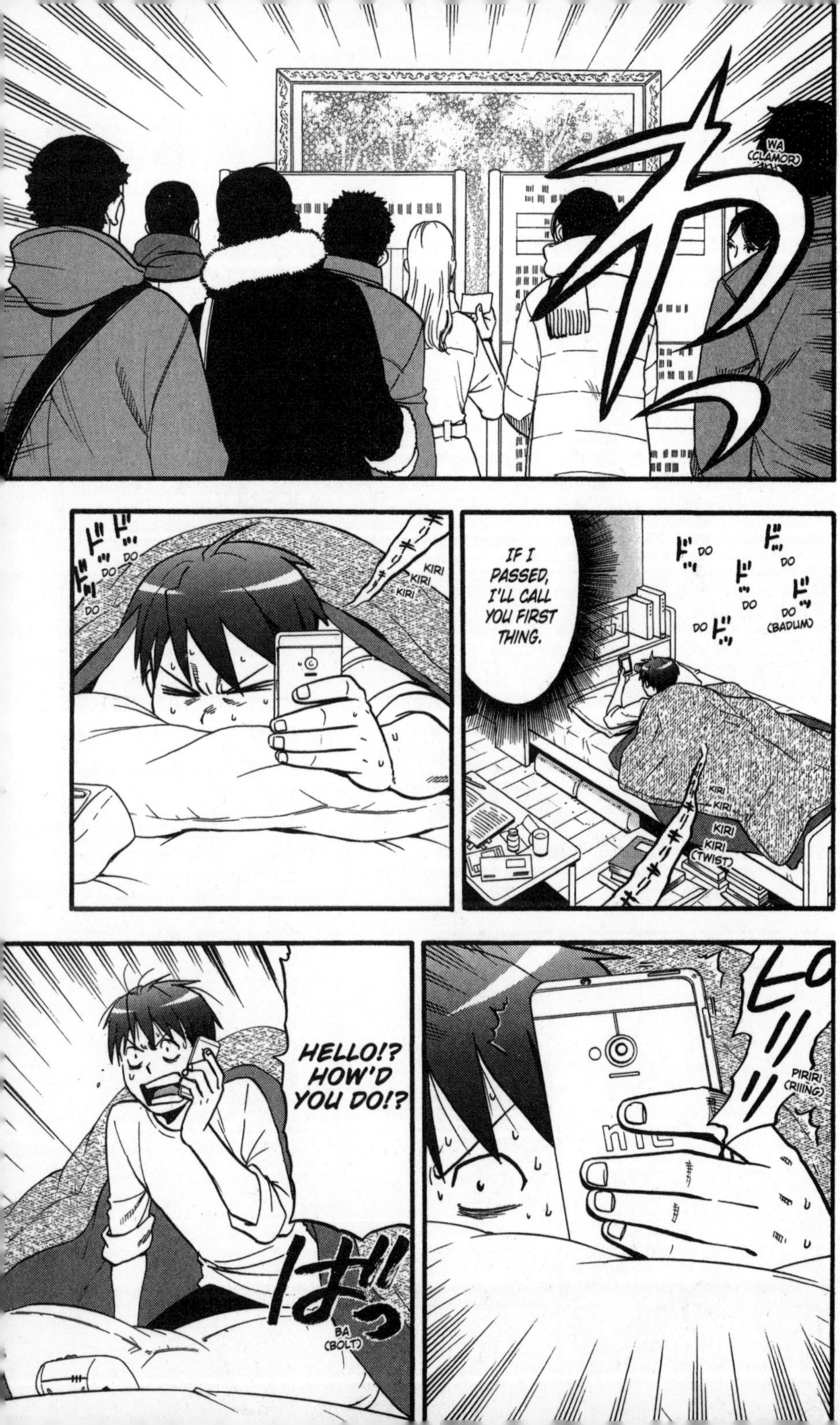
WA (CLAMOR)
IF I PASSED, I'LL CALL YOU FIRST THING.
DO DO DO DO DO (BADUM)
KIRI KIRI KIRI KIRI (TWIST)
DO DO DO
KIRI KIRI KIRI
PIRIRI (RIIING)
HELLO!? HOW'D YOU DO!?
BA (BOLT)

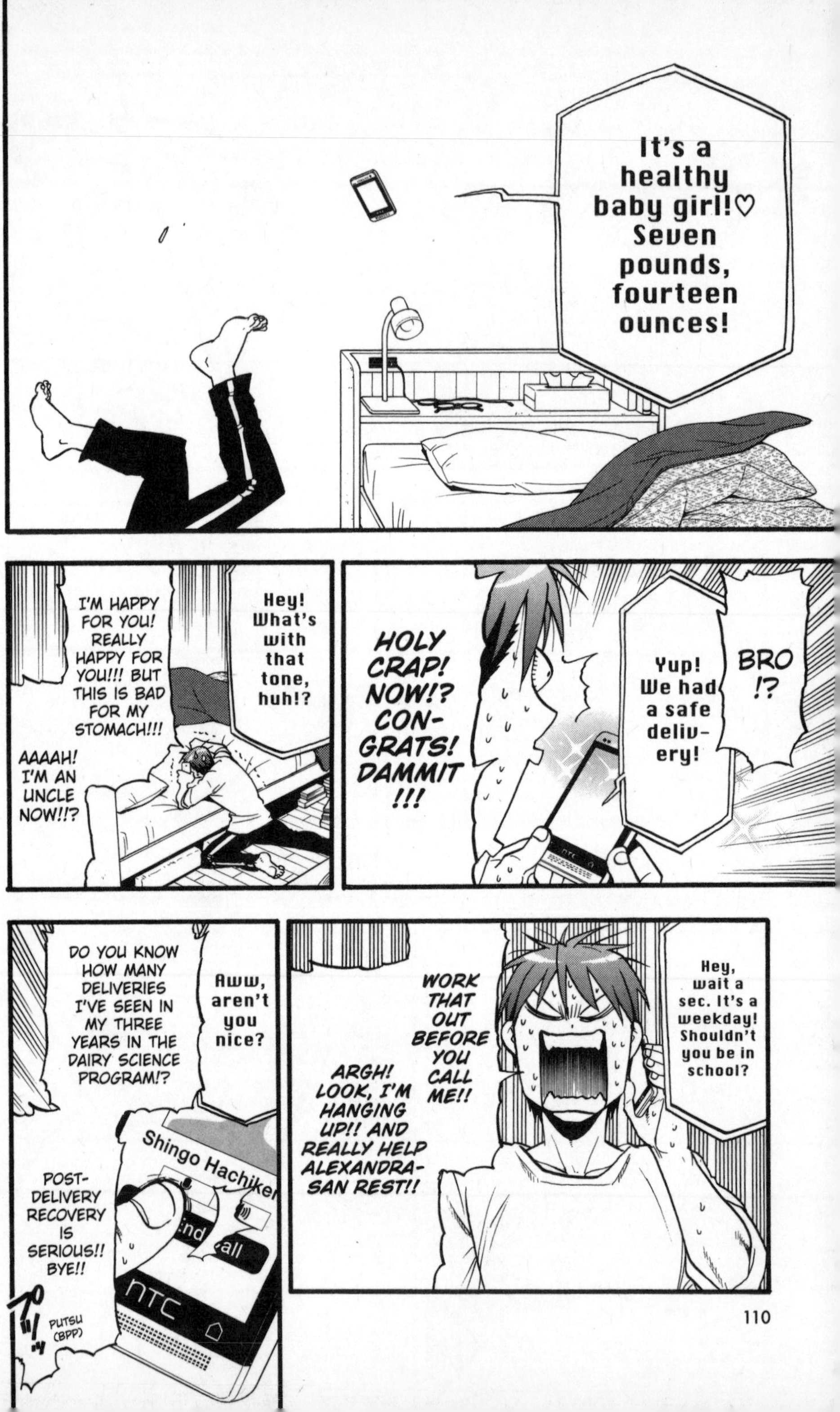
It's a healthy baby girl!♡ Seven pounds, fourteen ounces!
BRO !?
Yup! We had a safe delivery!
HOLY CRAP! NOW!? CON-GRATS! DAMMIT !!!
Hey! What's with that tone, huh!?
I'M HAPPY FOR YOU! REALLY HAPPY FOR YOU!!! BUT THIS IS BAD FOR MY STOMACH!!!
AAAAH! I'M AN UNCLE NOW!!?
Hey, wait a sec. It's a weekday! Shouldn't you be in school?
WORK THAT OUT BEFORE YOU CALL ME!!
ARGH! LOOK, I'M HANGING UP!! AND REALLY HELP ALEXANDRA-SAN REST!!
Aww, aren't you nice?
DO YOU KNOW HOW MANY DELIVERIES I'VE SEEN IN MY THREE YEARS IN THE DAIRY SCIENCE PROGRAM!?
Shingo Hachiken
POST-DELIVERY RECOVERY IS SERIOUS!! BYE!!
PUTSU (BPP)

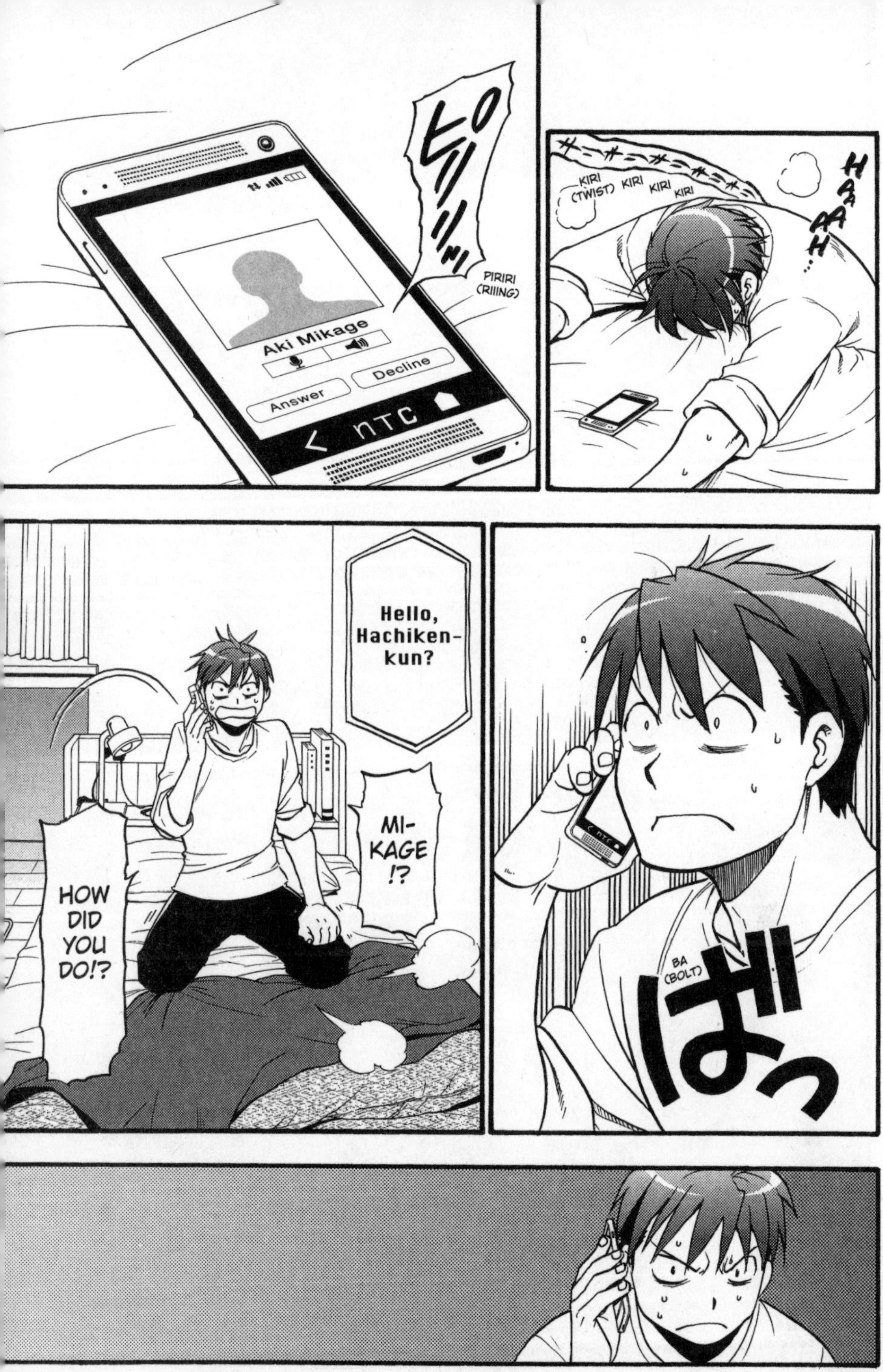
KIRI (TWIST) KIRI KIRI KIRI
HAAAH...
ピリリ
PIRIRI (RIIING)
Aki Mikage
Answer
Decline
BA (BOLT)
ばっ
Hello, Hachiken-kun?
MI-KAGE!?
HOW DID YOU DO!?

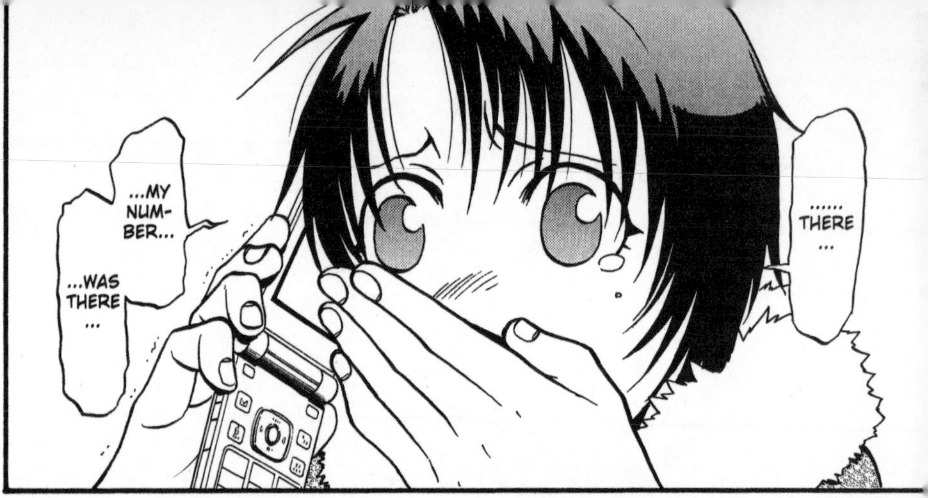
......THERE...
...MY NUM-BER...
...WAS THERE...

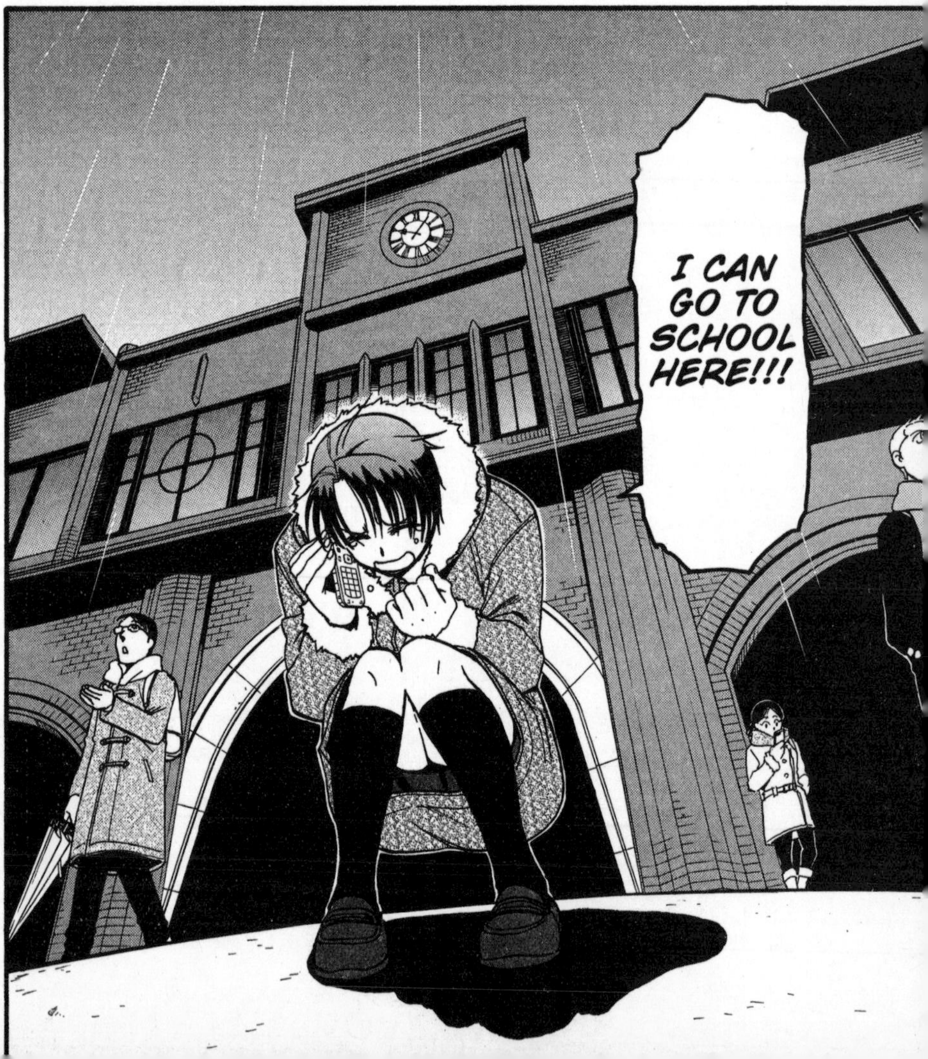
I CAN GO TO SCHOOL HERE!!!

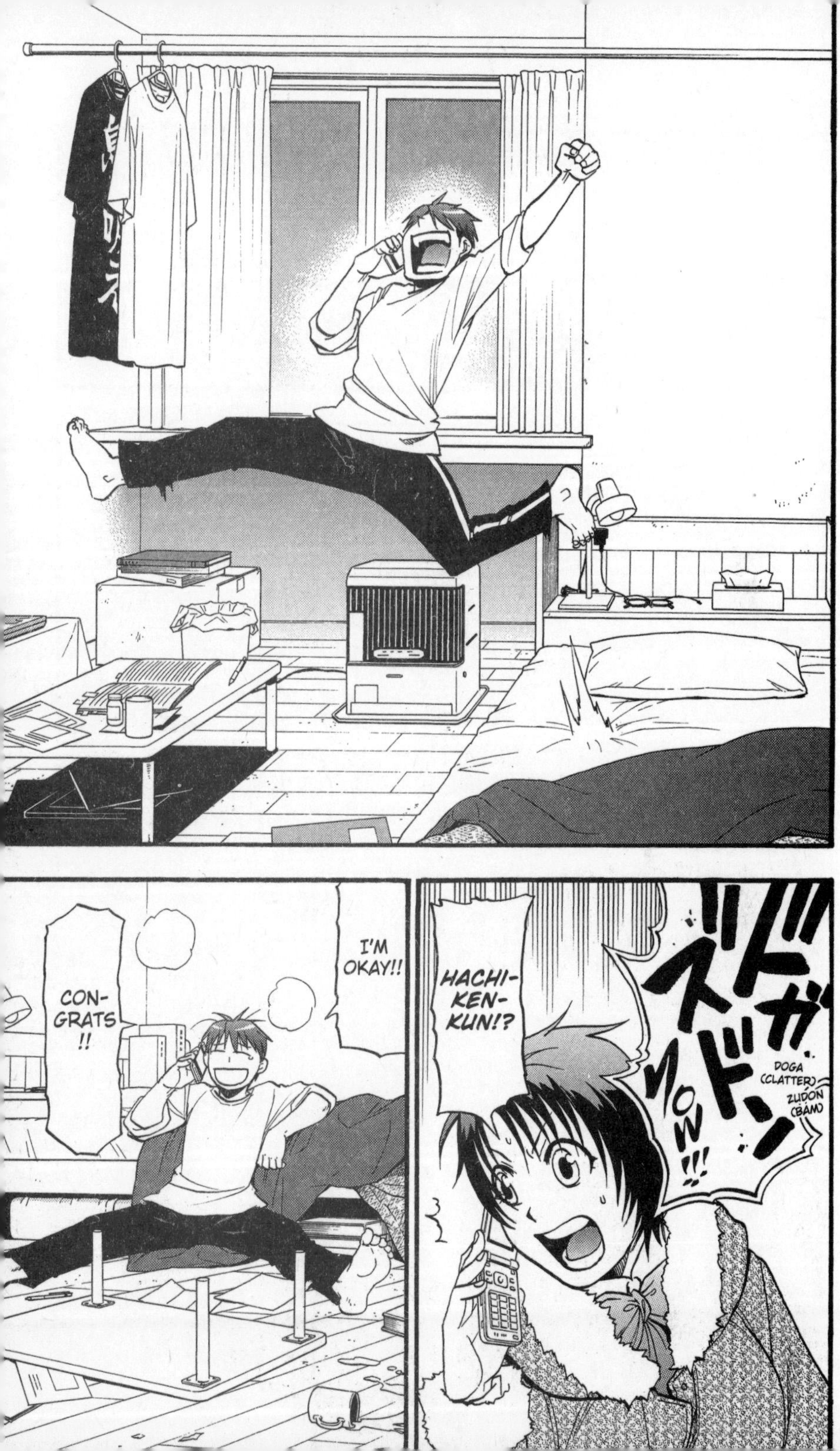
DOGA (CLATTER)
ZUDON (BAM)
OW!!!
HACHI-KEN-KUN!?
I'M OKAY!!
CON-GRATS!!

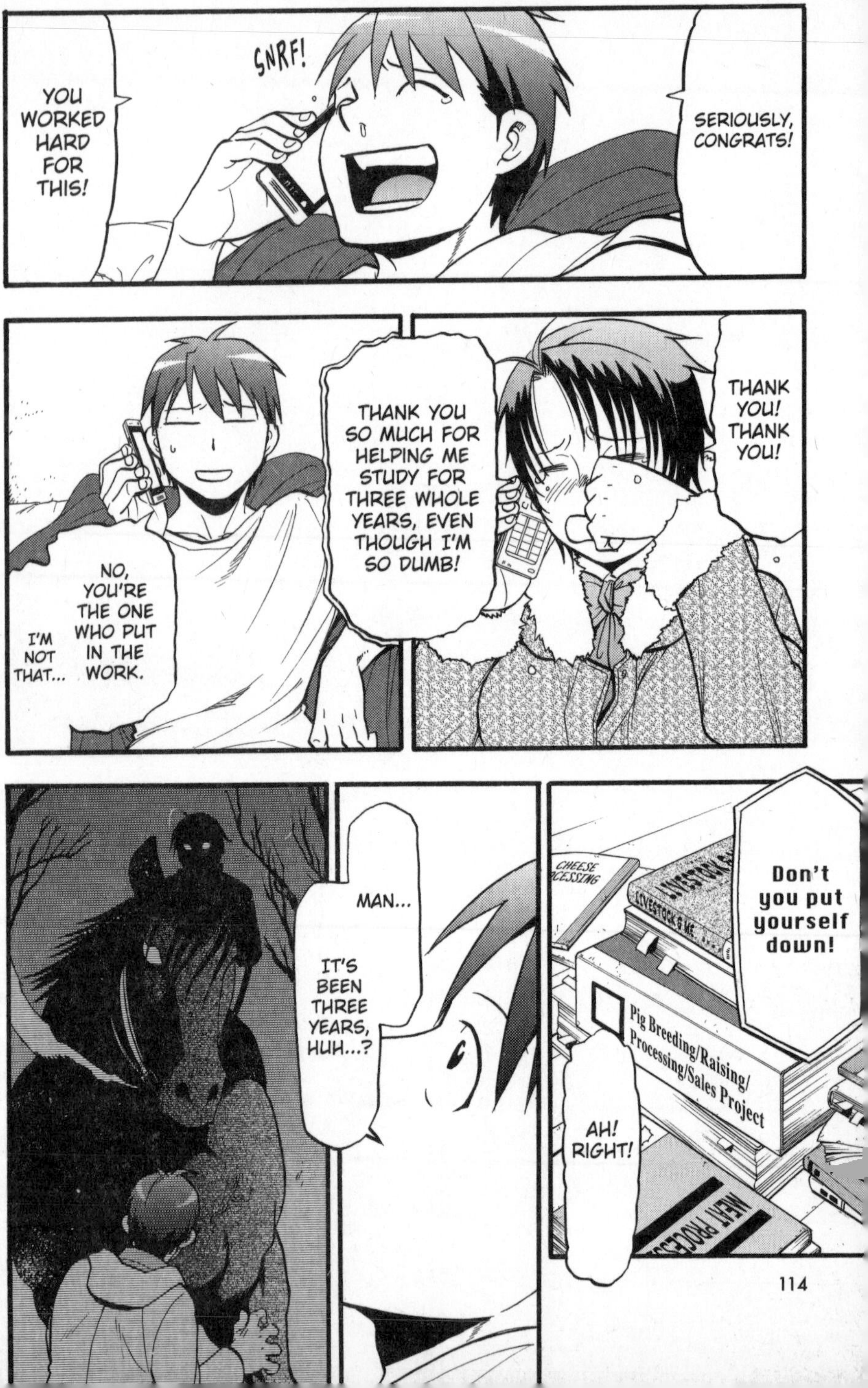
SERIOUSLY, CONGRATS!
SNRF!
YOU WORKED HARD FOR THIS!
THANK YOU! THANK YOU!
THANK YOU SO MUCH FOR HELPING ME STUDY FOR THREE WHOLE YEARS, EVEN THOUGH I'M SO DUMB!
NO, YOU'RE THE ONE WHO PUT IN THE WORK.
I'M NOT THAT...
Don't you put yourself down!
CHEESE PROCESSING
LIVESTOCK & ME
Pig Breeding/Raising/Processing/Sales Project
MAN...
IT'S BEEN THREE YEARS, HUH...?
AH! RIGHT!

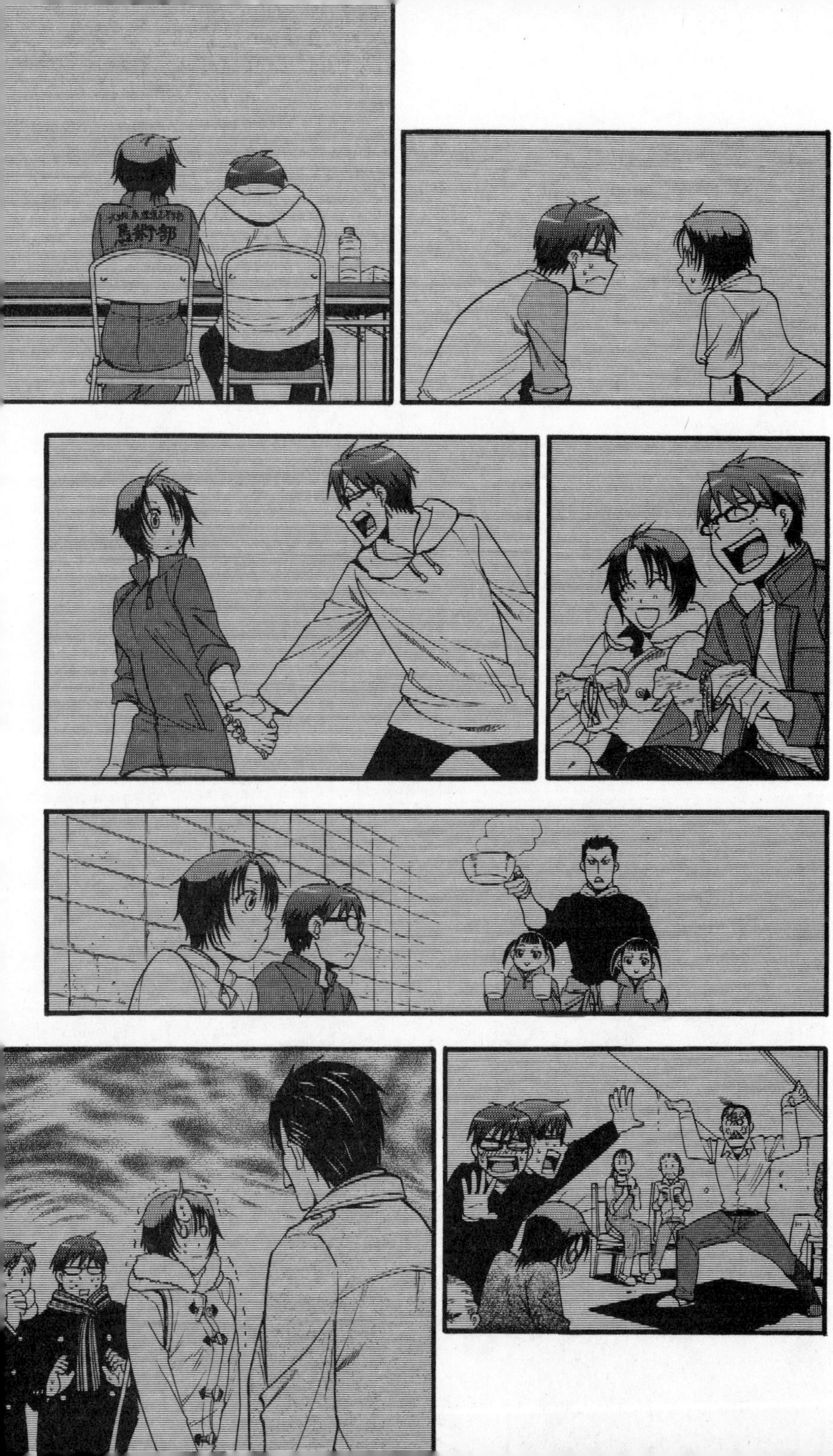
美術部

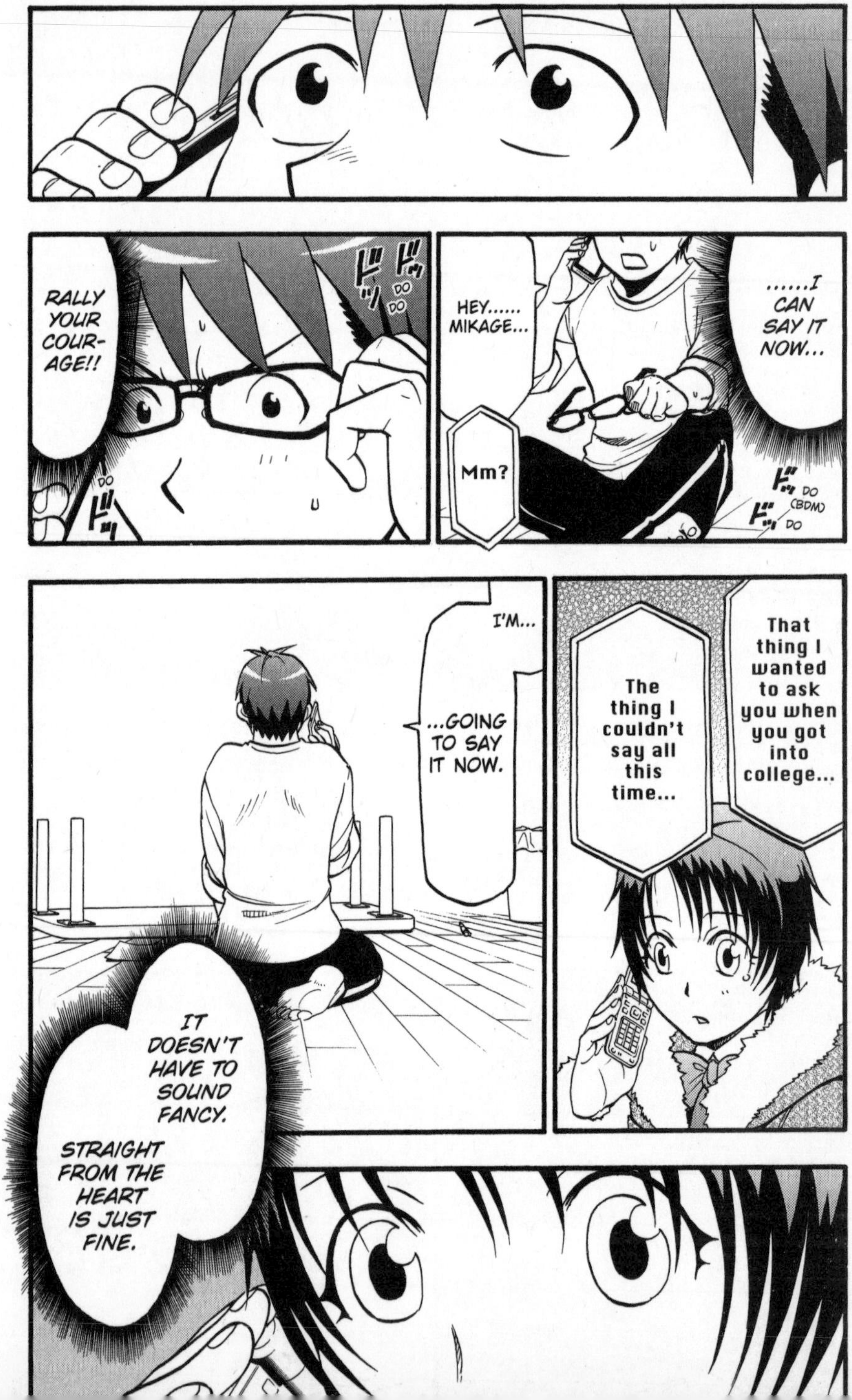
......I CAN SAY IT NOW...
HEY...... MIKAGE...
Mm?
DO
(BDM)
DO
RALLY YOUR COURAGE!!
DO
DO
DO
That thing I wanted to ask you when you got into college...
The thing I couldn't say all this time...
I'M...
...GOING TO SAY IT NOW.
IT DOESN'T HAVE TO SOUND FANCY.
STRAIGHT FROM THE HEART IS JUST FINE.

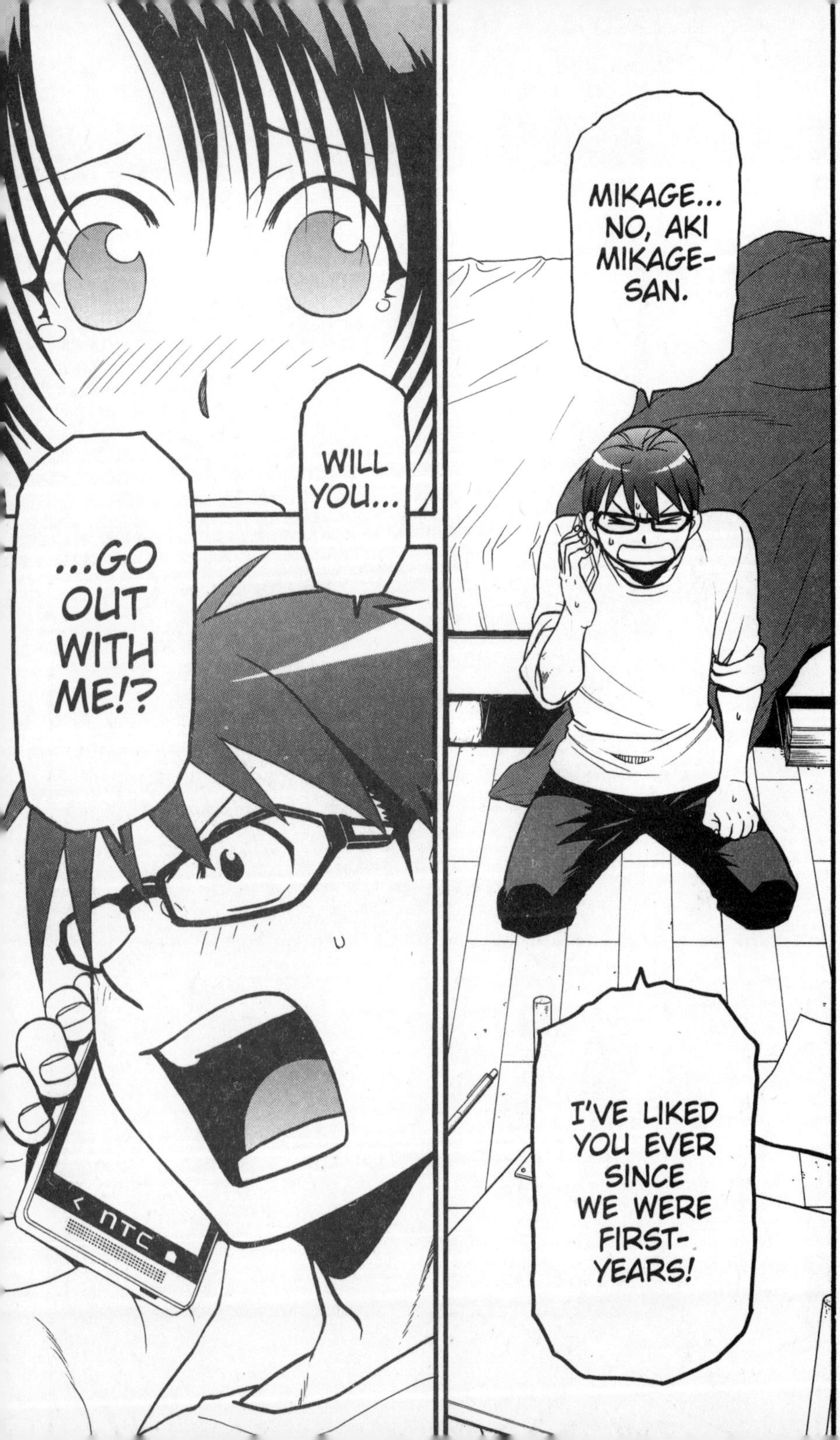
MIKAGE... NO, AKI MIKAGE-SAN.
I'VE LIKED YOU EVER SINCE WE WERE FIRST-YEARS!
WILL YOU...
...GO OUT WITH ME!?

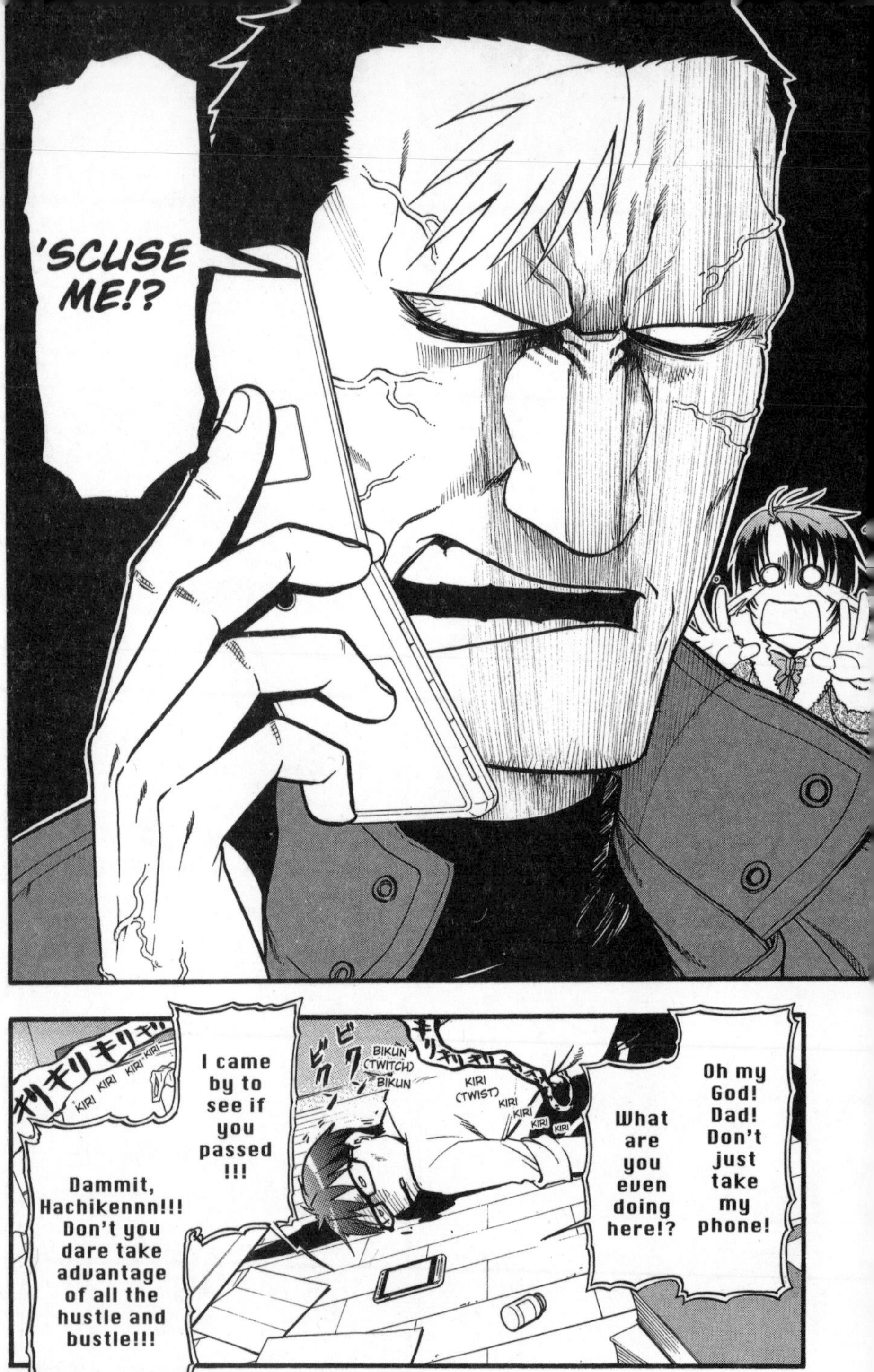
'SCUSE ME!?
Oh my God! Dad! Don't just take my phone!
What are you even doing here!?
KIRI (TWIST) KIRI KIRI KIRI KIRI
BIKUN (TWITCH) BIKUN
I came by to see if you passed!!!
KIRI KIRI KIRI KIRI
Dammit, Hachikennn!!! Don't you dare take advantage of all the hustle and bustle!!!

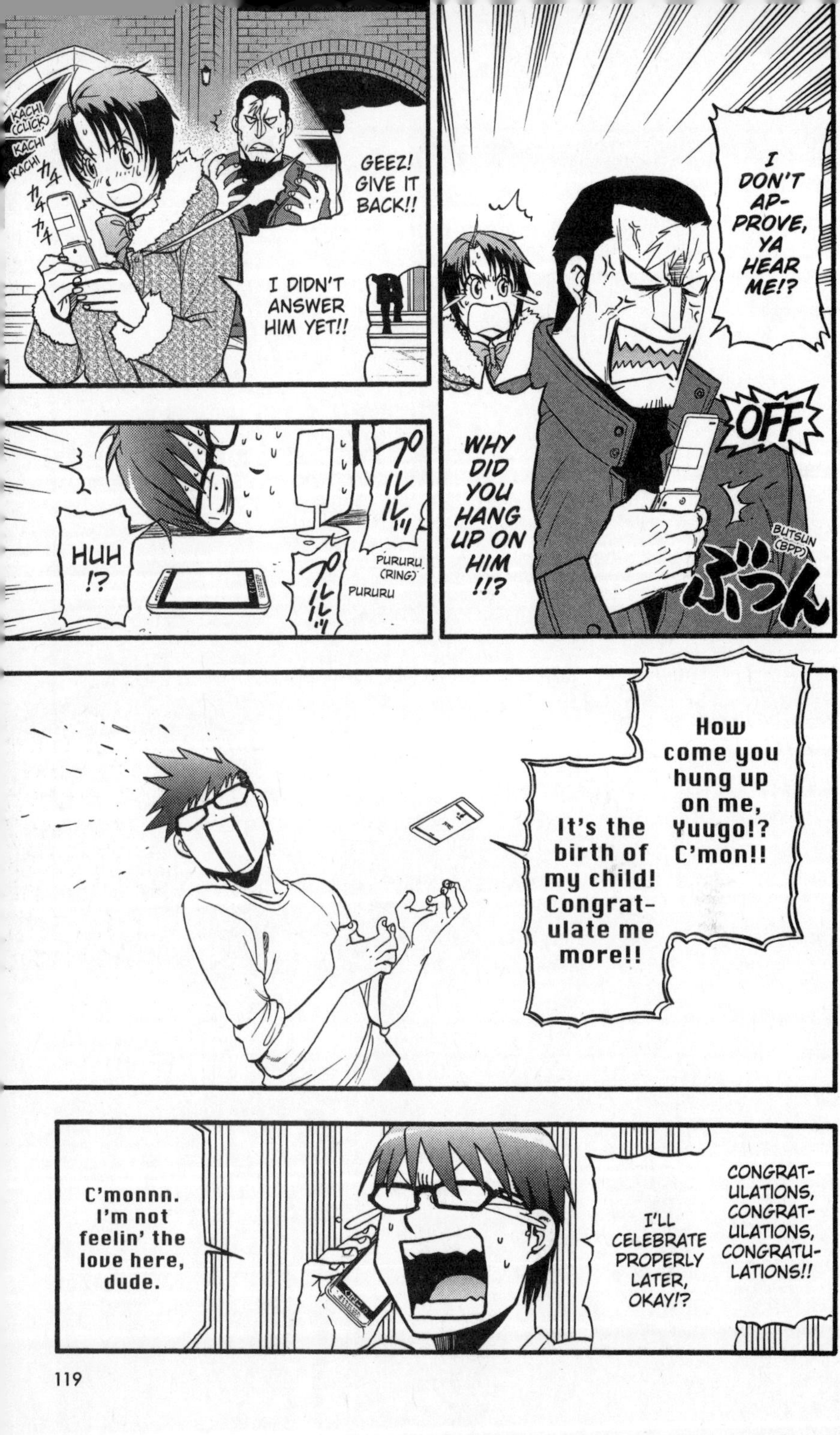
I DON'T AP-PROVE, YA HEAR ME!?
OFF
WHY DID YOU HANG UP ON HIM!!?
BUTSUN (BPP)
ぶつん
GEEZ! GIVE IT BACK!!
KACHI (CLICK) KACHI KACHI
カチカチカチ
I DIDN'T ANSWER HIM YET!!
プルルッ
PURURU (RING)
プルルッ
PURURU
HUH!?
How come you hung up on me, Yuugo!? C'mon!!
It's the birth of my child! Congrat-ulate me more!!
CONGRAT-ULATIONS, CONGRAT-ULATIONS, CONGRATU-LATIONS!!
I'LL CELEBRATE PROPERLY LATER, OKAY!?
C'monnn. I'm not feelin' the love here, dude.

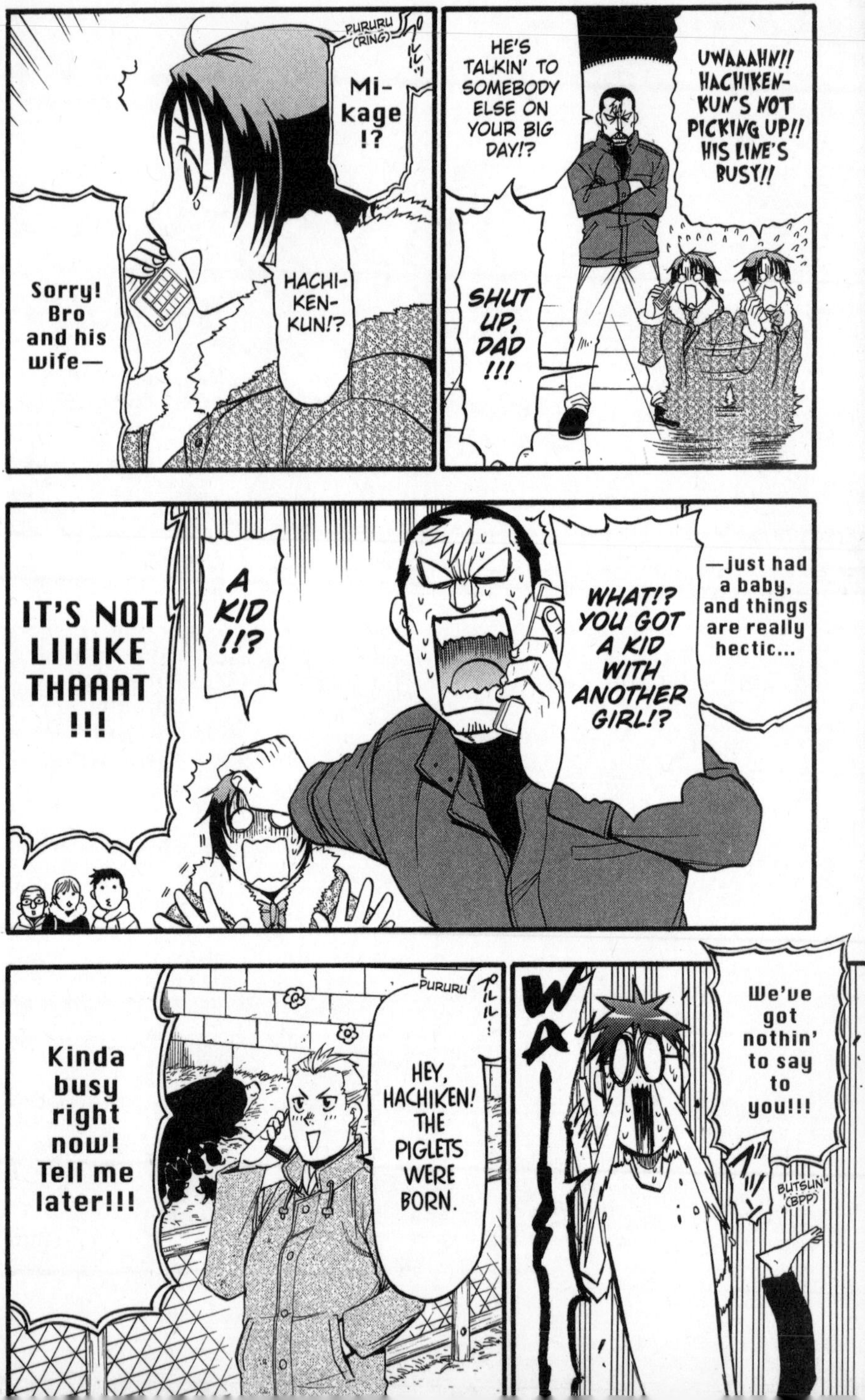
UWAAAHN!! HACHIKEN-KUN'S NOT PICKING UP!! HIS LINE'S BUSY!!
HE'S TALKIN' TO SOMEBODY ELSE ON YOUR BIG DAY!?
SHUT UP, DAD!!!
PURURU (RING)
Mi-kage!?
HACHI-KEN-KUN!?
Sorry! Bro and his wife—
—just had a baby, and things are really hectic...
WHAT!? YOU GOT A KID WITH ANOTHER GIRL!?
A KID!!?
IT'S NOT LIIIIKE THAAAT!!!
We've got nothin' to say to you!!!
BUTSUN (BPP)
PURURU
HEY, HACHIKEN! THE PIGLETS WERE BORN.
Kinda busy right now! Tell me later!!!

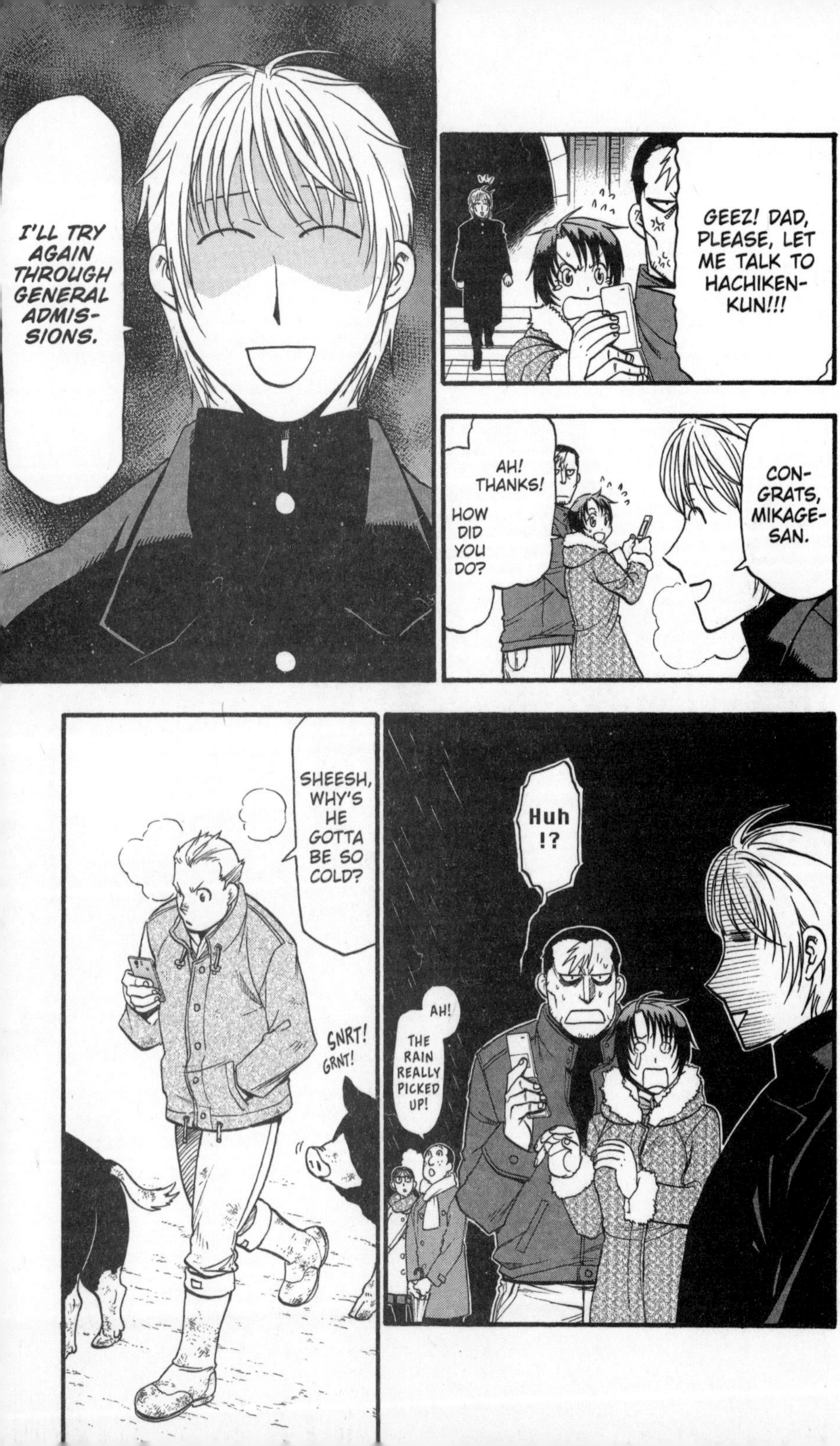
GEEZ! DAD, PLEASE, LET ME TALK TO HACHIKEN-KUN!!!
CON-GRATS, MIKAGE-SAN.
AH! THANKS!
HOW DID YOU DO?
I'LL TRY AGAIN THROUGH GENERAL ADMIS-SIONS.
Huh !?
AH!
THE RAIN REALLY PICKED UP!
SHEESH, WHY'S HE GOTTA BE SO COLD?
SNRT! GRNT!

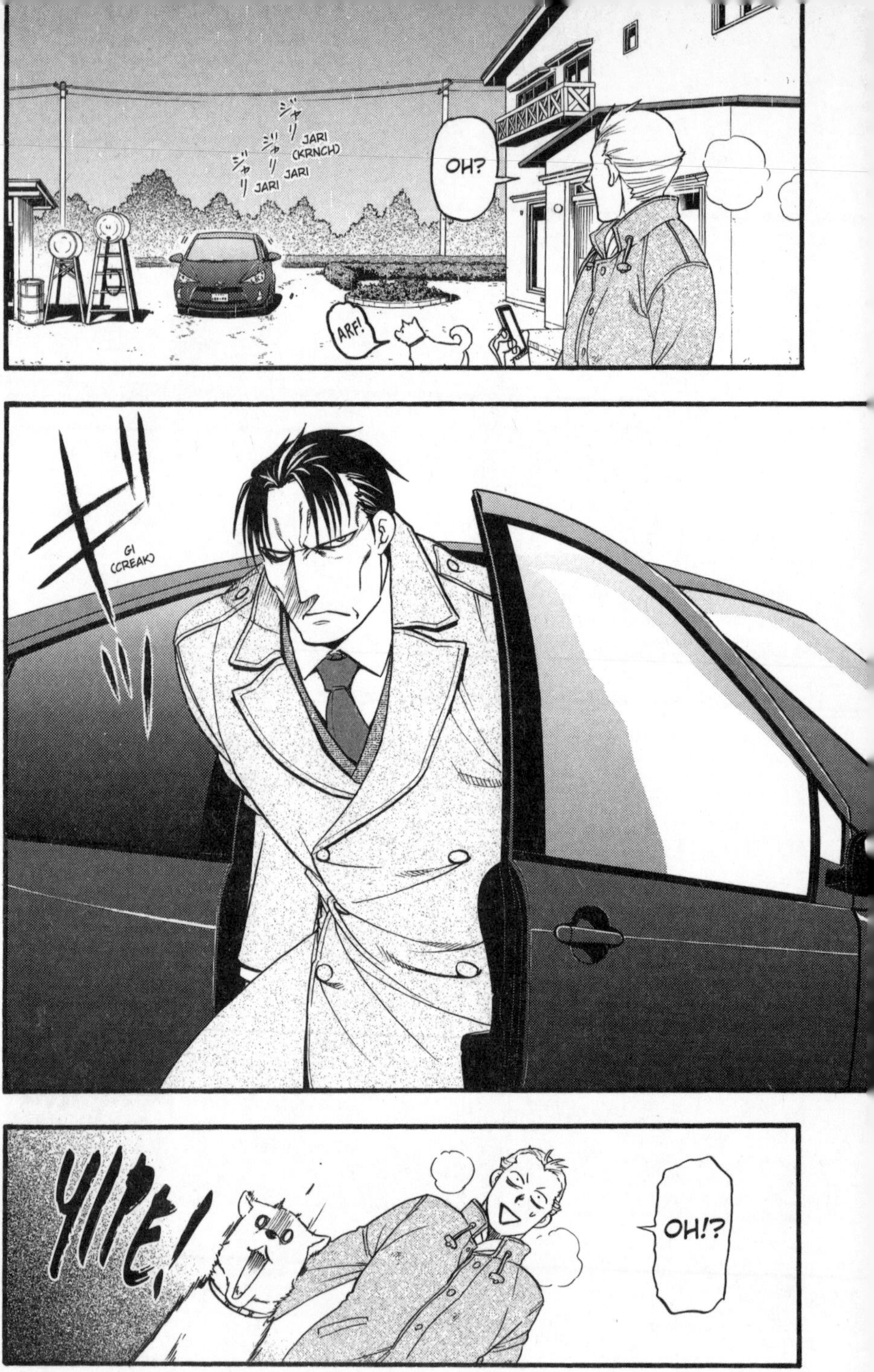
OH?
ジャリ JARI (KRNCH)
ジャリ JARI
ジャリ JARI
ARF!
ギリ GI (CREAK)
OH!?
YIPE!

Silver Spoon

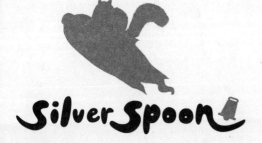

TOYONISHI-SENPAI

PROBABLY DOES
MARTIAL ARTS

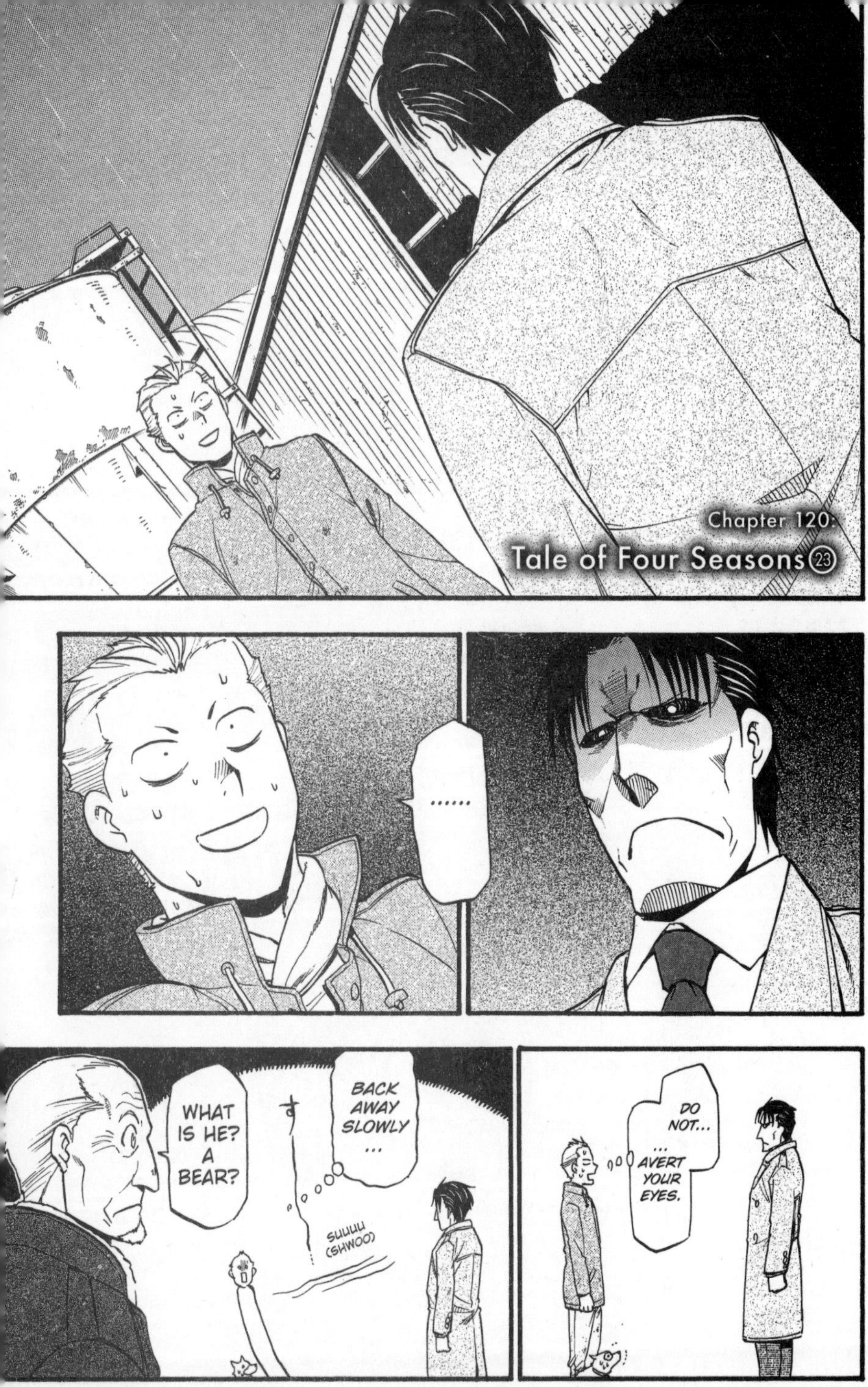
Chapter 120:
Tale of Four Seasons㉓
......
DO NOT... ...AVERT YOUR EYES.
BACK AWAY SLOWLY...
す
WHAT IS HE? A BEAR?
SUUUU (SHWOO)

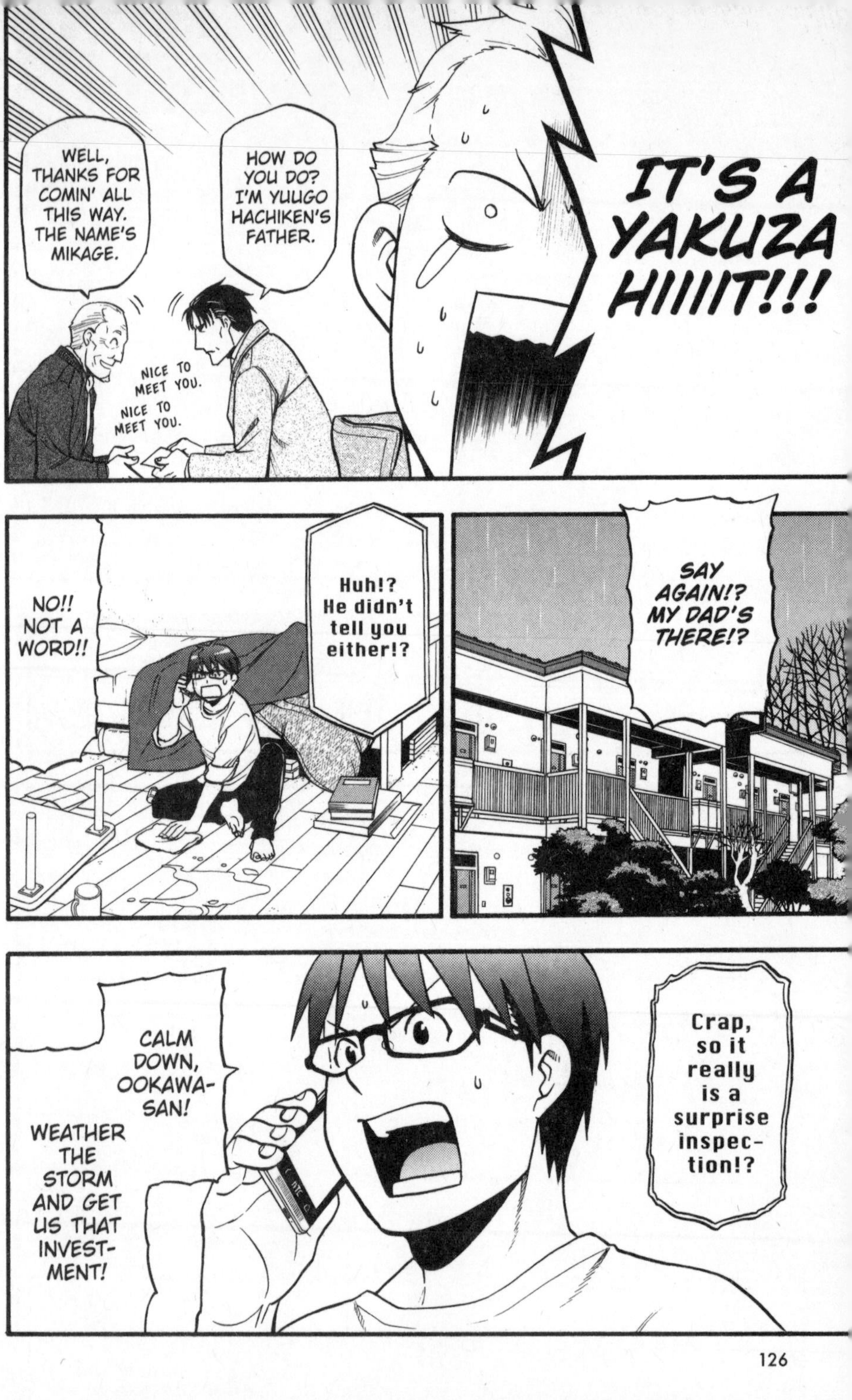
IT'S A YAKUZA HIIIIT!!!
HOW DO YOU DO? I'M YUUGO HACHIKEN'S FATHER.
WELL, THANKS FOR COMIN' ALL THIS WAY. THE NAME'S MIKAGE.
NICE TO MEET YOU.
NICE TO MEET YOU.
SAY AGAIN!? MY DAD'S THERE!?
Huh!? He didn't tell you either!?
NO!! NOT A WORD!!
Crap, so it really is a surprise inspection!?
CALM DOWN, OOKAWA-SAN!
WEATHER THE STORM AND GET US THAT INVESTMENT!

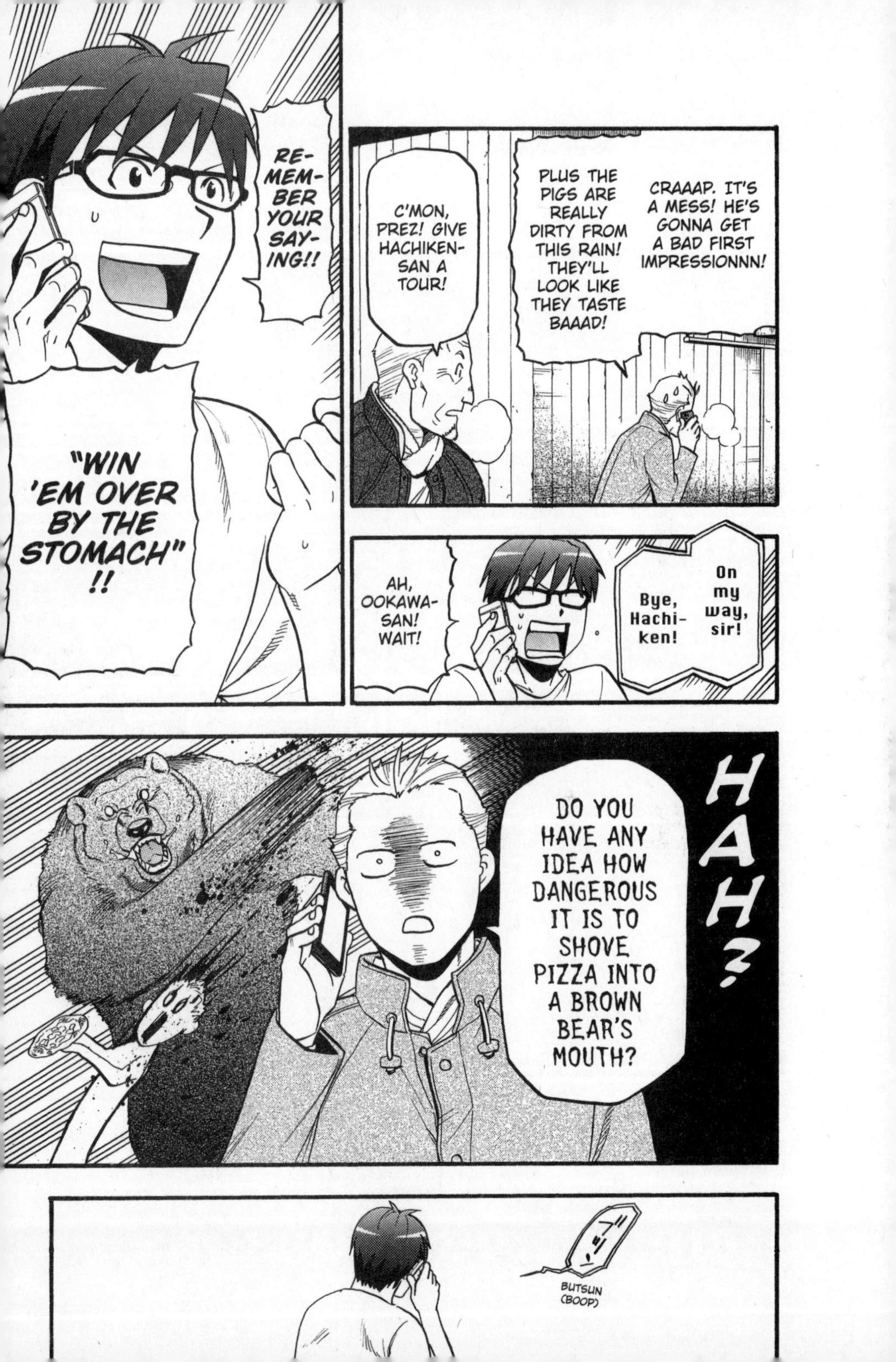
CRAAAP. IT'S A MESS! HE'S GONNA GET A BAD FIRST IMPRESSIONNN!
PLUS THE PIGS ARE REALLY DIRTY FROM THIS RAIN! THEY'LL LOOK LIKE THEY TASTE BAAAD!
C'MON, PREZ! GIVE HACHIKEN-SAN A TOUR!
On my way, sir!
Bye, Hachi-ken!
AH, OOKAWA-SAN! WAIT!
RE-MEM-BER YOUR SAY-ING!!
"WIN 'EM OVER BY THE STOMACH" !!
HAH?
DO YOU HAVE ANY IDEA HOW DANGEROUS IT IS TO SHOVE PIZZA INTO A BROWN BEAR'S MOUTH?
BUTSUN (BOOP)

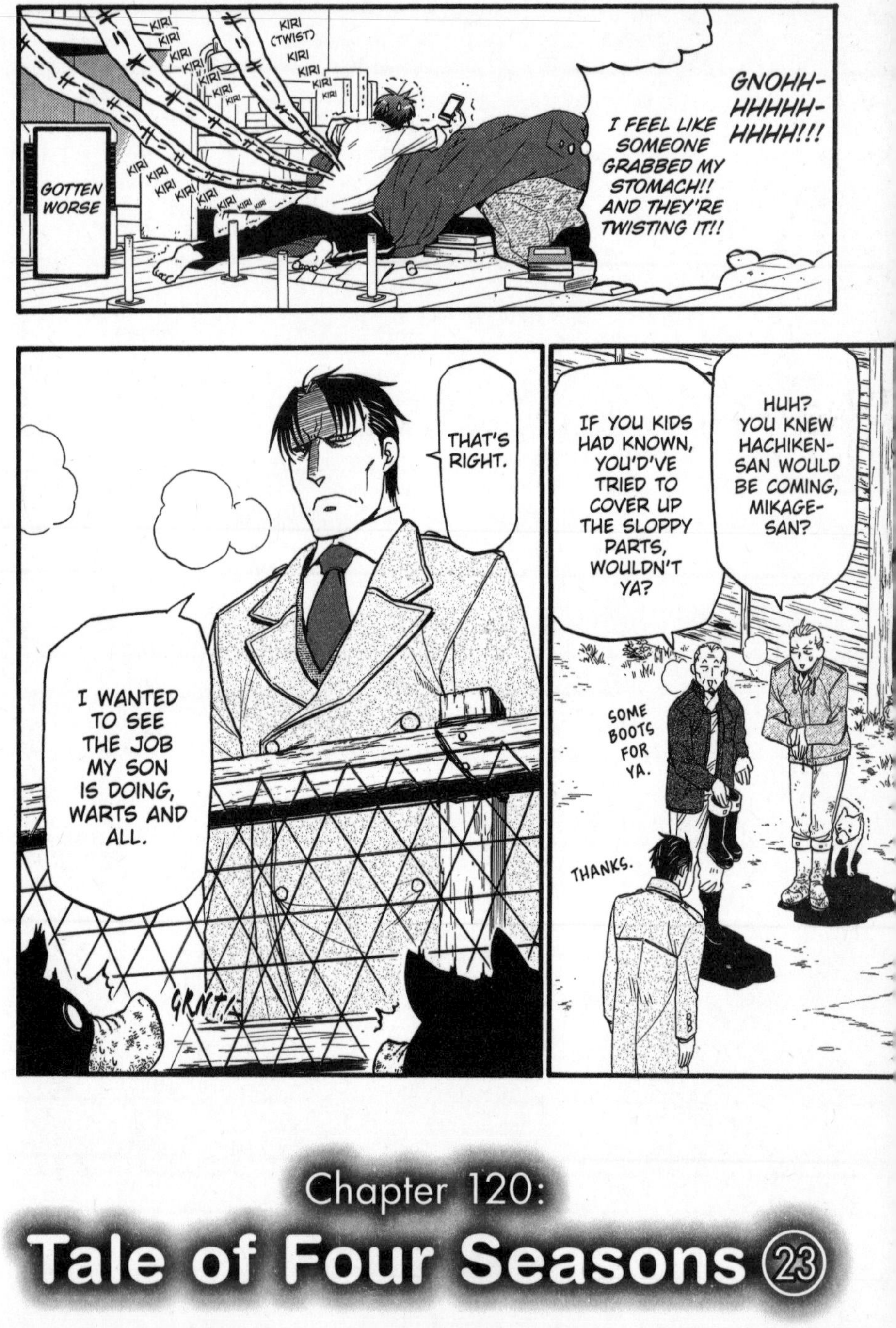
GNOHH-HHHHH-HHHH!!!
I FEEL LIKE SOMEONE GRABBED MY STOMACH!! AND THEY'RE TWISTING IT!!
KIRI (TWIST) KIRI KIRI KIRI
GOTTEN WORSE
HUH? YOU KNEW HACHIKEN-SAN WOULD BE COMING, MIKAGE-SAN?
IF YOU KIDS HAD KNOWN, YOU'D'VE TRIED TO COVER UP THE SLOPPY PARTS, WOULDN'T YA?
SOME BOOTS FOR YA.
THANKS.
THAT'S RIGHT.
I WANTED TO SEE THE JOB MY SON IS DOING, WARTS AND ALL.
GRNT!

Chapter 120: Tale of Four Seasons ㉓

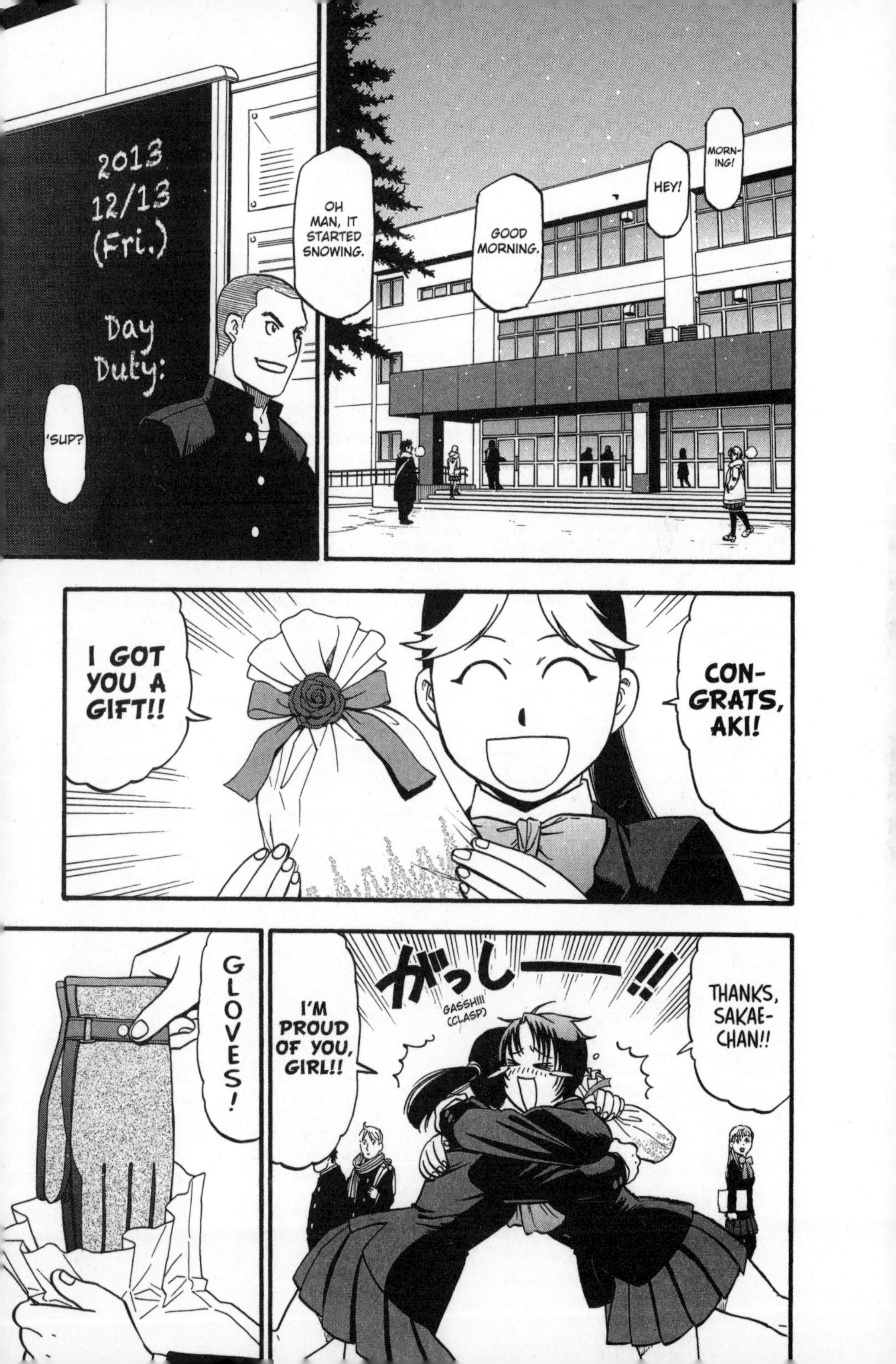
MORNING!
HEY!
GOOD MORNING.
OH MAN, IT STARTED SNOWING.
2013 12/13 (Fri.)
Day Duty:
'SUP?
CONGRATS, AKI!
I GOT YOU A GIFT!!
THANKS, SAKAE-CHAN!!
がっしー!!
GASSHIII (CLASP)
I'M PROUD OF YOU, GIRL!!
GLOVES!

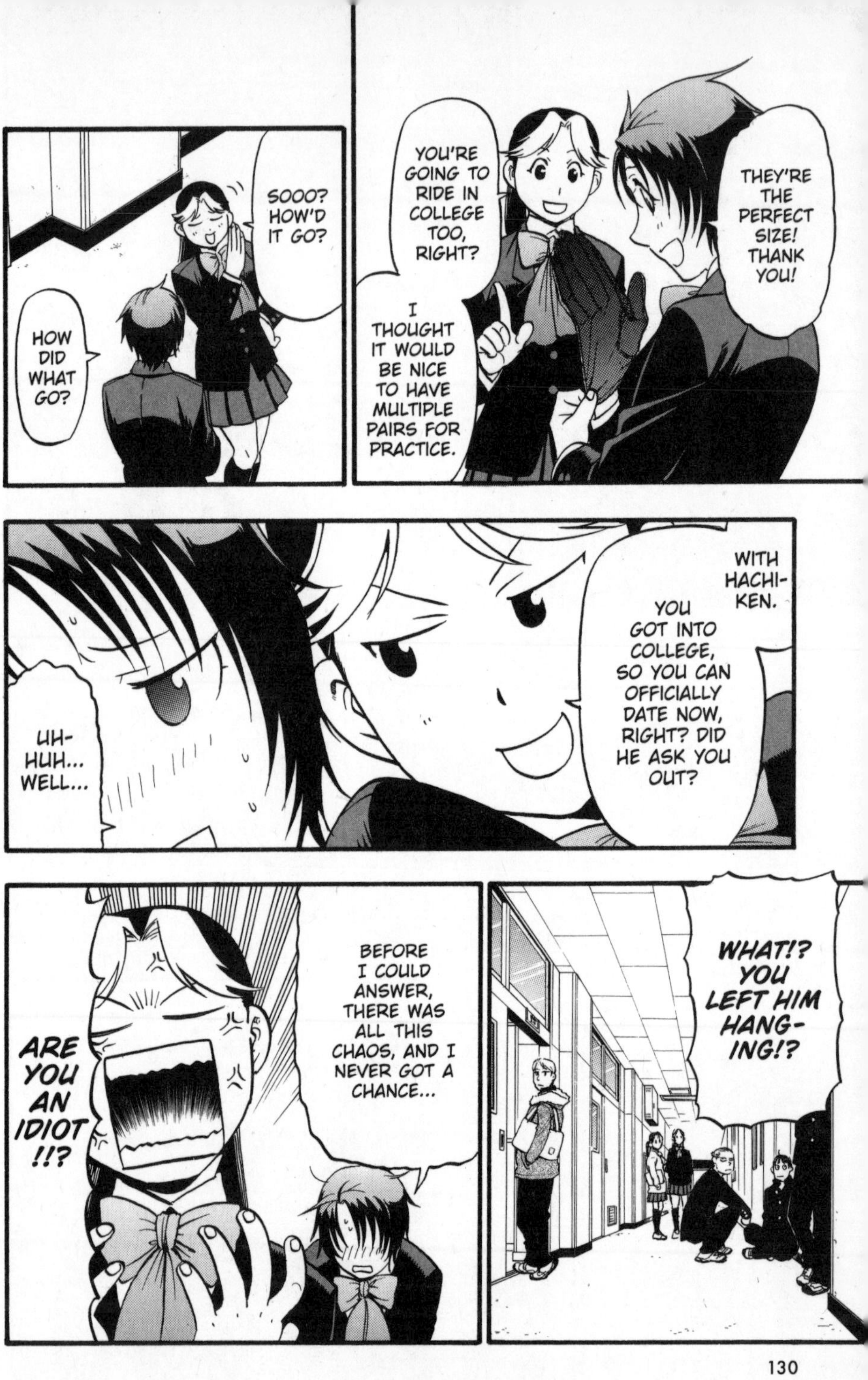
THEY'RE THE PERFECT SIZE! THANK YOU!
YOU'RE GOING TO RIDE IN COLLEGE TOO, RIGHT?
I THOUGHT IT WOULD BE NICE TO HAVE MULTIPLE PAIRS FOR PRACTICE.
SOOO? HOW'D IT GO?
HOW DID WHAT GO?
WITH HACHI-KEN.
YOU GOT INTO COLLEGE, SO YOU CAN OFFICIALLY DATE NOW, RIGHT? DID HE ASK YOU OUT?
UH-HUH... WELL...
WHAT!? YOU LEFT HIM HANGING!?
BEFORE I COULD ANSWER, THERE WAS ALL THIS CHAOS, AND I NEVER GOT A CHANCE...
ARE YOU AN IDIOT!!?

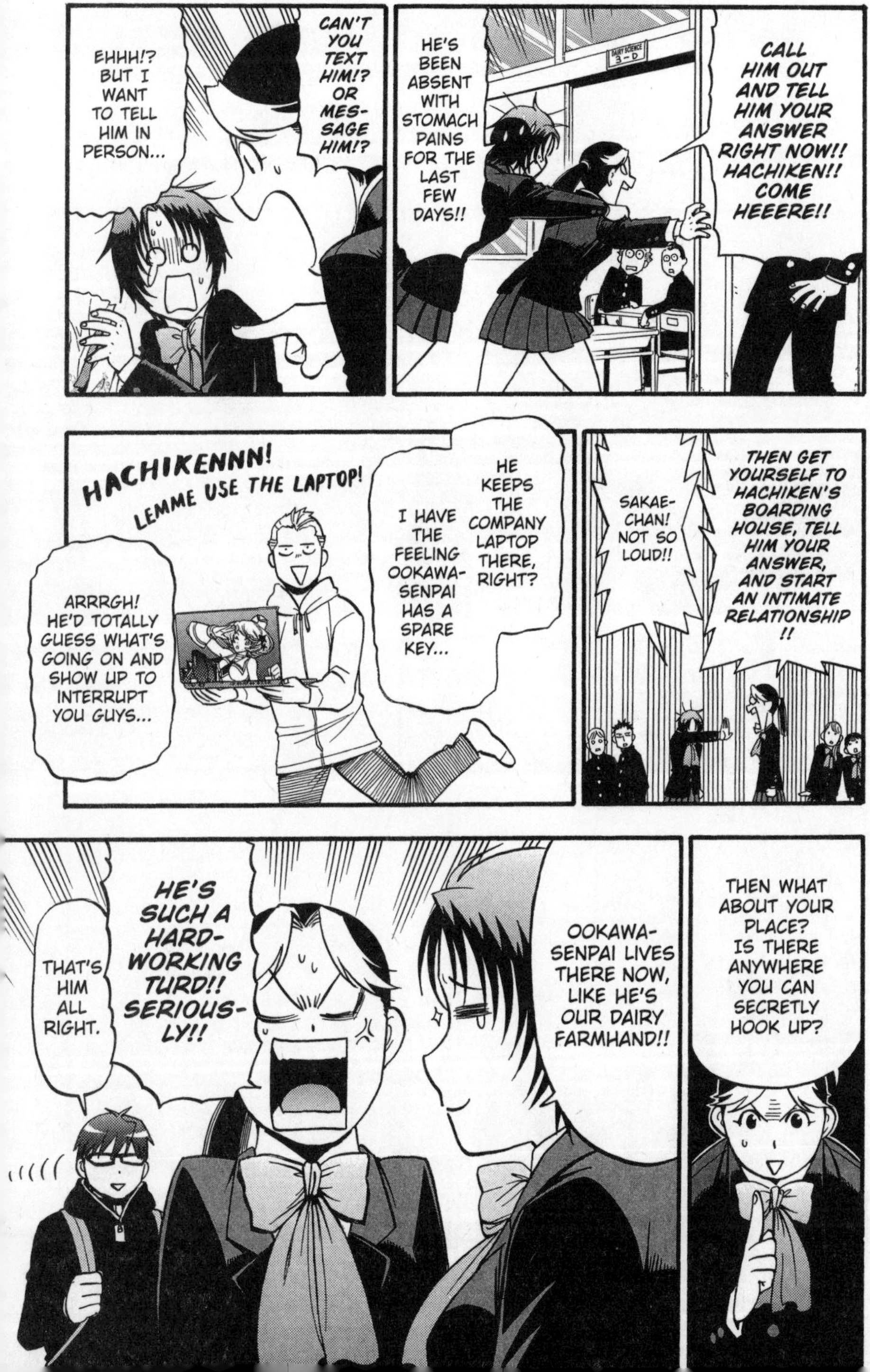
DAIRY SCIENCE 3-D
CALL HIM OUT AND TELL HIM YOUR ANSWER RIGHT NOW!! HACHIKEN!! COME HEEERE!!
HE'S BEEN ABSENT WITH STOMACH PAINS FOR THE LAST FEW DAYS!!
CAN'T YOU TEXT HIM!? OR MES-SAGE HIM!?
EHHH!? BUT I WANT TO TELL HIM IN PERSON...
THEN GET YOURSELF TO HACHIKEN'S BOARDING HOUSE, TELL HIM YOUR ANSWER, AND START AN INTIMATE RELATIONSHIP!!
SAKAE-CHAN! NOT SO LOUD!!
HE KEEPS THE COMPANY LAPTOP THERE, RIGHT?
I HAVE THE FEELING OOKAWA-SENPAI HAS A SPARE KEY...
HACHIKENNN! LEMME USE THE LAPTOP!
ARRRGH! HE'D TOTALLY GUESS WHAT'S GOING ON AND SHOW UP TO INTERRUPT YOU GUYS...
THEN WHAT ABOUT YOUR PLACE? IS THERE ANYWHERE YOU CAN SECRETLY HOOK UP?
OOKAWA-SENPAI LIVES THERE NOW, LIKE HE'S OUR DAIRY FARMHAND!!
HE'S SUCH A HARD-WORKING TURD!! SERIOUS-LY!!
THAT'S HIM ALL RIGHT.

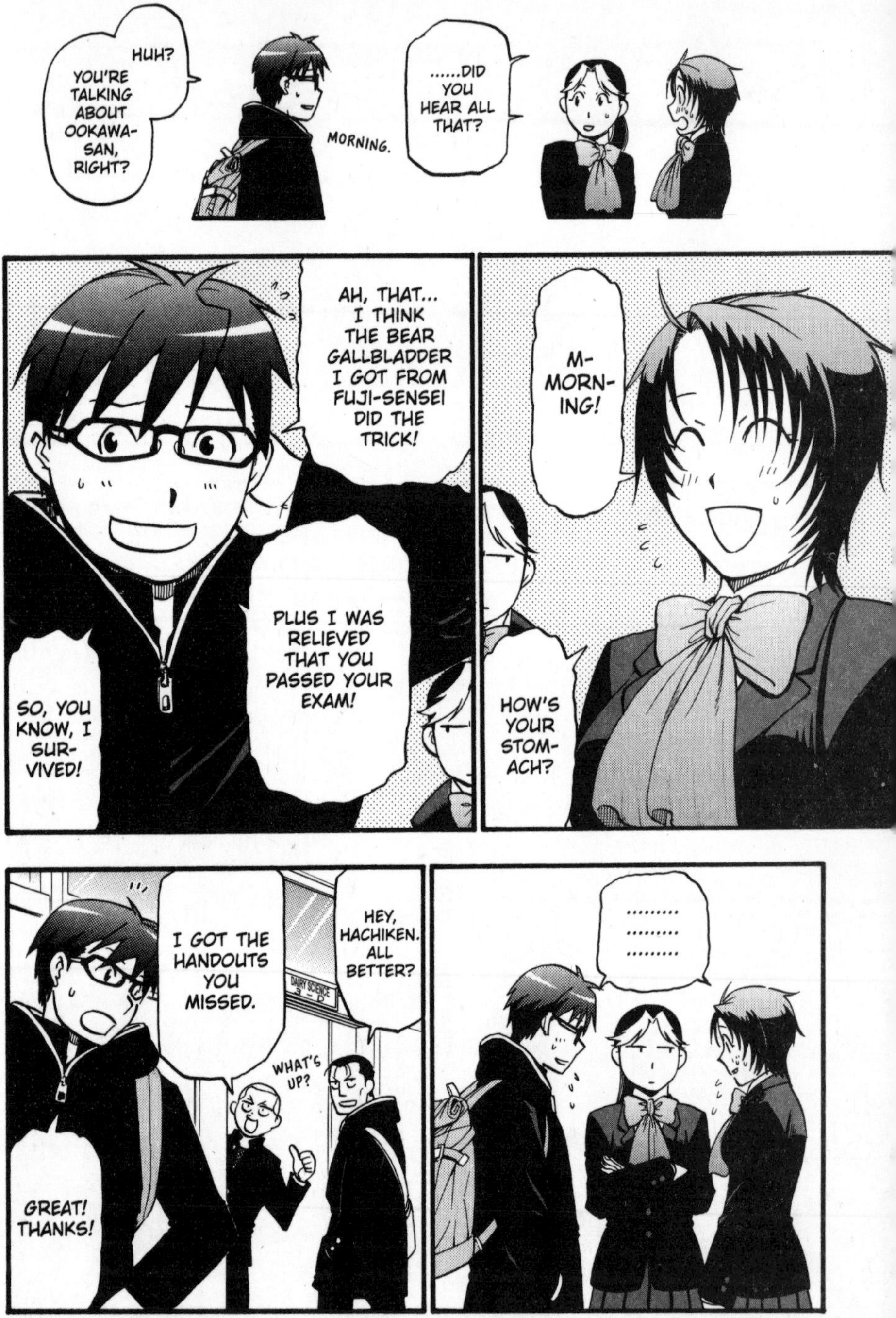
......DID YOU HEAR ALL THAT?
MORNING.
HUH? YOU'RE TALKING ABOUT OOKAWA-SAN, RIGHT?
M-MORNING!
HOW'S YOUR STOMACH?
AH, THAT... I THINK THE BEAR GALLBLADDER I GOT FROM FUJI-SENSEI DID THE TRICK!
PLUS I WAS RELIEVED THAT YOU PASSED YOUR EXAM!
SO, YOU KNOW, I SURVIVED!
....
....
....
HEY, HACHIKEN. ALL BETTER?
DAIRY SCIENCE
I GOT THE HANDOUTS YOU MISSED.
WHAT'S UP?
GREAT! THANKS!

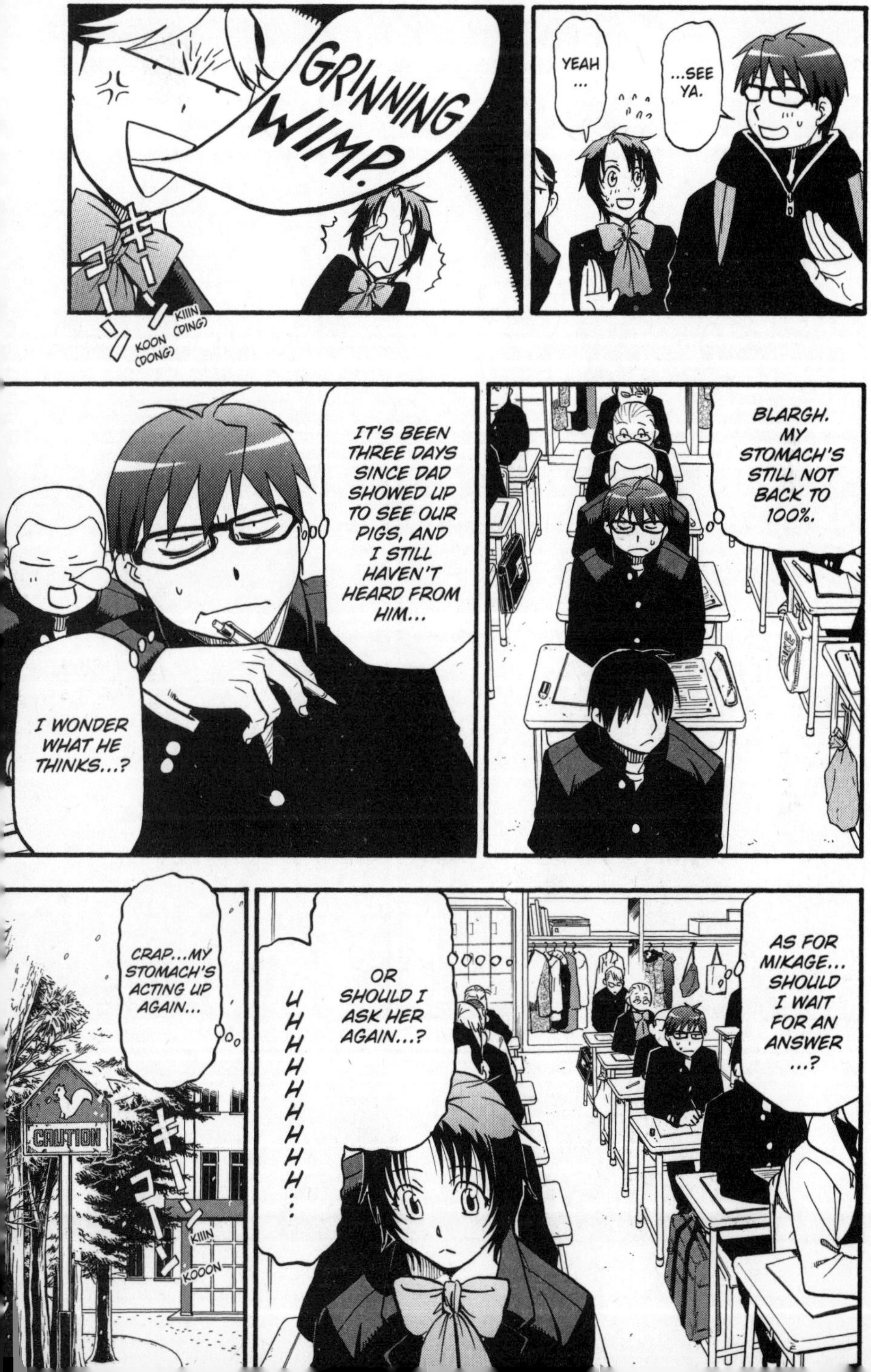
...SEE YA.
YEAH ...
GRINNING WIMP?
KIIN (DING)
KOON (DONG)
BLARGH. MY STOMACH'S STILL NOT BACK TO 100%.
IT'S BEEN THREE DAYS SINCE DAD SHOWED UP TO SEE OUR PIGS, AND I STILL HAVEN'T HEARD FROM HIM...
I WONDER WHAT HE THINKS...?
AS FOR MIKAGE... SHOULD I WAIT FOR AN ANSWER ...?
OR SHOULD I ASK HER AGAIN...?
UHHHHHHHH...
CRAP...MY STOMACH'S ACTING UP AGAIN...
CAUTION
KIIN
KOOON

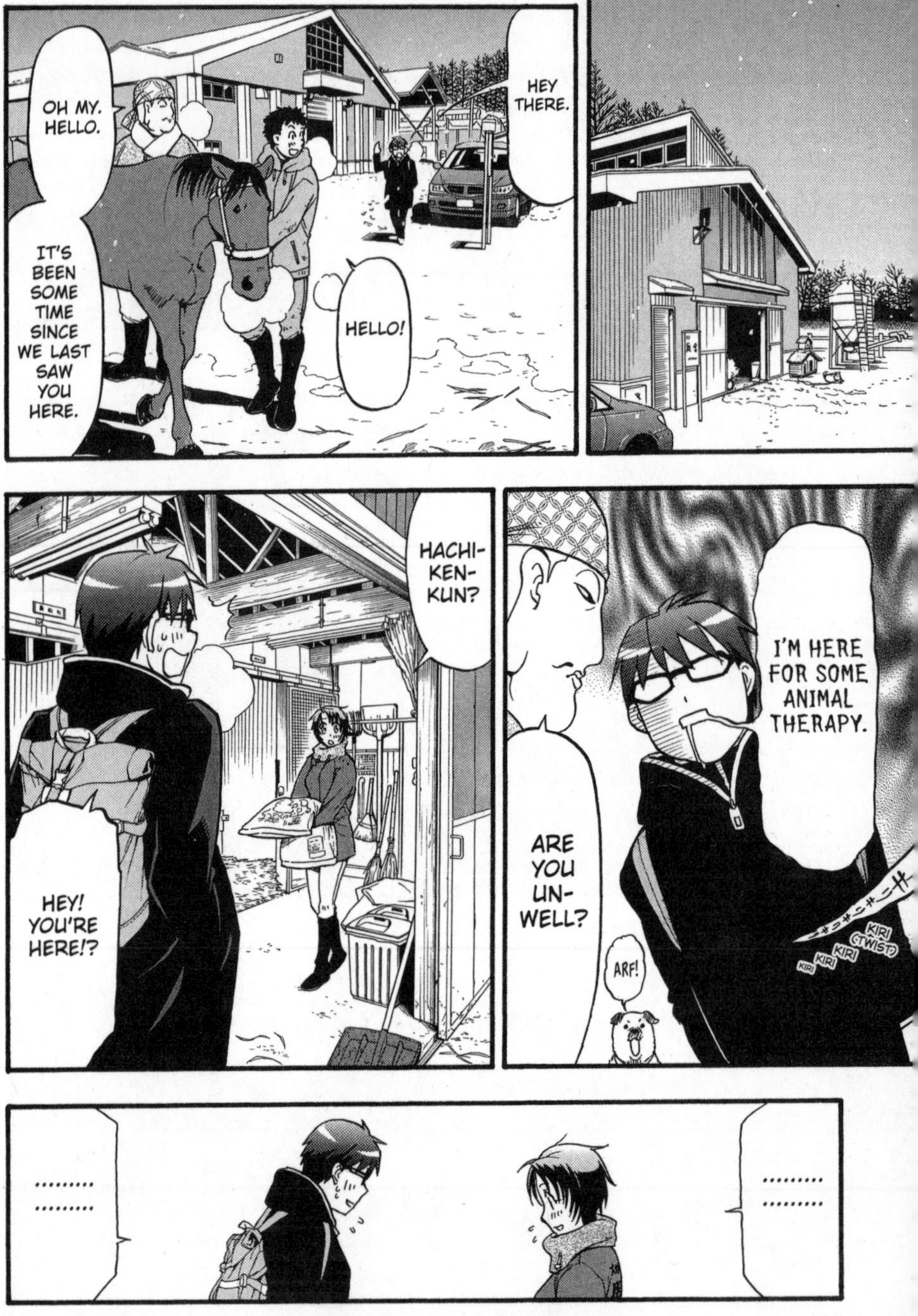
HEY THERE.
OH MY. HELLO.
HELLO!
IT'S BEEN SOME TIME SINCE WE LAST SAW YOU HERE.
I'M HERE FOR SOME ANIMAL THERAPY.
ARE YOU UN-WELL?
KIRI (TWIST) KIRI KIRI KIRI
ARF!
HACHI-KEN-KUN?
HEY! YOU'RE HERE!?
....
....
....
....

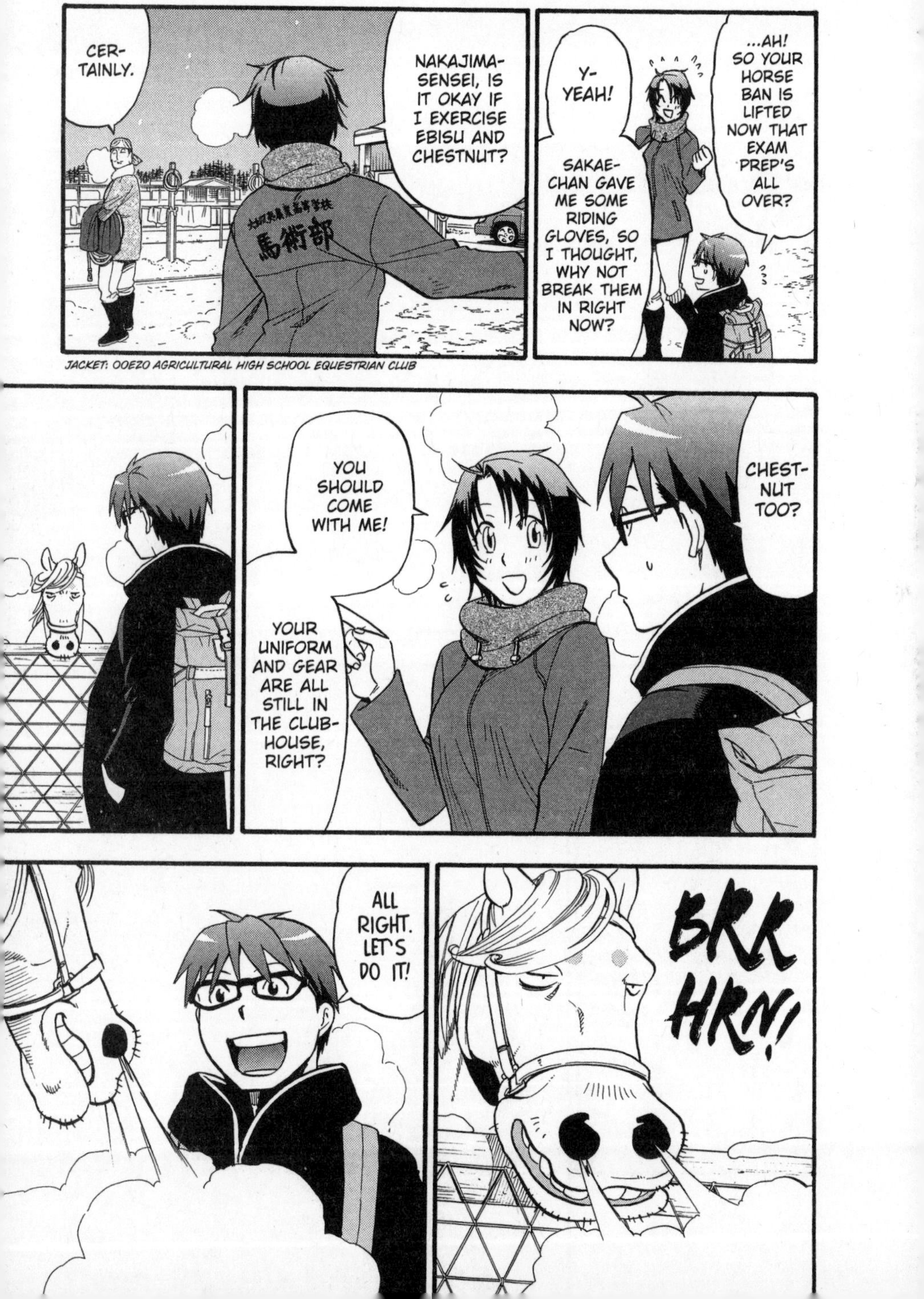
...AH! SO YOUR HORSE BAN IS LIFTED NOW THAT EXAM PREP'S ALL OVER?
Y-YEAH!
SAKAE-CHAN GAVE ME SOME RIDING GLOVES, SO I THOUGHT, WHY NOT BREAK THEM IN RIGHT NOW?
NAKAJIMA-SENSEI, IS IT OKAY IF I EXERCISE EBISU AND CHESTNUT?
馬術部
CER-TAINLY.
JACKET: OOEZO AGRICULTURAL HIGH SCHOOL EQUESTRIAN CLUB
CHEST-NUT TOO?
YOU SHOULD COME WITH ME!
YOUR UNIFORM AND GEAR ARE ALL STILL IN THE CLUB-HOUSE, RIGHT?
BRR HRN!
ALL RIGHT. LET'S DO IT!

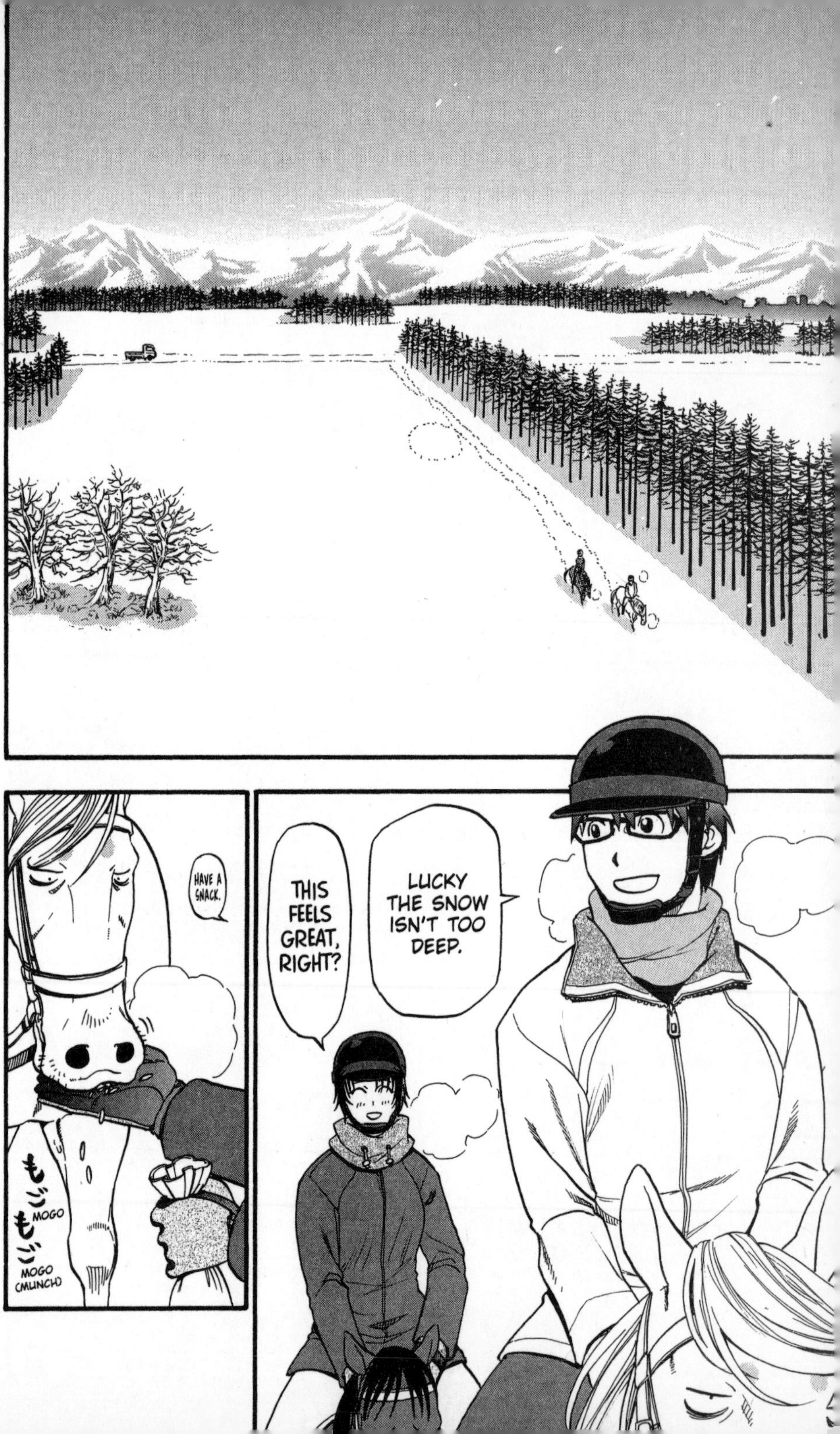
LUCKY THE SNOW ISN'T TOO DEEP.
THIS FEELS GREAT, RIGHT?
HAVE A SNACK.
もごもご MOGO MOGO (MUNCH)

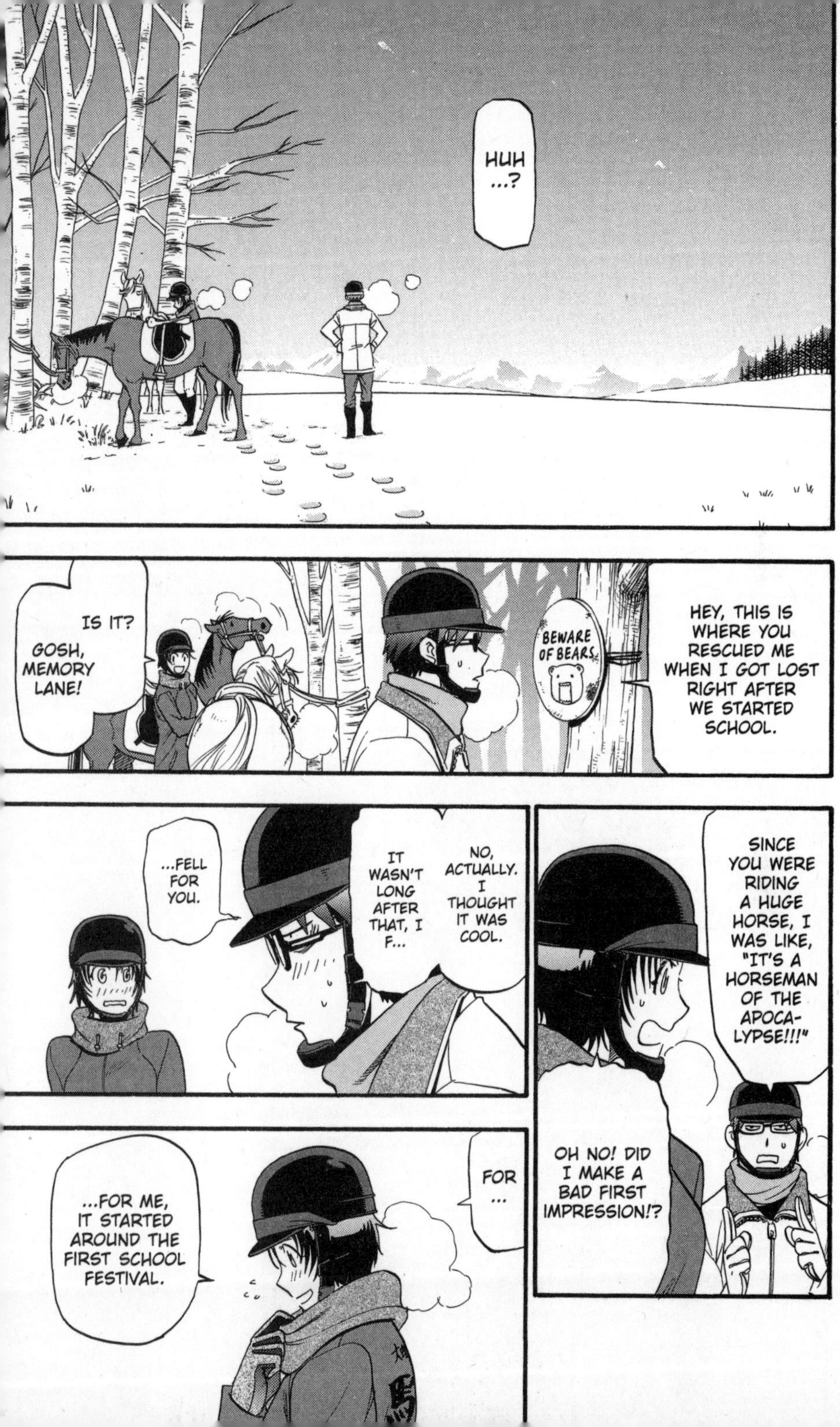
HUH ...?
HEY, THIS IS WHERE YOU RESCUED ME WHEN I GOT LOST RIGHT AFTER WE STARTED SCHOOL.
BEWARE OF BEARS
IS IT? GOSH, MEMORY LANE!
SINCE YOU WERE RIDING A HUGE HORSE, I WAS LIKE, "IT'S A HORSEMAN OF THE APOCA-LYPSE!!!"
OH NO! DID I MAKE A BAD FIRST IMPRESSION!?
NO, ACTUALLY. I THOUGHT IT WAS COOL.
IT WASN'T LONG AFTER THAT, I F...
...FELL FOR YOU.
FOR ...
...FOR ME, IT STARTED AROUND THE FIRST SCHOOL FESTIVAL.

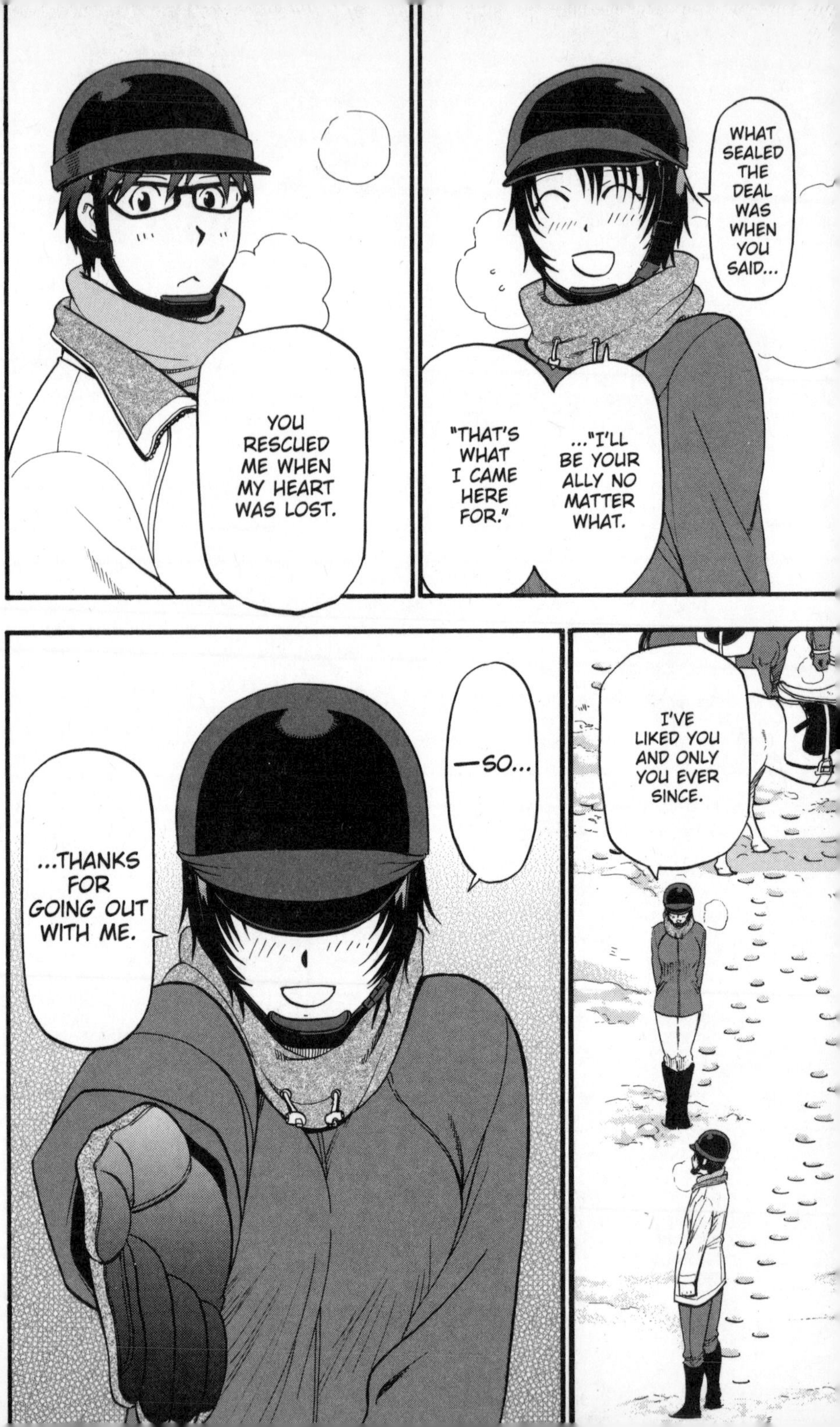
WHAT SEALED THE DEAL WAS WHEN YOU SAID...
..."I'LL BE YOUR ALLY NO MATTER WHAT.
"THAT'S WHAT I CAME HERE FOR."
YOU RESCUED ME WHEN MY HEART WAS LOST.
I'VE LIKED YOU AND ONLY YOU EVER SINCE.
—SO...
...THANKS FOR GOING OUT WITH ME.

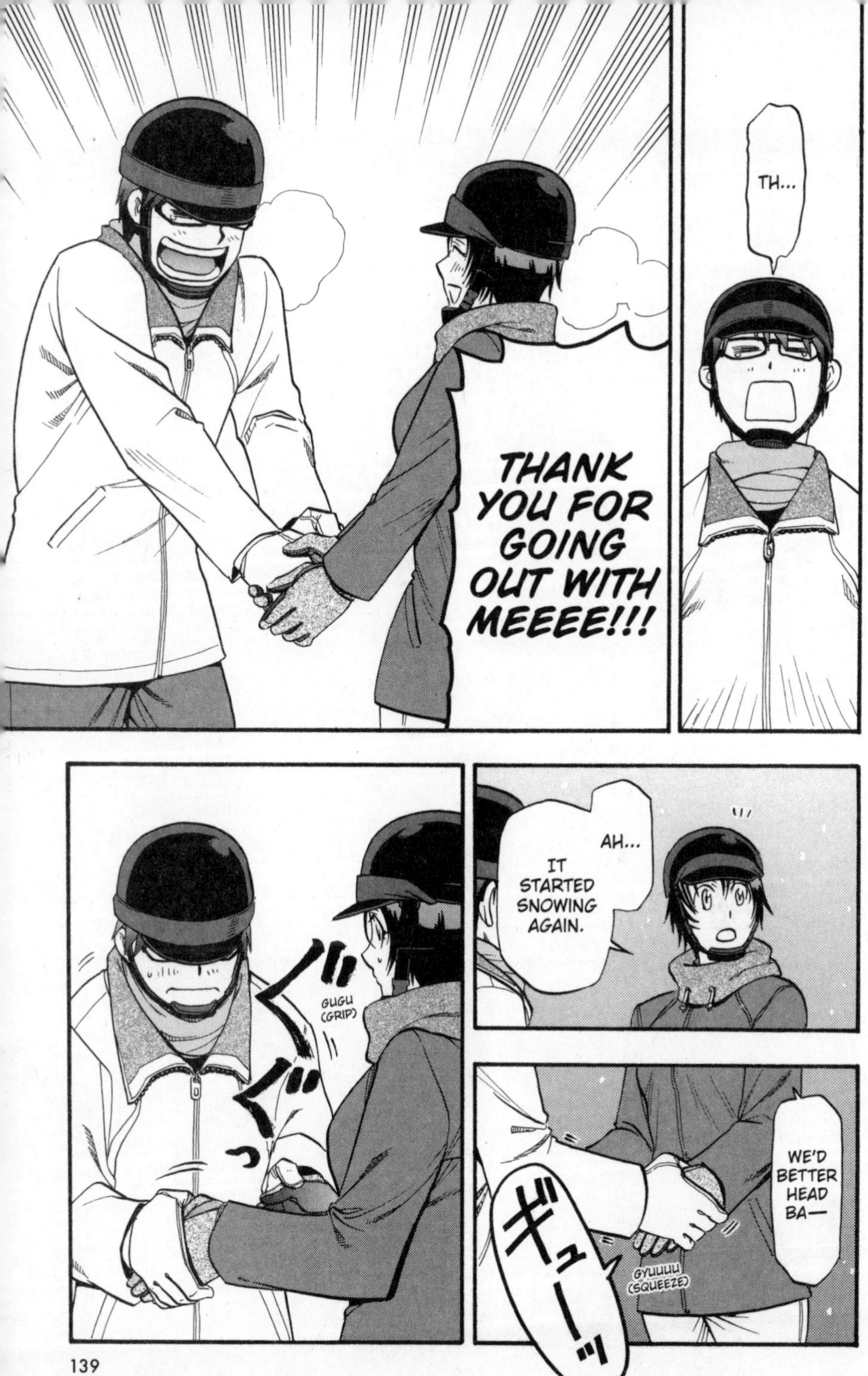
TH...
THANK YOU FOR GOING OUT WITH MEEEE!!!
AH...
IT STARTED SNOWING AGAIN.
WE'D BETTER HEAD BA—
ギューッ
GYUUUU (SQUEEZE)
GUGU (GRIP)

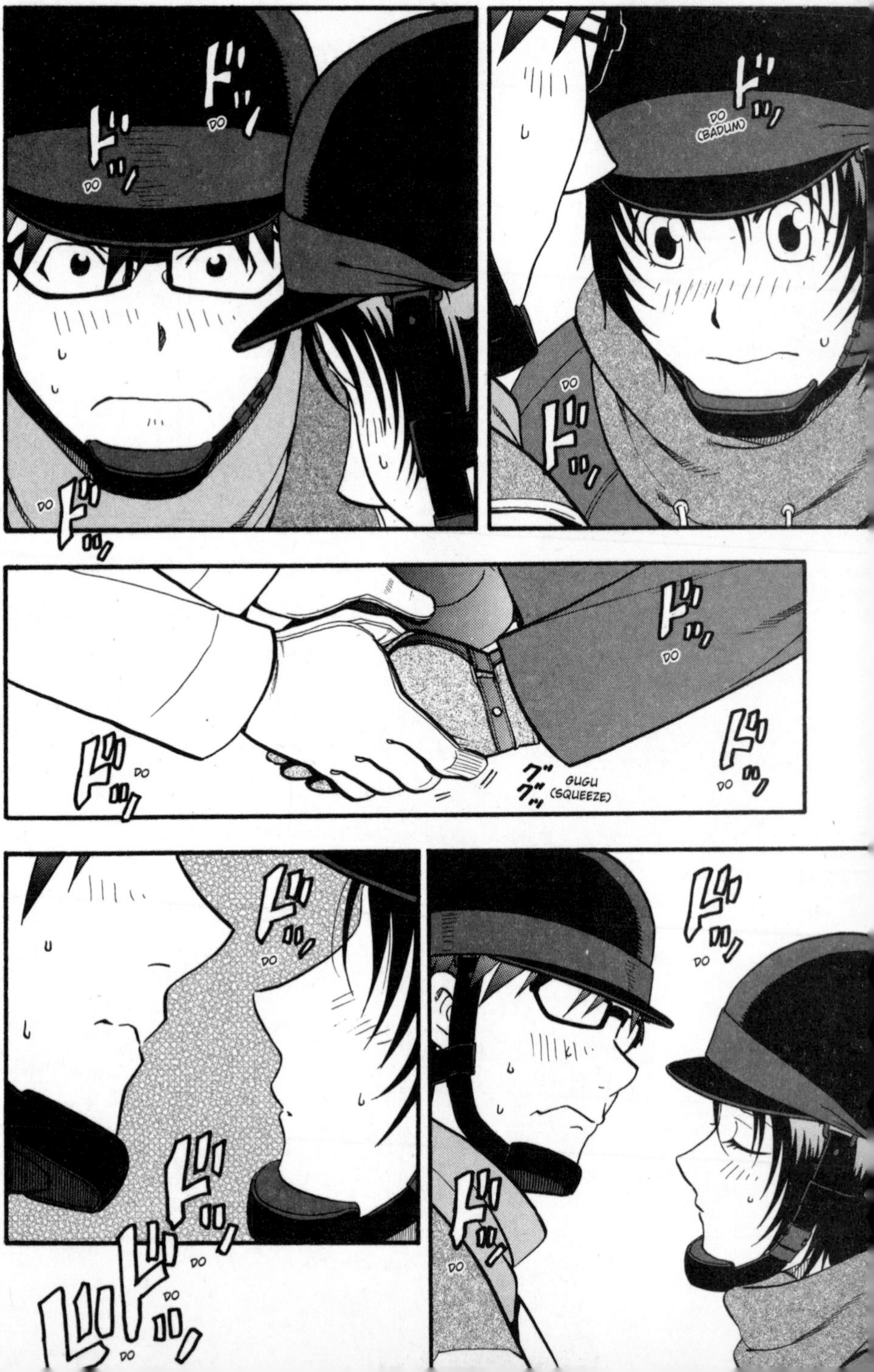
DO (BADUM)
DO
DO
DO
DO
DO
GUGU (SQUEEZE)
DO
DO
DO
DO
DO
DO
DO
DO

GON
(CLONK)

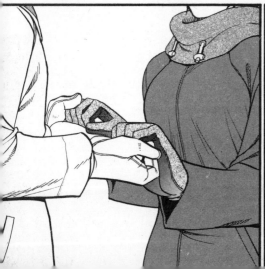

HWOO...

HAAH...

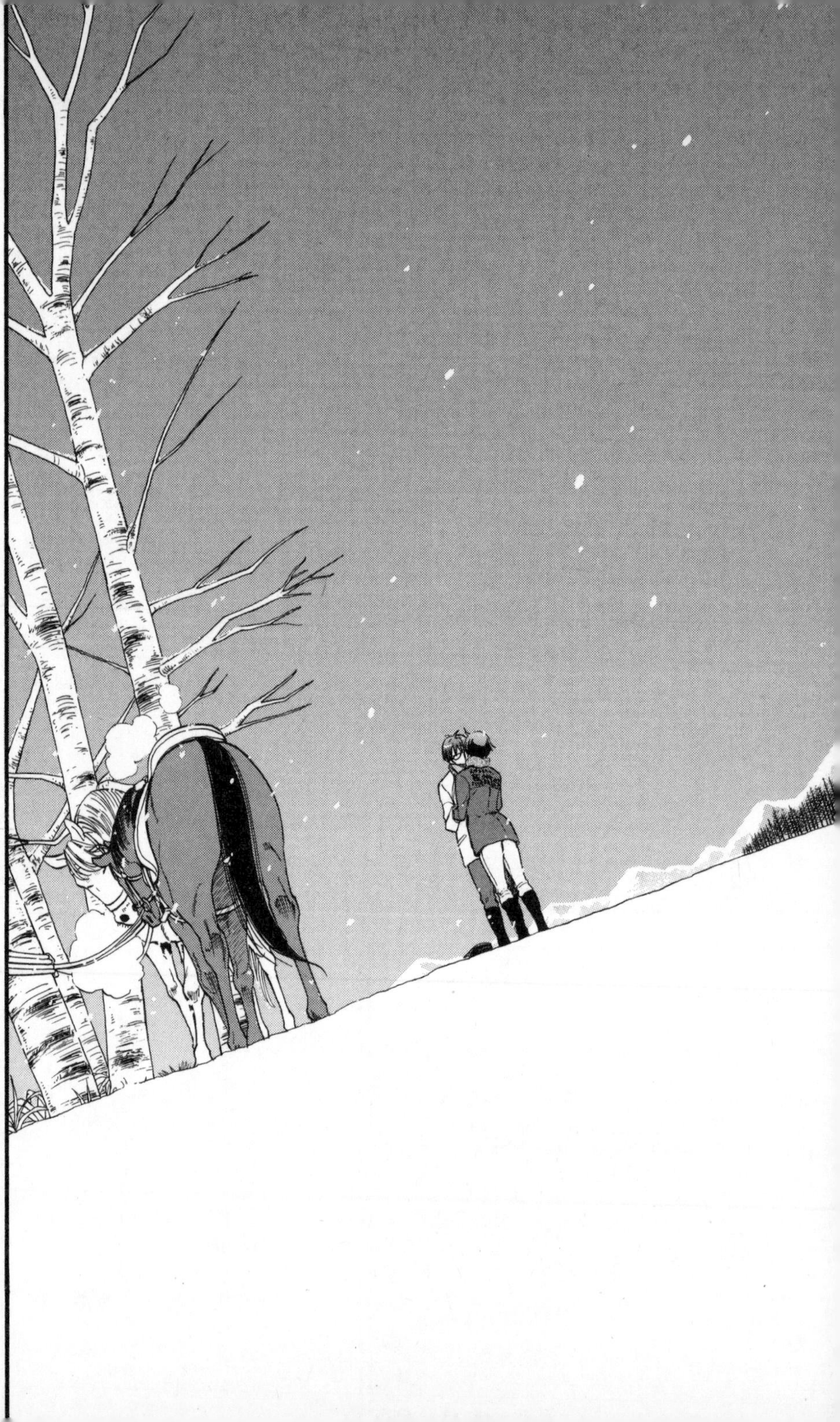

Silver Spoon

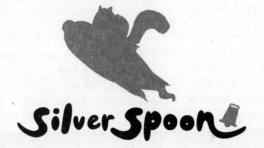

YODA-SENPAI

RX-8 (USED)

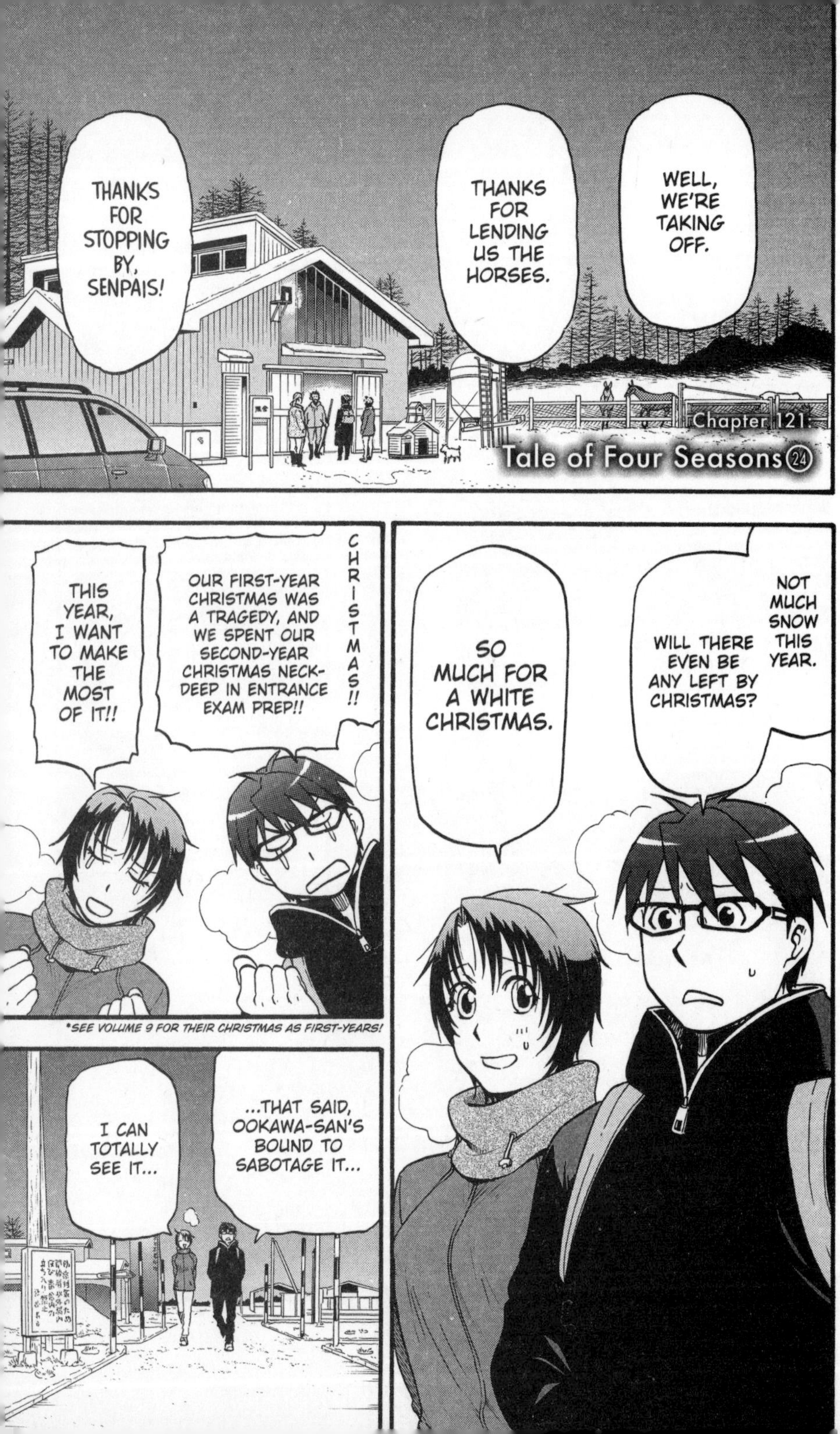
WELL, WE'RE TAKING OFF.
THANKS FOR LENDING US THE HORSES.
THANKS FOR STOPPING BY, SENPAIS!
Chapter 121: Tale of Four Seasons ㉔
NOT MUCH SNOW THIS YEAR.
WILL THERE EVEN BE ANY LEFT BY CHRISTMAS?
SO MUCH FOR A WHITE CHRISTMAS.
CHRISTMAS!!
OUR FIRST-YEAR CHRISTMAS WAS A TRAGEDY, AND WE SPENT OUR SECOND-YEAR CHRISTMAS NECK-DEEP IN ENTRANCE EXAM PREP!!
THIS YEAR, I WANT TO MAKE THE MOST OF IT!!
*SEE VOLUME 9 FOR THEIR CHRISTMAS AS FIRST-YEARS!
...THAT SAID, OOKAWA-SAN'S BOUND TO SABOTAGE IT...
I CAN TOTALLY SEE IT...

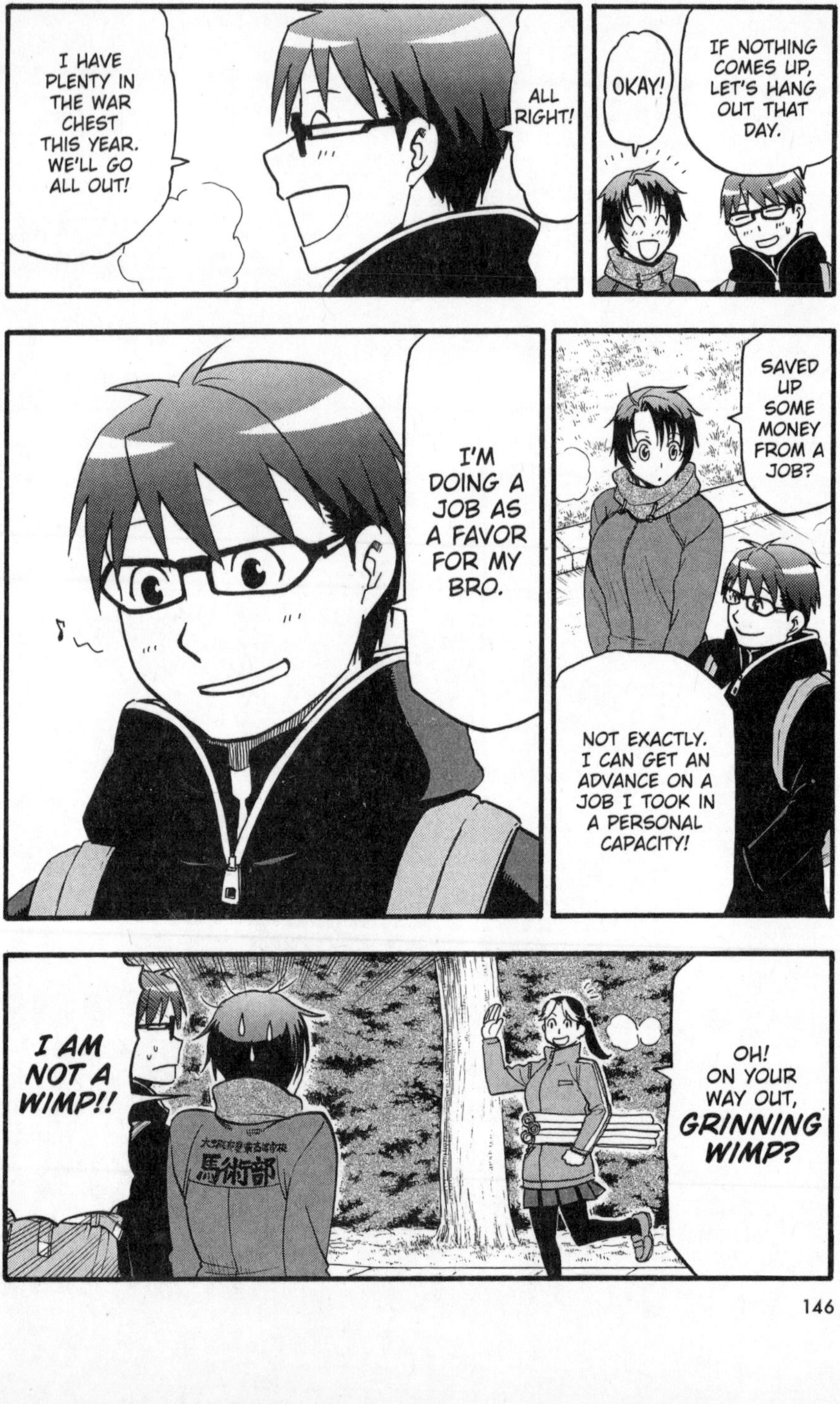
IF NOTHING COMES UP, LET'S HANG OUT THAT DAY.
OKAY!
ALL RIGHT!
I HAVE PLENTY IN THE WAR CHEST THIS YEAR. WE'LL GO ALL OUT!
SAVED UP SOME MONEY FROM A JOB?
NOT EXACTLY. I CAN GET AN ADVANCE ON A JOB I TOOK IN A PERSONAL CAPACITY!
I'M DOING A JOB AS A FAVOR FOR MY BRO.
OH! ON YOUR WAY OUT, GRINNING WIMP?
馬術部
I AM NOT A WIMP!!

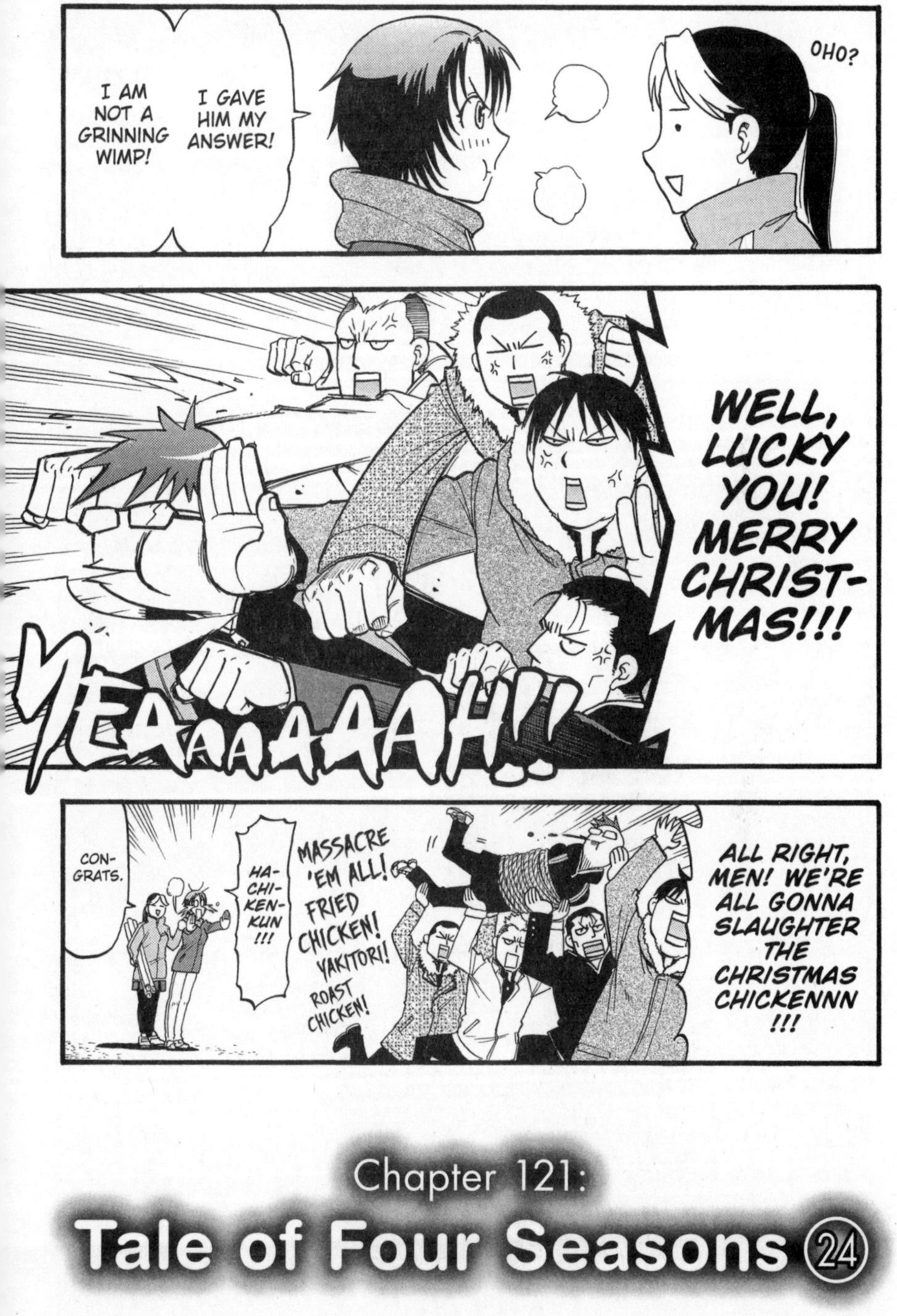
OHO?
I GAVE HIM MY ANSWER!
I AM NOT A GRINNING WIMP!
WELL, LUCKY YOU! MERRY CHRIST-MAS!!!
YEAAAAAAH!!
ALL RIGHT, MEN! WE'RE ALL GONNA SLAUGHTER THE CHRISTMAS CHICKENNN!!!
MASSACRE 'EM ALL! FRIED CHICKEN! YAKITORI! ROAST CHICKEN!
HA-CHI-KEN-KUN!!!
CON-GRATS.

Chapter 121:

Tale of Four Seasons ㉔

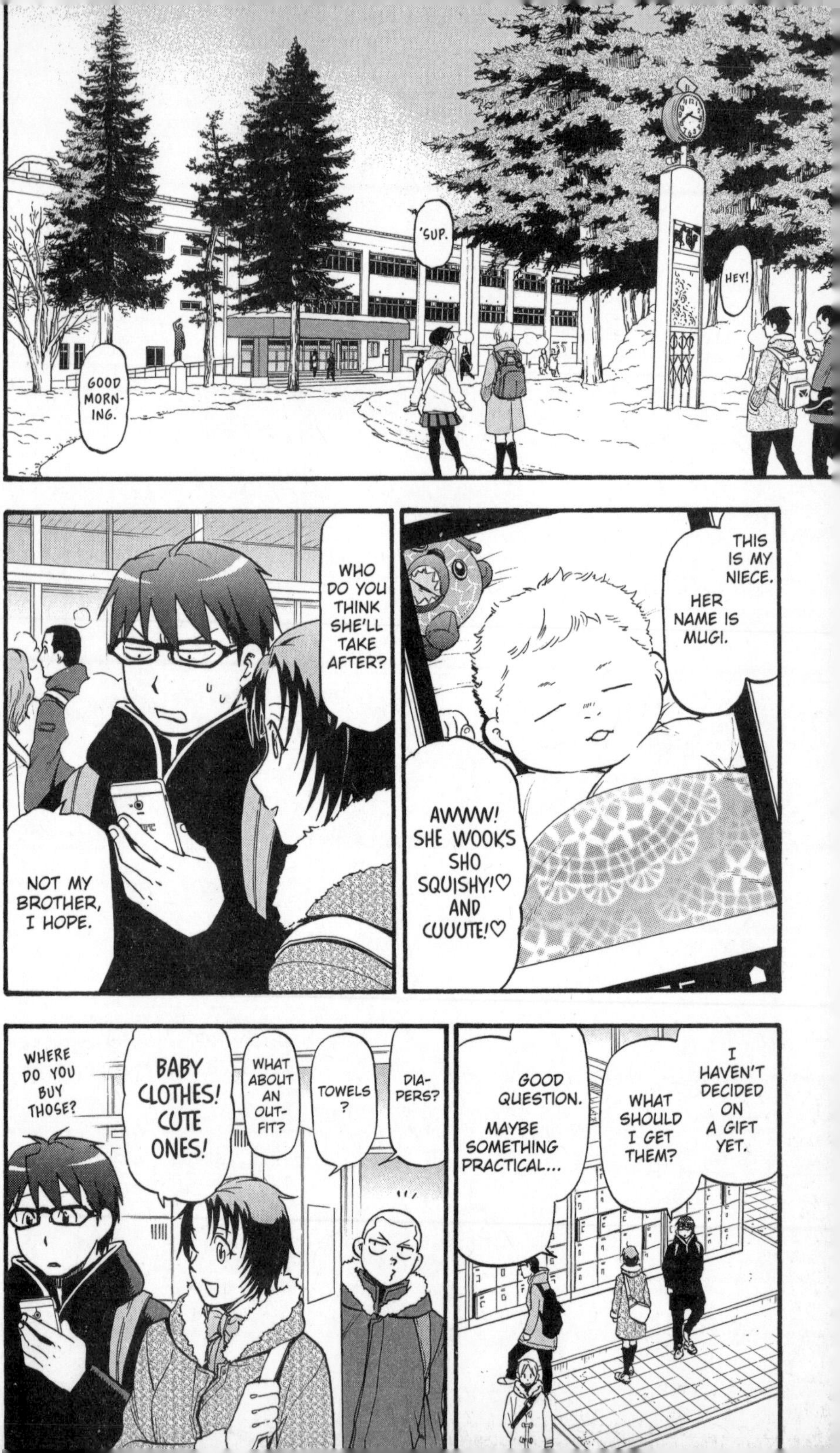
HEY!
'SUP.
GOOD MORNING.
THIS IS MY NIECE.
HER NAME IS MUGI.
AWWW! SHE WOOKS SHO SQUISHY!♡ AND CUUUTE!♡
WHO DO YOU THINK SHE'LL TAKE AFTER?
NOT MY BROTHER, I HOPE.
I HAVEN'T DECIDED ON A GIFT YET.
WHAT SHOULD I GET THEM?
GOOD QUESTION.
MAYBE SOMETHING PRACTICAL...
DIAPERS?
TOWELS?
WHAT ABOUT AN OUTFIT?
BABY CLOTHES! CUTE ONES!
WHERE DO YOU BUY THOSE?

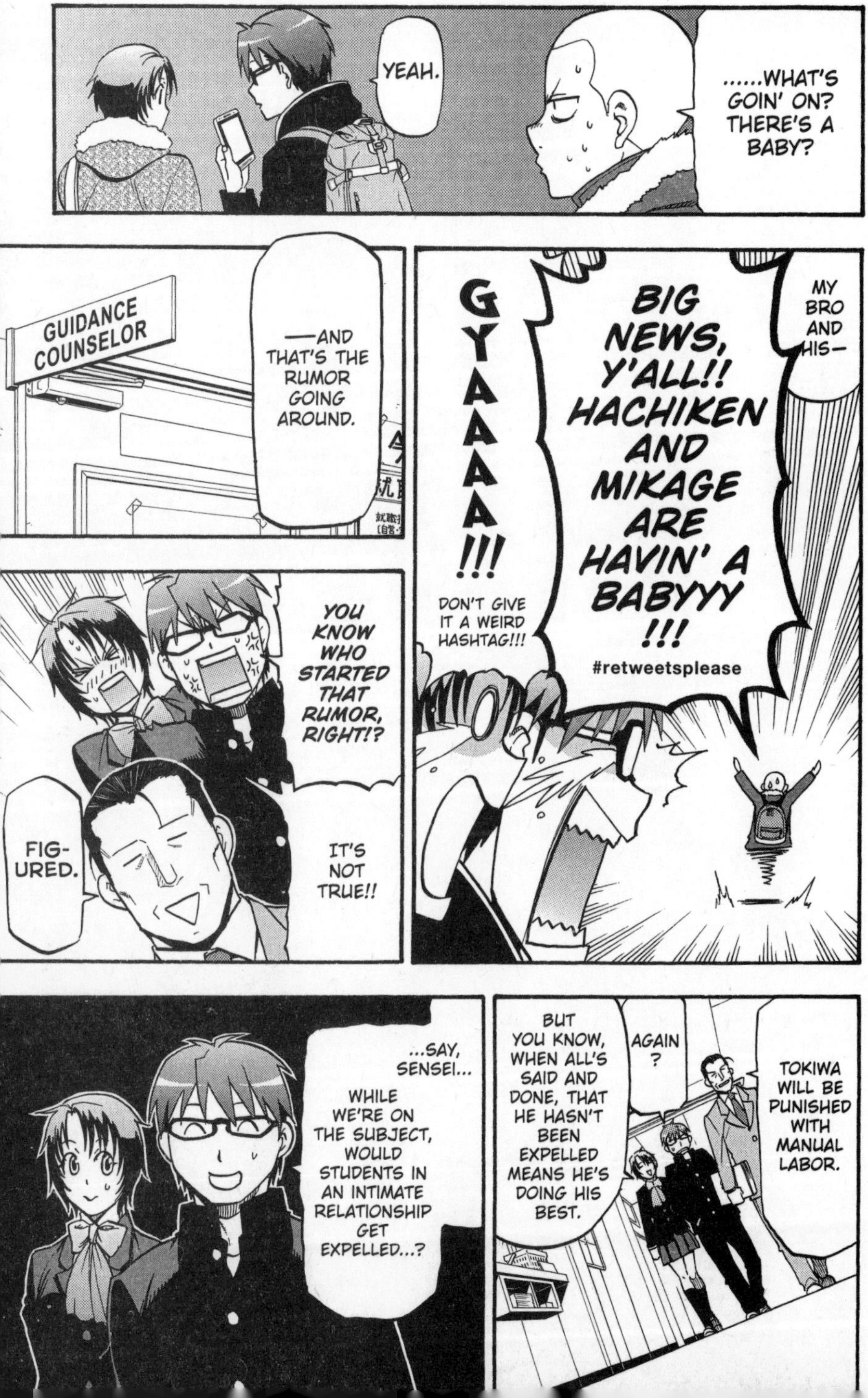

......WHAT'S GOIN' ON? THERE'S A BABY?
YEAH.
MY BRO AND HIS—
BIG NEWS, Y'ALL!! HACHIKEN AND MIKAGE ARE HAVIN' A BABYYY!!!
#retweetsplease
GYAAAAA!!!
DON'T GIVE IT A WEIRD HASHTAG!!!
GUIDANCE COUNSELOR
—AND THAT'S THE RUMOR GOING AROUND.
YOU KNOW WHO STARTED THAT RUMOR, RIGHT!?
IT'S NOT TRUE!!
FIG-URED.
TOKIWA WILL BE PUNISHED WITH MANUAL LABOR.
AGAIN?
BUT YOU KNOW, WHEN ALL'S SAID AND DONE, THAT HE HASN'T BEEN EXPELLED MEANS HE'S DOING HIS BEST.
...SAY, SENSEI...
WHILE WE'RE ON THE SUBJECT, WOULD STUDENTS IN AN INTIMATE RELATIONSHIP GET EXPELLED...?

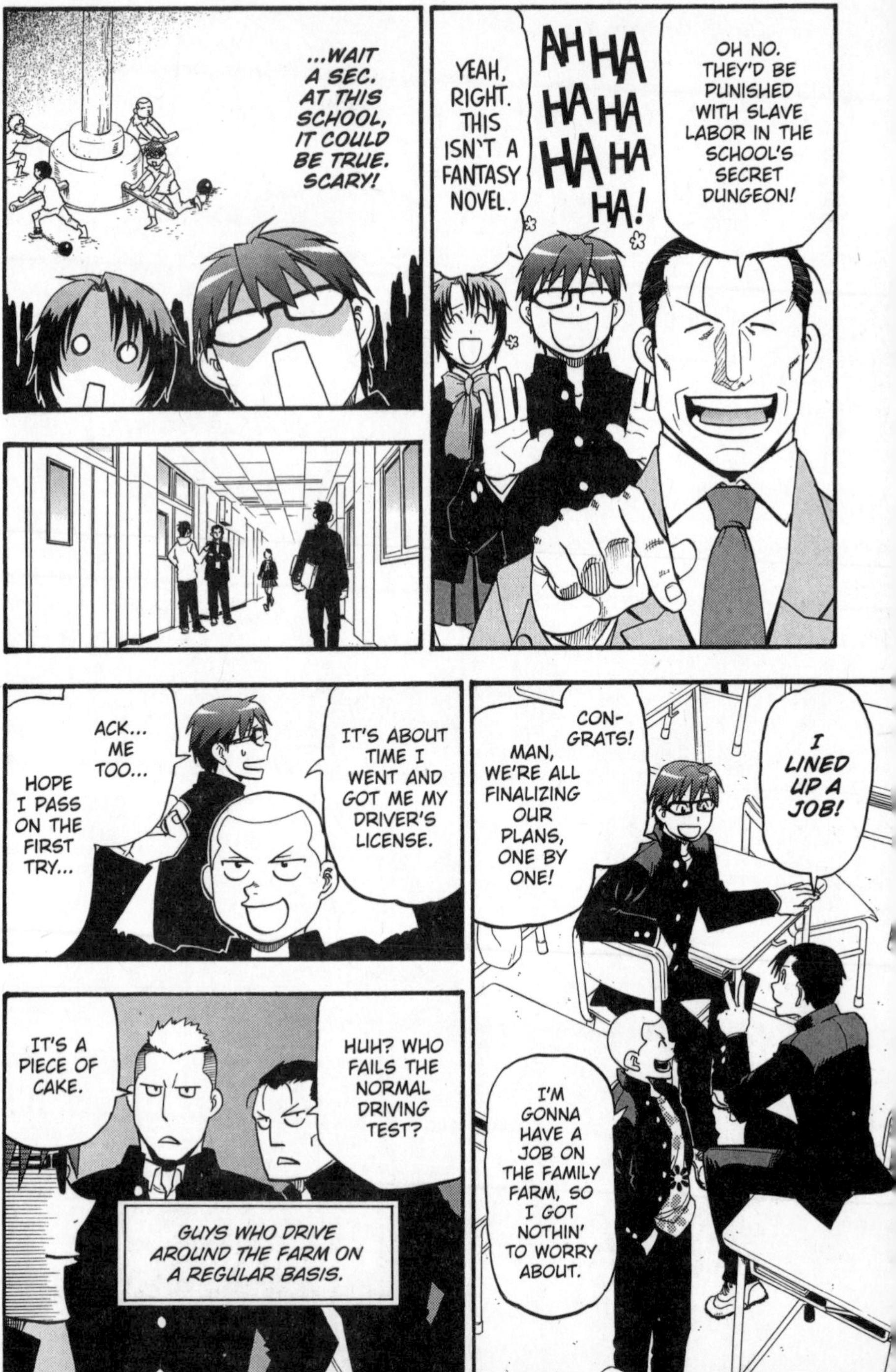
OH NO. THEY'D BE PUNISHED WITH SLAVE LABOR IN THE SCHOOL'S SECRET DUNGEON!
AH HA HA HA HA HA HA HA!
YEAH, RIGHT. THIS ISN'T A FANTASY NOVEL.
...WAIT A SEC. AT THIS SCHOOL, IT COULD BE TRUE. SCARY!
I LINED UP A JOB!
CON-GRATS!
MAN, WE'RE ALL FINALIZING OUR PLANS, ONE BY ONE!
I'M GONNA HAVE A JOB ON THE FAMILY FARM, SO I GOT NOTHIN' TO WORRY ABOUT.
IT'S ABOUT TIME I WENT AND GOT ME MY DRIVER'S LICENSE.
ACK... ME TOO...
HOPE I PASS ON THE FIRST TRY...
HUH? WHO FAILS THE NORMAL DRIVING TEST?
IT'S A PIECE OF CAKE.
GUYS WHO DRIVE AROUND THE FARM ON A REGULAR BASIS.

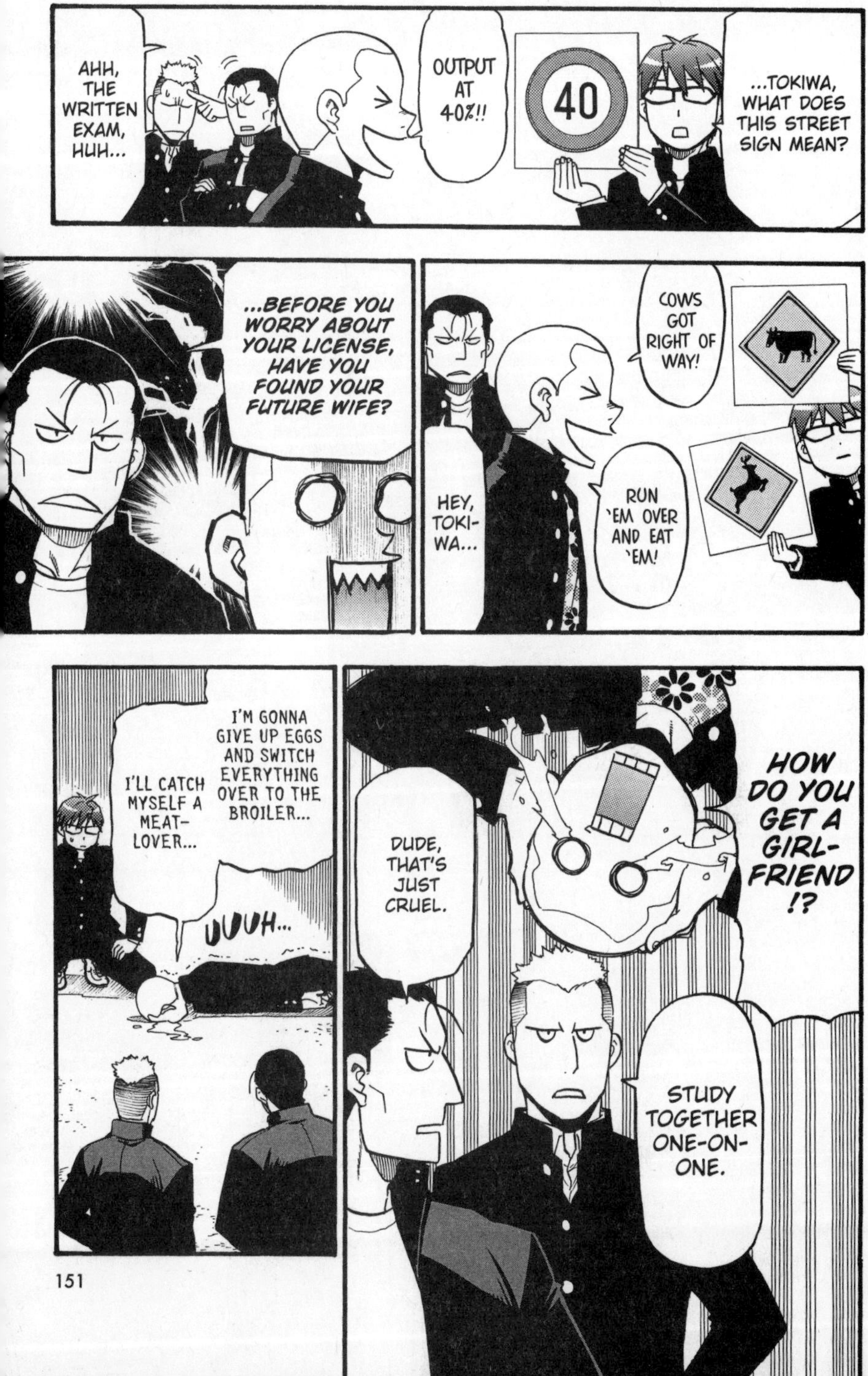
...TOKIWA, WHAT DOES THIS STREET SIGN MEAN?
40
OUTPUT AT 40%!!
AHH, THE WRITTEN EXAM, HUH...
COWS GOT RIGHT OF WAY!
RUN 'EM OVER AND EAT 'EM!
HEY, TOKI-WA...
...BEFORE YOU WORRY ABOUT YOUR LICENSE, HAVE YOU FOUND YOUR FUTURE WIFE?
HOW DO YOU GET A GIRL-FRIEND!?
DUDE, THAT'S JUST CRUEL.
STUDY TOGETHER ONE-ON-ONE.
I'M GONNA GIVE UP EGGS AND SWITCH EVERYTHING OVER TO THE BROILER...
I'LL CATCH MYSELF A MEAT-LOVER...
UUUH...

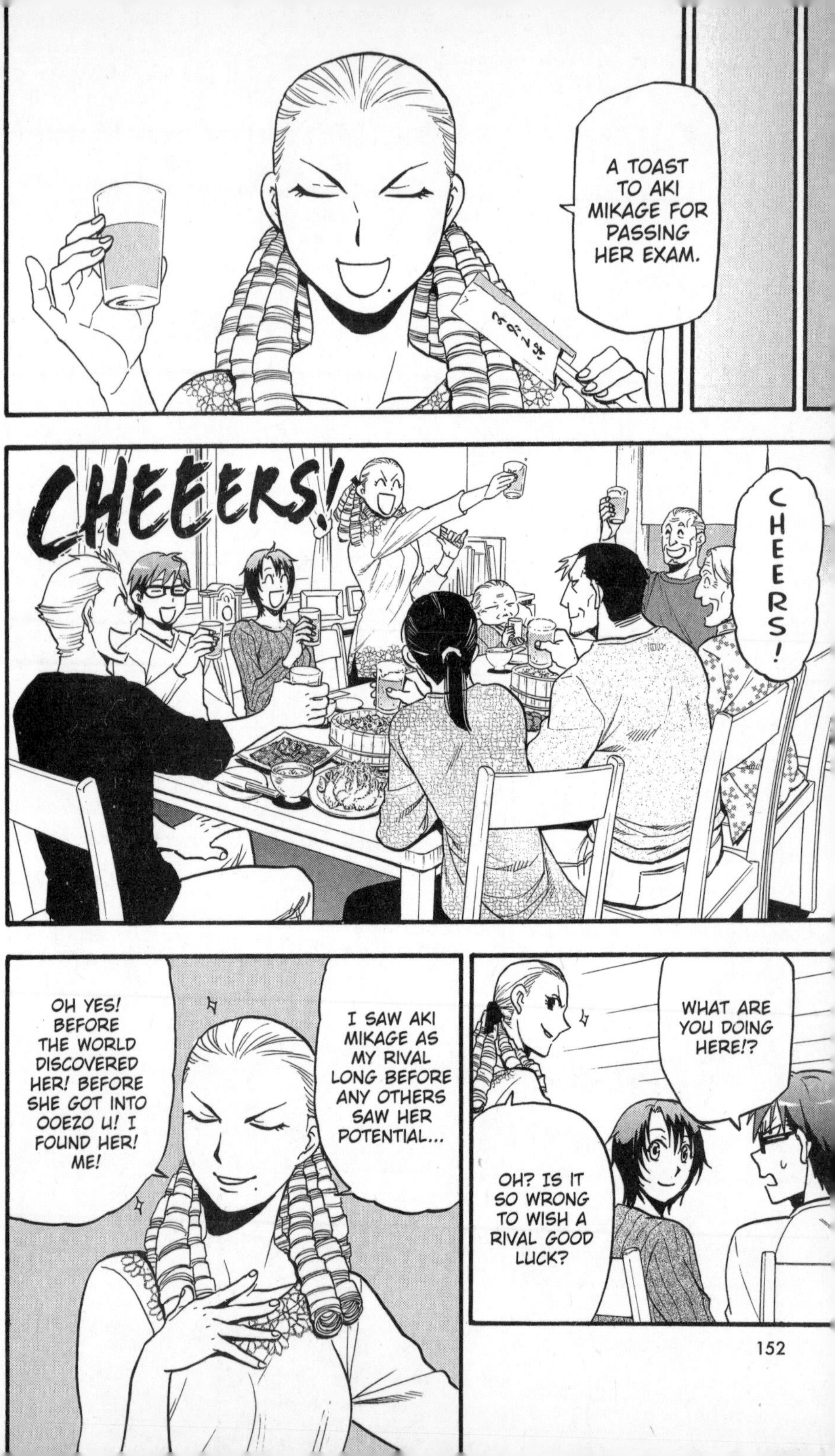
A TOAST TO AKI MIKAGE FOR PASSING HER EXAM.
CHEERS!
CHEEERS!
WHAT ARE YOU DOING HERE!?
OH? IS IT SO WRONG TO WISH A RIVAL GOOD LUCK?
I SAW AKI MIKAGE AS MY RIVAL LONG BEFORE ANY OTHERS SAW HER POTENTIAL...
OH YES! BEFORE THE WORLD DISCOVERED HER! BEFORE SHE GOT INTO OOEZO U! I FOUND HER! ME!

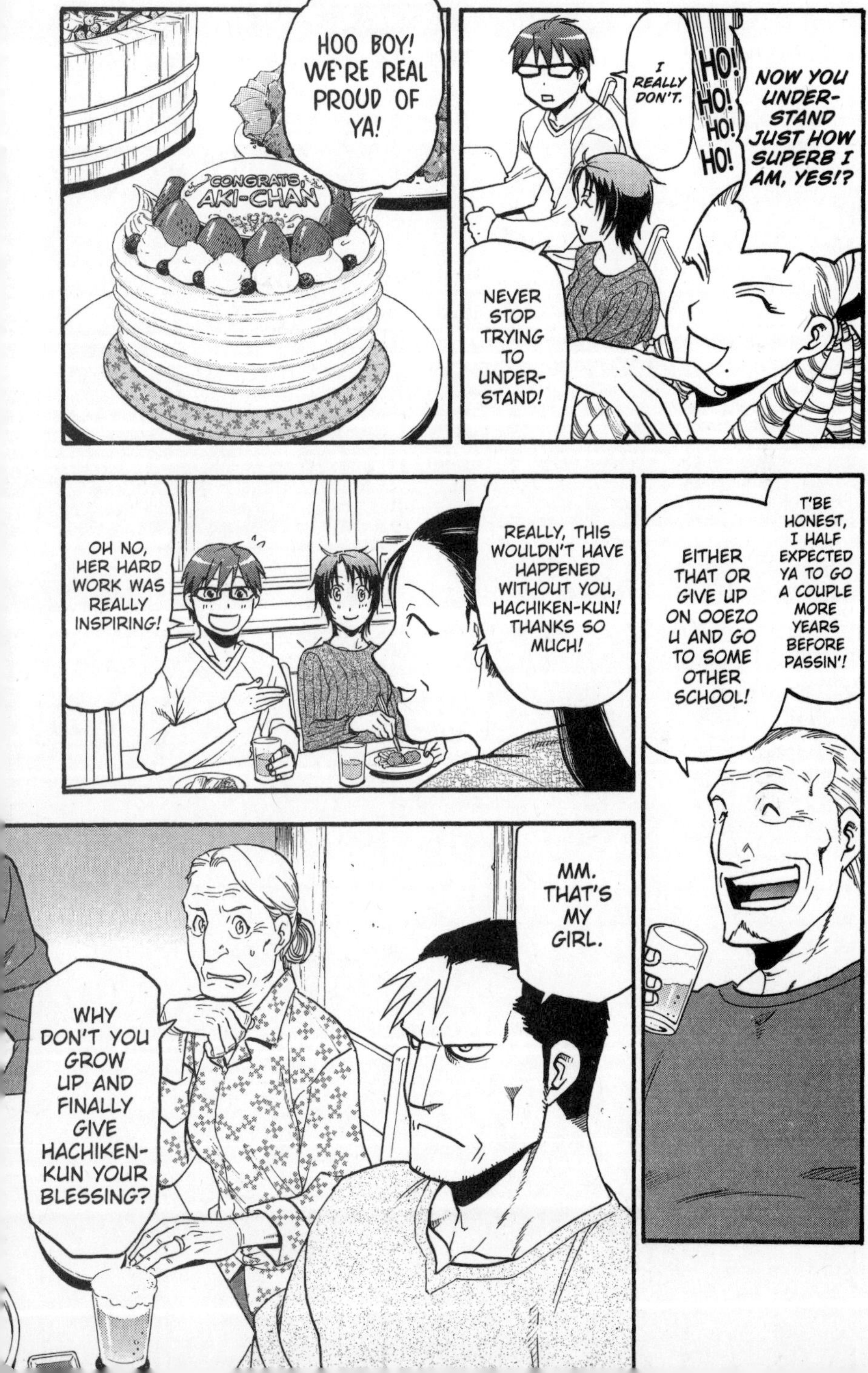

NOW YOU UNDERSTAND JUST HOW SUPERB I AM, YES!?
HO! HO! HO! HO!
I REALLY DON'T.
NEVER STOP TRYING TO UNDERSTAND!
HOO BOY! WE'RE REAL PROUD OF YA!
CONGRATS, AKI-CHAN
T'BE HONEST, I HALF EXPECTED YA TO GO A COUPLE MORE YEARS BEFORE PASSIN'!
EITHER THAT OR GIVE UP ON OOEZO U AND GO TO SOME OTHER SCHOOL!
REALLY, THIS WOULDN'T HAVE HAPPENED WITHOUT YOU, HACHIKEN-KUN! THANKS SO MUCH!
OH NO, HER HARD WORK WAS REALLY INSPIRING!
MM. THAT'S MY GIRL.
WHY DON'T YOU GROW UP AND FINALLY GIVE HACHIKEN-KUN YOUR BLESSING?

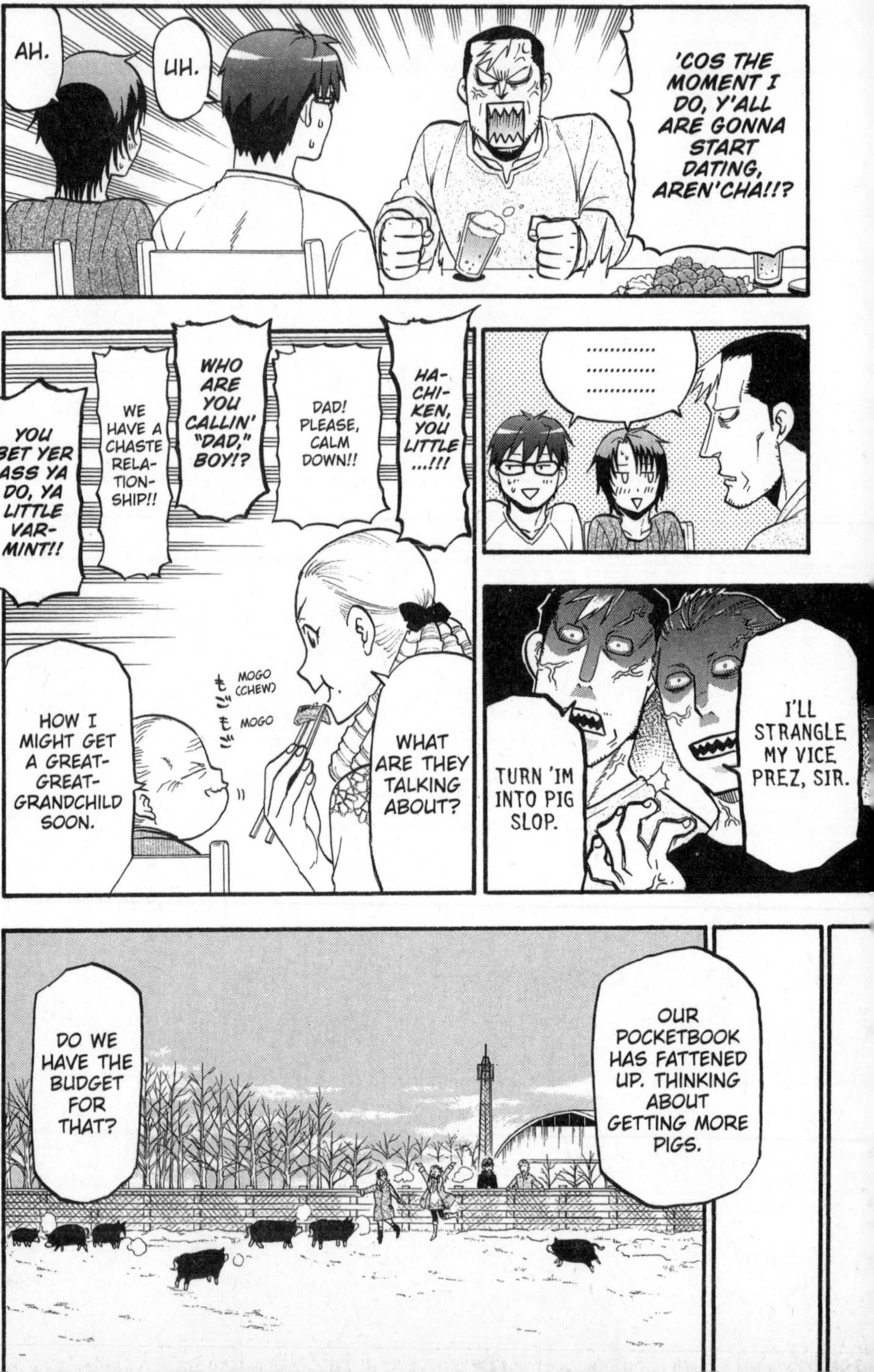
'COS THE MOMENT I DO, Y'ALL ARE GONNA START DATING, AREN'CHA!!?
UH.
AH.
....
I'LL STRANGLE MY VICE PREZ, SIR.
TURN 'IM INTO PIG SLOP.
HA-CHI-KEN, YOU LITTLE ...!!!
DAD! PLEASE, CALM DOWN!!
WHO ARE YOU CALLIN' "DAD," BOY!?
WE HAVE A CHASTE RELA-TION-SHIP!!
YOU BET YER ASS YA DO, YA LITTLE VAR-MINT!!
WHAT ARE THEY TALKING ABOUT?
もぐ MOGO (CHEW)
もぐ MOGO
HOW I MIGHT GET A GREAT-GREAT-GRANDCHILD SOON.
OUR POCKETBOOK HAS FATTENED UP. THINKING ABOUT GETTING MORE PIGS.
DO WE HAVE THE BUDGET FOR THAT?

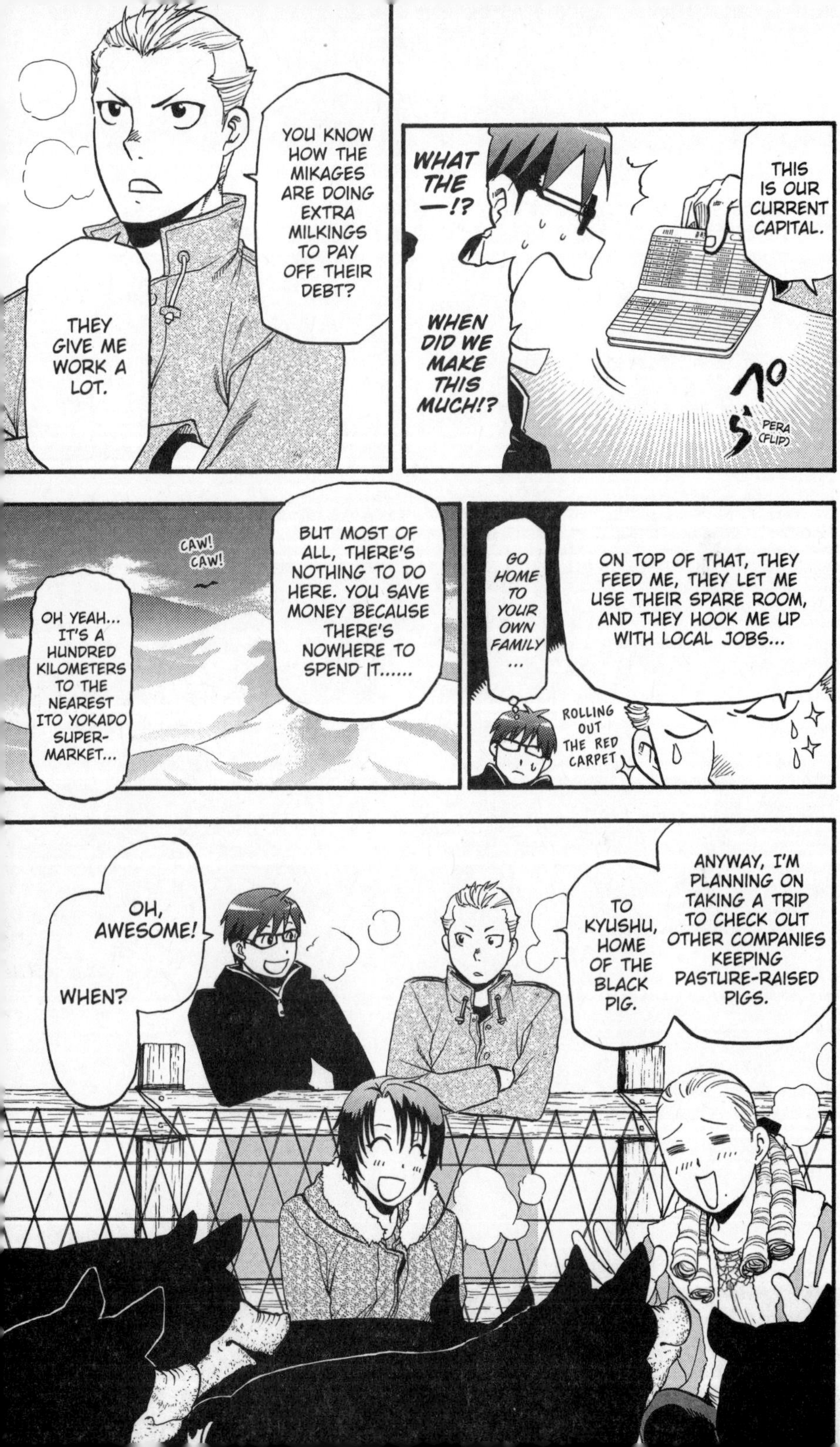
THIS IS OUR CURRENT CAPITAL.
WHAT THE—!?
WHEN DID WE MAKE THIS MUCH!?
PERA (FLIP)
YOU KNOW HOW THE MIKAGES ARE DOING EXTRA MILKINGS TO PAY OFF THEIR DEBT?
THEY GIVE ME WORK A LOT.
ON TOP OF THAT, THEY FEED ME, THEY LET ME USE THEIR SPARE ROOM, AND THEY HOOK ME UP WITH LOCAL JOBS...
GO HOME TO YOUR OWN FAMILY...
ROLLING OUT THE RED CARPET
BUT MOST OF ALL, THERE'S NOTHING TO DO HERE. YOU SAVE MONEY BECAUSE THERE'S NOWHERE TO SPEND IT......
CAW! CAW!
OH YEAH... IT'S A HUNDRED KILOMETERS TO THE NEAREST ITO YOKADO SUPER-MARKET...
ANYWAY, I'M PLANNING ON TAKING A TRIP TO CHECK OUT OTHER COMPANIES KEEPING PASTURE-RAISED PIGS.
TO KYUSHU, HOME OF THE BLACK PIG.
OH, AWESOME!
WHEN?

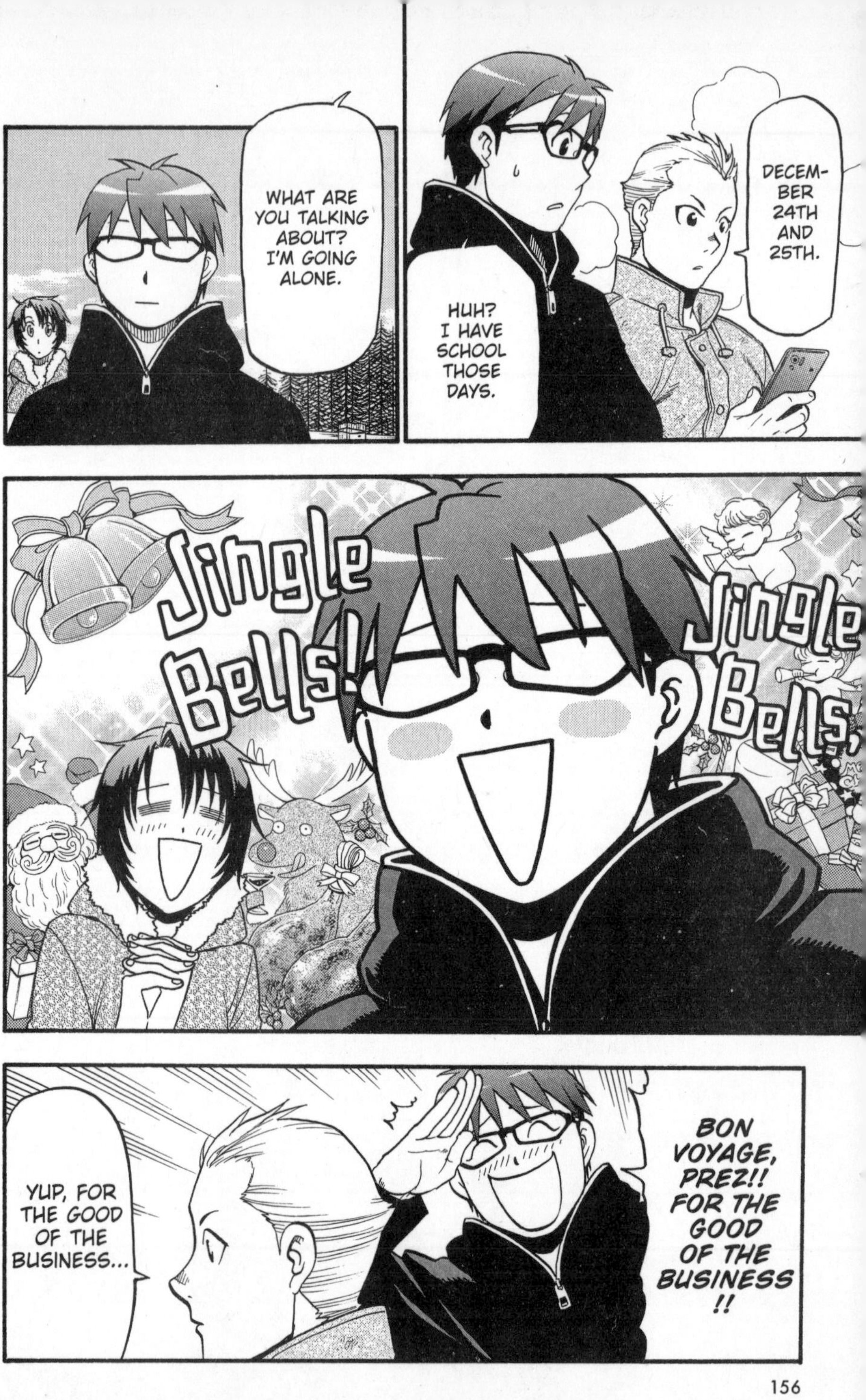
DECEMBER 24TH AND 25TH.
HUH? I HAVE SCHOOL THOSE DAYS.
WHAT ARE YOU TALKING ABOUT? I'M GOING ALONE.
Jingle Bells,
Jingle Bells!
BON VOYAGE, PREZ!! FOR THE GOOD OF THE BUSINESS!!
YUP, FOR THE GOOD OF THE BUSINESS...

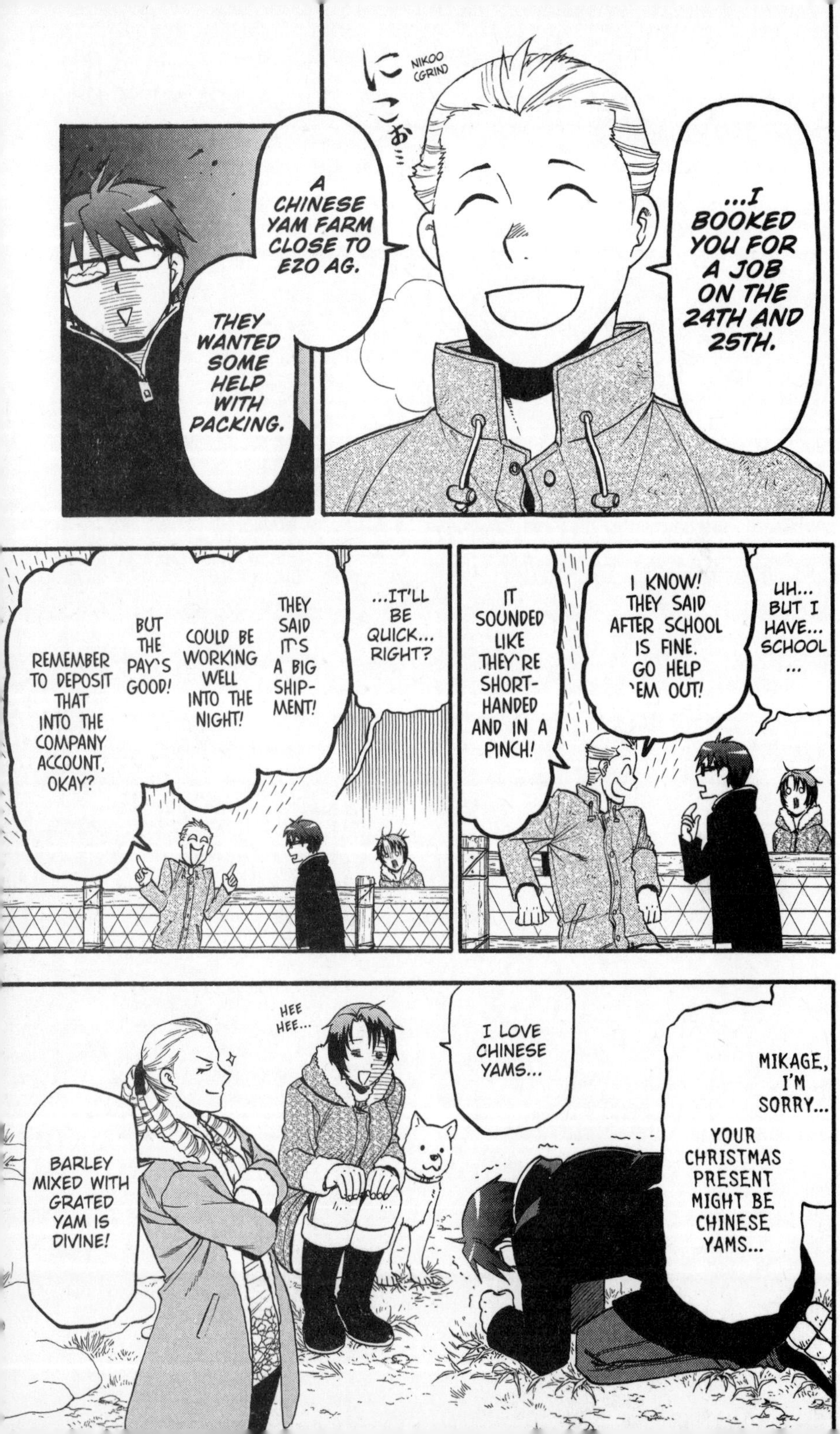
にっこぉ NIKOO (GRIN)
...I BOOKED YOU FOR A JOB ON THE 24TH AND 25TH.
A CHINESE YAM FARM CLOSE TO EZO AG.
THEY WANTED SOME HELP WITH PACKING.
UH... BUT I HAVE... SCHOOL ...
I KNOW! THEY SAID AFTER SCHOOL IS FINE. GO HELP 'EM OUT!
IT SOUNDED LIKE THEY'RE SHORT-HANDED AND IN A PINCH!
...IT'LL BE QUICK... RIGHT?
THEY SAID IT'S A BIG SHIPMENT!
COULD BE WORKING WELL INTO THE NIGHT!
BUT THE PAY'S GOOD!
REMEMBER TO DEPOSIT THAT INTO THE COMPANY ACCOUNT, OKAY?
MIKAGE, I'M SORRY...
YOUR CHRISTMAS PRESENT MIGHT BE CHINESE YAMS...
I LOVE CHINESE YAMS...
HEE HEE...
BARLEY MIXED WITH GRATED YAM IS DIVINE!

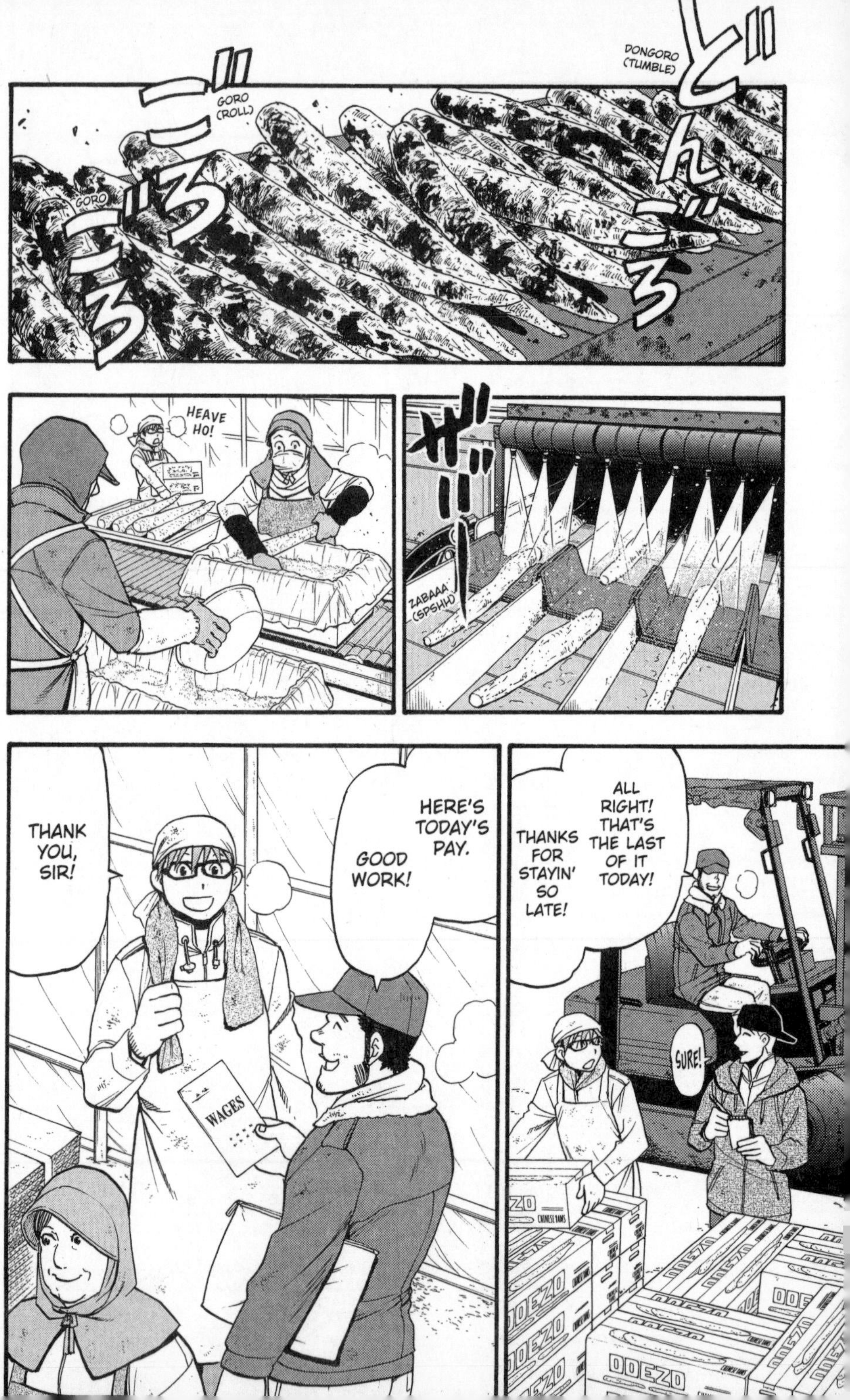

どんごろ
DONGORO (TUMBLE)
ごろ
GORO (ROLL)
ごろ
GORO
ザバー
ZABAAA (SPSHH)
HEAVE HO!
ALL RIGHT! THAT'S THE LAST OF IT TODAY!
THANKS FOR STAYIN' SO LATE!
SURE!
HERE'S TODAY'S PAY.
GOOD WORK!
THANK YOU, SIR!
WAGES
DOEZO
CHINESE YAMS

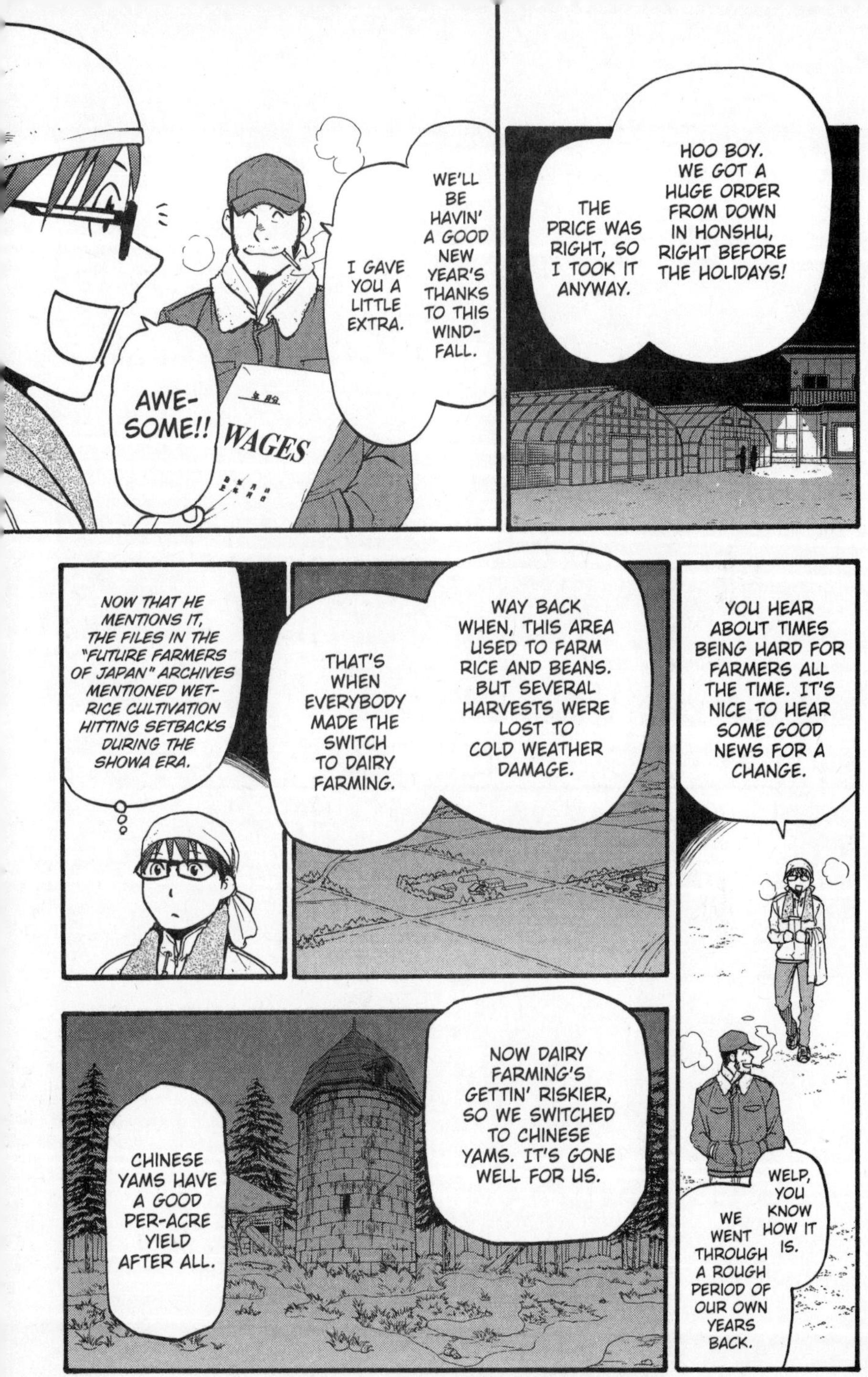
HOO BOY. WE GOT A HUGE ORDER FROM DOWN IN HONSHU, RIGHT BEFORE THE HOLIDAYS!
THE PRICE WAS RIGHT, SO I TOOK IT ANYWAY.
WE'LL BE HAVIN' A GOOD NEW YEAR'S THANKS TO THIS WIND-FALL.
I GAVE YOU A LITTLE EXTRA.
AWE-SOME!!
WAGES
YOU HEAR ABOUT TIMES BEING HARD FOR FARMERS ALL THE TIME. IT'S NICE TO HEAR SOME GOOD NEWS FOR A CHANGE.
WELP, YOU KNOW HOW IT IS.
WE WENT THROUGH A ROUGH PERIOD OF OUR OWN YEARS BACK.
WAY BACK WHEN, THIS AREA USED TO FARM RICE AND BEANS. BUT SEVERAL HARVESTS WERE LOST TO COLD WEATHER DAMAGE.
THAT'S WHEN EVERYBODY MADE THE SWITCH TO DAIRY FARMING.
NOW THAT HE MENTIONS IT, THE FILES IN THE "FUTURE FARMERS OF JAPAN" ARCHIVES MENTIONED WET-RICE CULTIVATION HITTING SETBACKS DURING THE SHOWA ERA.
NOW DAIRY FARMING'S GETTIN' RISKIER, SO WE SWITCHED TO CHINESE YAMS. IT'S GONE WELL FOR US.
CHINESE YAMS HAVE A GOOD PER-ACRE YIELD AFTER ALL.
※NOTE: 1 ACRE = 10 M X 10 M

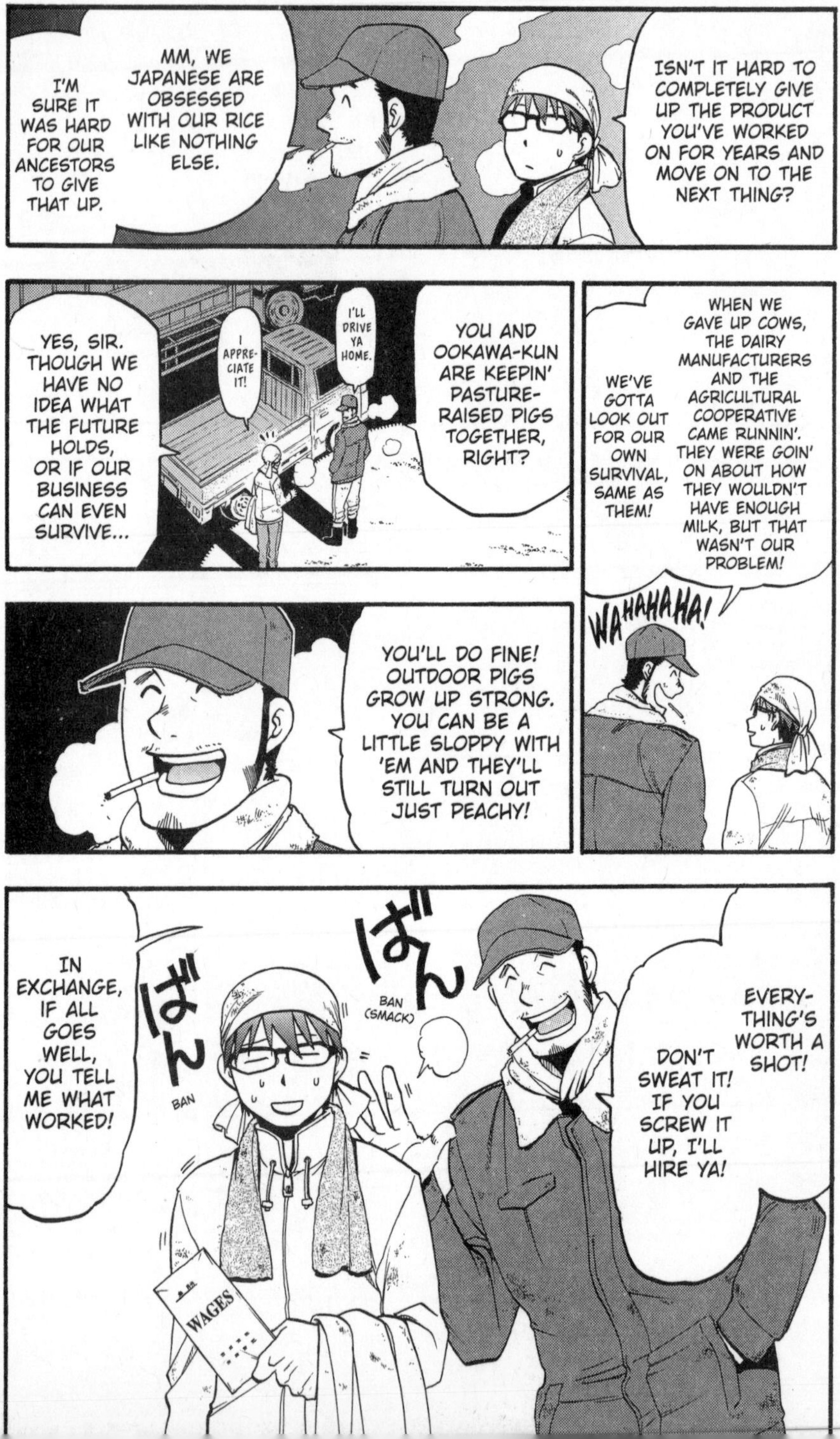
ISN'T IT HARD TO COMPLETELY GIVE UP THE PRODUCT YOU'VE WORKED ON FOR YEARS AND MOVE ON TO THE NEXT THING?
MM, WE JAPANESE ARE OBSESSED WITH OUR RICE LIKE NOTHING ELSE.
I'M SURE IT WAS HARD FOR OUR ANCESTORS TO GIVE THAT UP.
WHEN WE GAVE UP COWS, THE DAIRY MANUFACTURERS AND THE AGRICULTURAL COOPERATIVE CAME RUNNIN'. THEY WERE GOIN' ON ABOUT HOW THEY WOULDN'T HAVE ENOUGH MILK, BUT THAT WASN'T OUR PROBLEM!
WE'VE GOTTA LOOK OUT FOR OUR OWN SURVIVAL, SAME AS THEM!
WAHAHAHA!
YOU AND OOKAWA-KUN ARE KEEPIN' PASTURE-RAISED PIGS TOGETHER, RIGHT?
I'LL DRIVE YA HOME.
I APPRECIATE IT!
YES, SIR. THOUGH WE HAVE NO IDEA WHAT THE FUTURE HOLDS, OR IF OUR BUSINESS CAN EVEN SURVIVE...
YOU'LL DO FINE! OUTDOOR PIGS GROW UP STRONG. YOU CAN BE A LITTLE SLOPPY WITH 'EM AND THEY'LL STILL TURN OUT JUST PEACHY!
EVERY-THING'S WORTH A SHOT!
DON'T SWEAT IT! IF YOU SCREW IT UP, I'LL HIRE YA!
ばん
BAN (SMACK)
ばん
BAN
IN EXCHANGE, IF ALL GOES WELL, YOU TELL ME WHAT WORKED!
WAGES

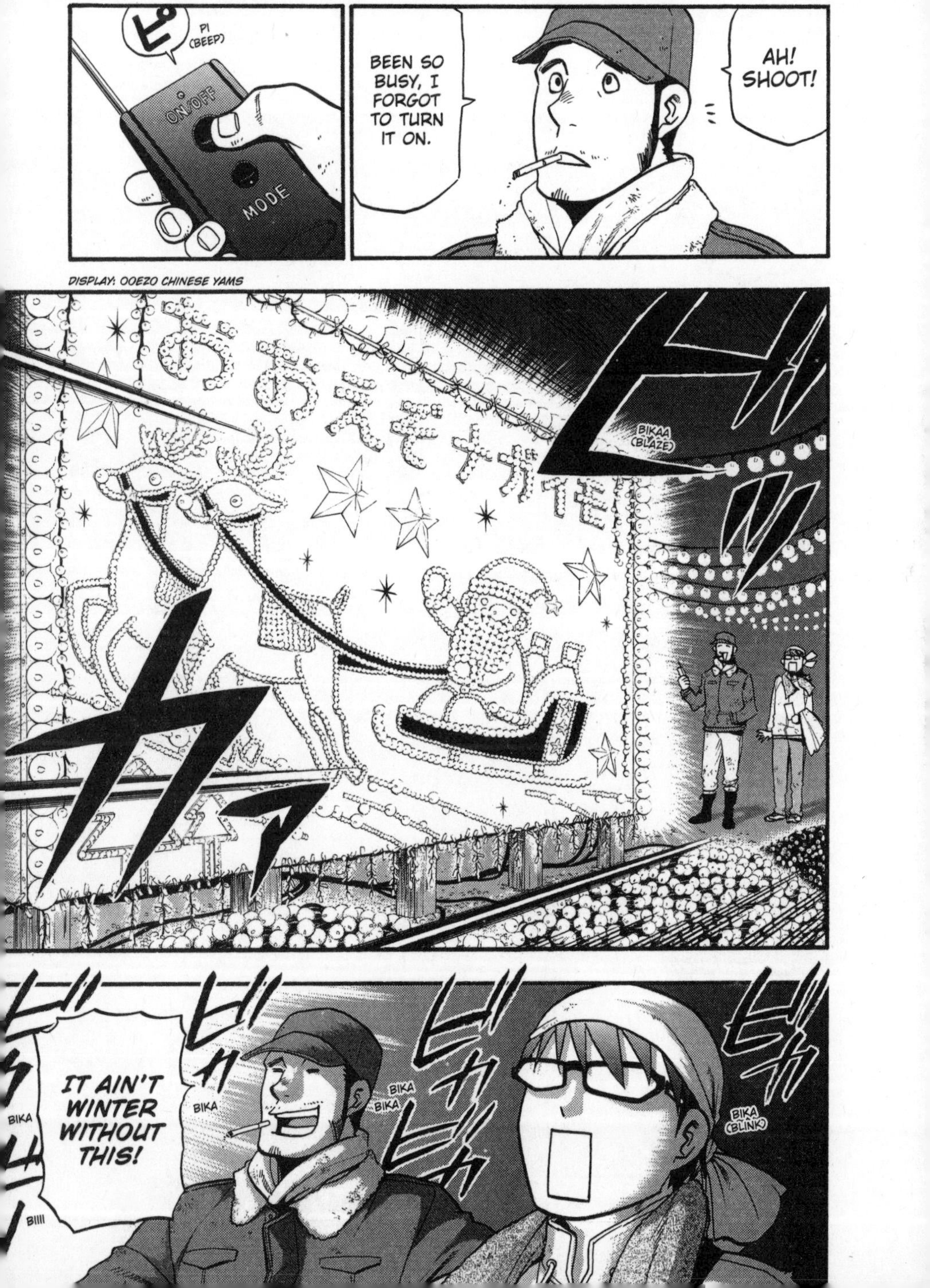
AH! SHOOT!
BEEN SO BUSY, I FORGOT TO TURN IT ON.
PI (BEEP)
ON/OFF
MODE
DISPLAY: OOEZO CHINESE YAMS
BIKAA (BLAZE)
BIKA (BLINK)
BIKA BIKA
BIKA
IT AIN'T WINTER WITHOUT THIS!
BIKA
BIIII

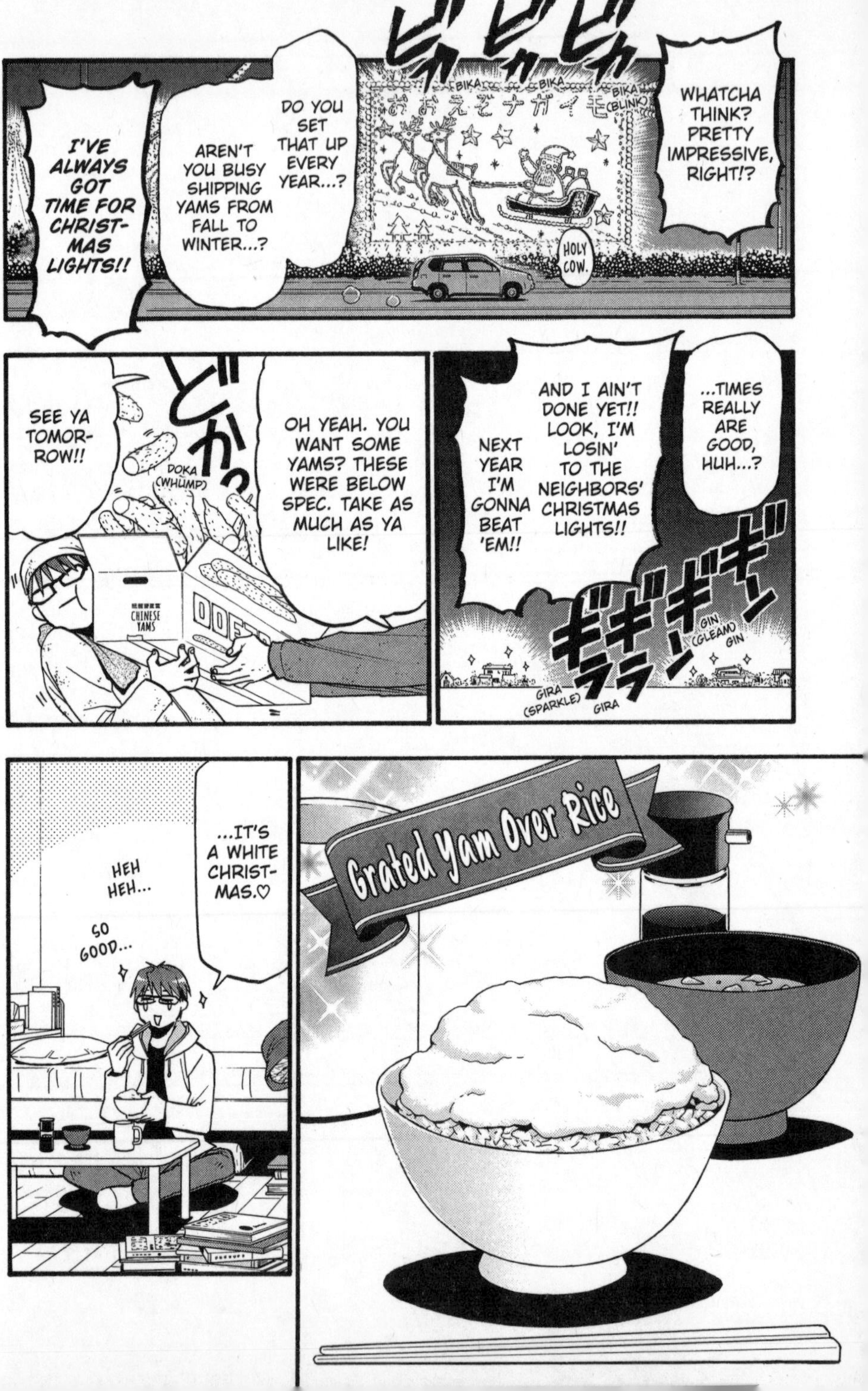
ビカビカビカ
BIKA BIKA BIKA (BLINK)
WHATCHA THINK? PRETTY IMPRESSIVE, RIGHT!?
HOLY COW.
DO YOU SET THAT UP EVERY YEAR...?
AREN'T YOU BUSY SHIPPING YAMS FROM FALL TO WINTER...?
I'VE ALWAYS GOT TIME FOR CHRISTMAS LIGHTS!!
...TIMES REALLY ARE GOOD, HUH...?
AND I AIN'T DONE YET!! LOOK, I'M LOSIN' TO THE NEIGHBORS' CHRISTMAS LIGHTS!!
NEXT YEAR I'M GONNA BEAT 'EM!!
ギンギン
GIN (GLEAM) GIN
ギラギラ
GIRA (SPARKLE) GIRA
OH YEAH. YOU WANT SOME YAMS? THESE WERE BELOW SPEC. TAKE AS MUCH AS YA LIKE!
どかっ
DOKA (WHUMP)
SEE YA TOMORROW!!
CHINESE YAMS
Grated Yam Over Rice
...IT'S A WHITE CHRISTMAS.♡
HEH HEH...
SO GOOD...

Silver Spoon

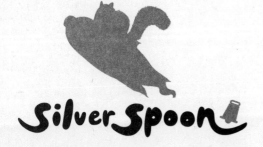

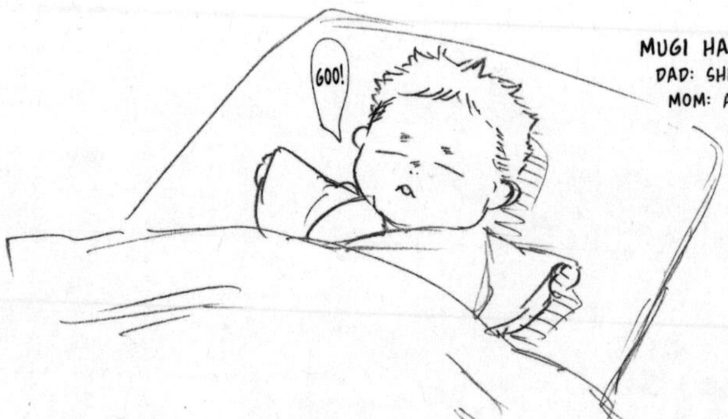
GOO!

MUGI HACHIKEN
DAD: SHINGO
MOM: ALEXANDRA

Chapter 122:
Tale of Four Seasons ㉕

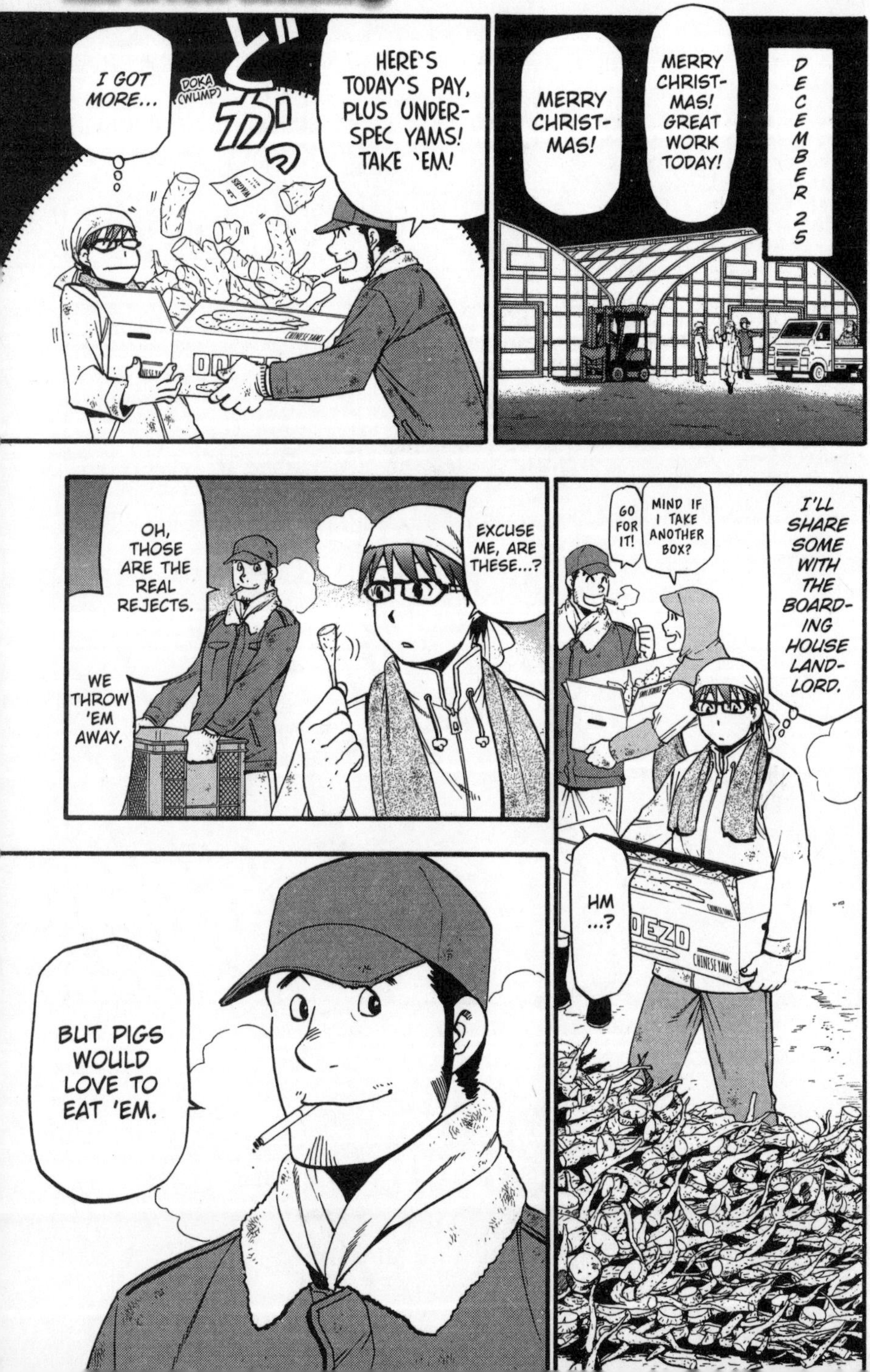
DECEMBER 25
MERRY CHRIST-MAS! GREAT WORK TODAY!
MERRY CHRIST-MAS!
HERE'S TODAY'S PAY, PLUS UNDER-SPEC YAMS! TAKE 'EM!
DOKA (WUMP)
I GOT MORE...
I'LL SHARE SOME WITH THE BOARD-ING HOUSE LAND-LORD.
MIND IF I TAKE ANOTHER BOX?
GO FOR IT!
HM ...?
EXCUSE ME, ARE THESE...?
OH, THOSE ARE THE REAL REJECTS.
WE THROW 'EM AWAY.
BUT PIGS WOULD LOVE TO EAT 'EM.

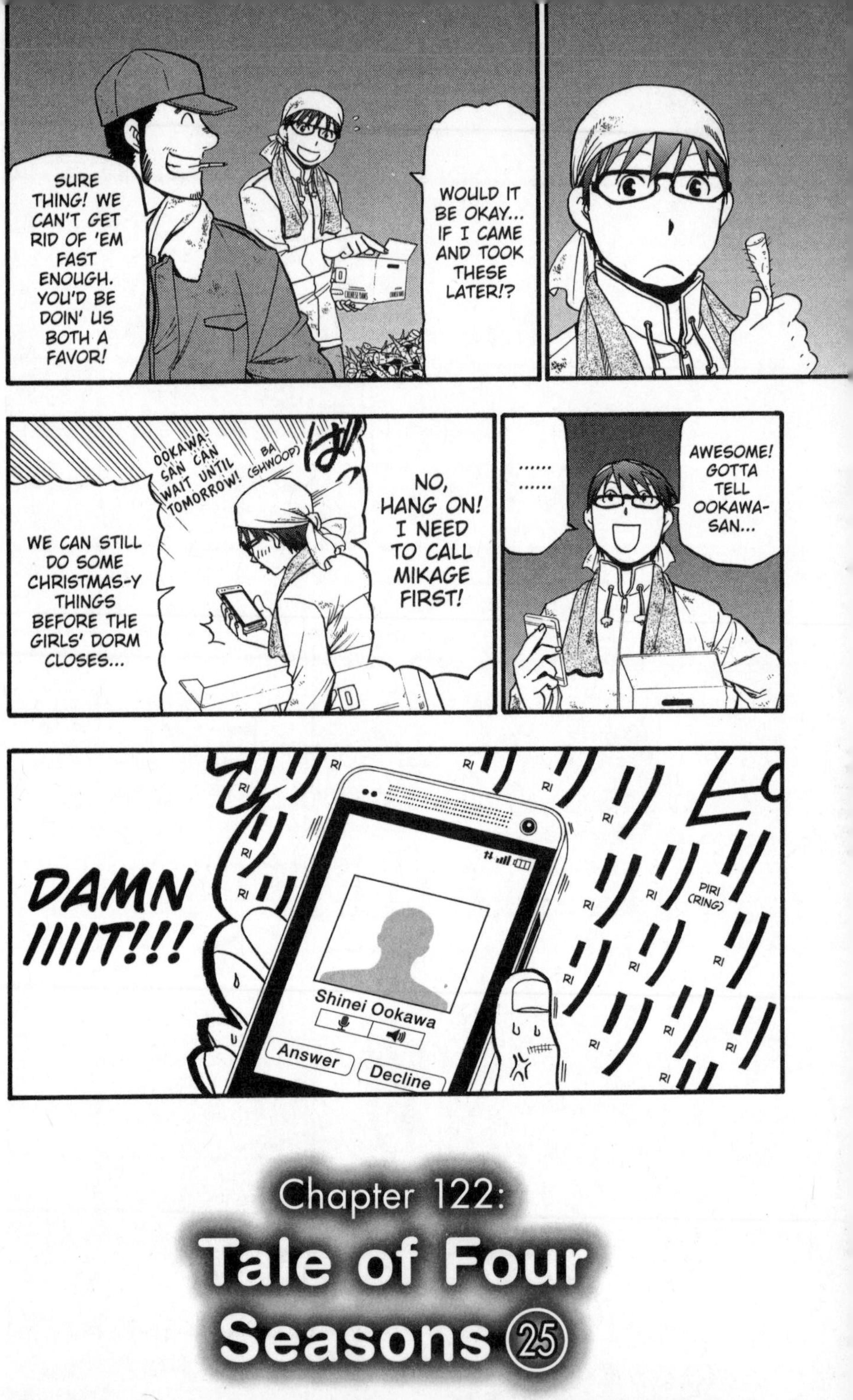
WOULD IT BE OKAY... IF I CAME AND TOOK THESE LATER!?
SURE THING! WE CAN'T GET RID OF 'EM FAST ENOUGH. YOU'D BE DOIN' US BOTH A FAVOR!
AWESOME! GOTTA TELL OOKAWA-SAN...
......
......
NO, HANG ON! I NEED TO CALL MIKAGE FIRST!
BA (SHWOOP)
OOKAWA-SAN CAN WAIT UNTIL TOMORROW!
WE CAN STILL DO SOME CHRISTMAS-Y THINGS BEFORE THE GIRLS' DORM CLOSES...
PIRI (RING)
RI
Shinei Ookawa
Answer
Decline
DAMN IIIIIT!!!

Chapter 122:

Tale of Four Seasons ㉕

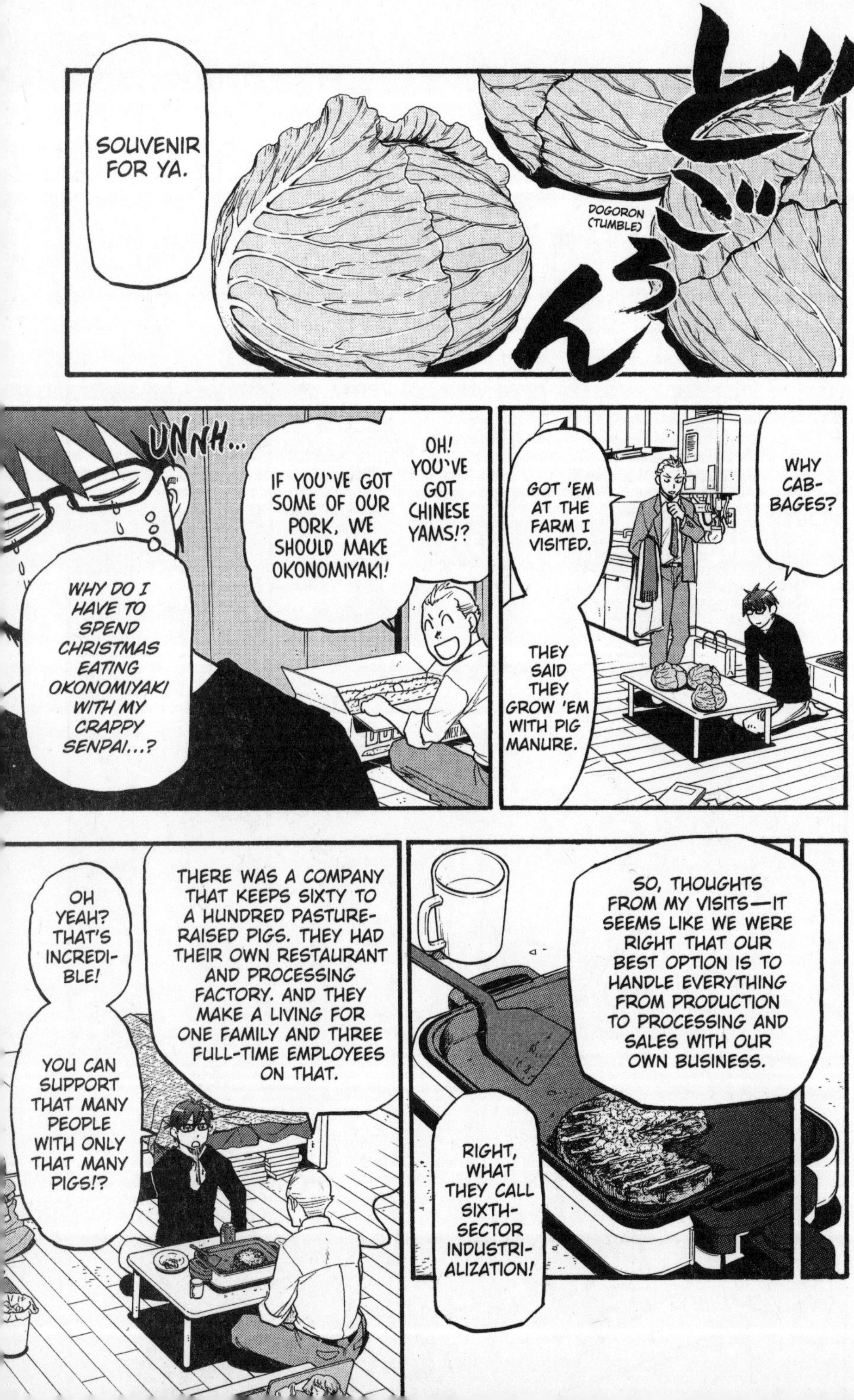
DOGORON (TUMBLE)
SOUVENIR FOR YA.
WHY CAB-BAGES?
GOT 'EM AT THE FARM I VISITED.
THEY SAID THEY GROW 'EM WITH PIG MANURE.
OH! YOU'VE GOT CHINESE YAMS!?
IF YOU'VE GOT SOME OF OUR PORK, WE SHOULD MAKE OKONOMIYAKI!
UNNH...
WHY DO I HAVE TO SPEND CHRISTMAS EATING OKONOMIYAKI WITH MY CRAPPY SENPAI...?
SO, THOUGHTS FROM MY VISITS—IT SEEMS LIKE WE WERE RIGHT THAT OUR BEST OPTION IS TO HANDLE EVERYTHING FROM PRODUCTION TO PROCESSING AND SALES WITH OUR OWN BUSINESS.
RIGHT, WHAT THEY CALL SIXTH-SECTOR INDUSTRI-ALIZATION!
THERE WAS A COMPANY THAT KEEPS SIXTY TO A HUNDRED PASTURE-RAISED PIGS. THEY HAD THEIR OWN RESTAURANT AND PROCESSING FACTORY. AND THEY MAKE A LIVING FOR ONE FAMILY AND THREE FULL-TIME EMPLOYEES ON THAT.
OH YEAH? THAT'S INCREDI-BLE!
YOU CAN SUPPORT THAT MANY PEOPLE WITH ONLY THAT MANY PIGS!?

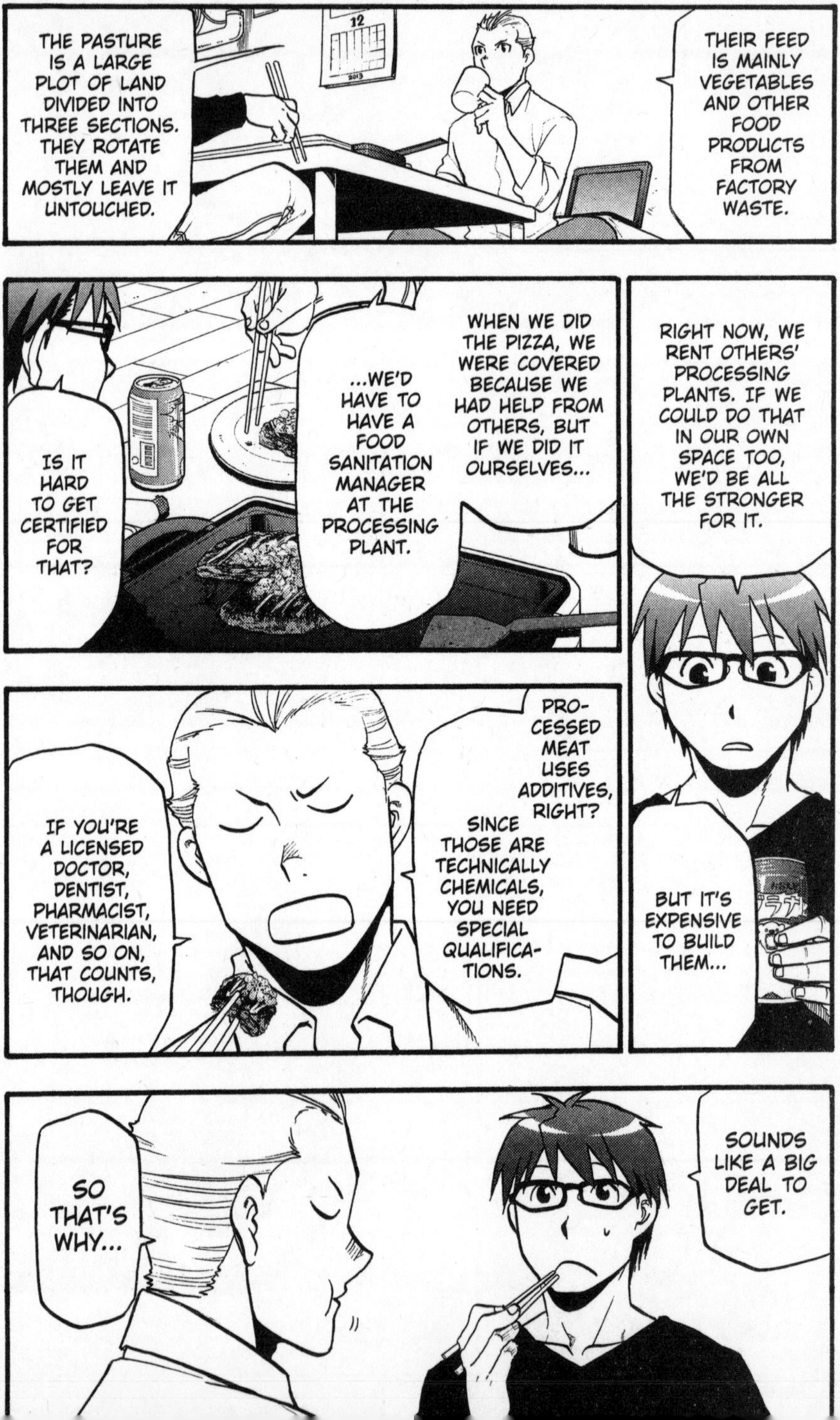
THEIR FEED IS MAINLY VEGETABLES AND OTHER FOOD PRODUCTS FROM FACTORY WASTE.
THE PASTURE IS A LARGE PLOT OF LAND DIVIDED INTO THREE SECTIONS. THEY ROTATE THEM AND MOSTLY LEAVE IT UNTOUCHED.
RIGHT NOW, WE RENT OTHERS' PROCESSING PLANTS. IF WE COULD DO THAT IN OUR OWN SPACE TOO, WE'D BE ALL THE STRONGER FOR IT.
BUT IT'S EXPENSIVE TO BUILD THEM...
WHEN WE DID THE PIZZA, WE WERE COVERED BECAUSE WE HAD HELP FROM OTHERS, BUT IF WE DID IT OURSELVES...
...WE'D HAVE TO HAVE A FOOD SANITATION MANAGER AT THE PROCESSING PLANT.
IS IT HARD TO GET CERTIFIED FOR THAT?
PRO-CESSED MEAT USES ADDITIVES, RIGHT?
SINCE THOSE ARE TECHNICALLY CHEMICALS, YOU NEED SPECIAL QUALIFICA-TIONS.
IF YOU'RE A LICENSED DOCTOR, DENTIST, PHARMACIST, VETERINARIAN, AND SO ON, THAT COUNTS, THOUGH.
SOUNDS LIKE A BIG DEAL TO GET.
SO THAT'S WHY...

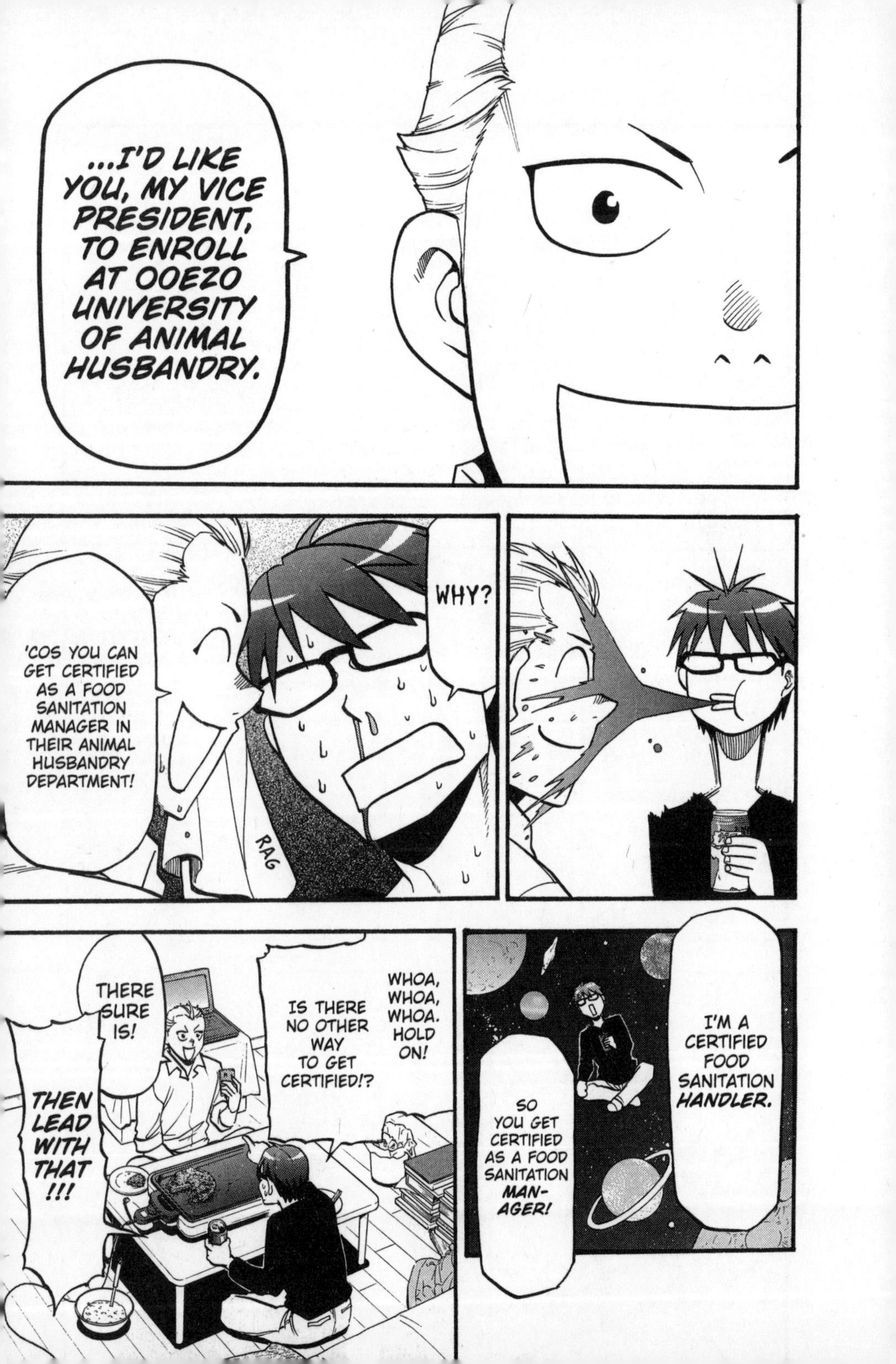
...I'D LIKE YOU, MY VICE PRESIDENT, TO ENROLL AT OOEZO UNIVERSITY OF ANIMAL HUSBANDRY.
WHY?
'COS YOU CAN GET CERTIFIED AS A FOOD SANITATION MANAGER IN THEIR ANIMAL HUSBANDRY DEPARTMENT!
RAG
I'M A CERTIFIED FOOD SANITATION HANDLER.
SO YOU GET CERTIFIED AS A FOOD SANITATION MAN-AGER!
WHOA, WHOA, WHOA. HOLD ON!
IS THERE NO OTHER WAY TO GET CERTIFIED!?
THERE SURE IS!
THEN LEAD WITH THAT!!!

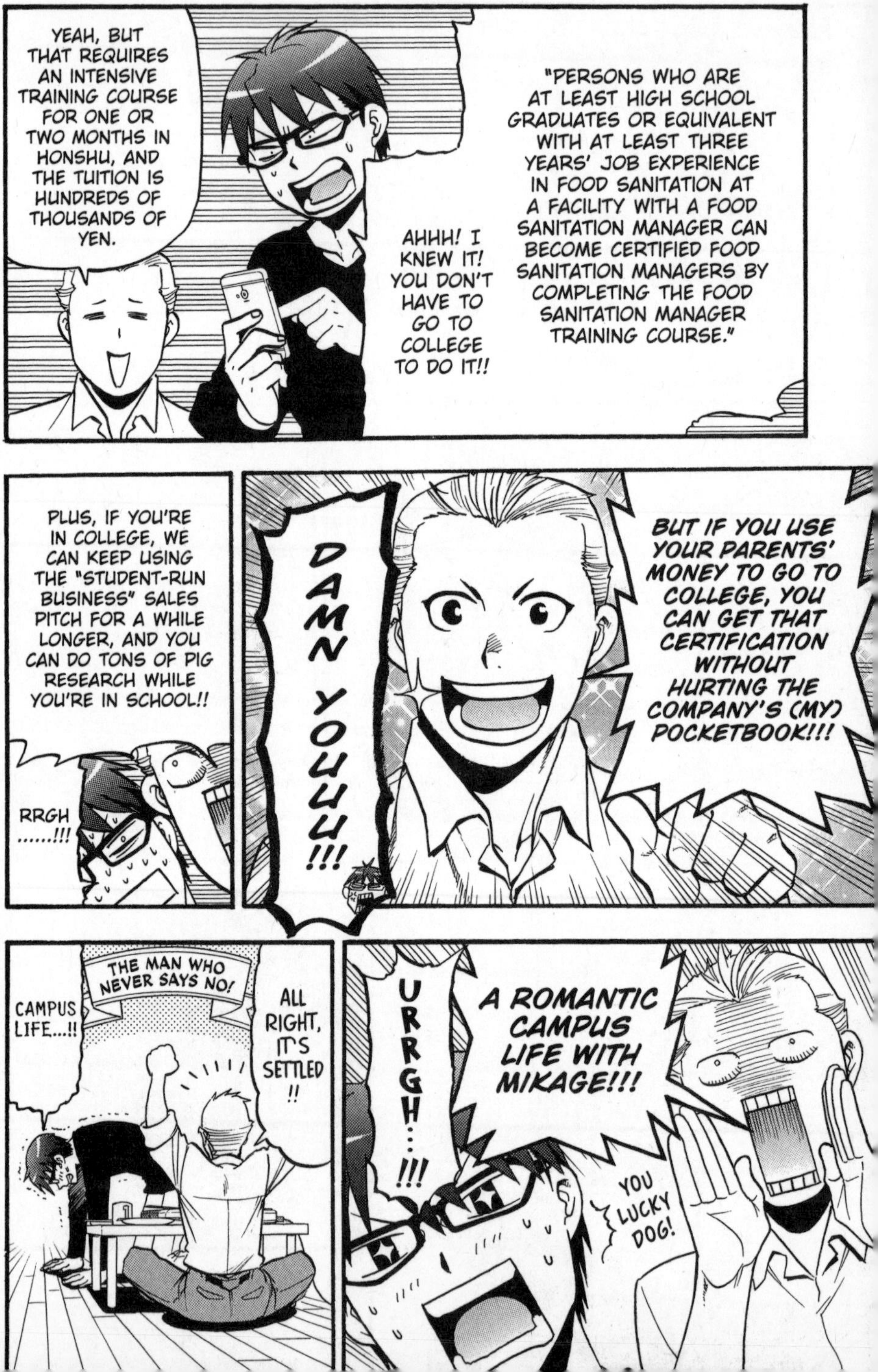
"PERSONS WHO ARE AT LEAST HIGH SCHOOL GRADUATES OR EQUIVALENT WITH AT LEAST THREE YEARS' JOB EXPERIENCE IN FOOD SANITATION AT A FACILITY WITH A FOOD SANITATION MANAGER CAN BECOME CERTIFIED FOOD SANITATION MANAGERS BY COMPLETING THE FOOD SANITATION MANAGER TRAINING COURSE."
AHHH! I KNEW IT! YOU DON'T HAVE TO GO TO COLLEGE TO DO IT!!
YEAH, BUT THAT REQUIRES AN INTENSIVE TRAINING COURSE FOR ONE OR TWO MONTHS IN HONSHU, AND THE TUITION IS HUNDREDS OF THOUSANDS OF YEN.
BUT IF YOU USE YOUR PARENTS' MONEY TO GO TO COLLEGE, YOU CAN GET THAT CERTIFICATION WITHOUT HURTING THE COMPANY'S (MY) POCKETBOOK!!!
DAMN YOUUUU!!!
PLUS, IF YOU'RE IN COLLEGE, WE CAN KEEP USING THE "STUDENT-RUN BUSINESS" SALES PITCH FOR A WHILE LONGER, AND YOU CAN DO TONS OF PIG RESEARCH WHILE YOU'RE IN SCHOOL!!
RRGH ......!!!
A ROMANTIC CAMPUS LIFE WITH MIKAGE!!!
URRGH...!!!
YOU LUCKY DOG!
ALL RIGHT, IT'S SETTLED!!
THE MAN WHO NEVER SAYS NO!
CAMPUS LIFE...!!

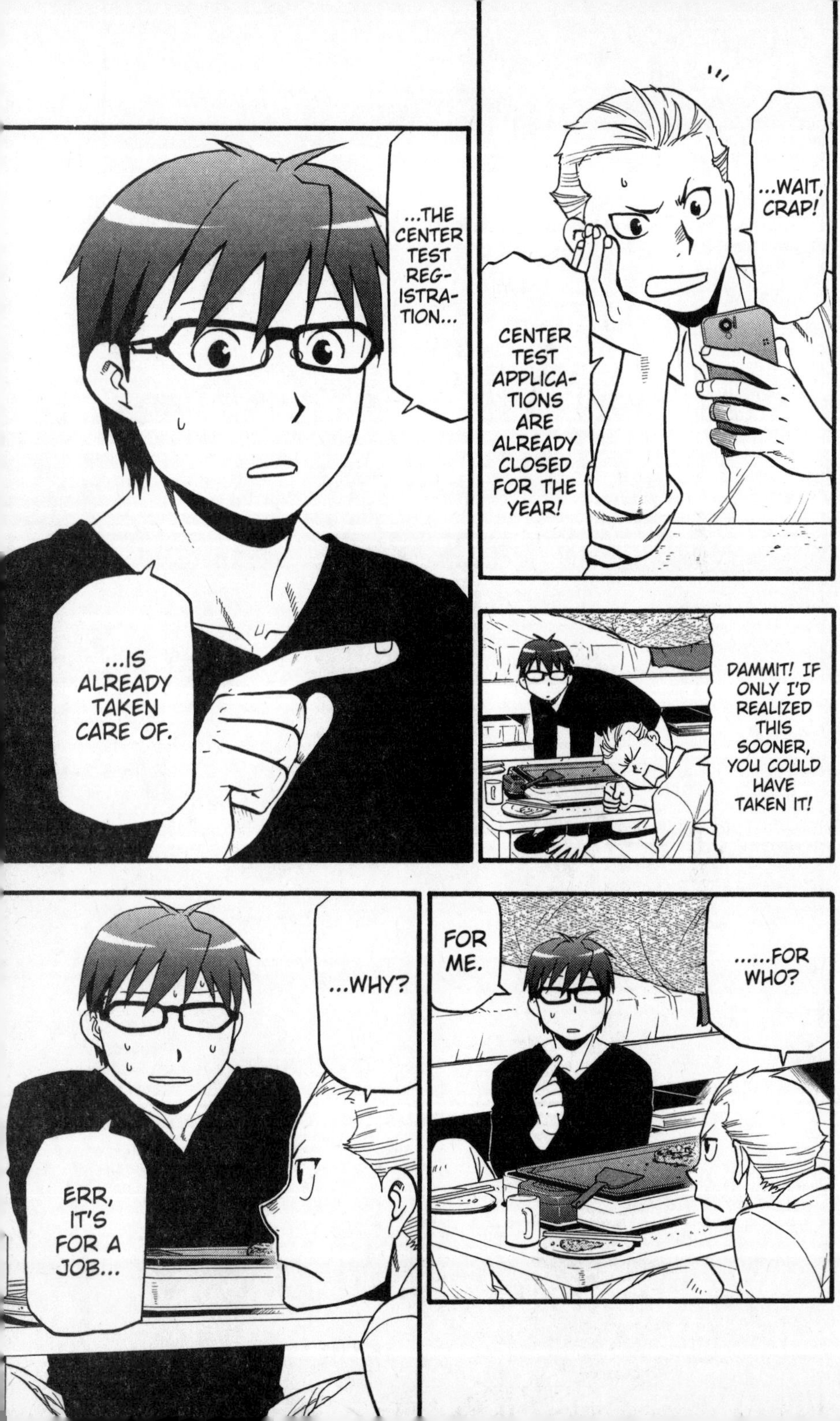
...WAIT, CRAP!
CENTER TEST APPLICATIONS ARE ALREADY CLOSED FOR THE YEAR!
DAMMIT! IF ONLY I'D REALIZED THIS SOONER, YOU COULD HAVE TAKEN IT!
...THE CENTER TEST REG-ISTRA-TION...
...IS ALREADY TAKEN CARE OF.
......FOR WHO?
FOR ME.
...WHY?
ERR, IT'S FOR A JOB...

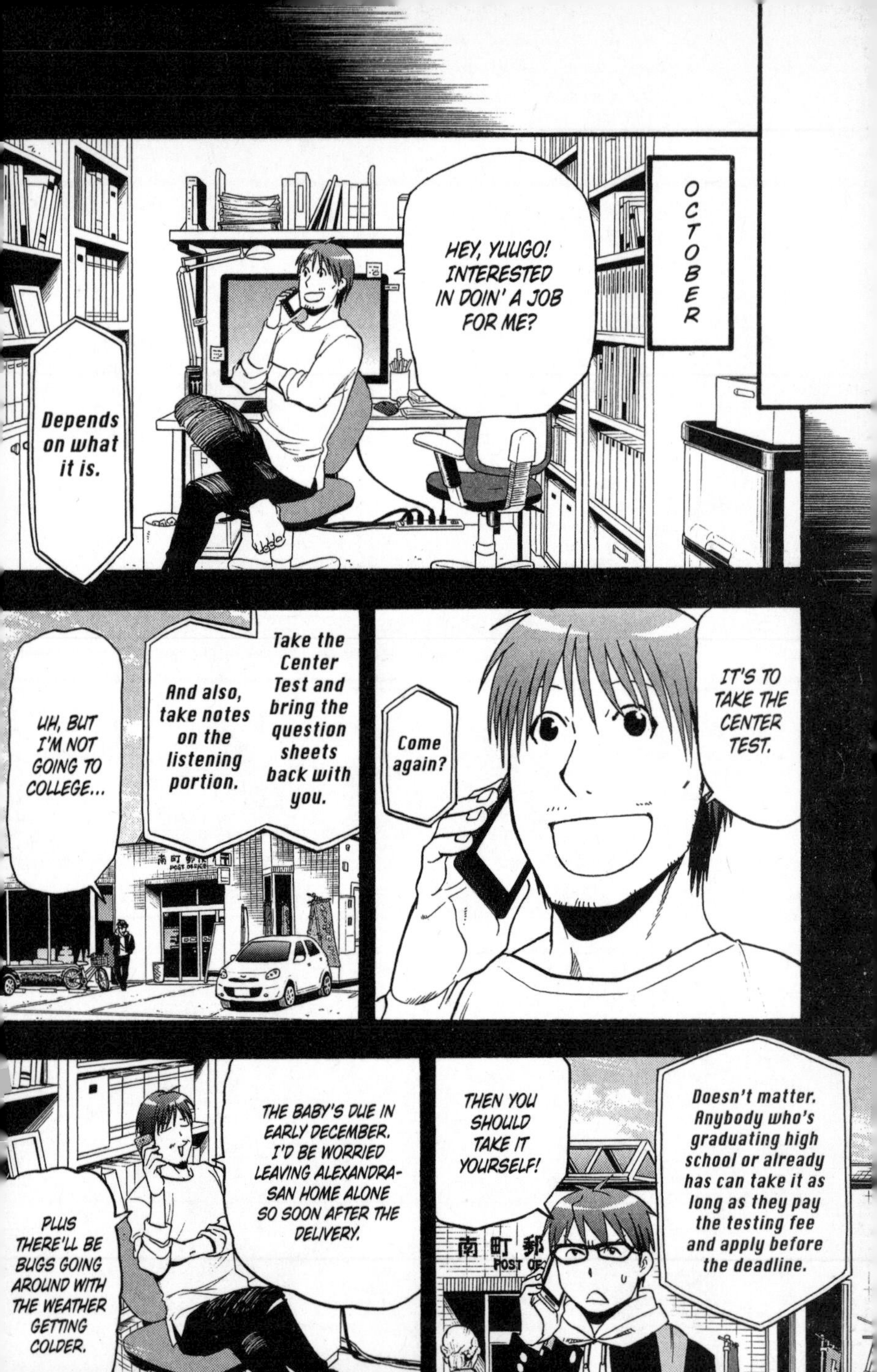
OCTOBER
HEY, YUUGO! INTERESTED IN DOIN' A JOB FOR ME?
Depends on what it is.
IT'S TO TAKE THE CENTER TEST.
Come again?
Take the Center Test and bring the question sheets back with you.
And also, take notes on the listening portion.
UH, BUT I'M NOT GOING TO COLLEGE...
Doesn't matter. Anybody who's graduating high school or already has can take it as long as they pay the testing fee and apply before the deadline.
THEN YOU SHOULD TAKE IT YOURSELF!
THE BABY'S DUE IN EARLY DECEMBER. I'D BE WORRIED LEAVING ALEXANDRA-SAN HOME ALONE SO SOON AFTER THE DELIVERY.
PLUS THERE'LL BE BUGS GOING AROUND WITH THE WEATHER GETTING COLDER.

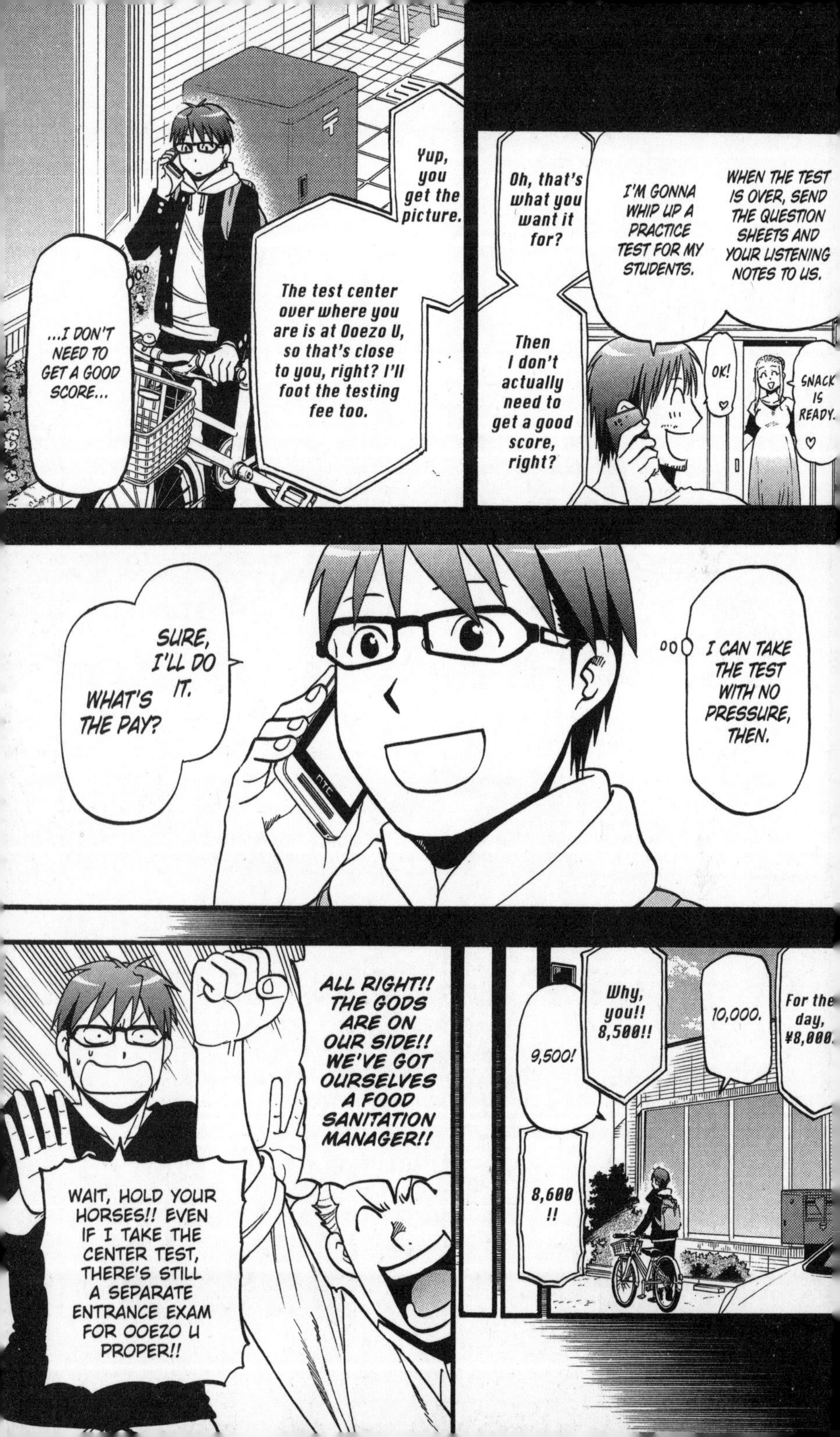
WHEN THE TEST IS OVER, SEND THE QUESTION SHEETS AND YOUR LISTENING NOTES TO US.
I'M GONNA WHIP UP A PRACTICE TEST FOR MY STUDENTS.
Oh, that's what you want it for?
SNACK IS READY.
OK!
Then I don't actually need to get a good score, right?
Yup, you get the picture.
The test center over where you are is at Ooezo U, so that's close to you, right? I'll foot the testing fee too.
...I DON'T NEED TO GET A GOOD SCORE...
I CAN TAKE THE TEST WITH NO PRESSURE, THEN.
SURE, I'LL DO IT.
WHAT'S THE PAY?
For the day, ¥8,000.
10,000.
Why, you!! 8,500!!
9,500!
8,600 !!
ALL RIGHT!! THE GODS ARE ON OUR SIDE!! WE'VE GOT OURSELVES A FOOD SANITATION MANAGER!!
WAIT, HOLD YOUR HORSES!! EVEN IF I TAKE THE CENTER TEST, THERE'S STILL A SEPARATE ENTRANCE EXAM FOR OOEZO U PROPER!!

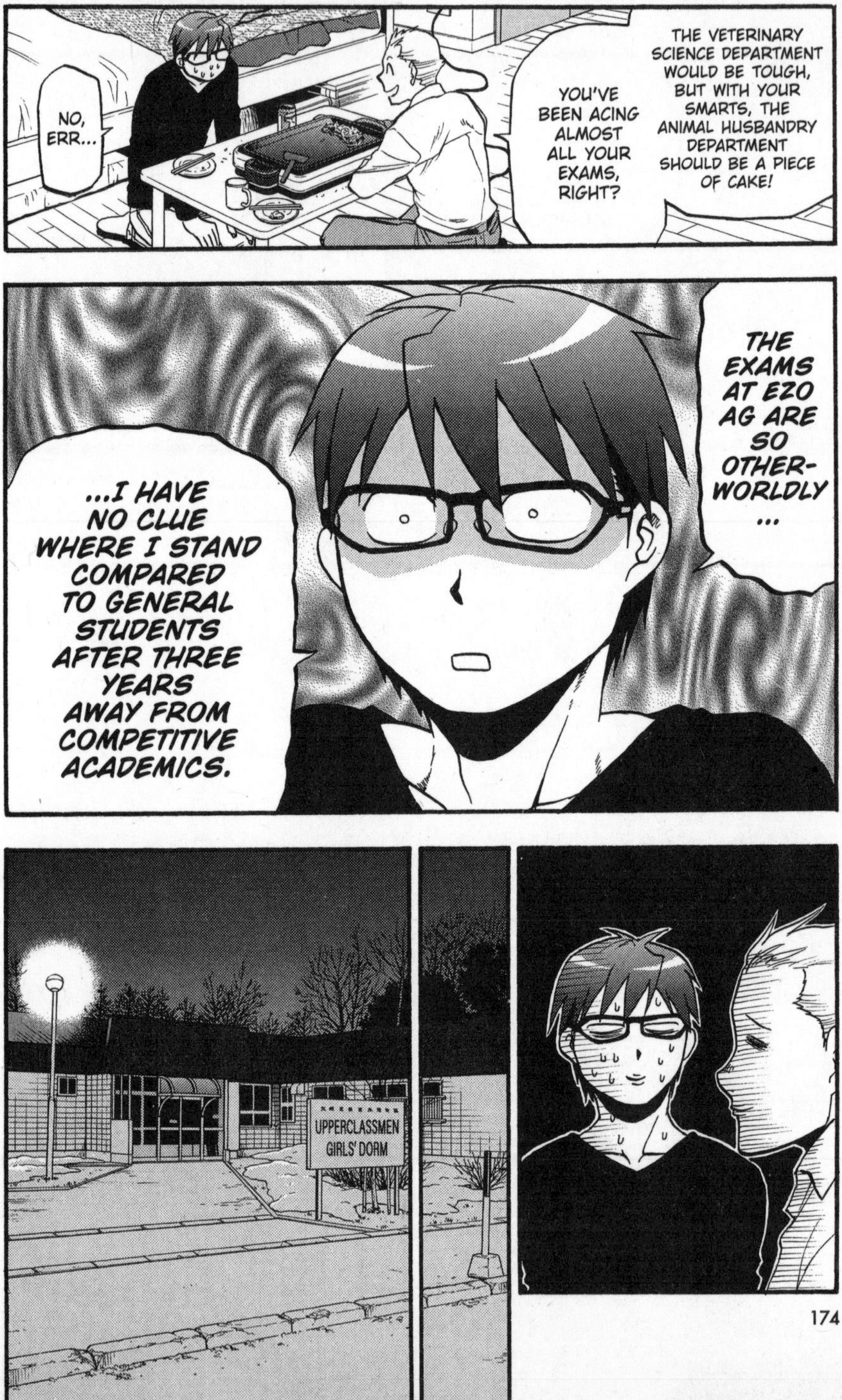
THE VETERINARY SCIENCE DEPARTMENT WOULD BE TOUGH, BUT WITH YOUR SMARTS, THE ANIMAL HUSBANDRY DEPARTMENT SHOULD BE A PIECE OF CAKE!
YOU'VE BEEN ACING ALMOST ALL YOUR EXAMS, RIGHT?
NO, ERR...
THE EXAMS AT EZO AG ARE SO OTHER-WORLDLY...
...I HAVE NO CLUE WHERE I STAND COMPARED TO GENERAL STUDENTS AFTER THREE YEARS AWAY FROM COMPETITIVE ACADEMICS.
UPPERCLASSMEN GIRLS' DORM

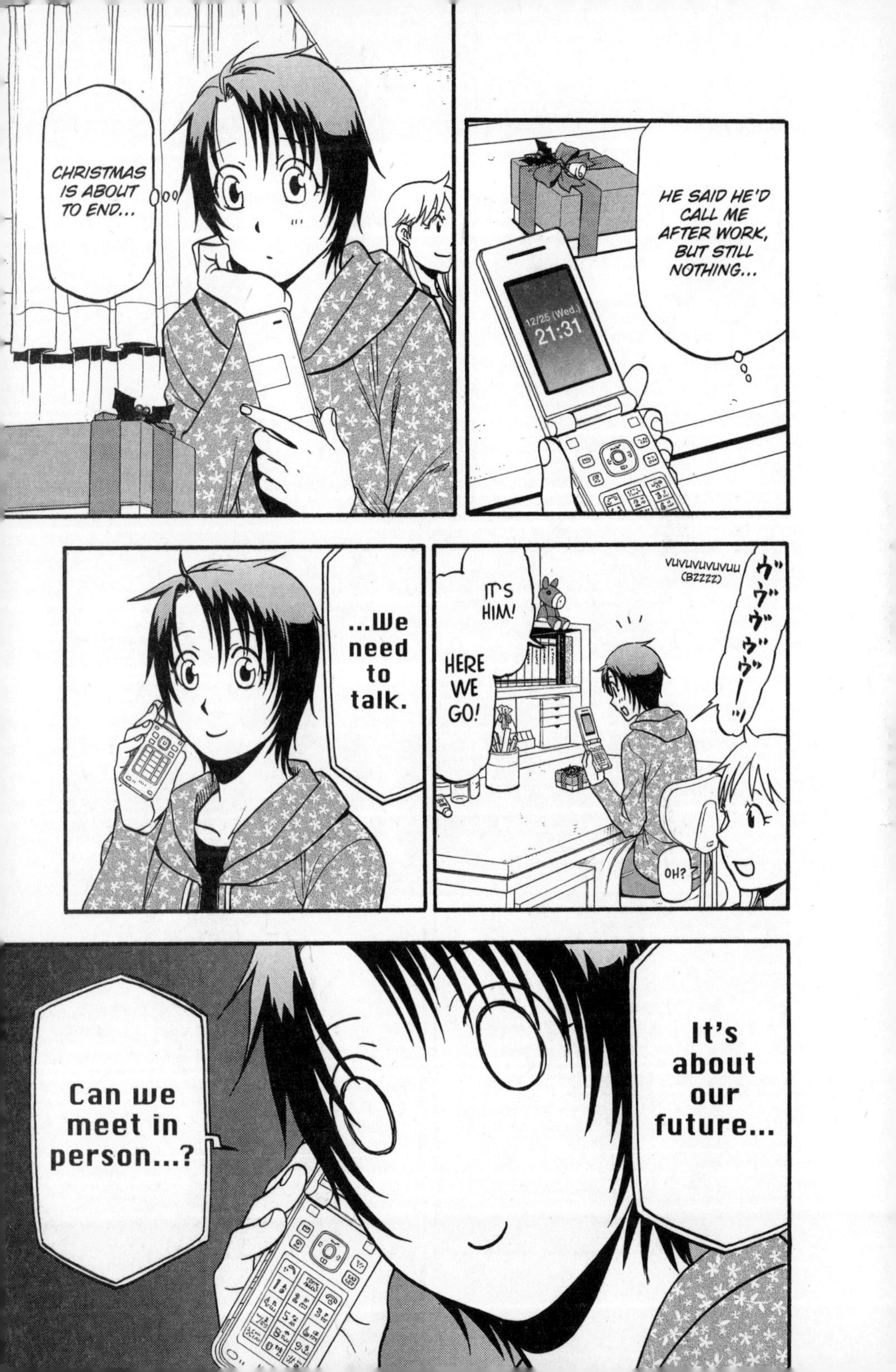
HE SAID HE'D CALL ME AFTER WORK, BUT STILL NOTHING...
12/25 (Wed.)
21:31
CHRISTMAS IS ABOUT TO END...
ヴヴヴヴヴーッ
VUVUVUVUVUU (BZZZZ)
IT'S HIM!
HERE WE GO!
OH?
...We need to talk.
It's about our future...
Can we meet in person...?

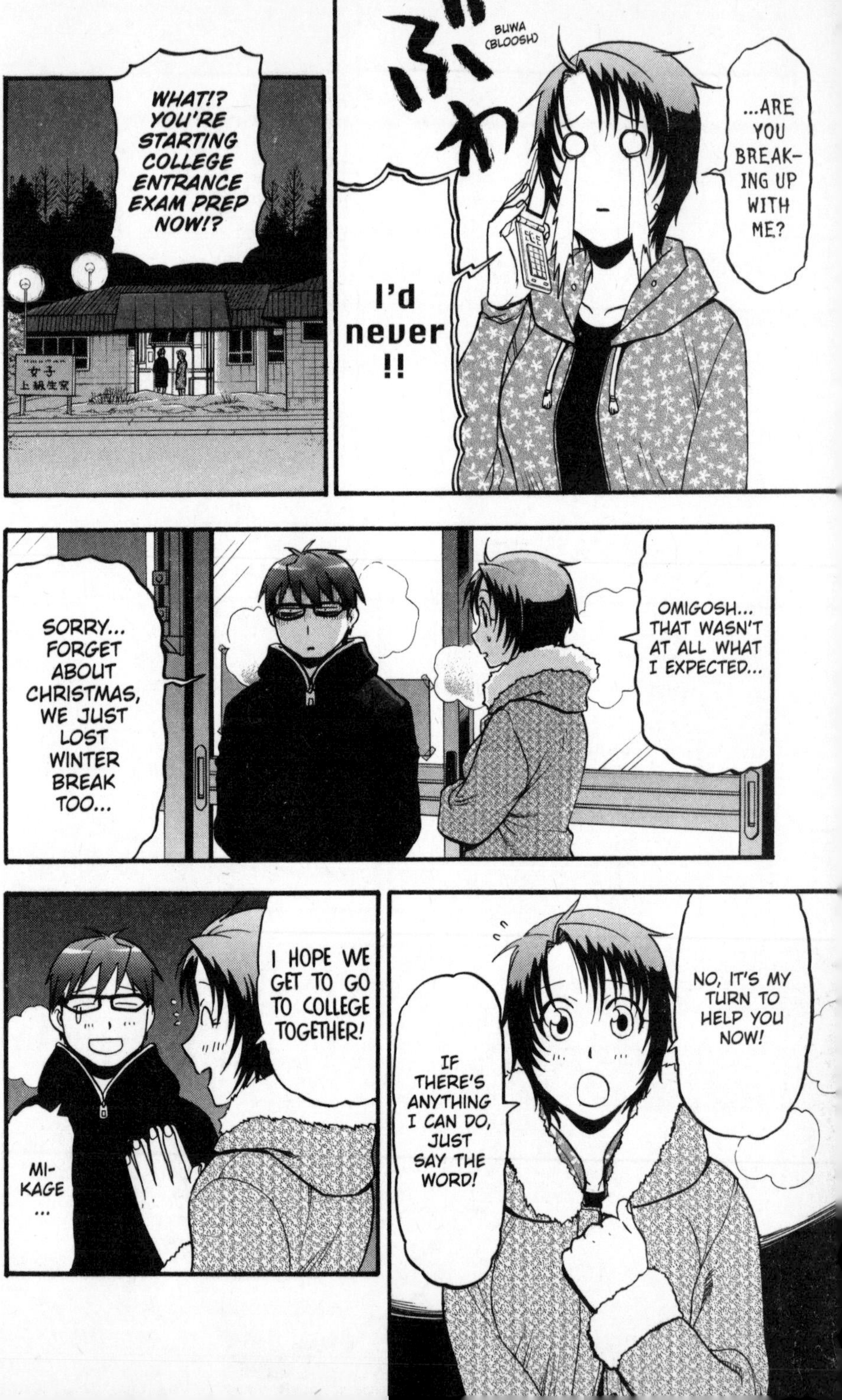
ぶわ
BUWA (BLOOSH)
...ARE YOU BREAKING UP WITH ME?
I'd never!!
WHAT!? YOU'RE STARTING COLLEGE ENTRANCE EXAM PREP NOW!?
OMIGOSH... THAT WASN'T AT ALL WHAT I EXPECTED...
SORRY... FORGET ABOUT CHRISTMAS, WE JUST LOST WINTER BREAK TOO...
NO, IT'S MY TURN TO HELP YOU NOW!
IF THERE'S ANYTHING I CAN DO, JUST SAY THE WORD!
I HOPE WE GET TO GO TO COLLEGE TOGETHER!
MI-KAGE...

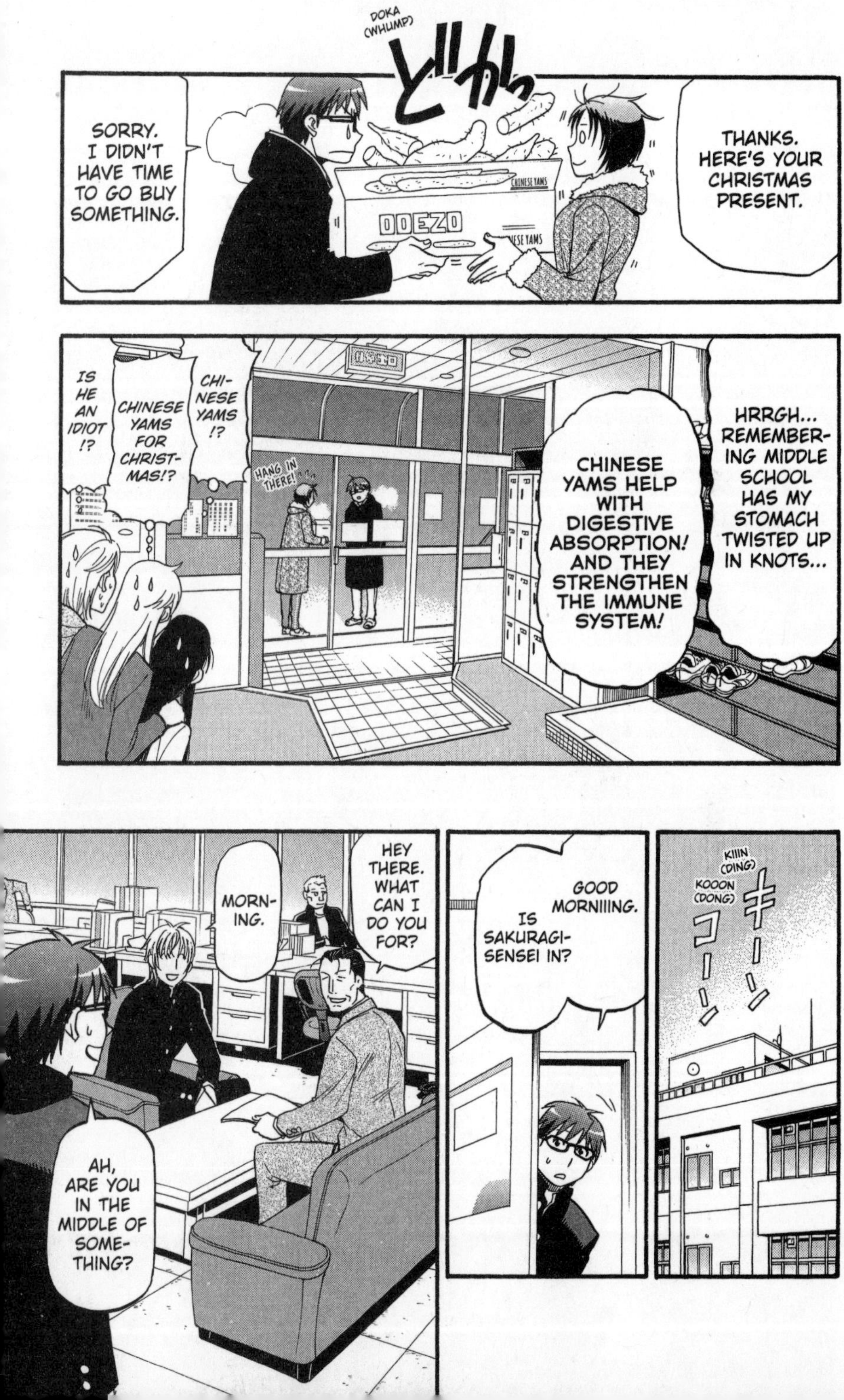
DOKA (WHUMP)
THANKS. HERE'S YOUR CHRISTMAS PRESENT.
CHINESE YAMS
OOEZO
CHINESE YAMS
SORRY. I DIDN'T HAVE TIME TO GO BUY SOMETHING.
HRRGH... REMEMBERING MIDDLE SCHOOL HAS MY STOMACH TWISTED UP IN KNOTS...
CHINESE YAMS HELP WITH DIGESTIVE ABSORPTION! AND THEY STRENGTHEN THE IMMUNE SYSTEM!
HANG IN THERE!
CHINESE YAMS!?
CHINESE YAMS FOR CHRISTMAS!?
IS HE AN IDIOT!?
KIIIN (DING)
KOOON (DONG)
GOOD MORNIIING.
IS SAKURAGI-SENSEI IN?
HEY THERE. WHAT CAN I DO YOU FOR?
MORNING.
AH, ARE YOU IN THE MIDDLE OF SOMETHING?

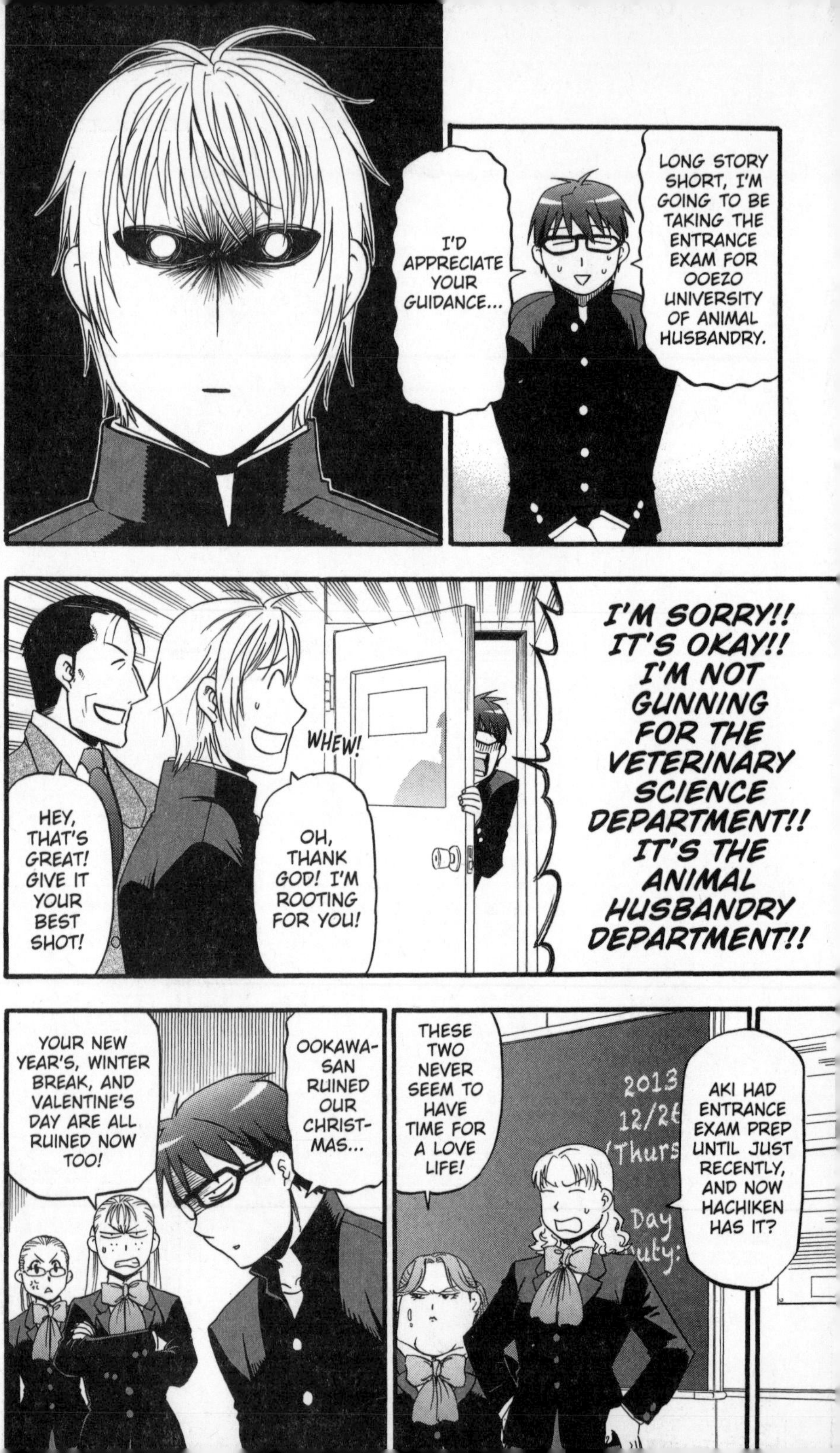
LONG STORY SHORT, I'M GOING TO BE TAKING THE ENTRANCE EXAM FOR OOEZO UNIVERSITY OF ANIMAL HUSBANDRY.
I'D APPRECIATE YOUR GUIDANCE...
I'M SORRY!! IT'S OKAY!! I'M NOT GUNNING FOR THE VETERINARY SCIENCE DEPARTMENT!! IT'S THE ANIMAL HUSBANDRY DEPARTMENT!!
WHEW!
OH, THANK GOD! I'M ROOTING FOR YOU!
HEY, THAT'S GREAT! GIVE IT YOUR BEST SHOT!
AKI HAD ENTRANCE EXAM PREP UNTIL JUST RECENTLY, AND NOW HACHIKEN HAS IT?
THESE TWO NEVER SEEM TO HAVE TIME FOR A LOVE LIFE!
OOKAWA-SAN RUINED OUR CHRIST-MAS...
YOUR NEW YEAR'S, WINTER BREAK, AND VALENTINE'S DAY ARE ALL RUINED NOW TOO!

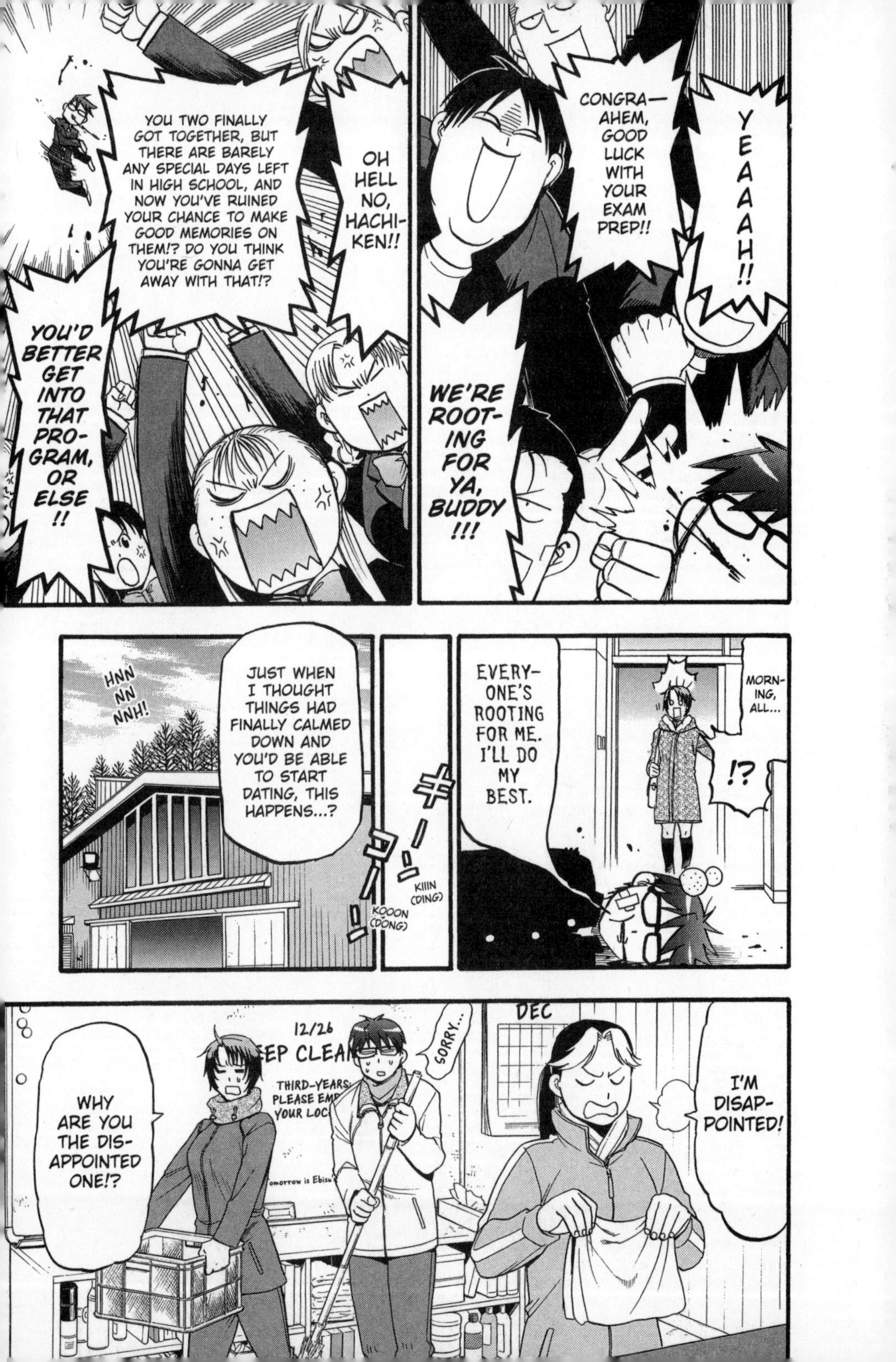
YEAAAAH!!
CONGRA— AHEM, GOOD LUCK WITH YOUR EXAM PREP!!
WE'RE ROOTING FOR YA, BUDDY!!!
OH HELL NO, HACHIKEN!!
YOU TWO FINALLY GOT TOGETHER, BUT THERE ARE BARELY ANY SPECIAL DAYS LEFT IN HIGH SCHOOL, AND NOW YOU'VE RUINED YOUR CHANCE TO MAKE GOOD MEMORIES ON THEM!? DO YOU THINK YOU'RE GONNA GET AWAY WITH THAT!?
YOU'D BETTER GET INTO THAT PROGRAM, OR ELSE!!
MORNING, ALL...
!?
EVERYONE'S ROOTING FOR ME. I'LL DO MY BEST.
KIIIN (DING)
KOOON (DONG)
JUST WHEN I THOUGHT THINGS HAD FINALLY CALMED DOWN AND YOU'D BE ABLE TO START DATING, THIS HAPPENS...?
HNNNNNNH!
I'M DISAP-POINTED!
DEC
SORRY...
12/26
EEP CLEA
THIRD-YEARS: PLEASE EMP YOUR LOC
Tomorrow is Ebisu's
WHY ARE YOU THE DIS-APPOINTED ONE!?

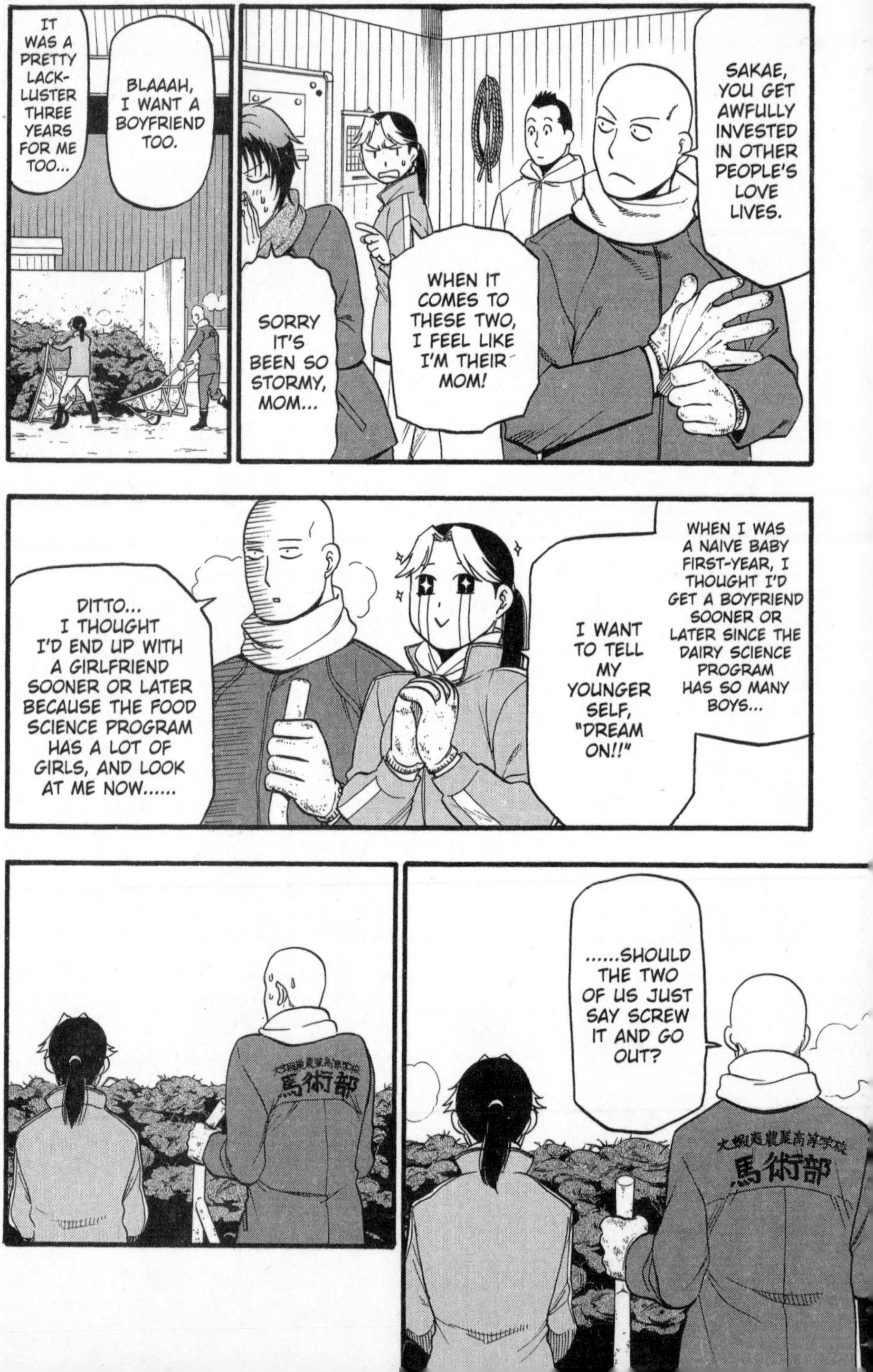
SAKAE, YOU GET AWFULLY INVESTED IN OTHER PEOPLE'S LOVE LIVES.
WHEN IT COMES TO THESE TWO, I FEEL LIKE I'M THEIR MOM!
SORRY IT'S BEEN SO STORMY, MOM...
BLAAAH, I WANT A BOYFRIEND TOO.
IT WAS A PRETTY LACK-LUSTER THREE YEARS FOR ME TOO...
WHEN I WAS A NAIVE BABY FIRST-YEAR, I THOUGHT I'D GET A BOYFRIEND SOONER OR LATER SINCE THE DAIRY SCIENCE PROGRAM HAS SO MANY BOYS...
I WANT TO TELL MY YOUNGER SELF, "DREAM ON!!"
DITTO... I THOUGHT I'D END UP WITH A GIRLFRIEND SOONER OR LATER BECAUSE THE FOOD SCIENCE PROGRAM HAS A LOT OF GIRLS, AND LOOK AT ME NOW......
......SHOULD THE TWO OF US JUST SAY SCREW IT AND GO OUT?
大蝦夷農業高等学校
馬術部

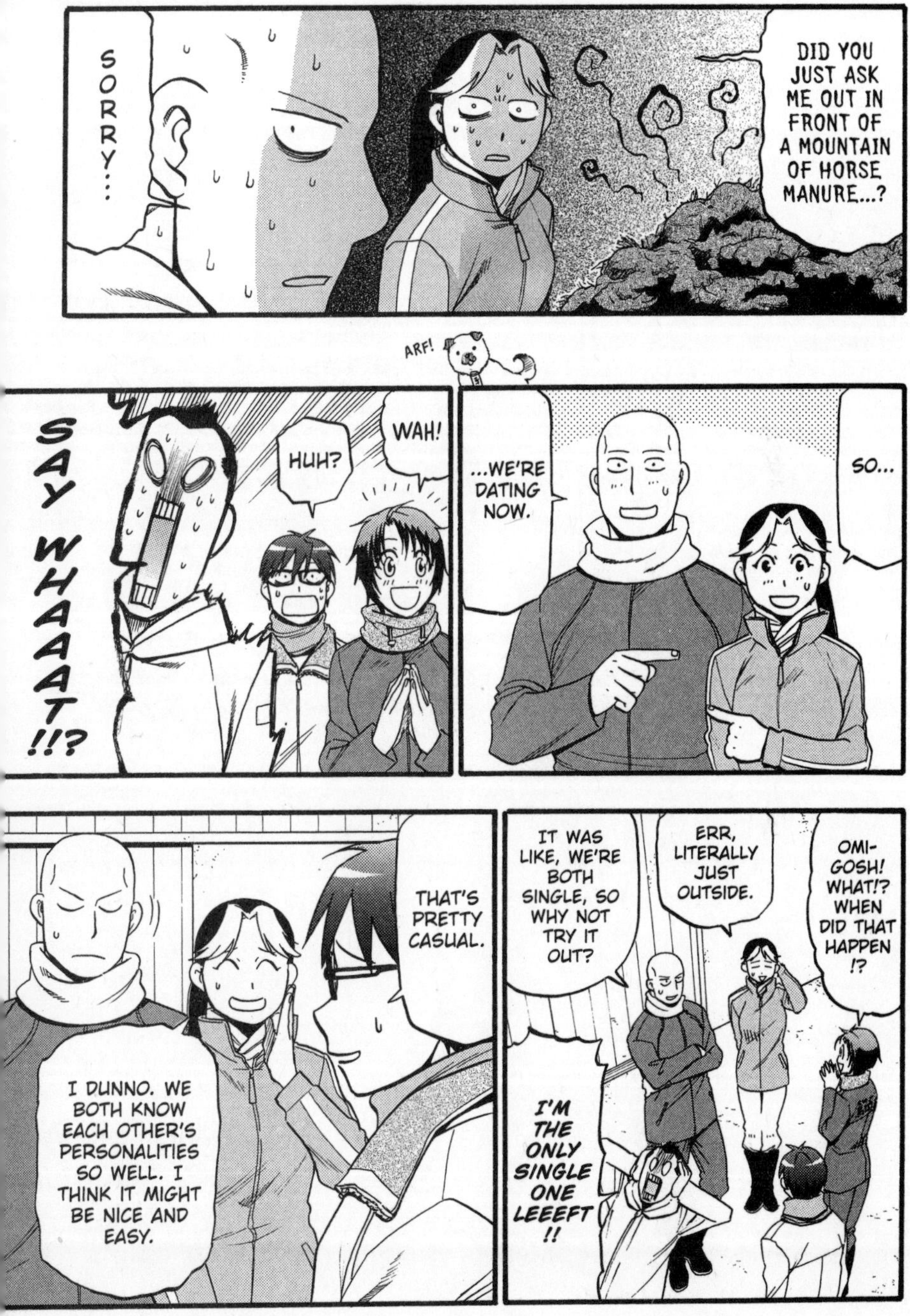
DID YOU JUST ASK ME OUT IN FRONT OF A MOUNTAIN OF HORSE MANURE...?
SORRY...
ARF!
SO...
...WE'RE DATING NOW.
WAH!
HUH?
SAY WHAAAAT!!?
OMI-GOSH! WHAT!? WHEN DID THAT HAPPEN!?
ERR, LITERALLY JUST OUTSIDE.
IT WAS LIKE, WE'RE BOTH SINGLE, SO WHY NOT TRY IT OUT?
I'M THE ONLY SINGLE ONE LEEEFT!!
THAT'S PRETTY CASUAL.
I DUNNO. WE BOTH KNOW EACH OTHER'S PERSONALITIES SO WELL. I THINK IT MIGHT BE NICE AND EASY.

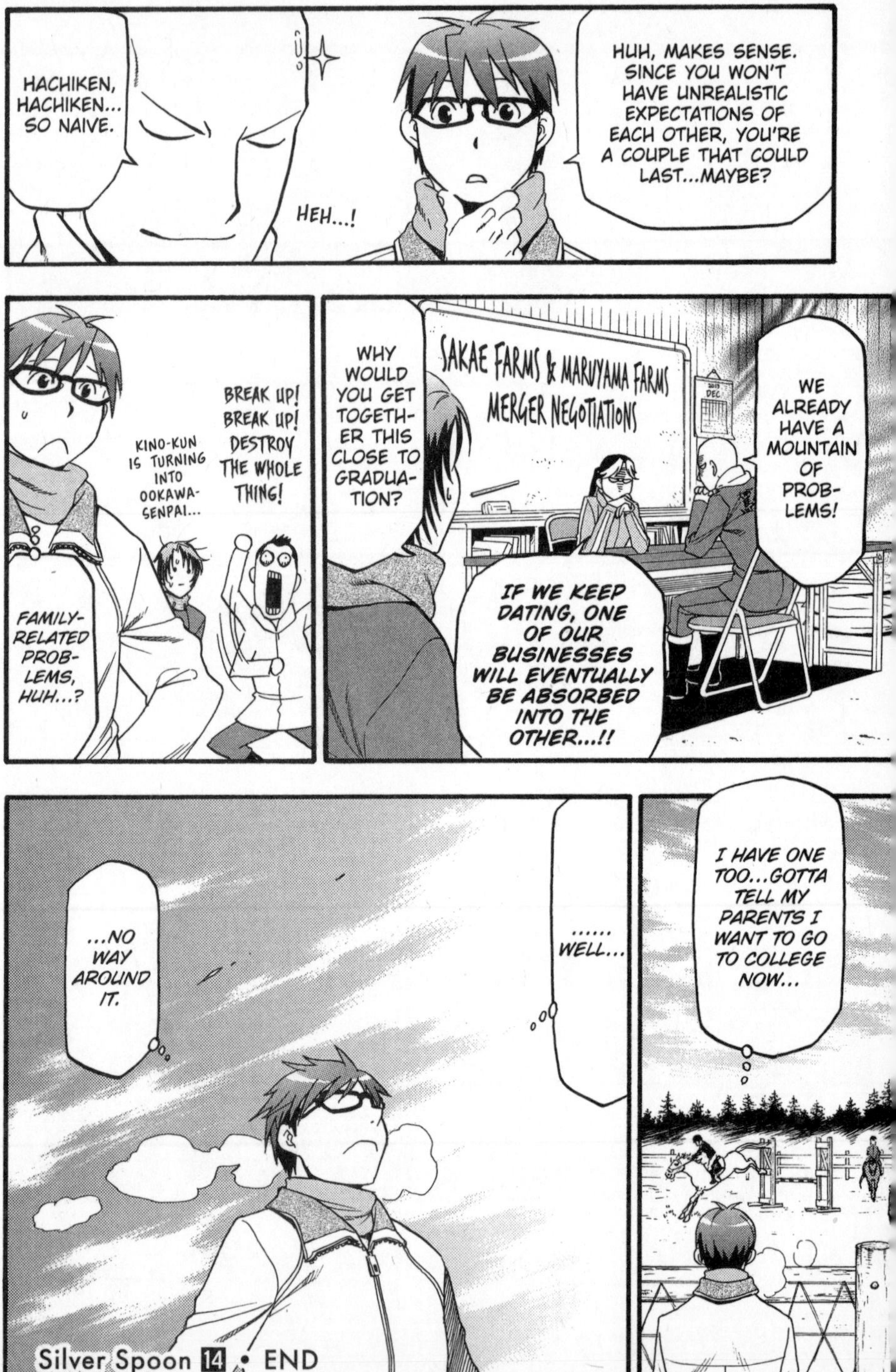
HUH, MAKES SENSE. SINCE YOU WON'T HAVE UNREALISTIC EXPECTATIONS OF EACH OTHER, YOU'RE A COUPLE THAT COULD LAST...MAYBE?
HACHIKEN, HACHIKEN... SO NAIVE.
HEH...!
WE ALREADY HAVE A MOUNTAIN OF PROBLEMS!
SAKAE FARMS & MARUYAMA FARMS MERGER NEGOTIATIONS
WHY WOULD YOU GET TOGETHER THIS CLOSE TO GRADUATION?
IF WE KEEP DATING, ONE OF OUR BUSINESSES WILL EVENTUALLY BE ABSORBED INTO THE OTHER...!!
BREAK UP! BREAK UP! DESTROY THE WHOLE THING!
KINO-KUN IS TURNING INTO OOKAWA-SENPAI...
FAMILY-RELATED PROBLEMS, HUH...?
I HAVE ONE TOO...GOTTA TELL MY PARENTS I WANT TO GO TO COLLEGE NOW...
...... WELL...
...NO WAY AROUND IT.
Silver Spoon 14 • END

Silver Spoon

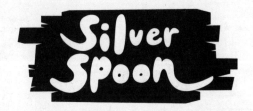

Bad.

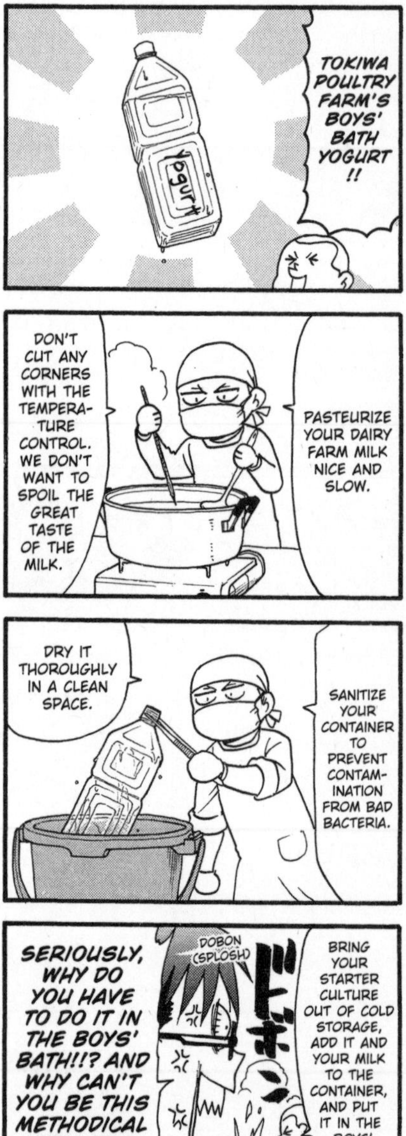

TOKIWA POULTRY FARM'S BOYS' BATH YOGURT!!
yogurt
PASTEURIZE YOUR DAIRY FARM MILK NICE AND SLOW.
DON'T CUT ANY CORNERS WITH THE TEMPERATURE CONTROL. WE DON'T WANT TO SPOIL THE GREAT TASTE OF THE MILK.
SANITIZE YOUR CONTAINER TO PREVENT CONTAMINATION FROM BAD BACTERIA.
DRY IT THOROUGHLY IN A CLEAN SPACE.
BRING YOUR STARTER CULTURE OUT OF COLD STORAGE, ADD IT AND YOUR MILK TO THE CONTAINER, AND PUT IT IN THE BOYS' BATH TO FERMENT...
DOBON (SPLOSH)
SERIOUSLY, WHY DO YOU HAVE TO DO IT IN THE BOYS' BATH!!? AND WHY CAN'T YOU BE THIS METHODICAL WITH YOUR SCHOOLWORK!!?

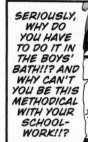

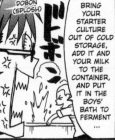

Cow Shed Diaries: The "Horse Stuff" Chapter

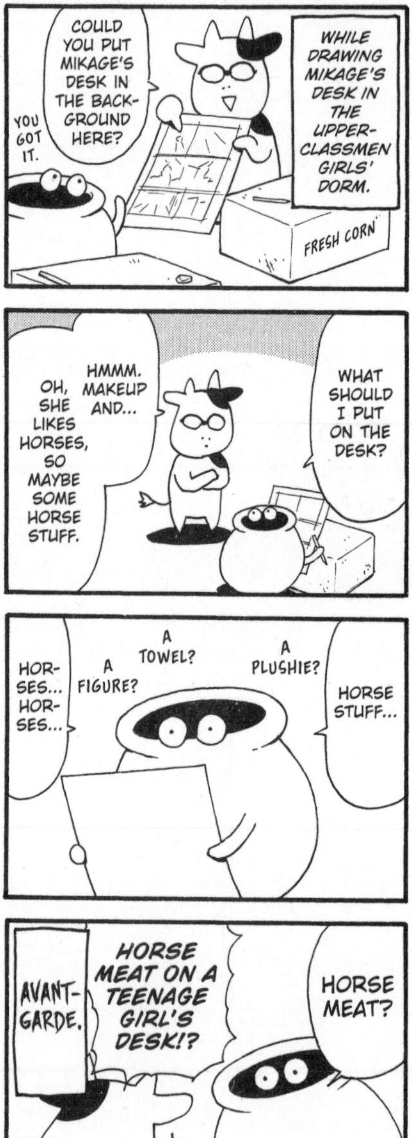

WHILE DRAWING MIKAGE'S DESK IN THE UPPERCLASSMEN GIRLS' DORM.
COULD YOU PUT MIKAGE'S DESK IN THE BACKGROUND HERE?
YOU GOT IT.
FRESH CORN
WHAT SHOULD I PUT ON THE DESK?
HMMM. MAKEUP AND...
OH, SHE LIKES HORSES, SO MAYBE SOME HORSE STUFF.
HORSE STUFF...
A PLUSHIE?
A TOWEL?
A FIGURE?
HORSES... HORSES...
HORSE MEAT?
HORSE MEAT ON A TEENAGE GIRL'S DESK!?
AVANT-GARDE.

Cow Shed Diaries: "The Series Endgame Storm" Chapter

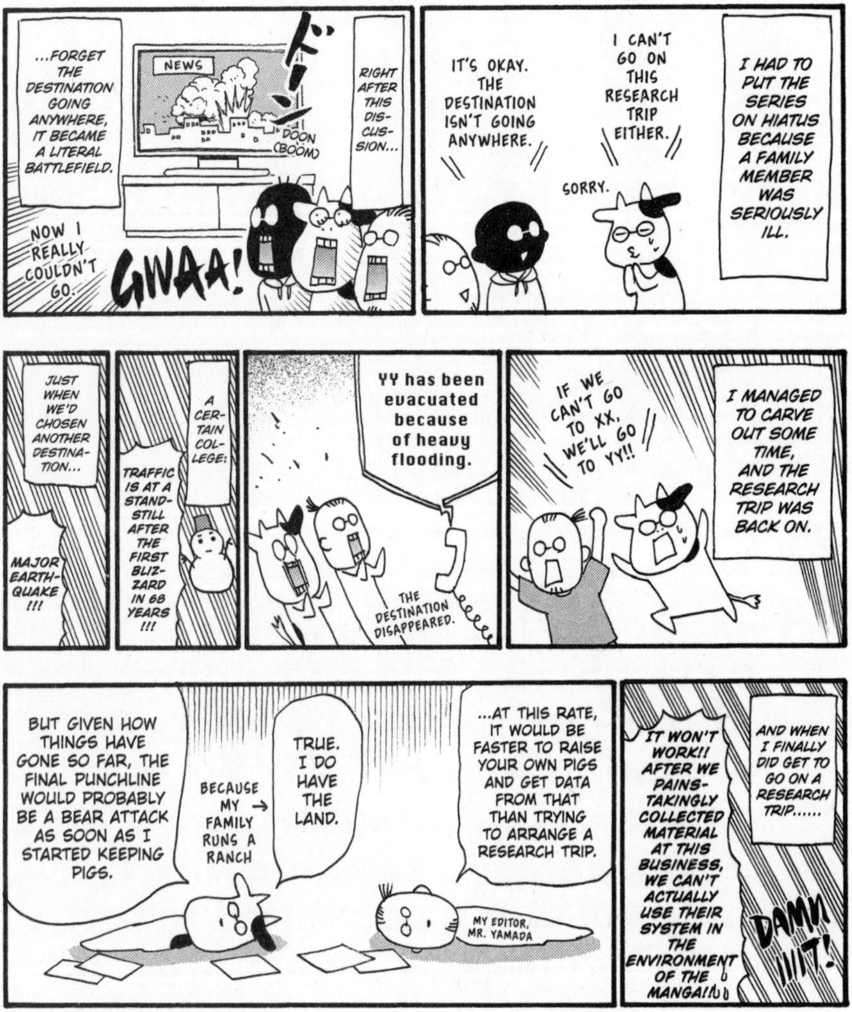
I HAD TO PUT THE SERIES ON HIATUS BECAUSE A FAMILY MEMBER WAS SERIOUSLY ILL.
I CAN'T GO ON THIS RESEARCH TRIP EITHER.
SORRY.
IT'S OKAY. THE DESTINATION ISN'T GOING ANYWHERE.
RIGHT AFTER THIS DISCUSSION...
ド
DOON (BOOM)
NEWS
...FORGET THE DESTINATION GOING ANYWHERE, IT BECAME A LITERAL BATTLEFIELD.
GWAA!
NOW I REALLY COULDN'T GO.
I MANAGED TO CARVE OUT SOME TIME, AND THE RESEARCH TRIP WAS BACK ON.
IF WE CAN'T GO TO XX, WE'LL GO TO YY!!
YY has been evacuated because of heavy flooding.
THE DESTINATION DISAPPEARED.
A CERTAIN COLLEGE:
TRAFFIC IS AT A STANDSTILL AFTER THE FIRST BLIZZARD IN 68 YEARS!!!
JUST WHEN WE'D CHOSEN ANOTHER DESTINATION...
MAJOR EARTHQUAKE!!!
AND WHEN I FINALLY DID GET TO GO ON A RESEARCH TRIP......
IT WON'T WORK!! AFTER WE PAINSTAKINGLY COLLECTED MATERIAL AT THIS BUSINESS, WE CAN'T ACTUALLY USE THEIR SYSTEM IN THE ENVIRONMENT OF THE MANGA!!
DAMN IIIT!
...AT THIS RATE, IT WOULD BE FASTER TO RAISE YOUR OWN PIGS AND GET DATA FROM THAT THAN TRYING TO ARRANGE A RESEARCH TRIP.
TRUE. I DO HAVE THE LAND.
BECAUSE MY FAMILY RUNS A RANCH
BUT GIVEN HOW THINGS HAVE GONE SO FAR, THE FINAL PUNCHLINE WOULD PROBABLY BE A BEAR ATTACK AS SOON AS I STARTED KEEPING PIGS.
MY EDITOR, MR. YAMADA

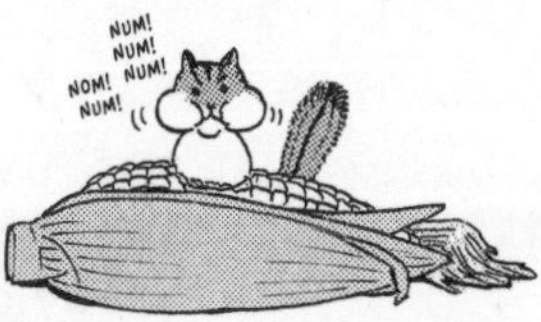
NUM! NUM! NUM!
NOM! NUM!

Silver Spoon 14!
I went on a research trip somewhere five minutes from my folks' place, but I didn't have time to visit them (lol).

~ Special Thanks ~

Everyone who helped with collecting material; all of my assistants; everyone who helped with consulting; my editor, Mr. Tsubouchi (Thanks for all you've done since the launch of the series!!); my editor, Mr. Yamada; **AND YOU!!**

NEXT......

I HAVE TO DO IT...
THERE'S NO TIME...
IT'S ALREADY THE END OF THE YEAR...
I'M HOME.
ぬ
NU (LOOM)
YUUGO.
Y-YES!?

Hachiken once ran away because he hated being forced to compete. So too has he raised his voice in rebellion against rejection. The unpleasant memories haven't disappeared, the inferiority complex can't be waved away, and he's painfully aware that the wall in his way is impregnable!

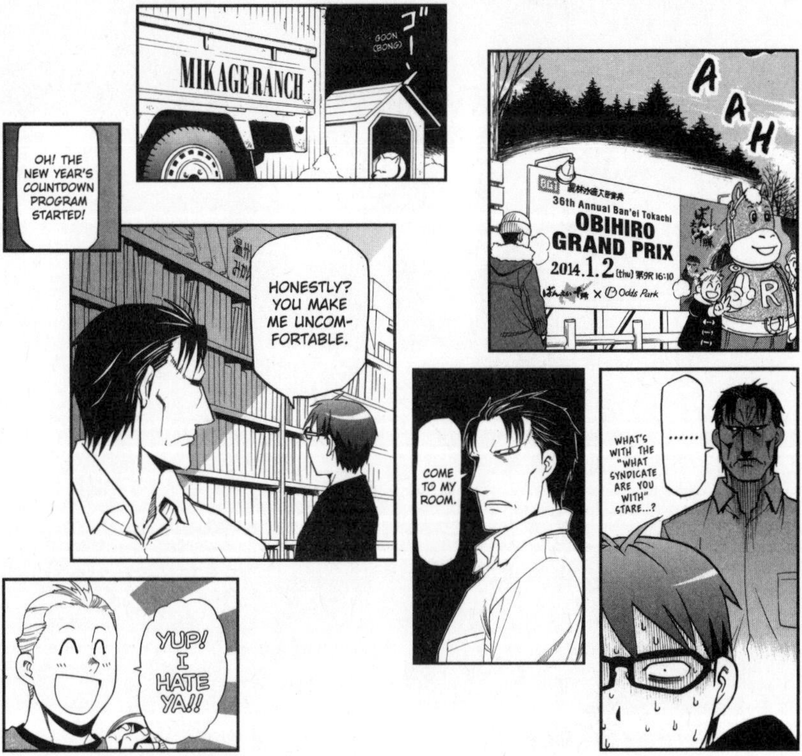
AAH
36th Annual Ban'ei Tokachi
OBIHIRO GRAND PRIX
2014.1.2 (thu) 16:10
Odds Park
MIKAGE RANCH
GOON (BONG)
OH! THE NEW YEAR'S COUNTDOWN PROGRAM STARTED!
HONESTLY? YOU MAKE ME UNCOM-FORTABLE.
......
WHAT'S WITH THE "WHAT SYNDICATE ARE YOU WITH" STARE...?
COME TO MY ROOM.
YUP! I HATE YA!!

But Hachiken has to come face-to-face with his fears. For the sake of the goal he chose for himself... In *Silver Spoon* 15, Hachiken will take a step forward. Don't miss it!!

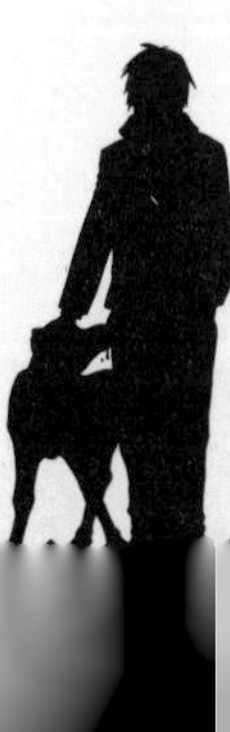

to be continued......

Silver Spoon

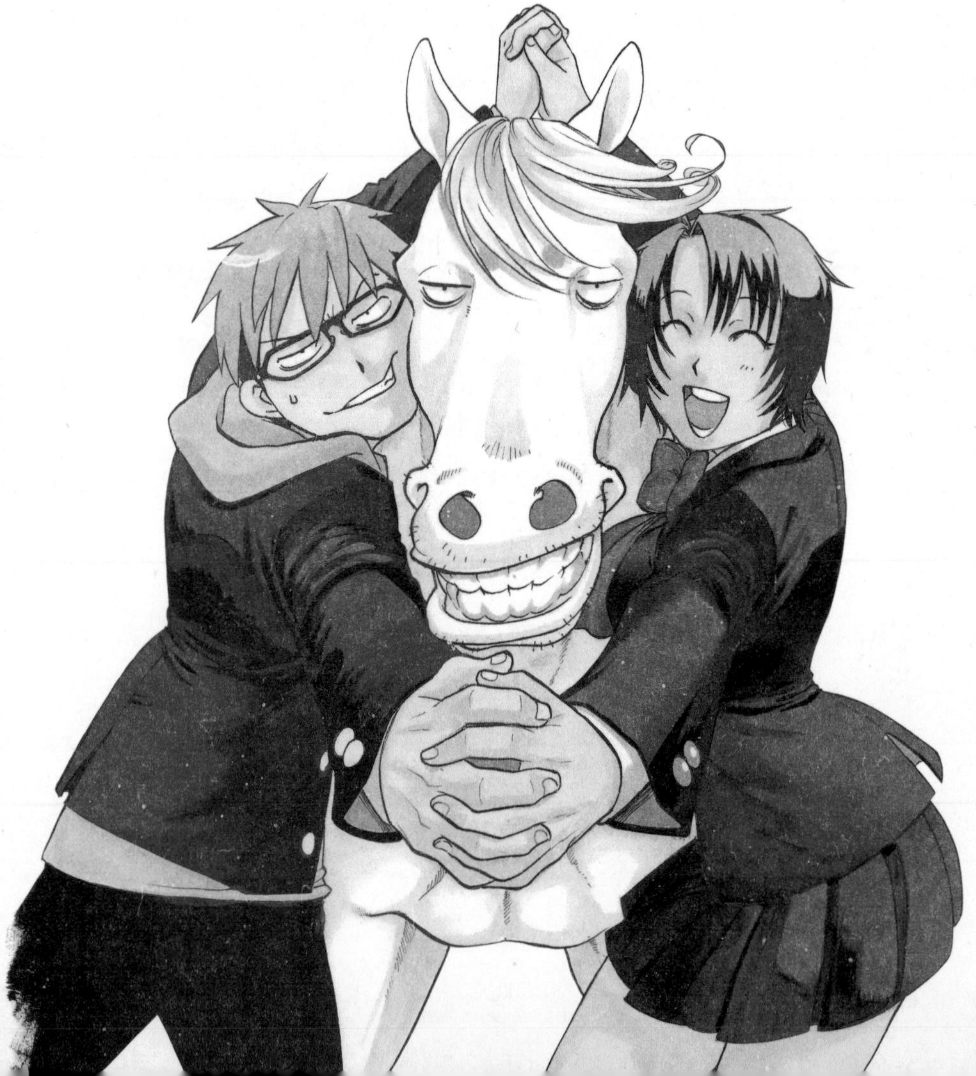

MIKAGE RANCH FINALLY GETS A CELL SIGNAL!!
YAAAY!
THEY BUILT A BASE STATION IN THE AREA.
MAN! IT'LL BE NICE TO BE ABLE TO CHECK THE MARKET IN REAL TIME WHILE I WORK!
THE AGE OF TECH-NOLOGY!
WE'VE REACHED THE AGE OF TECH-NOLOGY!
TOTALLY! PLUS IT'LL BE EASIER TO GET AHOLD OF EACH OTHER NOW!
LIVESTOCK MARKET
OUR PLACE GETS A SIGNAL NOW TOO!
MOM BOUGHT US CELL PHONES!
OH! YOU GUYS GOT PHONES ALREADY, HUH!?
YEAH, IT IS USEFUL TO BE ABLE TO CALL HOME!
NUH-UH. IT'S 'COS THEY GET BEAR ALERTS FROM CITY HALL.
WE DON'T MAKE MANY CALLS.
DING! DING!
EMER-GENCY ALERT! EMER-GENCY ALERT!
VRR! VRRR!
...I SEE.
THAT'S GREAT... YEAH...

Translation Notes

Common Honorifics

no honorific: Indicates familiarity or closeness; if used without permission or reason, addressing someone in this manner would constitute an insult.

-san: The Japanese equivalent of Mr./Mrs./Miss. If a situation calls for politeness, this is the fail-safe honorific.

-sama: Conveys great respect; may also indicate the social status of the speaker is lower than that of the addressee.

-kun: Used most often when referring to boys, this honorific indicates affection or familiarity. Occasionally used by older men among their peers, but it may also be used by anyone referring to a person of lower standing.

-chan, -tan: An affectionate honorific indicating familiarity used mostly in reference to girls; also used in reference to cute persons or animals of either gender.

-sensei: A respectful term for teachers, artists, or high-level professionals.

-niisan, nii-san, aniki, etc.: A term of endearment meaning "big brother" that may be more widely used to address any young man who is like a brother, regardless of whether he is related or not.

-neesan, nee-san, aneki, etc.: The female counterpart of the above, nee-san means "big sister."

Currency Conversion

While conversion rates fluctuate, an easy estimate for Japanese yen conversion is ¥100 to 1 USD.

Page 19
Akihabara is considered Tokyo's "holy land" for anime fans like Nishikawa.

Page 39
Pork omelet (butatama) is a specific variety of okonomiyaki (a savory pancake) made with pork.

Page 48
Honshu is Japan's biggest main island. Major cities Tokyo, Kyoto, and Osaka are located there.

Page 50
The Trans-Pacific Partnership, or TPP, is a multinational trade agreement that first came into effect at the end of 2018.

Page 52
In Japanese, sketchy/exploitative companies are called "black companies" ("burakku kigyou"), so it's ironic that the company Yoshino is interviewing with is called the White Cheese Factory.

Page 88
Keiko Toda is the voice actress who played fan-favorite character Matilda Ajan in the original Mobile Suit Gundam anime. All of the audio clips Nishikawa plays on his phone are iconic lines of hers from the series. Matilda is more of a cool big sister figure than Nishikawa's usual cute anime girls, defining her as more of a "-san" than a "-tan," and she's addressed as "Matilda-san" in Gundam too.

Page 145
In Japan, Christmas is better known as a big date night than a family or religious occasion. This is why Hachiken and Aki are hoping to spend it together, and why Ookawa would be extra gleeful to stop them from doing so.

Page 154
In Japan, you would generally address your significant other's parents as "Mom" and "Dad." Aki's father's reaction is yet another rejection of their relationship.

Page 155
Kyushu is Japan's third-largest and southernmost main island.

Page 159
The Showa Era corresponds to the reign of Emperor Showa, who ruled from the end of 1926 to early 1989.

Page 167
Okonomiyaki (literally "cooked how you like it") is a savory pancake that can contain a variety of ingredients; cabbage is popularly one of them.

Page 171
The Center Test (National Center Test for University Admission) is a standardized test used for public and some private university admissions in Japan, similar to how SAT or ACT test scores are used for American college admissions.

Silver Spoon

Silver Spoon

HIROMU ARAKAWA

Translation: **Amanda Haley** Lettering: **Abigail Blackman**

This book is a work of fiction. Names, characters, places, and incidents are the product of the author's imagination or are used fictitiously. Any resemblance to actual events, locales, or persons, living or dead, is coincidental.

GIN NO SAJI SILVER SPOON Vol. 14
by Hiromu ARAKAWA
© 2011 Hiromu ARAKAWA
All rights reserved.
Original Japanese edition published by SHOGAKUKAN.
English translation rights in the United States of America, Canada, the United Kingdom, Ireland, Australia and New Zealand arranged with SHOGAKUKAN through Tuttle-Mori Agency, Inc.

English translation © 2020 by Yen Press, LLC

Yen Press
150 West 30th Street, 19th Floor
New York, NY 10001

Visit us at yenpress.com
facebook.com/yenpress
twitter.com/yenpress
yenpress.tumblr.com
instagram.com/yenpress

First Yen Press Edition: April 2020

Yen Press is an imprint of Yen Press, LLC.
The Yen Press name and logo are trademarks of Yen Press, LLC.

The publisher is not responsible for websites (or their content) that are not owned by the publisher.

Library of Congress Control Number: 2017959207

ISBNs: 978-1-9753-5315-5 (paperback)
978-1-9753-1208-4 (ebook)

10 9 8 7 6 5 4 3 2 1

WOR

Printed in the United States of America